LORDS & LADIES
COLLECTION

*Two Glittering Regency
Love Affairs*

Ten Guineas on Love
by Claire Thornton
&
The Rake
by Georgina Devon

The *Regency*

LORDS & LADIES

COLLECTION

The Regency

LORDS & LADIES
COLLECTION

*Claire Thornton &
Georgina Devon*

MILLS & BOON®

*First published in Great Britain 2006 by
Harlequin Mills & Boon Limited,
Eton House, 18-24 Paradise Road, Richmond, Surrey TW9 1SR*

THE REGENCY LORDS & LADIES COLLECTION
© Harlequin Books S.A. 2006

The publisher acknowledges the copyright holders of the
individual works as follows:

Ten Guineas on Love © Alice Thornton 1992
(originally published in Great Britain in 1996 under the name
Alice Thornton)
The Rake © Alison J Hentges 2000

ISBN-13: 978 0 263 85107 6
ISBN-10: 0 263 85107 9

138-0906

*Printed and bound in Spain
by Litografia Rosés S.A., Barcelona*

Ten Guineas on Love
by
Claire Thornton

Claire Thornton grew up in Sussex. It is a family legend that her ancestors in the county were involved in smuggling. She was a shy little girl, and she was fascinated by the idea that she might be distantly related to bold and daring adventurers of the past – who were probably not shy! When she grew up she studied history at York University, and discovered that smugglers were often brutal men whose main ambition was to make money. This was disappointing, but she still feels justified in believing in – and writing about – the romantic and noble heroes of earlier ages.

For Sally

Chapter One

"**M**r Canby! Are you telling me that unless we can find *twenty thousand* pounds by the end of the month we are going to lose our home?" Charity demanded.

"I—er—that is to say—yes, Miss Mayfield," the attorney replied miserably.

For a moment there was silence as Charity gazed at Mr Canby in disbelief and Mr Canby stared dismally at the faded library carpet.

"Why?" said Charity at last.

"Your father used Hazelhurst as security for a loan," Mr Canby explained. "According to the terms of the agreement, he had one year to repay the money, with the total sum due on the first of March 1766—but unfortunately he was killed within two days of signing the agreement."

"Yes, I understand that," said Charity impatiently. She was holding a copy of the document in her hand. "What I don't understand is why he borrowed the money in the first place—and why it is only now, nearly a year later, that you tell us about it."

The attorney began to look rather hunted.

"It…it's entirely my fault," he stammered. "I knew about the agreement from the beginning—I'm sure Mr

Mayfield meant to repay...but then he was...and it was at that time that our youngest died...and Mrs Canby so upset—I really feared for her. Everything to do with business went clean out of my head.''

His distress was so palpable that when he briefly raised his eyes to Charity's face she found herself nodding reassuringly at him.

Her father had died almost eleven months ago, and at nearly the same time the Canbys had lost their last and youngest child. Mrs Canby had been hysterical with grief—for a while it had been feared that she might never regain her reason—and Mr Canby had been distracted with anxiety on her behalf. It was understandable if he had temporarily neglected his work.

The attorney sighed, grateful for Charity's forbearance, and continued with his explanation.

''The document got lost under other papers and by the time I could attend to things properly I...I'm afraid I'd forgotten it. I only found it again yesterday evening. I came at once. I hope... I'm sorry.'' He fell once more into dejected silence.

''I see,'' said Charity. She walked over to the window and stared out at the snow-covered garden. February snow. By the beginning of March she and her mother would have to leave Hazelhurst. The glare of reflected sunlight hurt her eyes and when she turned back to Mr Canby the room seemed very dark in comparison.

''I still don't understand what can have prompted Papa to make such an agreement,'' she said. ''I didn't even know he knew the Earl...'' she paused, glancing down at the document in her hand, searching for the name ''...the Earl of Ashbourne,'' she continued. ''What did he want the money for? And how did he think he was going to repay it?''

The enormity of the situation was finally coming home to Charity and her voice rose as she asked the last question.

The attorney shuffled his feet and concentrated his attention on the carpet. He'd been hoping to avoid the need to explain that part of the story.

"I think…I believe…"

The clock on the mantel suddenly began to chime the hour, and Mr Canby started with surprise. He looked up at the clock-face, almost as if he expected to find the answer to Charity's question there, and, without quite realising what he was doing, he began to count the chimes.

…Eight, nine, ten. Ten o'clock in the morning, and all was not well.

"Mr Canby!"

"It was a gambling debt," he said desperately.

"A gambling debt. Dear God!" Charity sat down suddenly and put her hands up to her face.

She had been hoping that, although her father had borrowed the money, he hadn't had time to spend it. She'd been hoping that they might be able to recover it and use it to repay the loan—but if it was a gambling debt it was gone forever.

Mr Canby looked down at her anxiously, but her face was hidden from him. All he could see were the wayward dark curls which, despite the prevailing fashion, she invariably wore unpowdered. She was a pretty, vivacious girl, with expressive hands that she used to emphasise everything she said. But today she seemed unnaturally still and her usually merry brown eyes looked strained and sombre when she raised her head and smiled bleakly at Mr Canby.

"That's it, then," she said. "I was hoping…but never mind. We must start making arrangements for the move. Can you…?" She stopped abruptly, an arrested expression in her eyes.

"What about the money Uncle Jacob left me?" she asked suddenly, wondering why she hadn't remembered it at once. "Isn't there some way we could use that to pay the debt?"

"Not until you are thirty," Mr Canby replied. "Mr Kelland's will is very clear on that point."

"And I couldn't borrow, using it as security?" Charity frowned, wishing her uncle hadn't been quite so firmly convinced that wisdom could only be acquired with age.

The attorney pursed his lips and shook his head slowly.

"Possibly, he said, "but, even if you could find a lender who would agree to such terms, I wouldn't advise such a course. A great deal could happen in the next seven years—and I'm sure that Mr Mayfield would not have wanted you to burden yourself with such a debt."

Mr Canby winced a little as he said those last few words—whatever Mr Mayfield's intentions might have been, he had hardly set his daughter a good example—but Charity simply nodded. Her immediate impulse was to do anything she could to save the family estate, but she had no desire to take on an enormous debt that she would be unable to repay for years to come.

"You won't be destitute," Mr Canby pointed out, glad that the situation was not totally black. "There's still your mother's jointure and the quarterly allowance Mr Kelland left to you. You will be able to live quite comfortably—but not here." Mr Canby bit his lip; he didn't think his words of reassurance had helped much.

"No, not here," said Charity.

Then she remembered her duties as a hostess and managed to smile at the attorney.

"I'm sorry, Mr Canby, I haven't offered you any refreshment, and it's a bitter day to be out," she said. "Would you like some tea, or perhaps some brandy? It's a fair ride back to Horsham.''

''No, no, thank you, Miss Mayfield,'' he replied uncomfortably, thinking how like Charity it was to be thinking of his comfort even at such a time. In all her dealings with him, both before and after the death of her father, she had been unfailingly generous and good-natured. She deserved better than this, Mr Canby thought wretchedly.

So did Mrs Mayfield, of course, but Mr Canby had always found her a more difficult woman and he had been secretly rather glad that a minor indisposition had kept her in bed that morning and obliged him to make his explanations directly to Charity. Charity could always be relied upon to listen rationally to what was said to her.

''I'm so sorry!'' he burst out suddenly. ''If only I'd remembered sooner…''

''Perhaps it was better that you didn't,'' Charity said quickly. She'd had enough of the attorney's regrets and self-recriminations. All she wanted now was to be left alone so that she could think, but she was too kind-hearted to dismiss Mr Canby without saying anything to assuage his guilt.

''There was nothing we could have done and we've had nearly an extra year here without having to worry about the future,'' she pointed out. ''Now, have you heard from Lord Ashbourne yet?''

''No,'' Mr Canby replied, gazing at her in some bewilderment. Her brisk assumption of a businesslike manner rather confounded him.

''Then I think you'd better contact him,'' said Charity. ''I'd also like you to come back tomorrow when I've had time to consider the situation in more detail. There will be a great many arrangements to make—and I must also tell Mama…''

She paused, and he suddenly saw that her eyes were suspiciously bright. She was very close to tears, though she was doing her best to hide it.

"Of course," he said quietly. "I'll see myself out."

He turned to go, then paused with his hand on the door-handle as he remembered something.

"I meant to tell you—there will be other changes in the neighbourhood soon," he said. "I heard only yesterday that Lord Riversleigh is dead."

"Lord Riversleigh? Good heavens!" said Charity faintly. At any other time the fortunes of her neighbours, even those of one she disliked as much as Lord Riversleigh, would have been of considerable interest to her. Now she hardly cared.

"What did he die of? Apoplexy?" she asked, with rather disconcerting bluntness.

Lord Riversleigh's bad temper and feuds had been a by-word for miles around. He'd given every indication of having loathed his one surviving son, and Charity had good reason to know that his treatment of his grandson had been no better.

"His carriage overturned in London," Mr Canby replied, reflecting that no one could accuse Miss Charity of being mealy-mouthed.

"Mr Harry Riversleigh was also with him. I think they were both killed. Of course, I may have been misinformed," he added pedantically, "but I don't think I was. No doubt we'll be seeing Master Edward—I mean, Lord Riversleigh back at the Hall before long. Well, I must be going. Please let me know if there's any way I can be of assistance to you. Good day, Miss Mayfield."

He closed the library door quietly, unconcerned that Charity hardly seemed to be aware that he was leaving and rather pleased with himself that even at such a black moment he had been able to give a new direction to her thoughts. Everyone knew that Miss Charity and young Edward Riversleigh had always been uncommonly friendly.

For a while after Mr Canby had gone Charity continued to be preoccupied by his final piece of news, partly because at that moment she would have welcomed anything that distracted her from her own troubles, but mainly because, as Mr Canby had suspected, she was genuinely interested in what happened to Edward.

In her opinion there hadn't been much to choose between Harry Riversleigh and his father: one had been an elderly tyrant, the other a middle-aged bully; she couldn't pretend to grieve for either of them.

Edward, on the other hand, she most definitely liked, and she was glad that for once he seemed to be having good luck. Harry had never married, and Edward was the child of the late Lord Riversleigh's youngest son. He had been orphaned at an early age and he had been brought up at Riversleigh Hall in an atmosphere of contention, his wishes constantly thwarted by his uncle or his grandfather. In the circumstances, it said a great deal for Edward that he should have grown into a generous and likeable man. Charity thought he deserved his good fortune and she was pleased for him—then she remembered that she wasn't likely to be there to see him enjoy it, and she sighed.

The library seemed cold and she was more aware than ever of the draughts coming in through the cracks in the mullioned windows. The heavy curtains stirred restlessly as a particularly large gust of wind hit the corner of the house, and outside the snow began to drift. If the weather continued so the roads would become impassable. It wasn't a good time to have to leave one's home.

When Charity entered her mother's room Mrs Mayfield

was sitting up in bed, a shawl wrapped round her shoulders and a cup of chocolate in her hands. She had taken a chill the previous day and the cold weather had inclined her to stay in bed longer than usual. She smiled when she saw her daughter and patted the edge of her bed invitingly.

"Hello, love. Come and sit down. Tabby tells me we had a visitor this morning—Mr Canby. I'm glad I missed him. Such a well-meaning man, but he does fidget me so. What did he want? You look cold. Good heavens, your hands are like ice. What *have* you been doing? Why don't you ring for some chocolate?"

"I am a little cold," Charity acknowledged, grateful for her mother's habit of never requiring an answer to more than one or two of the questions that invariably formed such a large part of her conversation. "I think the wind must be in the east; it's certainly very draughty in the library."

"I hate winter." Mrs Mayfield shivered and instinctively pulled her shawl more tightly about her, though in fact her room was one of the cosiest in the house. Her dislike of the cold was well known and her maid, Tabitha, always made sure that the fire was blazing in the hearth before she allowed her mistress to venture from her bed.

"Well, perhaps the cold weather will soon be over," said Mrs Mayfield hopefully when Charity, did not immediately reply to her previous comment. "Tabby told me she saw several snowdrops yesterday. Spring must be on its way."

"Yes, Mama." Charity tried to smile. "I saw them as well. I'll pick you some later."

"Thank you, dear. Oh, I *do* hope the weather improves," said Mrs Mayfield, her gentle voice running on without pause. "I'm so looking forward to the Leydons' party, and if the weather is too bad we won't be able to go. Though it will be worse if it rains, of course. Nothing is as bad for the roads as a flood. I still haven't forgotten that dreadful time when I went to London with your father and the coach got stuck above the axles in the mud and there was no inn for *five miles!* I had to wait in the most *uncomfortable* cottage for *hours* before we could continue our journey.''

''Papa said it was only forty-five minutes,'' Charity said mildly.

''It was nearly three hours,'' said Mrs Mayfield firmly. ''You should have known better than to believe what *Papa* had to say on such a matter. You know how he always used to make light of even the most dreadful situations.''

''He was an optimist,'' said Charity. ''Mama, there's something I have to tell you.''

''Really, dear? Do you know, I've been wondering what I ought to wear to Sir Humphrey's party? Do you think that gown I had made up in Horsham last November would—''

''*Mama!*'' Charity interrupted, suddenly unable to endure her mother's flow of gentle chatter any longer.

''Yes, love?'' Mrs Mayfield said in surprise. Then she saw the look on Charity's face and her own expression altered abruptly. ''What is it?'' she asked.

Charity hesitated, then she gripped her hands tightly together, took a deep breath and began to tell Mrs Mayfield what Mr Canby had told her.

It was late that evening before Charity could even consider going to bed. Mr Canby's news had thrown the whole household into turmoil. Not only Mrs Mayfield but the servants too were anxious about their future, and no sooner had Charity managed to calm her mother than she had had to face worried questions from the housekeeper.

She had done her best to reassure Mrs Wendle, but she was ruefully aware that she hadn't entirely succeeded. She was also resigned to the fact that soon the whole parish would know of their troubles. It wouldn't be long before they received visits from the more sympathetic—or curious—of their neighbours. She could only hope the cold weather would keep them at home for as long as possible.

She sighed, and put another log on the library fire. Everyone else was in bed but now she needed time alone to think, and for some reason she'd always felt more at peace surrounded by the shelves of old books than she did in any other room in the house.

The wind had died down, but she knew that if she pulled back the curtains she would see large white flakes of snow, falling down against the darkness beyond. She tucked up her feet beneath her, rested her chin on her hand, and gazed into the fire as she considered ways and means.

Whatever they did would be up to her. Mrs Mayfield had never been a decisive woman, and ever since the death of her husband she had increasingly allowed Charity to take on the responsibility for managing their affairs. It was a task which Charity relished and, even now, she was aware of a small spark of excitement at the thought of the new challenge she had been set. Somehow she would manage, not only for her mother, but for everyone on the Hazelhurst estate.

It was well past midnight when she finally thought of a way to do it.

She turned the plan over in her mind a couple of times in case there was a flaw, then, with typical energy, she set about executing it.

She'd been sitting in the firelight, but now she lit a candle and put it on the desk while she found the necessary materials to write a letter. She moved the candle once, so that it cast no shadow upon the paper, dipped the pen in the ink, and began to cover the sheet with bold, confident writing.

My dear friend,

Today I heard the news of your unexpected change of fortune and I write at once to congratulate you. I dare say that perhaps I ought to commiserate with you also, but we know each other too well for such *commonplace* utterances to be necessary. I don't suppose there is a single person at Riversleigh Hall, or on the rest of the estate for that matter, who is not thanking heaven that it is you, not Harry, who will be their new master.

I wish that I need do no more than send you my congratulations but, unfortunately, on the same day that I learnt of your advancement I received news which may have disastrous consequences for all of us here at Hazelhurst. However, on reflection I think the coincidence may be fortuitous, and that, now you are Lord Riversleigh, it may be possible for us to be of mutual service to each other.

Just before he died, Papa ran up monstrous gambling debts and now—because, of course, we can't pay them—his entire property is forfeit! We have to leave Hazelhurst within the month! You can't think what a relief it is to be able to tell that to someone who won't moan and wring their hands and say, ''But Miss Charity, what are we going to *do?*''

Poor Mrs Wendle; it must have come as a dreadful shock to her—she's been living at Hazelhurst for more than forty years, ever since she first began as a chambermaid. Well, none of that's relevant now, of course.

Charity paused briefly, biting the end of the pen. In the relief of being able to express herself freely she had nearly strayed completely from the point, and it was going to cost Edward enough to receive this letter without her adding unnecessary digressions. She dipped the pen in the ink again and carried on writing.

At first I didn't know what we should do, but, after thinking about it, I believe I might have come up with a solution. One that may be of benefit to both of us—you as well.

Do you remember Mama's brother, Jacob Kelland, who'd been sent to India in disgrace years ago? The one who suddenly turned up here at Hazelhurst about three years ago and demanded to be taken in? He was such a fusspot. He drove Mama to distraction, worrying about the price of candles, and when he started telling Papa how to manage the estate Papa was provoked into saying that India must have ruined his disposition, as well as his health and his fortune! Anyway, he stayed for weeks—we thought we'd never get rid of him—then one morning we got up to find that he'd left in the night without even telling us; it was so peculiar—and not at all polite—but Mama was relieved. Though, I must admit, I quite liked him—he used to make me laugh.

Oh, dear, I've wandered off the point again. The point is that Mama and I found out only last autumn that he hadn't been poor at all. He knew that his health had been undermined by the Indian climate and he suddenly took a quixotic notion into his head to come back to England—posing as a poor man—and see which of his relatives most deserved to inherit his fortune! When he'd made his decision he didn't tell anyone, he just went back to India and carried on getting richer until he died! It's hard to believe he was Mama's brother.

Anyway, for some reason he decided that I was the

most trustworthy person to receive his worldly goods. That's how he described me in his will—trustworthy.

Charity paused again, remembering the less than courteous epithets which her uncle had used to describe her parents. She didn't intend to share those with anyone—even Edward. She continued.

I'm afraid I've been gossiping on here, but I'll try to make the rest briefer. Uncle Jacob left me his entire fortune, but I cannot have access to it until I am thirty—or until I am married. Apparently he didn't think I was *that* trustworthy!

Anyway, Mama and I agreed not to tell anyone about it, because I'm happy as we are, and I don't want my *prospects* to be more attractive to the people I meet than I am.

But now it occurs to me that I can save Hazelhurst myself—if only I can find a husband before the end of February!

I know that an early marriage has never been part of your plans. And I suspect that, even now, you are more concerned with pursuing your studies than you are with other, more worldly considerations—but, even so, I think Uncle Jacob's fortune may be able to serve both our interests.

It's no secret that Riversleigh is mortgaged to the hilt and, however conscientiously you may discharge your duties, it will be years before the estate is back on its feet. Such a situation can only be to your disadvantage, particularly as your interests lie elsewhere.

If you were to marry me, Uncle Jacob's fortune could buy back Hazelhurst, release Riversleigh from the most crippling of its debts, and still provide you with sufficient funds to visit Rome and the other places you have been longing to see.

I dare say that it is very *unladylike* for me to make such a suggestion, but it does seem to me to be an extremely *practical* solution to both our problems, and I do hope that you will agree to it.

Yours hopefully
Charity

She signed the letter boldly and was just about to fold and seal it when she suddenly thought of something and opened the paper up again.

PS The lease on Bellow's farm has now expired and, since Mr Bellow had decided to go and live with his daughter in Middlesex, you will need to look for a new tenant. Your grandfather favoured Cooper, but both Mr Guthrie and I think Jerry Burden would be a much better choice. I hope you will look into this matter *as soon as possible* because it is not profitable to you or Jerry to leave the farm untenanted for long.

She glanced quickly through what she had written, refolded the letter, sealed it and wrote the direction on the outside. Then she sat back with a sigh of satisfaction that she had at least done something towards saving Hazelhurst. Now all she had to do was send the letter off and wait for Edward to reply.

Chapter Two

"Good morning, Mr Guthrie. Isn't it a lovely day?"

"Aye, so it is, Miss Charity," replied Mr Guthrie, the land agent for the Riversleigh estate. "Though I'm told all this melted snow has rendered the roads well nigh impassable halfway to London."

"But the sky is blue, the sun is shining and I've found some snowdrops. Look!" Charity held the flowers up in the bright morning light for the land agent to see. "Who cares about a little mud?" she finished exultantly. It was true that earlier that morning she had been quite worried in case the mail-coach foundered. But out in the sunshine her doubts could not linger, and now she was convinced that it would not be long before Edward would be reading her letter.

It was only two days since Mr Canby had visited, but the weather had broken and Charity had been unable to stay indoors a moment longer. She had gone out into the garden and then, enticed by the crisp fresh air, she had walked down the drive to the gate. It had been while she was standing there that Mr Guthrie had passed by.

The land agent's dour expression softened slightly as he

looked down at Charity and the fragile blooms she held in her hand.

''I've always had a fondness for the brave wee flowers, growing in the snow,'' he said, managing to give the impression that he was rather ashamed to admit to such a weakness; then he swung down stiffly from his horse.

''Does your leg hurt?'' Charity asked, concerned to see how awkwardly the land agent was moving.

''No, no. Mebbe the cold weather aggravates it—but nothing to speak of,'' he said impatiently, his Scottish accent more pronounced than usual.

''So don't *fuss,* woman!'' Charity finished for him.

Mr Guthrie looked at her disapprovingly. ''You ought to mind that pert tongue of yours,'' he said. ''One day it will get you into trouble.''

''It already has—many times,'' Charity agreed, undaunted by the grim expression on his weather-beaten face. ''Would you like some snowdrops?''

Without waiting for a reply, she stood on tiptoe and carefully inserted a small bunch of flowers into Mr Guthrie's buttonhole.

''Thank you,'' he said gruffly. ''Is it true you must leave Hazelhurst?'' he continued, his sharp eyes scanning her face intently as she stepped back to admire her handiwork. ''You're looking more cheerful than I had expected.''

''There, it's amazing what a difference a buttonhole can make,'' Charity said. ''If you'd only smile a bit more often you'd look quite festive. Yes, it's true. But I hadn't expected the news to get out *quite* so soon.''

''You sent Charles to post a letter for you yesterday. I dare say the whole village knows by now,'' said Mr Guthrie drily.

''So I did; I'd forgotten that,'' Charity said ruefully. ''Never mind, it was bound to come out sooner or later, and I dare say people will lose interest very quickly. I think *your* news is much more dramatic. It must have been a terrible shock to you, Lord Riversleigh and Mr Riversleigh being killed at the same time like that,'' she added in her forthright manner.

"It was," said the land agent grimly. "There'll be great changes at Riversleigh now, I don't doubt."

"For the better, surely?" said Charity.

She had known Mr Guthrie for a long time and she was well aware that he had shared her dislike for his late master. In fact, she had often wondered why the land agent had remained at Riversleigh, and she had been sure he would be pleased with the unexpected course of events.

"I know Edward's always dreaming of designing the perfect building," she said, "but he must be an improvement on his grandfather!"

"Aye, but…"

"Miss Charity! Miss Charity! Mrs Wendle says, please can you come at once?" A maid came running down the drive towards them, stumbling over her gown in her haste.

Mr Guthrie's mare shied back and tossed her head nervously, and the land agent seized her bridle and spoke soothingly to her while Charity turned to greet the girl.

"What is it?" she asked.

"It's Mrs Mayfield," Ellen gasped. "She was trying to decide which furniture to take and she got upset! Please come quickly, miss!"

"Of course. Excuse me, Mr Guthrie." Charity smiled briefly but warmly at the land agent, then she picked up her skirts and ran back to the house, with Ellen following behind her.

Mr Guthrie watched until she had disappeared, then he sighed and put his foot in the stirrup and dragged himself into the saddle. He had broken his right leg in a riding accident nearly fifteen years ago and it was aching more than usual today. I must be getting old, he thought; but he'd known Charity since she was a child, and he was going to miss her.

"Miss Charity!"

"I'm here, Charles. What is it?" Charity looked up as the footman picked his way towards her through the crowded and dusty attic.

It was nearly a week later and Charity had finally persuaded her mother that it would do her good to visit the Leydons, and now she was taking advantage of Mrs Mayfield's absence to sort through the attic, trying to decide if there was anything up there worth taking with them.

"Lord Riversleigh is here to see you, miss!" Charles announced, and, even in the gloom, Charity thought she caught sight of a conspiratorial gleam in his eyes.

Charles had only been working at Hazelhurst for a few months, but he was already devoted to Charity and it had been he who had posted the letter for her. She had asked him not to tell anyone else she was writing to Lord Riversleigh and, as far as she was aware, he had not done so. But no doubt someone must have told him she had always been on very friendly terms with Edward Riversleigh. Never mind; if her plan succeeded he was welcome to share some of the credit.

"He's in the library, miss," said Charles as he followed Charity out of the attic. "That being the only room apart from Mrs Mayfield's where a fire's been lit."

"Thank you, Charles," Charity called over her shoulder. In her haste she was already halfway down the stairs and she didn't pause in her headlong flight until she had burst impetuously through the library door.

"Edward! I'm so pleased you could…" She stopped short.

The tall man standing by the window was not Edward Riversleigh. Edward could never have appeared so casually elegant, nor could he have imposed his presence on a room so completely that his surroundings faded into insignificance. Yet the stranger had done nothing dramatic, he had simply turned at the sound of the opening door and looked at Charity; but, as her eyes met his, she was instantly aware that he possessed an aura of strength and sophistication which seemed quite out of place in the small, comfortably shabby library.

"I…I beg your pardon, sir," she stammered, dazedly wondering how Charles could possibly have mistaken this man for the far from grand Edward. "I was expecting someone else. How…how do you do? May I help you?" she finished rather breathlessly.

"Thank you, you are very kind," the gentleman replied, and even in her confusion Charity could not help noticing that his voice was deep and melodious. "But I am afraid it is I who should apologise to you."

He came towards her as he spoke and as the light from the window fell on his face she could see that he had grey eyes, a firm chin and a decisive mouth.

He halted before her and bowed courteously over the hand she instinctively offered him.

"You…you *should?*" Charity said, still somewhat confused by his presence, and disconcertingly aware of the firm clasp of his fingers on hers.

"Certainly." The gentleman straightened up and released her hand. His expression was grave, but there was a distant glint of amusement in his grey eyes as he looked at Charity, though she was far too bewildered to notice it.

"I believe I have the honour of addressing Miss Mayfield…Miss Charity Mayfield?'' he said, his eyebrow lifting enquiringly as he spoke.

"Yes, but…''

"It's always wise to make certain of these things, don't you think?'' he continued smoothly. "My name is Jack Riversleigh.''

"Jack Riversleigh?'' Charity echoed, staring up at him blankly.

"Richard's son,'' he explained. "Richard was the late Lord Riversleigh's second son.''

"Oh!'' Charity gazed, open-mouthed, at her unexpected visitor, still so stunned that it was several minutes before she understood the significance of what he had said.

"You mean *you* come before Edward in the succession?'' she said at last.''

"I'm afraid so,'' he agreed.

"But I thought Richard died in disgrace years ago!'' Charity burst out, losing some of her awe in her amazement at this remarkable turn of events.

Lord Riversleigh smiled.

"My father died in the most respectable of circumstances seventeen years ago,'' he said. "I believe it was only the late Lord Riversleigh who held him in such aversion.''

"I'm sorry.'' Charity blushed, painfully aware of what a poor impression she must be making. "I didn't mean to be rude. It's just that…it's all rather surprising. Good grief!'' she exclaimed suddenly. "You must have received my letter!''

"Yes, ma'am,'' Jack Riversleigh said gently. "It was that which prompted my visit today. I thought, in the circumstances, you would prefer to be appraised of your misapprehension in private.''

"Oh, how dreadful!'' Charity put up her hands to her burning cheeks and closed her eyes, not really listening to what he was saying as she realised with horror that she had proposed marriage to a stranger!

"Come, I think you should sit down," he said, and he guided her unresistingly to a chair. "You've had quite a shock."

"No, no, I'm all right," she said mechanically.

Her thoughts were in such a turmoil of confusion and embarrassment that she hardly knew what to say—or do— but almost instinctively she sought refuge in her role as hostess.

"I'm so sorry, I should have invited you to sit down, my lord," she said with an attempt at polite formality, which she immediately spoiled by bursting out impetuously, "Oh, dear! You must have formed the most *dreadful* impression of me!"

"No." Suddenly, and quite unexpectedly, he laughed. "No, Miss Mayfield, dreadful is not the word I would have used. I apologise for startling you; I should have introduced myself less baldly."

Charity looked at him doubtfully. Then she smiled hesitantly. Now that her first shock was receding she could see that the strength in his face was tempered by humour, and she began to feel slightly more at ease with him. She thought that perhaps it was his fine black coat which had made him seem so grand—and then realised almost immediately that he must be in mourning for his grandfather.

She felt relieved to have discovered the reason for her unexpected lack of composure earlier, and instantly resolved never to be impressed by fine clothes again. Then, just as she was about to make a polite comment on the weather, or the state of the roads, or some other bland, innocuous topic—to indicate her own level of unconcern and sophistication—it suddenly dawned on her that he was finding the situation amusing, and she began to feel flustered all over again.

She raised startled and rather alarmed eyes to his—and then began to feel more comfortable as she realised that, although he was certainly amused, he was equally definitely not gloating over her discomfiture. She even thought she detected a gleam of sympathy in his expression.

She thought ruefully that he might well find it amusing to receive a proposal of marriage from a woman whose existence he had hitherto been completely unaware of and cursed herself for not having addressed the letter more precisely.

"Good," he said when he saw she had recovered at least partially from her initial astonishment. "I was sure you would have too much presence of mind to be overset by my visit. I believe, in fairness to you, I ought to explain how this peculiar situation has arisen—if you're interested?"

"Oh, yes!" said Charity, leaning forward eagerly and momentarily forgetting her embarrassment in her desire to find out just how it had come about that Riversleigh had been inherited by a complete stranger. "Oh, I beg your pardon." She blushed again as she suddenly remembered all her mother's lectures on decorum. In a belated attempt to make amends for her unmannerly interest she sat up straight and folded her hands demurely in her lap. "I mean, thank you, that would be very kind of you."

Jack smiled. He had been slightly concerned by Charity's earlier evident confusion, but now that she had regained much of her composure his amusement at the situation in which he found himself had revived, though he was careful not to show it too openly. He was also slightly surprised by the lack of interest she had so far shown in the fate of the man she had just proposed to. It did not seem to suggest that her heart was inextricably bound to Edward.

"Well, as I said before," he began, "my father, Richard, was the late Lord Riversleigh's second son, and Edward's father was his third son. But my father left Riversleigh thirty years ago, and when he did so Lord Riversleigh declared that as far as he was concerned he now had only two sons—Richard was dead to him."

"How *inhuman!*" Charity gasped, her eyes fixed on Jack's face, her dark curls dancing with indignation. "I *never* liked him! He behaved most unkindly to Edward for no good reason at all. Was there any reason for him to dislike your papa? Oh, dear! I mean...I mean..." She floundered to a halt, uncomfortably aware that once again she had allowed her tongue to run away with her.

"No," said Jack. "My father refused to be ruled by my grandfather, but he never behaved dishonourably."

"I never suspected he did!" Charity exclaimed indignantly. "Lord Riversleigh disliked Edward for being conscientious in his studies—and if that isn't a crackbrained attitude for a guardian to hold I don't know what is!"

"Quite." Jack's lips twitched, but he maintained an admirable gravity. "Anyway, my father married my mother not long after he left Riversleigh and, no doubt much to Lord Riversleigh's annoyance, I was one of the consequences."

"Did he know you existed?" Charity asked curiously. The workings of the late Lord Riversleigh's mind had always been a mystery to her; she had never understood how he could be so cruel to those who should be closest to him.

"Oh, yes," Jack replied. "I met him once, after my father died. I made it my business to do so—I wanted to know what kind of man he was—but when he discovered who I was he refused to acknowledge me. It didn't greatly concern me. I had no idea that I might eventually succeed him.''

''Nor had anyone else,'' said Charity. ''At least... Edward didn't know, did he?''

''No,'' Jack said. ''I believe my grandfather gave orders that my father's name was never to be mentioned again. Over the years people must have forgotten, and even those who did know wouldn't have spoken of the matter.''

''Of course not,'' said Charity. ''He could be quite... Poor Edward; I wonder what he'll do now.''

In her first amazement she had not considered how Edward must feel about the whole thing, but now she felt sad that once more he had been unlucky. She stood up and walked over to the window, looking out at the holly tree that stood up against the blue sky beyond.

''You mustn't think I'm not pleased for you, my lord,'' she said. ''But it must have been rather hard on Edward. Not that he wanted the title, but even if he hadn't accepted my propo— I mean, at the very least the revenues of the estate could probably have provided him with a trip to Rome... Where is he?''

She swung round to face Jack as she suddenly realised that, interesting though all this was, she still didn't have the one piece of information which was essential for the success of *her* plans.

''I'm afraid he's already on his way to Italy,'' Jack said quietly, watching Charity's face carefully as he spoke.

He suspected that this news would be a great disappointment to her and, though he was not above being amused by the situation, he was reluctant to give her tidings which he was afraid would cause her real distress.

''Italy? But how on earth...?''

''As you said, it was something he'd wanted to do for a long time,'' Jack continued smoothly. ''I believe when he had the opportunity the excitement drove all other thoughts from his head. I'm sure he'll be writing to you soon.''

"You mean, someone's going to help him in his efforts to become an architect?'' Charity asked incredulously.

"Yes."

"Oh, I'm so glad!'' she exclaimed, forgetting her own problems in her relief at Edward's good fortune. "He's worked so hard, and had so little support. He'll enjoy that much more than being Lord Riversleigh!''

"I hope so," said Jack, relieved at Charity's reaction.

"He will,'' Charity assured him. "Last time I saw him he insisted on reading me extracts from a book he'd just acquired about the ruins of some palace at Spal… Spally…"

"Spalatro,'' Jack supplied. "I believe you mean the book by Robert Adam on *The Ruins of the Palace of the Emperor Diocletian at Spalatro in Dalmatia.*"

"That's it!'' said Charity. "How on earth did you know?''

"I've read it,'' said Jack apologetically.

"Oh.'' She looked at him blankly. "Are you an architect too, sir?''

"No, but I've always been interested in a variety of different crafts. It's important not to have too narrow a viewpoint,'' Jack said, and changed the subject abruptly. "At the risk of being impertinent, may I ask you a question, Miss Mayfield?''

"Of course. What is it?'' Charity glanced at him apprehensively, suddenly reminded that he had read her letter and consequently knew far more about her than she might have wished.

"Are you very disappointed by the turn of events?'' he asked. "As I'm sure you've realised, I'm afraid I read your letter. I must apologise for that—I don't make a habit of reading other people's correspondence, and I assure you I will treat what I read in confidence—but at first I didn't quite know what to make of it.'' He paused.

"No, I understand,'' said Charity; she looked down at her hands, feeling very self-conscious.

"I hope so. When I realised you'd intended it for Edward I would have forwarded it to him unread, but it seemed as if you needed his assistance urgently *because* he was Lord Riversleigh, so I hoped that I might be able to help instead. I'm sorry that I can't. But if you wish I'll do everything in my power to get your message to him as soon as possible.''

"Thank you,'' she said. "But it would be too late. Edward was my first choice, but I dare say I can manage without him. I shall just have to look about me again.''

"You mean, you're going to ask someone *else* to marry you?'' Jack had been leaning back negligently in his chair, but he sat up straight at this.

"No,'' said Charity. "Unfortunately Edward is the only man I know who can be relied upon to be sensible about such things. Next time I must try and persuade *them* to propose to *me*.''

"Good God!'' said Jack. For the first time during the interview he looked startled—he hadn't expected this. "But what about Edward?''

"What about him?'' Charity looked puzzled.

"Less than ten days ago you asked him to marry you!'' Jack pointed out.

"Yes, but that was when I thought he was available. He's no good to me in Italy!''

"No, I suppose not,'' said Jack. He had relaxed again, his surprise giving way to amusement. "I gathered from your letter that you had very little time at your disposal, but I hope you will forgive me if I tell you that you seem to have a rather prosaic view of matrimony.''

"No, just practical," Charity replied. "One should always be practical, don't you think?"

"An admirable philosophy," Jack agreed. "May I ask if you have anyone in particular in mind? I imagine the supply of eligible bachelors is fairly limited in this part of Sussex—though being an heiress must widen your choice."

"You mean, you can't imagine why anyone should want me without the sweetener of Uncle Jacob's fortune?" Charity demanded, seizing on his last comment.

"No, of course not!" he replied quickly as he saw the flash in her dark eyes. "I was thinking aloud and what I said was very badly phrased. I only meant that for various reasons most heiresses have, or could have, a wider circle of acquaintances than many other ladies. More—perfectly unexceptional—doors are open to you. That must be useful if you're looking for a husband."

"Possibly," said Charity cautiously. "Lord Riversleigh, may I ask a great favour of you? Until now, nobody apart from Mama and me—and our lawyer, of course—has known about Uncle Jacob's fortune. I didn't want them to. I still don't."

"Yes, I see," said Jack slowly. "You mentioned something about that in your letter; I should have remembered. Don't be alarmed; I'll keep your secret."

"Thank you." She smiled with relief. "As you said, there aren't a great many suitable men in the neighbourhood, but at least I know them, and I needn't worry about their motives if one of them…" She paused, an arrested expression in her eyes. "Yes, yes, definitely," she said after a moment as if she was speaking to herself—which she was. Then she suddenly recollected herself.

"Good heavens! How remiss of me. I haven't even offered you any refreshment. Would you like some tea, my lord? Or some wine?" she asked brightly.

"Thank you." Jack watched her pull the bell, and then allowed her to steer the conversation on to more mundane matters until after Charles had arrived with the tray and then departed, desperate with curiosity to know more of what was happening in the library.

"Is it really essential that you be married?" Jack asked when they were alone again. "I've no wish to appear impertinent, but our acquaintance began in such an unusual way that I trust you won't be offended if I seem a little outspoken."

Charity looked at him suspiciously, but his expression was perfectly grave and it was impossible to accuse him of laughing at her.

"No, it's not essential," she said at last. "But, since you've read my letter, you know why I need a husband."

"To retain your home," he said. "I can understand why you would wish to do that." He looked appreciatively round the library as he spoke. "It's a fine old house. When was it built?"

"Just before the Civil War," Charity replied. "There were Mayfields living here for at least a century before that, but the old house was in a sad state of decay by the beginning of Charles I's reign, and Thomas Mayfield had this one built. That's Thomas there."

She pointed at a portrait hanging on the chimney breast. It was quite a dark, almost a gloomy picture, certainly not by the hand of a master. But somehow it seemed to capture something of the spirit of the man it depicted. He was not a handsome man, but he looked both amiable and sensible—and his gaze was as direct as Charity's.

"Unfortunately he didn't have long to enjoy the house," Charity continued. "He died a few years later, fighting for the Royalist cause, but his baby son inherited it and it's remained in the family ever since."

She sighed, and some of the animation died out of her face. She loved her home, and now that she had recovered from her initial astonishment at Jack Riversleigh's unexpected arrival she was feeling sadly deflated. She hadn't realised until now how much she had been counting on Edward.

"I'm sorry," said Jack. "Is there no other way to save it?"

"No." Charity shook her head.

"I see. It did occur to me that you would have to leave your home anyway, if you were married. Doesn't that rather defeat your purpose?" Jack asked delicately.

"Yes, I know," Charity replied impatiently. "But Mama would be able to continue here, and the rest of the household. It's been their home for so long... Oh, well," she continued more briskly, "I shouldn't be burdening you with our problems, my lord. At least..." She paused, a speculative expression in her eyes as they rested on his face.

"Are you married, sir?" she asked at last.

Jack blinked and then gave a shout of laughter. "No, Miss Mayfield, nor do I have any immediate plans to be. Thank you."

"Are you sure?" said Charity. "After all, the same considerations apply to you as did to Edward. Riversleigh is still mortgaged; it will still be difficult for you to pull it out of debt."

"Miss Mayfield, you don't know me," Jack said more soberly. "Don't think I'm not flattered, but I hope you don't intend to fling yourself at every man you meet until the end of February. That's a sure way to come to grief— particularly if you intend to offer them a fortune at the same time!"

"No, of course not," said Charity impatiently. "You may think I'm a hoyden, but I assure you I'm not entirely lacking in sense. If you had agreed to marry me you would have kept the bargain—wouldn't you?''

''Do you think every man would?'' Jack asked, without answering her question.

''No. But I shan't ask one who won't.''

''I hope you don't,'' he said quietly, and stood up. ''I must be going; I have already stayed far too long. Thank you for your hospitality. I trust your schemes will meet with success.''

''So do I.'' Charity held out her hand and felt a curious moment of regret as his lips lightly brushed her fingers.

''Who is your next target?'' he asked. ''You've decided already, haven't you?''

She looked at him consideringly. ''I don't think I'll tell you that,'' she said at last. ''You might warn him.''

He laughed. ''You do me an injustice,'' he said. ''I look forward with interest to our next meeting. Your servant, Miss Mayfield.''

When he was gone the library seemed oddly empty without his presence to fill it. Charity sat in the window-seat and gazed with unfocused eyes at the holly tree. All her plans had been completely overturned and now she would have to begin again, with ten days already wasted.

She was only roused when she heard her mother's voice in the hall and realised Mrs Mayfield had returned from the Leydons'. No doubt she had already heard that Lord Riversleigh had visited. Charity suddenly woke up to the fact that she was going to have to tell her mother that Edward *wasn't* the new Lord Riversleigh, and to explain why *Jack* Riversleigh had come to call!

She gasped and quickly tried to think of an excuse. And by the time the door opened and Mrs Mayfield came into the library she was able to smile at her mother quite calmly, ready for any question.

Chapter Three

The morning after Jack Riversleigh's unexpected visit Charity went out early for a walk. Mrs Mayfield was still in bed and Charity needed some peace away from the house to think. Her mind seemed to be divided: part of her was busy planning for their departure; part of her was hoping they'd never have to leave.

Mr Canby had visited again to tell her that Lord Ashbourne's agent would soon be arriving to discuss the transfer, and Charity was trying to get everything in order before he did so. Mr Canby was doing what he could to help, and Mr Guthrie had offered his services also, but there were a great many things which only Charity *could* do.

Yet all the time she was adding up the household and farm accounts, or overseeing the packing of boxes, a voice in her head kept telling her that none of this was necessary, that everything would turn out fine in the end.

She shook her head irritably in an effort to clear it and walked briskly down the lane. There had been no rain since the last of the snow and, despite Mrs Mayfield's fears and Mr Guthrie's comments, the roads had remained surprisingly good. Charity had only to pick her way round the odd

puddle and to avoid those boggy patches which never dried
out except during exceptionally fine summers.

She still thought her plan of getting married was a good
one, and Lord Riversleigh had been correct when he had
suspected that she already had someone in mind.

Owen Leydon was much of an age with Edward Riversleigh and she had known him, like Edward, all her life.
He would not have been her first choice—indeed, he hadn't
been—but she thought he would suit her purposes very
well. The only difficulty was that she would have to adopt
more circuitous means to achieve her end. With Edward
you could be as blunt as you liked and he wouldn't take
offence—but she had always had to coax Owen round to
her viewpoint. In fact, there had been occasions when his
stubbornness had driven her to distraction, but this time she
was determined to be subtle.

The hedges on both sides of the lane were thick and well
tended and, because she couldn't see much over the top of
them, she was glad when she reached a gate. There was no
stock in the field and the gate had been left open, so she
walked through it and stood looking out across the rolling
farmland—Hazelhurst land. The sun was shining and it was
surprisingly warm. It was the kind of morning when Charity found that it was impossible to stay indoors.

She took a deep breath and looked about her. To the
right the field was edged by a hazel coppice, and in the
centre a huge old oak tree raised its branches to the sky.
She had climbed that tree as a child, and every year since
she could remember she had come nutting here in autumn.
She wondered if Lord Ashbourne liked hazelnuts, but, even
if he did, he was unlikely to pick his own.

She would miss this when she left Hazelhurst. She would
miss the easy access to the countryside, and the freedom
she had always enjoyed there—but it wasn't just memories

she would be leaving behind her. She had worked hard and accomplished a great deal in the past few years and now, just as she felt she was really beginning to get somewhere, she had to hand over everything to a stranger.

Hazelhurst was a small estate, consisting only of the home farm and two tenant farms, but in the last few years, even before her father's death, Charity had started to increase its efficiency. It wasn't easy: the heavy Sussex Wealden clay didn't lend itself to all the improvements possible in Norfolk or even further south on the Sussex Downs or coastal regions; and the impatience of her father and the old-fashioned notions of one of the tenants hadn't helped.

But Charity had persisted. She had watched and waited and made tactful suggestions whenever the opportunity arose, coaxing change—never forcing it—and at last she was beginning to see the reward for her patience in the increased yields from all three farms. Only days ago she had been optimistic about the future, busy making plans for further improvements—and now she was to lose it all.

Soon she would be sitting meekly in a shabby drawing-room in a provincial town, with nothing more exciting to think about than her embroidery or the gossip of her neighbours.

I'll go mad, she thought. But, of course, if her plans succeeded she would be married to Owen and living at Leydon House. For a moment her courage failed her—was that really the best solution? The memory of her conversation with Lord Riversleigh rose unbidden in her mind and once again she experienced an unaccountable sense of regret. But then she thought of Mrs Mayfield and Mrs Wendle and all the other people for whom Hazelhurst was home, and her resolve to marry Owen returned. To be sure, her household didn't know she was planning their salvation, but, all the same, she couldn't let them down.

There were catkins in the hedge and she picked some, meaning to take them back for Mrs Mayfield. In the distance she could hear the sound of hounds in full cry and she was dimly aware that the hunt was out, but it was not until the fox ran straight past her and out through the gate that she realised how close it was. She swung round and saw the first of the hounds racing towards her across the field.

Later she couldn't explain what she did next, but at the time she was only aware of a sudden uncharacteristic anger at the dogs. Perhaps she felt a momentary affinity with the fox because she felt it was being driven from its home in much the same way that she was being driven from hers.

Whether that was the case or not, with Charity thinking inevitably led to action. She dropped the bunch of catkins, heaved the heavy gate up on its hinges and staggered round to close it, letting it fall back in place just as the first of the huntsmen came over the opposite hedge, hard on the heels of the hounds. At the same moment the enormity of what she had done occurred to her—and she realised that she had shut herself in on the wrong side of the gate.

She wasn't frightened of the hounds, but the dogs would be followed by men, and even Charity's courage failed her at the thought of what Sir Humphrey Leydon would have to say about what she'd done!

She began to edge her way along the hedge, hoping that in the heat of the chase no one would notice her. The hounds had already reached the gate and checked. They couldn't get through it, or below it—it was too low to the ground and the bars were too closely spaced. They whined and spread out on either side of it, forcing their way through gaps in the thick hedge. The first of them were through, but they checked again: they had temporarily lost the scent.

Charity kept walking along the hedge and, to her relief, it seemed that nobody had noticed her, or knew what she had done. She spotted Sir Humphrey and some red-faced tenant farmers and a thin-faced man she didn't recognise, but none of them saw her. They were anxious for the gate to be opened, for the chance to continue the chase.

There was a fuss and some delay. It was a heavy gate, not easily opened from the back of a horse, and one of the whippers-in had to dismount. Then the last of the hounds went through, followed by the riders, and Charity was alone again, listening to the sounds of the retreating hunt.

"Charity! What the *devil* did you do that for? How *dare* you ruin my father's hunt?"

Charity stopped and turned round slowly.

Owen Leydon was riding up behind her—and he was furious.

"I don't know what you mean," she said weakly; she couldn't afford to argue with Owen now!

"I saw you close the gate. How *dare* you do such a thing?" Owen was almost shaking with rage at what he considered to be her unpardonable interference; and his anger was undoubtedly made worse because until she'd closed the gate they'd been enjoying one of the best chases of the season.

"Oh." She realised he must have been the first rider over the hedge, and she could hardly deny his accusation.

"I...I don't know what came over me," she said, trying to propitiate him, but unfortunately only increasing his anger by her procrastination. "I think I must have been startled when I suddenly saw all those hounds bearing down on me!"

"Nonsense!" Owen might have been conciliated if Charity had made an immediate and frank apology, but he had known her far too long to be convinced by what he considered a very feeble excuse. "I don't believe you. You're no more frightened of the hounds than I am. You were deliberately trying to sabotage the hunt! What were you trying to do? Make my father look like a fool? Don't you know we have an important visitor from London staying with us?"

"Indeed I don't know. How should I?" Any intention Charity might have had to apologise disintegrated completely at this unfounded accusation. "Why *should* I want to ruin your stupid hunt?"

"I don't know," Owen said disagreeably, the heat of his fury having died down into sullen animosity. "I've never understood the crazy notions you take in your head. But I do know a more contrary, obstinate, self-willed girl can't exist!"

"I beg your pardon?" By now Charity was so rigid with indignation that she hardly cared what she said. "But this is Hazelhurst land you're riding across—and cutting up with all your pounding hoofs—and if I want to close the gate on my own land I have every right to do so!"

"Not when the hounds are running! Well, all I can say is that it's fortunate my father doesn't know what you did. Good day, Miss Mayfield," Owen ended, and wheeled about to follow the hunt without waiting for Charity to reply.

She stepped back to avoid the mud thrown up from the horse's hoofs and tripped over a rut in the ground, falling heavily.

It hurt; but instead of calling out she sat up and rubbed her elbow ruefully, watching Owen disappear through the gate, unaware of her accident.

"And a perfect opportunity missed," said an amused voice behind her.

She looked up quickly to see Lord Riversleigh dismounting from a fine bay gelding.

"Are you hurt, Miss Mayfield?" He pulled the reins over the horse's head and led him over to her.

"No, of course not!" Charity exclaimed, feeling rather annoyed at being discovered in such an undignified position by someone who seemed so very point-device. Nevertheless, she accepted the hand he offered her and allowed him to pull her to her feet.

"Thank you. What are you doing here? What do you mean, 'a perfect opportunity'?" she asked, running one question straight on from the other.

"And I'm delighted to meet *you* again, Miss Mayfield. Very fine weather we're having for the time of year, don't you think?" Jack said, looking at her in some amusement. She was so unselfconsciously outspoken that he found the impulse to tease her irresistible.

Charity blinked at him, then she laughed and held out her hand. "I'm sorry, I've never been very good at polite conversation. How do you do?"

"Very well, thank you." He took her hand and kissed it gracefully, and she felt her fingers tingle at the touch of his lips.

"As to your first question, I was out riding when I heard the sound of the hunt and I thought I'd watch it pass," he explained as he straightened up. "And as to your second…am I by any chance correct in suspecting that that's the young man who is destined to take Edward's place in your plans?"

"What if he is?" Charity asked cautiously. She was trying, ineffectually, to brush the mud and pieces of dead twig from her skirts, and feeling at a decided disadvantage.

"Then I stand by my first opinion: you did indeed miss a perfect opportunity," Jack declared.

"I don't understand," Charity said. She was still feeling ruffled from her encounter with Owen and she wasn't at all sure she cared for the amused expression in Lord Riversleigh's grey eyes. He was so entirely different from the other men she knew that she couldn't predict his reactions at all.

"You should have cried out when you fell," he explained gravely. "A few tears, perhaps a little raillery against his brutish conduct in causing you to fall, and he would have been your devoted servant. You could probably have had the whole thing settled in a trice."

Charity gasped. "How could you think me so ungentlemanly?" she demanded. "It wasn't Owen's fault I fell over. I should scorn to use such devious methods!"

Jack shook his head in mock sadness, an appreciative gleam in his eyes as they rested on the riot of dark curls which framed a face both unselfconsciously pretty and very feminine.

"Then I fear that if you cannot bring yourself to be ungentlemanly in the pursuit of a husband you are destined to remain a spinster, Miss Mayfield," he said.

"I am not!" Charity declared, outraged. "I wager you ten guineas I'm married by the end of the month."

Lord Riversleigh laughed. "Come, allow me to escort you home," he said, and offered her the support of his arm.

She stepped away from him and put her hands behind her back.

"Are you refusing my wager, sir?"

"Well, it's certainly not my habit to make bets on such a subject." Jack looked at her in some exasperation. "Are you coming down to the gate or are you going to try to force your way through the hedge?"

Charity stopped backing away—it was perfectly true that the sharp hawthorn twigs were beginning to dig into her—

and looked at him challengingly. ''I think you're afraid I'll win,'' she said scornfully.

There was a moment's silence. Then, ''Very well, Miss Mayfield,'' Lord Riversleigh replied. ''I accept your wager. If I lose I'll buy you a wedding present—unless you'd prefer cash.''

''Thank you,'' Charity said regally. ''But perhaps you'd better not make the wager after all. I'm afraid you'll soon be sadly out of pocket.''

''I hope so, Miss Mayfield,'' said Jack politely. ''I would hate to see you dwindle into an old maid.''

For a moment they stared at each other, then Charity laughed and took his proffered arm.

''I wouldn't like it either,'' she confided. ''It wouldn't suit my plans at all. How are you settling in at the Hall? Do you feel at home?''

''I wouldn't say that it much resembles my notion of a home,'' said Jack precisely as they made their way over the uneven ground towards the gate. ''Too much decaying grandeur for my taste. You must realise, I'm a simple man, Miss Mayfield. On the other hand, the people have been very welcoming.''

''I expect they're curious,'' said Charity, without mentioning that his notions of simplicity didn't quite tally with hers. ''Besides, *anyone* would be a better master than Lord Riversleigh was, or Harry would have been,'' she continued.

''It's not what I've been brought up to,'' said Jack, ''but I shall do my best not to disappoint them.'' And Charity heard an unaccustomed note of seriousness in his voice as he spoke.

''There's no need to come any further with me,'' she said as they reached the gate. ''If you're going back to the

Hall our paths lie in opposite directions. Are you really going to do your best for Riversleigh?"

"Certainly." He looked down at her. "I did not ask for the responsibility, but I have no intention of shirking it."

"You could milk the estate for all it's worth and live the high life in London, just like your grandfather," Charity said. "But I hope you won't. Lord Riversleigh was a bad landlord—sometimes I think Mr Guthrie despaired of him."

"Yes, I trust I shall do better than my grandfather," said Jack. He gathered up the reins and swung easily into the saddle.

"Good morning, Miss Mayfield; I hope all your plans meet with success," he said, but as he glanced down at her upturned face it occurred to him that it might be a pity if she was too successful. His impression of Owen Leydon was necessarily imperfect, but he was afraid that Charity's more unusual and delightful qualities would be wasted on the young man.

"I look forward to our next meeting," he said. "I shall be anxious to hear of your progress with your friend—or shall I say victim?" He smiled at her wickedly and touched his heels to the bay's sides before Charity could think of a suitable response.

She watched him go, fulminating at his impertinence. Then her mood changed abruptly and she sighed. Her conversations with Lord Riversleigh seemed destined to follow unusual channels, but at least he had never exasperated her with his stupidity. How different he was from Owen—or even Edward, who had never been more than half aware of the world around him. But Edward was on his way to Rome, and Owen was the only hope of saving Hazelhurst.

She turned and began to walk home, hoping that she could get back into the house without anyone seeing her, because if they did she'd no doubt be drawn into a tedious explanation about how she had come to be covered in mud. She seemed to be spending all her time at the moment explaining awkward circumstances—and she was annoyed with herself for having lost her temper first with Owen and then a second time with Lord Riversleigh. How could he have provoked her into making such a foolish wager? And now she had to find some way of ingratiating herself with Owen again.

"Well, m'lord?" Mr Guthrie asked, his eyes on Lord Riversleigh's face.

"Not well at all," said Jack. He sat back and looked at the land agent, a book of accounts open on the desk before him. "Even from my cursory glance at the accounts I can see that things are in a bad way and, from my understanding, the whole of Riversleigh is in a run-down or dilapidated state."

"Aye, m'lord," said Mr Guthrie drily.

"Very well." Jack tapped his fingers thoughtfully on the desk once or twice before continuing. "Now, as you know, my experience hitherto has been entirely confined to the City, and, whatever success I might have had there, I am a complete novice at estate management. On the other hand, I see no reason why I shouldn't learn—and my father always spoke very highly of *your* capabilities, so..." suddenly he smiled "...I don't see any reason why between us we can't bring Riversleigh about."

"It won't be easy," the land agent warned. "It needs money to be put into it, not taken out—there'll be no easy profits here."

"Do I look like your idea of a complaisant banker, Guthrie?" Jack asked gently.

"No, m'lord." The land agent looked at him thoughtfully. "I'm bound to say you lack sufficient girth to be convincing in the role."

"Thank you." Lord Riversleigh inclined his head ironically. "I'll need to study the books at greater leisure, of course. And I'd like you to show me over the estate as soon as possible. I have a lot to learn."

"Whenever it's convenient." Mr Guthrie stood up, wincing a little as he took his weight on his bad leg. "There is one matter that should be dealt with urgently, m'lord."

"What is it?"

"You're in need of a tenant for one of your farms. The present lease has expired, and Bellow doesn't want to renew it."

"I see." Jack remembered the reference to Bellow in Charity's letter to Edward; he also remembered her advice as to his choice of tenant, but he didn't mention that the matter was already familiar to him. Instead he asked, "Do you have anyone in mind?"

"Yes, sir. Jerry Burden. He's the eldest son of one of the Mayfields' tenants. He's young, but he's learned a lot from his father, and Sam Burden is one of the best farmers in the area. I think he would be a good choice. Of course..." Mr Guthrie hesitated "...I should tell you that your grandfather disagreed with me," he said at last, somewhat reluctantly. "He favoured Nat Cooper."

"But you didn't," said Jack. "Well, my knowledge of farming may be limited, but I believe I'm a fair judge of men. You say this young man lives on the Mayfield estate? I'll ride over tomorrow and meet him."

"I could have him come to the hall," Mr Guthrie offered.

"No, don't do that; I'd rather meet him on his home ground when he's *not* expecting me."

"Do you wish me to accompany you?"

''Thank you, no. I'll find my own way,'' Jack said as he stood up. If the luck favoured him—and Jack had a way of influencing his own luck—he might meet Charity again; and he had no particular desire for the land agent to be present at such a meeting.

He had been quite sincere when he had told Charity that he had no immediate plans for marriage, but it was also true that he had found her an extremely stimulating and entertaining companion. He was certainly looking forward to further encounters with her and, though he had no real expectation that her scheme to inveigle Owen into proposing would be successful, their wager gave him an excellent excuse to seek her out. All in all, his stay in Sussex promised to be far more pleasurable than he had anticipated.

He dismissed that train of thought from his mind and said to Guthrie, ''I won't need you in the morning, but if you have no other pressing business to attend to I'd like to see the rest of Riversleigh tomorrow afternoon.''

''Very well, m'lord.'' Mr Guthrie bowed stiffly and went out. To all appearances, his new master was a vast improvement on the old, and the land agent had always liked Richard Riversleigh, but Guthrie was not in the habit of making hasty decisions and he would reserve judgement for a little longer.

''Mr Leydon, ma'am,'' Charles announced.

''Owen! Good heavens! Whatever can he want?'' Mrs Mayfield exclaimed. ''How very peculiar. Yes, of course, show him in, Charles.''

''Mrs Mayfield.'' Owen bowed punctiliously in her direction and then turned with a hint of awkwardness in his manner to Charity.

''Good evening, Owen,'' she said cautiously, hoping he wasn't going to say anything embarrassing in front of her mother. She'd told Mrs Mayfield she'd tripped in the lane; she didn't want any more lectures on her unladylike behaviour.

"Charity." He stood in the middle of the room, looking uncomfortable. "I came… I wanted… That's a very pretty cap you're wearing, ma'am," he finished desperately, addressing himself to Mrs Mayfield as his courage failed him.

"Thank you," she smiled, delighted at the compliment. "Won't you sit down? I'll ask Charles to bring us some wine. How dark it is already. These short winter days pass so quickly, don't they? Ring the bell, Charity."

"Yes, Mama." Charity stood up, grateful for an opportunity to hide her face.

"And how is dear Lady Leydon?" Mrs Mayfield said, continuing to address herself to Owen. "To be sure, I only visited her yesterday. She seemed in very good health."

"Yes," said Owen baldly. Then he realised that Mrs Mayfield was looking at him and he stumbled into speech again. "That is to say, I believe she is very well. Lord Travers came to visit us yesterday, and I think she's been looking forward to his arrival."

"Of course; she told me he was coming," Mrs Mayfield said. "I hope I shall have the opportunity of meeting him. But no doubt I shall on the fourteenth."

"The fourteenth?" said Owen, looking as if he hadn't got a clue what she was talking about.

"The day of your party," Mrs Mayfield said reprovingly.

"Oh, the party; yes, of course." Owen took a steadying gulp of his wine. "I'm looking forward to it. I hope…I hope you'll be able to come, Charity." He looked at her, his expression half appealing and half belligerent.

"Of course she'll be there," said Mrs Mayfield, then she sighed. "Oh, dear, I don't suppose we'll be going to many more parties.

"Of course we will, Mama," Charity said bracingly, but the thought had depressed Mrs Mayfield and she suddenly fell silent. Unfortunately her silence daunted Owen almost as much as her earlier loquacity, and he suddenly jumped to his feet, declaring that he was expected at home.

"Let me fetch your coat," said Charity, taking pity on his obvious desire to speak to her alone. Besides, she wanted the opportunity to further her own plans.

"Thank you," he said. But once they were in the hall he picked up a candle from the small table and pulled her into the front parlour, which was otherwise unlit and un-heated.

"Charity, I had to come," he burst into speech. "I meant…I wanted to tell you I didn't mean what I said this morning. I ought to have my tongue cut out! But when I get angry I can't help myself. I hope you'll forgive me." He looked at her miserably, holding the candle at an angle.

"Owen! Of course I do!" Charity exclaimed, genuinely touched by his generosity. She took the candle away from him as she spoke and made a mental note that she must get Ellen to scrape the melted wax from the carpet tomorrow. "Besides, it was all my fault. I behaved abominably."

"No, you didn't," he said, not necessarily because he believed it, but rather because he hated them to be at odds with one another, and Sir Humphrey had always told him to make allowances for the peculiar fancies of the weaker sex. "I said some terrible things in the heat of the mo-ment… I'm sure your motives were excellent—but what on earth made you shut the gate? You must have known it would spoil the sport!" he finished, forgetting some of his good intentions.

Charity was just about to make a sharp retort when she remembered that not only the future of Hazelhurst but also the fate of her ten guineas were riding on the outcome of this interview. So, with a remarkable piece of self-discipline, she hung her head and confessed that she'd felt sorry for the fox.

"Sorry for the fox!" Owen exclaimed, looking at her as if she were mad. "How very singular. But you always did take some odd notions into your head. Well, I'm glad that's settled. I'll be off now. We're taking the hounds out again tomorrow. Father was mortified that we couldn't show Lord Travers better sport today."

"Oh," said Charity, "I see. The fox got away, then, did it?"

"Yes. Now, where's my coat?" Owen followed Charity back into the hall.

"It's here. Are you sure you wouldn't like to stay any longer?" Charity smiled meltingly at him. Unfortunately Owen was too busy struggling into his greatcoat to notice.

"And next time you hear the hounds running, make sure you don't interfere with them," he said severely as he buttoned it up.

"Yes, Owen," she said meekly. "Owen!" She had a sudden inspiration. "Won't you come and see me tomorrow? I have so much to arrange before we move and I would really value your advice."

"Oh, yes…yes, certainly," he said, puffing up. "Yes, I'll come tomorrow without fail."

He would have to give up his sport, but the idea that his advice was invaluable flattered his pride, and he was really very good-natured. He didn't like to think of Charity struggling alone with all the problems of moving house.

"I'm so glad," she said gratefully. But as she closed the front door after him she was trying to think of which particular piece of unimportant business she could get Owen to help her with. She had a much higher opinion of his good will than she did of his good sense.

Chapter Four

Charity woke up suddenly at two o'clock in the morning and lay quietly in the darkness, wondering what had roused her. Her room was directly above the library and, as she lay listening, she thought she heard a noise in the room below.

She sighed. She'd had the windows opened that day to air the room and she supposed that Ellen had neglected to shut them. It wasn't the first time that such a thing had happened, and once she had gone downstairs to find that the wind-blown curtains had knocked over one of Mrs Mayfield's favourite vases.

She wondered whether it was worth getting up and then decided that it probably was. If she didn't she was bound to find all her papers blown about by morning. She slid out of bed and put on her robe, not bothering to light a candle because she knew the way so well—and because it was always such a bothersome business to strike a spark from the steel and flint. She could probably be downstairs and back in bed again before she got the tinder to catch light.

She padded silently downstairs, feeling her way with one hand on the banister, and opened the library door. After the darkness of the hall the room seemed quite light because the curtains were drawn back and the moon was nearly full. She saw with some irritation that the window was indeed open, and went over to close it.

At that moment she heard a startled exclamation from the shadows and realised, unbelievably, that she wasn't alone. There was a dark figure standing by the bookshelves.

"Who's there?" she said sharply. "Charles, is that you?"

The next minute she was pushed violently aside. She fell heavily against the oak table, bruising her hip and sending a chair crashing to the floor. She pushed herself up, intending to grab the poker from the fireplace, and briefly saw a dark shape in the window, silhouetted against the moonlight. Then she was alone.

She sat down suddenly, annoyed to find that her legs felt weak with reaction. Her hip was aching and she rubbed it absently. The next minute the library door burst open and her heart leapt nervously—then she heard Charles's voice demanding to know what was going on, and she sank back in relief.

"Miss Charity, is that you?" he asked, confused. "Is something the matter?"

"Not any more," she said. "We had an intruder, but he's gone now. Please close the window and then light some candles."

"An intruder!" he exclaimed, without moving.

"Charles! The window!"

"I'm sorry, miss. I'll close it at once." Charles hurried across the room and drew it shut. "Did he hurt you, Miss Charity?" he asked anxiously.

"Not really. I think I frightened him as much as he frightened me," Charity said; she was beginning to feel more like herself.

"Whatever did you want to go and tackle him on your own for?" Charles wondered.

"I didn't know anyone was in here. I thought Ellen had forgotten to close the window," Charity explained. "Could you light the candles, please?"

"I'll fetch a tinder-box." Charles turned round and cannoned straight into the housekeeper, who let out a small scream.

"Goodness! Is that you, Mrs Wendle?" Charity asked weakly. "I hope you weren't disturbed by all the noise."

Before the housekeeper could reply both women were electrified by a scream from the hall.

"Good grief! What's happened now?" Charity leapt up and hurried to the door.

"It's Ellen, miss," said Charles's voice apologetically from the hall. "She's fainted. I bumped into her in the darkness. I must have frightened her."

"I see." Charity took a deep breath. "Mrs Wendle, would you please go and tell Mama that everything is all right while I try and revive Ellen? And for heaven's sake provide us with some light, Charles!"

"Yes, miss. But should I lay Ellen down on the floor?"

"No, no. Bring her in here and put her on the sofa." Charity crossed to the parlour and held the door open for Charles to carry Ellen through.

"Now," she said, "if you would just fetch some candles. And I think perhaps you'd better get dressed as well." The footman was wearing nothing but his nightshirt.

"Oh, yes, miss, of course." Charles blushed in the darkness and hurried away.

Charity let out her breath in a long sigh and turned her attention to Ellen.

It was not until long after dawn, when Mrs Mayfield was eating breakfast in the comforting presence of Mrs Wendle, that Charity finally had a moment's respite. She sighed with relief and slipped quietly out of the house and into the garden, grateful for the chance to be alone. She couldn't remember ever having had such a dreadful night. Her encounter with the intruder had been the least part of it.

Not only had Ellen had hysterics when she had recovered from her faint, but Mrs Mayfield too had become extremely nervous when she had discovered that they'd almost been burgled. She'd insisted that Charles check every room and by the time he had done this, and checked that every door and window was securely fastened, everyone had been far too jumpy to go back to bed.

Charity was exhausted. Charles was certainly willing, but the unexpected events of the night seemed to have fuddled his wits so much that she'd had to continually remind him of what to do next; and everyone else had been suffering from an extreme agitation of the nerves. It was only with the daylight that they'd all begun to feel somewhat reassured.

Charity leant against an old apple tree and closed her eyes, feeling the sun on her face. The wind was quite strong, but in the shelter of the garden it was remarkably warm and she wondered how much longer the fine weather would last.

"Miss Mayfield!"

She jumped visibly, putting her hand up to her throat as she felt a sickening jolt of surprise.

"I'm sorry, I didn't mean to startle you." Lord Riversleigh was standing just behind her, his approach having been muffled by the short grass. He frowned, an expression of concern on his face as he saw the alarm in Charity's startled eyes. "Is something wrong?"

"No. I just didn't hear you coming," Charity said.

She was both relieved and unexpectedly pleased to see who it was; yet she felt a slight, unfamiliar flutter, almost of nervousness, as she looked up at him. Then she remembered how their last meeting had begun and in an effort of liveliness she held out her hand politely.

''Good morning, my lord. Isn't it mild for the time of year?''

''Very.'' He took her hand and held it for a moment, looking down into her face. ''What's the matter?'' he asked abruptly.

''Nothing really.'' She drew her hand away and tried to laugh. ''Were you coming to see us? I'm sure my mother would like to meet you.''

''Not exactly, although I would, of course, be delighted to meet Mrs Mayfield. In fact, I was riding past on my way to visit Jerry Burden when I saw you in the garden. So I thought I'd stop to let you know how assiduously I was following your advice.''

''What?'' Charity stared at him blankly for a minute. ''Oh! You mean in my letter to Edward.''

''Of course.'' Jack looked at her searchingly. He could see the signs of weariness and past alarm in her face, and he felt a sudden surge of admiration for her. She was facing the difficult situation in which she found herself with such good-humoured courage that it was easy to underestimate how badly she must be hurt by the imminent loss of her home.

''Miss Mayfield, are you sure you're quite yourself?'' he asked. ''Is there anything I can do?''

''You mean, you've been talking to me for a whole five minutes and I haven't said anything outrageous yet,'' Charity said, pulling herself together and smiling ruefully.

''I would have said, rather, that you seem a little subdued,'' he replied. ''Is it something to do with leaving Hazelhurst? Perhaps I can help. I'm not unacquainted with matters of business.''

''No. Thank you. But it's very kind of you to offer,'' Charity replied gratefully, but without offering to explain her uncharacteristic behaviour. Despite her occasionally disastrous outspokenness, she nevertheless possessed a good deal of reserve and she had always been reluctant to share her problems with others.

''I'm glad you're going to see Jerry,'' she said. ''You certainly don't waste any time, my lord.''

Jack smiled. ''As I recall, you wanted the matter dealt with 'as soon as possible','' he said. ''I'm simply complying with your wishes.''

''Oh, dear.'' Charity blushed. ''I'd never have written so if I'd known you weren't Edward. Things used to slip his memory, you know.''

''I didn't know, but I can well imagine they might,'' Jack replied, ''and also that you'd have had no hesitation in reminding him if they did! I'm glad you approve of my promptness. And now I must be on my way. I'm afraid I've already intruded upon you long enough. Please convey my compliments to Mrs Mayfield.'' He stepped back and bowed with the careless grace which characterised all his movements.

Charity felt a flicker of disappointment. She enjoyed talking to Lord Riversleigh, and after the alarms of the previous night she found his presence remarkably reassuring. She didn't want him to leave, and it occurred to her that it might, after all, be a relief to discuss what had happened with someone who could be relied upon to take her meaning without tedious explanations—and who would certainly *not* have the vapours.

''We had an intruder last night,'' she said abruptly, without any form of preamble. ''I heard a noise downstairs and thought Ellen must have left a window open, so I went down to close it and surprised a burglar. He escaped through the window. No harm was done.''

''Were you hurt?'' Jack came back to her, a gleam of concern in his grey eyes which Charity found almost disconcerting. She wasn't used to people being worried about her.

''No.'' she looked away, annoyed to find she was blushing. ''I think I frightened him more than he frightened me. But in his haste to get away he pushed me aside and I knocked over a chair,'' which woke up the household. Poor Mama was very upset.''

''Very understandably so, I imagine,'' Jack said. Without conscious thought he had taken Charity's hand in his, and now he held it in a comforting clasp. ''Are you sure he didn't hurt you?''

''No, indeed he didn't,'' she assured him.

He had braced his free hand against the branch over her head and he was standing so close to her that she had to tip her head back to meet his gaze. He seemed very strong, and she was intensely aware of how much taller than her he was. The half-formed thought even flitted across her mind that it might be rather nice to be able to cast her problems on to somebody else's broad shoulders. Most people were so used to the way she always dealt with every problem that arose that they tended to take it for granted that she could manage.

So she could, she reminded herself. Nevertheless, it was very pleasant to stand quietly beside him, and she was quite content for him to break the lengthening silence.

The early-morning sun was behind her head and, though she didn't realise it, it lit up her hair until it almost seemed as if she wore a halo. She looked so gallant and vulnerable as she smiled up into his eyes that Jack felt a strong desire to take her into his arms, and he suddenly realised that he was becoming more involved than he had intended. His hold on her hand tightened briefly—but only briefly. He knew that, despite her slightly misleading outspokenness, she had in many respects led a very cloistered life. It showed in so many ways, including the way in which she smiled up at him with such open trust—and it was not his practice to play games with innocent young women.

For an instant Charity had felt an unaccustomed fluttering breathlessness as she had gazed up at Jack. But then he released her hand, although he continued to lean against the apple tree, and she realised he was speaking to her. With an effort she tried to concentrate on what he was saying.

"Would you recognise the intruder again?" he asked.

"I don't think so," she replied, with commendable composure. "I never saw his face. At first he was standing in the shadows, then he was silhouetted in the window. I never saw him properly at all. And he didn't take anything—I checked this morning—so even if he was caught there wouldn't be any way of identifying him. I don't think there's any point in pursuing him," Charity concluded. "That's what you were trying to find out, isn't it?"

"Yes." Jack smiled faintly. "You have a remarkable trick of taking disaster in your stride," he observed. "Has anything ever overset you for long, Miss Mayfield?"

"Once or twice," Charity replied, unexpectedly serious; she was remembering her grief at the death of her father, a grief that time had still not entirely mended. Then her expression lightened and she reverted to her more characteristic manner.

"One must be *practical* about these things, after all," she said, and took the opportunity to move slightly away from him.

"A very sensible attitude to take," Jack agreed, turning so that he was still facing her.

"Now you're laughing at me," Charity said amiably, feeling more relaxed now that she had the open space of the garden, rather than the apple tree, behind her. "Never mind; would you like to come in and meet Mama?" she asked. "She's very anxious to find out what... I mean, I'm sure she'd be delighted to make your acquaintance."

"I imagine I must be an object of curiosity to quite a lot of people," Jack agreed. "I'll be very happy to meet Mrs Mayfield, and perhaps even divert her mind from the alarms of last night. But what did I ought to do about my horse?" He pointed to where the handsome bay gelding he had been riding the previous day was tied to the post of the kitchen garden gate.

"Well! I don't know how you can reprove *me* for impropriety when you can say things like *that!*" Charity said after a moment. "Though it's perfectly true I did think you might give Mama something else to think about. Bring him through and we'll take him to the stables."

"Across the kitchen garden?" Jack asked.

"Well, he's not going to do it much harm if you lead him round the edge," Charity said. "Besides, it'll soon be Lord Ashbourne's garden—and I don't suppose he cares much one way or another."

"I don't suppose he does," Jack agreed gravely, untying the reins from the gatepost. He clicked his tongue and the bay walked willingly towards him. "Lead the way, Miss Mayfield."

"Lord Riversleigh! How wonderful to meet you! Do sit down. Charity, get Charles to bring in some tea." Mrs Mayfield was indeed delighted with her unexpected visitor, the more so because she was comfortably aware that she must be one of the first people in the neighbourhood to meet him.

"I'm afraid you find us in rather a turmoil," she continued brightly. "We had a burglar last night and we're all still in something of a flutter."

"Yes, Miss Mayfield told me," Jack said. "I hope it's not an inconvenient moment for me to call. I was riding past when I saw Miss Mayfield in the garden, and when I stopped to speak to her she invited me in."

"And I'm so glad she did!" Mrs Mayfield exclaimed. "I've been longing to thank you in person for the kind message you brought us from Edward. So thoughtful of him, and of you."

"Not at all, ma'am," said Jack immediately, without a flicker of surprise.

"Mama was very touched that in the midst of all his preparations Edward remembered us and commissioned you especially to bring us his good wishes," Charity explained hastily, wishing she'd thought to tell Lord Riversleigh the excuse she'd given her mother for his visit two days earlier.

"And for your own kindness in bringing us the message so quickly," Mrs Mayfield assured him.

"I beg you won't mention it," Jack said smoothly. "Edward spoke very highly of you and he particularly desired that you should receive good news of him."

"Yes. Well, I'm sure he'll have a wonderful time in Rome," said Charity, anxious to change the subject. She could imagine all too clearly how horrified Mrs Mayfield would be if she ever found out Charity had proposed to a stranger!

"Will you be staying up at the Hall long, Lord Riversleigh?" she continued.

"I'm not entirely sure. Thank you." Jack leant forward

and accepted the cup of tea she was offering him. "I have affairs in town which cannot be neglected for too long, but there is also a great deal of work to be done here."

"Your home is in London?" Mrs Mayfield pounced on this snippet of information eagerly. She was fascinated by the deliciously mysterious way in which the unknown heir had suddenly appeared.

"Yes, ma'am." Jack sipped his tea. He gave the impression of being a man who, while perfectly willing to answer questions, had no intention of volunteering gratuitous information about himself. Charity thought he was quietly amused by her mother's good-natured curiosity. Whether that was the case or not, Mrs Mayfield rose handsomely to the challenge and within half an hour, without once appearing vulgarly inquisitive, she had discovered a number of interesting facts about her visitor.

Charity listened in amazement. It suddenly occurred to her that she had been remarkably incurious about Jack Riversleigh. Yet she guessed he must be nearly thirty years old, and somehow she had gained the impression that he had made his mark on whatever world he had inhabited during those years. Perhaps her lack of curiosity had been caused by the peculiar nature of their first meeting—or perhaps it was because of a subconscious awareness that if she allowed herself to be too curious about him he might begin to intrude uncomfortably upon her thoughts. She had stern and important schemes afoot and she couldn't allow herself to be distracted.

Mrs Mayfield was far more interested in Jack's family than in any other aspect of his life and, as a result of her efforts, she learned that he had two sisters, Elizabeth and Fanny; that Elizabeth was married and that Fanny, who was only twenty-one, lived with his mother. She also learned that he wasn't married, a fact that Charity had already discovered on their first meeting, though she'd lost interest in it after he'd refused to take Edward's place in her schemes.

"Well, I dare say you will find things quite different, now you are Lord Riversleigh," said Mrs Mayfield comfortably. "I'm sure your mother and sisters must be very pleased. You will be able to launch Miss Riversleigh into society in some style now."

"I think Fanny will probably launch herself," Jack murmured irrepressibly.

"The Riversleigh town house will be an excellent setting for her introduction to the highest ranks of society," Mrs Mayfield continued, not really attending. "I beg your pardon, my lord, did you say something?"

"Nothing of importance," he assured her, and stood up. "Thank you for your hospitality, but I believe I must be going now. I'm on my way to visit the son of one of your tenants, to discuss a lease."

"Oh?" Mrs Mayfield looked blank. She'd never bothered to pay much attention to the management of the estate.

"Jerry Burden, Mama," Charity explained.

"Oh, Jerry!" Mrs Mayfield said, relieved. "Yes, Jerry is a fine young man. I'm sure he'll answer your purposes excellently. I wonder…?" She paused; she'd obviously had an idea. "Do you know the way, my lord? Perhaps Charity ought to show you. She's been cooped up indoors for days now, planning this wretched move of ours. I'm sure the fresh air would do her good."

"Oh, no!" said Charity instinctively. "I've far too much to do this morning. I'm sure Lord Riversleigh can find his own way; it's not at all difficult."

"But you said you were going to see Mrs Burden today, anyway," Mrs Mayfield pointed out.

She'd had a sudden, delightful vision of her daughter as Lady Riversleigh and both their futures assured. To be sure, everyone knew Riversleigh was heavily mortgaged, but living in debt at Riversleigh had to be better than living in lodgings in Horsham. Besides, even in the short time she had known Jack Riversleigh, she'd decided that she liked him a great deal better than Owen Leydon, and Charity didn't know many other men. Mrs Mayfield, in fact, had her own scheme for ensuring the future happiness of herself and her daughter—and paying off the debt on Hazelhurst wasn't part of it.

"Very well." Charity capitulated suddenly. "Can you wait while I get ready, my lord?"

"Certainly, Miss Mayfield." Jack sat down again and smiled at Mrs Mayfield.

"I'm so glad she's going out riding with you," Mrs Mayfield confided when they were alone. "She's had so much to worry her with all the arrangements for the move, and then last night—it was Charity who found the burglar, you know!"

"Yes, ma'am," said Jack gently.

"You don't think he'll come back, do you?" Mrs Mayfield twisted her handkerchief nervously in her hands. "Charity says he won't, but I can't help worrying…"

"No, ma'am," Jack said, his deep voice very reassuring. "I'm sure he won't be back. But if you're nervous, have a couple of your manservants sleep downstairs for a few days."

"That's a good idea." Mrs Mayfield seemed relieved. "I'll suggest it to Charity."

"Thank you for not telling Mama why you really came to see me that first day!" Charity said as she rode beside Lord Riversleigh on a placid grey mare, her groom a discreet distance behind them.

"You didn't think I would, did you?" he sounded amused.

"I didn't know," she confessed. "I suppose not, but I meant to warn you anyway, just in case. I forgot." She seemed annoyed with herself.

"You have a great deal on your mind," he said soothingly. "Even you can't expect to remember everything."

"I don't see why not," Charity said. "Are you really going to give Jerry the lease?"

"How can I tell until I meet him?" Jack replied. "What I *would* like to know, however, is why both you and Guthrie appear so set against Cooper."

"I don't like him," Charity admitted frankly. "But, apart from that, I really think Jerry would make a better tenant. Cooper already leases two farms, and he just wants the opportunity to increase his profits and his consequence. He's more experienced than Jerry and he'd be a safe choice—that's why your grandfather favoured him—but I think Jerry would be a better investment. He's very young, but he's learnt a lot from his father, and he's not only hardworking and enthusiastic but he's also desperate for a chance to prove himself. I think if you gave him that chance it would be very profitable for both of you."

"I see," said Jack slowly. "You seem to have a remarkable head for business, Miss Mayfield."

"It seemed like common sense to me," Charity said, rather surprised.

"Possibly, but if that's the case it's amazing how few people possess it," Jack replied, smiling slightly. "Have you had much to do with the management of Hazelhurst?"

"I've always been interested, and Papa wasn't…" Charity caught herself up just in time before she criticised her father to Lord Riversleigh. She knew Mr Mayfield hadn't always been very consistent in the management of his affairs, but she was far too loyal to say so.

"I've always been interested in it," she amended her reply, "and since my father died it's been entirely in my hands—apart from Sam Burden's help, of course. I don't know what we'd have done without Sam—he oversees the home farm for us. But you mustn't think there's anything grand about Hazelhurst," she added hastily, in case he'd gained the wrong impression. "It's not like Riversleigh, or even Sir Humphrey's estate. We only have two tenants and then the home farm. It's not difficult to manage. May I ask you a question, my lord?"

"Of course." Jack hadn't missed her fleeting reference to Mr Mayfield, though he was far too polite to remark upon it.

"What is your business?"

Jack smiled, apparently not at all offended by her blunt question.

"I'm a banker."

"A *banker!* Good gracious!" Charity exclaimed, rather startled. "I must say, you don't look like one."

"No, Guthrie didn't think I was stout enough, either," Jack remarked humorously. "Perhaps I ought to do something to rectify the matter."

"That's not what I meant at all!" said Charity firmly, although there was a slight, tell-tale blush to her cheeks. "But however did you get to be a banker? Somehow it seems such an unlikely occupation for *Lord Riversleigh's* grandson."

"It does, doesn't it?" Jack grinned, thinking of all the money Lord Riversleigh had borrowed during his lifetime. "But it isn't at all an unlikely occupation for Joseph Pembroke's grandson. Besides, strangely enough, it was my father who had most to do with developing that side of the business.''

''Joseph Pembroke was your mother's father?'' Charity said, trying to get Jack's family tree untangled in her mind. ''Was *he* a banker, then?''

''Eventually,'' Jack replied. ''He was originally apprenticed as a goldsmith, but the two professions have always had very close links, so it was a fairly natural development—particularly after he'd met my father. By all accounts, Father was fascinated by the business and played a large part in developing it, even though he'd had no previous experience.''

''He must have been a very different kind of man from *his* father or his brother Harry,'' Charity said. ''They only seemed to take pleasure in destroying things.''

Jack smiled. ''He was,'' he said.

''When you said that your grandfather was a goldsmith,'' said Charity, going back to the other point that interested her, ''do you mean that he could actually make things in gold?''

''Oh, yes,'' Jack replied, looking amused. ''Though in fact, despite the name, most goldsmiths usually work in silver. But, of course, once grandfather became more involved in banking he had less time to devote to the workshop.''

''You mean, he gave up his craft?'' Charity exclaimed, surprising Jack with her vehemence. ''How could he? Surely it must be more rewarding to create a beautiful object than it is to…to…?''

''Deal in filthy lucre?'' Jack supplied when she seemed at a loss. ''Perhaps I should have said that my grandfather didn't entirely abandon his craft. He and my father did become preoccupied with banking, but his other partner was, and still is, very much a working goldsmith—and an important part of the business.''

He didn't sound annoyed, but Charity blushed painfully as she realised that once again she had been more outspoken than courtesy demanded.

"I'm sorry, my lord,'' she said. "I didn't mean to offend you. It's just that I have so little talent myself that it seems almost criminal to me when people who do have a skill waste it.''

"Are you thinking of Edward?'' Jack asked, beginning to understand her reaction.

"I suppose so,'' Charity replied slowly. "But not because he deliberately wasted his talent—quite the contrary. In fact, I think it's probably because I watched him struggling against so many obstacles that I feel so strongly on the subject.''

For a moment she gazed over the winter landscape almost as if she was remembering something. Then she roused herself and laughed.

"There were times when I almost envied him,'' she confessed. "Painting, sketching, carving—it all came so easily to him. As I said, I've no talent for that kind of thing at all, and perhaps that was partly why I liked him. Nearly everyone else used to get annoyed with him because he seemed so vague, half foolish even. But I saw him when he was sketching, and heard him talk about the things he really cared about—and he was a different person then, so quick and decisive.''

She smiled reminiscently.

"Do you miss him very much?'' Jack asked abruptly, responding to the almost wistful note in Charity's voice. "I'm sure, if you wish it, it would be possible to contact him—even recall him to England.''

Yet, even as he spoke, he was aware of a reluctance to

carry out his own suggestion, and he suddenly realised that the unfamiliar—and hitherto unnamed—sensation he was experiencing was jealousy. The knowledge shook him. He had thought he knew himself better than that and he damned himself silently for his folly—nevertheless, he was relieved when he heard Charity's surprised rejection of his offer.

"Oh, no!" she exclaimed. "I do miss him; he was like the older brother I never had—and he used to side with me against Owen. But I'd never deny him this opportunity. Besides, I only asked him to marry me when I thought we could be of mutual assistance to each other—and now he's already on the way to Rome he doesn't need my help."

She turned her head and smiled at Jack.

"But I do thank you," she said. "It was very kind of you to offer to help."

"It would have been my pleasure," Jack replied formally, but the more familiar gleam of humour had returned to his eyes. He found Charity's unusual out-spokenness very entertaining—and her unthinking reference to Owen very revealing. He was less inclined than ever to believe that she really intended to marry him.

Charity laughed.

"You do the grand manner very well," she said. "It wouldn't have been a pleasure at all—but that only makes your offer all the more generous. Are you acquainted with Lord Ashbourne?"

"Lord Ashbourne?" Jack repeated, wondering if he'd missed part of the conversation. He still wasn't used to Charity's tendency to change the subject in almost mid-sentence.

"He's the man who lent Papa the money," Charity explained. "Didn't I mention it in my letter?"

''Not as far as I remember,'' Jack replied slowly. ''What was it you wanted to know?''

''Only if you'd ever met him,'' Charity said. ''It didn't occur to me before, but when you told us this morning that you live in London I wondered if you knew him. I believe he also spends a great deal of time there.''

She smiled ruefully.

''Mama and I have never met him, and I can't help being slightly curious about the man who will soon own our home,'' she admitted.

''Of course,'' said Jack. ''It must seem very odd. But I'm afraid...'' He paused, looking absently ahead. ''No, I'm afraid that I can't be of much help to you,'' he continued at last. ''I have occasionally encountered the Earl, but he moves in the most fashionable of circles and my home has always been in the City. The two worlds are not always...compatible.''

''I just wondered, but it's not important,'' said Charity quickly.

It had suddenly occurred to her that perhaps the reason the Earl and Jack had encountered each other was because Lord Ashbourne had ordered some silver from Jack. If that was the case the two men were hardly likely to be on intimate terms—especially if the Earl hadn't yet paid his bill. And Charity knew that the aristocracy were notorious for procrastinating over their debts to tradesmen!

''We live in such a small community here that we all know each other,'' she continued, trying to steer the conversation on to a less potentially embarrassing subject. ''I'm afraid I tend to imagine that the same is true of London, but of course it isn't—it's so much bigger.''

''With so many more inhabitants,'' Jack agreed humorously. He didn't know exactly what Charity was thinking, though he could make a fair guess.

Charity looked at him doubtfully. She thought he seemed amused, but she couldn't understand why and she wasn't sure what to say next. She glanced ahead and then pointed towards some roof-tops just becoming visible over the brow of the hill.

"Look, we're nearly there," she said.

Chapter Five

"Well, you've met Jerry now. Are you going to give him the lease?" Charity asked as they rode back across the field to Hazelhurst.

"Yes, I think so," Jack replied. "I'd say you summed him up very accurately earlier."

"I'm so glad!" Charity exclaimed. "What a relief it will be to Mrs Burden. She's very anxious about the changes Lord Ashbourne might want to make when he takes over. The Burdens have a twenty-one-year lease, you know, but it has only four years left to run. Of course, I always intended to renew it, but now… Still, at least they won't have to worry about Jerry any more."

"Yes, it's a difficult time for everyone," Jack said quietly, not that he had ever doubted it, but his conversation with Sam and Jerry Burden had confirmed it very forcefully.

He and Charity had met the Burdens just outside their house and, after introducing them to each other, Charity had left the three men alone together while she went in to see Mrs Burden. It was only after the business part of their discussion had been concluded that Sam had invited Lord Riversleigh into the house.

For Jack it had been an enlightening meeting in more ways than one. Not only had he come to the conclusion that Guthrie and Charity were right in their assessment of the younger Burden's capabilities, but he had also learnt far more about Charity. He had always suspected that beneath her somewhat scatter-brained exterior she had a great deal of common sense, but he had not hitherto realised just how much she had had to do with management of Hazelhurst. Both Sam and Jerry clearly held her in great respect, not only because of who she was, but also because of her hard work and diligence in doing everything she could to improve the estate.

Jack was no fool and, despite the fact that nothing had openly been said, he had guessed that Mr Mayfield had been an indifferent landlord. From various sources he had gained the impression that Charity's father had been a man of grand visions and generous impulses, but that he had always lacked the stamina or patience to see his plans through to their completion. During his lifetime Mr Mayfield had probably never realised how much Charity had contributed to the smooth running of his affairs—and since his death she had dealt with everything.

''You must find it very galling, having to give up Hazelhurst after all the work you've put into it,'' Jack said quietly, putting his thoughts into words.

Galling! It's more than…'' Charity broke off sharply, biting her lip in vexation. ''Let's race!'' she exclaimed. ''I haven't had a good gallop for days. To the oak in the next field.'' She touched her heel to the mare's side as she spoke and suddenly the sleepy air left the grey horse. She sprang forward like a charger.

Lord Riversleigh was taken by surprise and the bay skittered nervously sideways—then Jack had him under control and was urging him on.

The grey mare was running like a steeplechaser, anxious for the first jump, and for a moment Jack thought she was bolting. Sudden fear for Charity filled him and he leant forward, urging the bay on in an effort to overtake her—but the grey mare hated to be passed, and when she heard the thunder of hoofs behind her she put back her ears and lengthened her stride.

They were approaching a thick hawthorn hedge, not an impossible obstacle, but challenging, and from their outward journey Jack remembered that the drop on the other side was longer than on the take-off.

He was still convinced that the mare had run away with Charity and he forced the bay on, intending to turn the grey before she took the jump. Then the horses were abreast and, as he glanced sideways at Charity, he saw that she had the mare under complete control. He felt a surge of anger at the alarm she had caused him; then he concentrated on the jump. Both horses thundered on towards the hedge—there was a heart-stopping silence as they took off at almost the same moment, and then they both landed safely.

At that point Jack stopped worrying about Charity and turned his attention to winning the race. The bay was willing, and Jack a clever horseman, but the grey mare wouldn't give up and both horses went past the oak tree together.

In the distance, the groom trotted sedately on, heading for the gate. He was grinning to himself, thinking what a fright Miss Charity must have given his lordship—*he* couldn't know that she was the best horsewoman in Sussex. Gregory was partial, of course, but then most people who worked for Charity were.

Charity slowed the mare to a walk and leant forward, patting her neck.

Jack drew alongside her, his first impulse to give vent to

his anger at the alarm she had caused him. Then he remembered the expression on her face just before she'd set the grey mare running and changed his mind.

"That is a remarkably deceptive animal, Miss Mayfield!" he exclaimed.

Charity laughed; her cheeks were flushed and her eyes were bright with excitement.

"She looks as if she's so tired that she's in danger of tripping over her own feet, doesn't she?" she said. "But she runs like an angel, and when she hears the huntsman's horn she goes away like a demon. She was Papa's horse and everyone told him he was a fool to buy her, but the first time he rode her she went at a jump so hard that she threw him and finished the hunt on her own, up with the leaders to the end. Then she came quietly back to the stable for her hot mash like a true veteran. Sir Humphrey was most impressed. He's tried to buy her several times, but Papa wouldn't sell. How did you know?"

"Miss Mayfield?" The bay was fidgeting, excited by the race, and Jack soothed him.

"Even Guthrie doesn't really understand," Charity continued, sitting easily as the mare stretched out her neck and shook her head. "He thinks it's sad that we must lose our home—but that's all. He told me the other day that he thinks it's a good thing that I won't have to worry about the estate any more—as if it ought to come as a relief to me! As if I ought to be *glad* to hand over everything I've worked for to someone else! Someone who won't even *care!*"

She turned her head away as she finished speaking, but the anguish in her voice was unmistakable, and painful to hear.

"I knew how you felt, because I know how I'd feel if the same thing happened to me," Jack said quietly.

Her distress wrenched at his heart and he wanted to take her in his arms to comfort her; but he knew that, at that moment, her thoughts were far away from him, and he was reluctant to do, or say, anything which might upset her even more.

For a second or two longer Charity continued to gaze away across the fields, then she turned and looked at him—and saw in his eyes that he really did understand. She felt the tears threaten and instinctively put up her hand to cover her eyes. Until that moment she'd received a great deal of sympathy—but no one had really understood how she felt. She'd never expected that they would.

"Miss Mayfield?" Jack said gently.

"Sometimes I feel so angry," she said, without looking at him, and dashed the tears from her cheeks. "I shouldn't. It's not right to feel so angry."

"I'd be angry—very angry. There's no reason to feel guilty. It's a measure of how much you care," Jack said.

"Perhaps. But it's not… Well, never mind, there's no point in talking about it. Shall we go on, my lord?"

"In a minute." Jack leant forward and took hold of the grey mare's bridle, drawing her to a halt. "What were you about to say?"

"Nothing important." Charity tried unsuccessfully to laugh. "I'm sure we should be going, my lord. You must have a great many things to do."

"Nothing that won't wait." Jack released the mare's bridle, but he didn't encourage the bay to walk on. "I'm not trying to force your confidence, but I'm usually considered a good listener—and I'm not easily shocked."

"Do you think I'm going to say something shocking?" Charity tried to smile, but there wasn't much humour in her expression.

"No." Jack's voice was deeper than ever, slow and curiously reassuring.

"I'm angry with Papa!" she bursts out, and felt a sudden, overwhelming relief that she'd finally told someone what she was really thinking. She knew that most of the neighbourhood were probably harbouring critical thoughts about her father, but until that moment she had never done anything but defend him. Even to herself she'd tried to make excuses for what he'd done.

"I'm angry with Papa," she said again, more temperately, "and then I'm angry with myself. Because I *know* what he was like. How can I be angry with him for being himself? And he's not even here to defend himself."

"No. But he should be, shouldn't he?" said Jack. "It wasn't fair to leave you in such a fix."

Charity looked at him, shaken by how accurately he had guessed her feelings.

"How did you know?" she whispered.

Jack smiled wryly. "It seemed like a natural reaction," he said. "You're too hard on yourself. How did he die?"

"He was shot by a highwayman. By all accounts it was the most farcical situation. Typical of Papa." Charity tried to laugh, but Jack knew she wasn't far from tears. "He was on his way home when he came across a coach being held up by three highwaymen. Being Papa, he couldn't ignore it, so he decided to intervene. Apparently he charged down on them, shouting like a madman and waving his pistol. I can almost see him doing it." She smiled affectionately. She had happy as well as sad memories of her father.

"He was trying to take them by surprise, of course," she continued, "and he did. At first it looked as if everything was going to turn out all right—but one of the highwaymen couldn't control his horse at all. They said afterwards that he'd never meant to fire, that his pistol had gone off by accident—but Papa was in the way.''

"He must have been a brave man," said Jack.

"For getting shot!" Charity flashed, and there was hostility in the glance she threw at Jack. She was afraid he was mocking her.

"No," said Jack equably. "For trying to help. The odds were against him, were they not?"

"Yes." Charity looked down. "Poor Papa; somehow they always were. I think we should go back now, my lord." She shortened her reins and chirruped to the mare.

Jack brought the bay round and they began to walk slowly back to Hazelhurst.

For a moment neither of them spoke; then, without looking at Jack, Charity said, "Thank you. I'm sure I shouldn't have said some of the things I have, and I hope you will forget that I did, but...well, thank you." She glanced at him briefly as she finished speaking, then looked away again.

"I was honoured by your confidence," Jack replied quietly, and he meant it. "As to the rest...my memory is at your disposal."

Charity looked at him gravely for a moment, then she smiled, as warmly and as openly as a daisy might unfurl its petals in the morning sun.

Jack looked down at her, unable to take his eyes from her face. Ever since he had met her Charity had been trying to manipulate events in her favour—even now she was busy trying to inveigle Owen Leydon into marrying her—yet Jack could not remember ever having met such an honest woman. It was a quality he prized highly. He knew how difficult it could be to speak the truth, or to say what one really felt, without fear of ridicule or censure. A friend with whom one could be oneself, without pretence, was a friend worth knowing—and a woman with whom one could be oneself…

Charity saw the warmth in his eyes and turned her head away. She felt embarrassed and vaguely uncomfortable, yet at the same time reassured. She could not remember ever having spoken so openly to anyone before and she felt very vulnerable, yet it never occurred to her that she couldn't trust Jack with her secrets. She knew he could be relied on not to hurt or betray her; she didn't even wonder how she knew. And he had helped her, not because he had offered trite words of sympathy, but because he had understood her mixed feelings towards her father. He had not been shocked or horrified, and that meant a great deal to her.

On the other hand, she was afraid that he might pursue the subject, and she didn't want that. She had already opened herself up far more than she had intended and she needed time to adjust, and to regain her equilibrium. She began, with a hint of awkwardness in her manner, to discuss his plans for Riversleigh, and felt a sudden surge of relief when he answered in kind. But it was only when she saw Owen in the distance that she finally lost her self-consciousness and was once more completely herself.

"There's Owen!" she exclaimed. "I quite forgot, he's coming to see me today."

Yet, despite the fact that this was what she had wanted, she felt a tinge of regret as she realised that now she would have to cut short her conversation with Lord Riversleigh. Then she told herself severely that she had more important concerns to think about than her own pleasure. She had made her decision to save Hazelhurst and it was not Jack but Owen who was going to help her do it. She should be pleased to see Owen.

"You're back on speaking terms, then?" Jack said, a

hint of amusement in his voice—he still didn't take her matrimonial plans entirely seriously.

"Of course we are!" Charity pulled herself together, chiding herself for having let her mind wander. "He came to see me yesterday evening just to apologise. I was very relieved; it saved a great deal of time."

"So you're going ahead with your scheme?" Jack asked.

"Well, of course!" She sounded surprised that he should have doubted it. "I never give up something once I've started! I wasn't immediately sure how to proceed, but I had a brilliant idea last night, and now I'm afraid your ten guineas are in great jeopardy."

"Are they, indeed? And may I ask what your brilliant idea is?" Jack said. "Have you decided to tell him about your inheritance, after all?"

"Certainly not," said Charity firmly. "The money wouldn't make any difference to Owen."

Even as she spoke she wondered if she was right, but she pushed the thought aside as unworthy of both Owen and herself.

"It might even have the opposite effect," she said. "He can be *very* stubborn. No, my idea was completely different, but I'm not sure I ought to tell you." She looked at him doubtfully. "You might try to make me lose the bet."

"Miss Mayfield!" Jack said, outraged. "Are you suggesting I might *cheat?*" But even as he spoke he realised that that was precisely what he intended to do—though he wasn't yet prepared to admit as much to his companion.

For a moment Charity was taken aback—the haughty indignation in Jack's voice was so real that she was suddenly reminded of how grand he had seemed on their first meeting—then she saw the twinkle in his eye and relaxed.

"Please accept my apologies…" she began formally, then interrupted herself almost immediately. "Oh, good

heavens! He's almost upon us! You must know I asked him
to give me his advice with all the arrangements I have to
make. He was immensely flattered, and I have great hopes
for our meeting this afternoon.''

"And do you wish for his advice?" Jack asked mildly.

"Of course not," Charity replied. "But that's not important. He'll *think* I need his advice, and that's what
counts."

"You don't think that's rather a poor basis for a lifelong
partnership?" Jack asked.

"I don't see why. As long as he leaves the management
of everything to me, I dare say we'll do splendidly," Charity said firmly.

"Poor fellow," said Jack provocatively. "Perhaps I
ought to warn him of the dreadful fate in store for him."

"Don't you dare!" Charity exclaimed hotly. "It would
be…it would be…"

"Ungentlemanly?" Jack suggested helpfully as she cast
around for a word strong enough to condemn such underhand conduct.

"Worse than that," she began darkly, but Owen was
already within earshot and she had to turn her attention to
him.

Owen had sacrificed a day's sport to ride over to help
Charity. Consequently he felt rather aggrieved to find her
jaunting about the countryside with a total stranger as if
she hadn't a care in the world. His manner was decidedly
stiff as he greeted Charity and her escort and, when he
found out who Jack was, he became quite hostile.

"Lord Riversleigh, eh?" he said, looking at Jack suspiciously. "I don't believe I've ever had the pleasure of meeting you before, my lord. Will you be staying in Sussex
long?"

"I'm not entirely sure," Jack replied, amused rather than

offended by Owen's ungraciousness. He found it impossible to imagine Charity united in blissful wedlock with this hot-headed young man.

"But I certainly have unfinished business that will keep me here until the end of the month," he continued.

"Unfinished business?"

"A contract," Jack explained, a slight chill in his polite voice, "the terms of which cannot be fulfilled until the end of February."

He heard Charity gasp as she realised he was talking about their wager, but he gave no indication of his amusement as he continued smoothly, "I won't bore you with the details. Are you much interested in business, Mr Leydon?" He raised his eyebrows, a faint, and not altogether encouraging, smile on his lips.

Owen looked into the cool grey eyes and suddenly felt rather hot. He knew that somehow he had been put at a disadvantage and he was afraid that his annoyance with the stranger had led him beyond the bounds of courtesy.

"No, no, not at all," he stammered. He was angry with himself, and angrier still with Jack, but most of all he was angry with Charity. He thought that he had been made to look a fool, and he was sure it was her fault.

"We've been over to see the Burdens," Charity explained. "Lord Riversleigh is going to lease Bellow's farm to Jerry, and I went with him to show him the way."

"I see," said Owen stiffly; he looked very put out. "I thought you wanted *me* to come and see you today, but if you've changed your mind…"

"No, no, indeed I haven't," Charity said hastily. "I'm so glad you've come. There's something I particularly need to ask you.

"Lord Riversleigh," she turned to Jack, "thank you for giving Jerry the lease; I'm sure you won't regret doing so.

And thank you for escorting me so far of the way home. I don't think I need to trespass on your time any further— I'm sure Owen will be happy to see me the rest of the way.''

''The pleasure has been all mine, Miss Mayfield,'' Jack replied politely, accepting his dismissal gracefully. His expression was grave, but she thought she saw amusement in his eyes and she acknowledged it with a slightly rueful look in her own.

''Mr Leydon.'' Jack took his leave of Owen. Then he turned the bay and considerately urged him into a steady canter. He thought Owen, and therefore Charity, would probably be glad to see the back of him as quickly as possible. It was very difficult to have a good argument when the cause of it was still within earshot—and the more Charity and Owen argued, the better.

''I thought you were going to be busy today,'' said Owen belligerently as he watched Jack disappear from view. ''Couldn't Gregory have shown that fellow where the Burdens live just as well? There was no need for you to make a spectacle of yourself, riding about the fields with a total stranger!''

''I *am* busy,'' Charity retorted, ''but I had to see Mrs Burden anyway. She's very anxious about all the changes that are going to happen. Besides, 'that fellow' is not a total stranger, he's Lord Riversleigh, and a perfectly respectable gentleman.''

''Respectable gentleman!'' Owen exclaimed. ''I heard he's nothing but the grandson of a common tradesman. He may possess the title, but he certainly doesn't have any breeding. Father was saying only last night that it's not surprising the old Lord should have disowned his son if he married so far beneath him. He must be turning in his grave at the thought of such an upstart stepping into his shoes!''

"If that's what Sir Humphrey thinks then he must be a narrow, bigoted fool!" Charity declared, her eyes sparkling with indignation. "I'd rather see an honest *coal-heaver's* son as Lord of Riversleigh than the mean-spirited, bullying, apology for a man who would otherwise have inherited it. *Harry's* birth might have been unimpeachable, but the only man I've ever respected less was his father!"

"Well, I know the late Lord wasn't exactly…" Owen was beginning, somewhat taken aback by Charity's vehemence and precluded by his innate honesty from defending the late Riversleigh, when he suddenly remembered what she'd said about Sir Humphrey.

"How dare you speak about my father so? At least he's not a worthless wastrel who gambled away his family's inheritance, and left his wife and children to be turned out of their home!" Owen stopped, appalled at what he had just said.

Charity stared at him, her face deathly pale. She was too shocked even to be angry, and she didn't say a word.

"Charity, I'm sorry! I never meant to say that…you just made me so angry. Charity! Don't look like that!"

In his agitation Owen leant over and gripped Charity's arm, shaking it in an effort to get through to her.

The grey mare didn't like being crowded so close, and snorted. Then she tossed up her head and sidled away.

"No. You didn't mean to say it, but it was what you were thinking," Charity said, her voice cold and even. "And who shall blame you? It must be what everyone in the country is thinking. But don't ever say so in my presence again, Owen."

"No, I promise. I'll go now," said Owen humbly. This cold, calm Charity was new to him, and much more disturbing than the old hot-tempered Charity who flared up at the slightest annoyance.

He began to ride away, and Charity watched him go.

The groom watched with interest. Miss Charity was certainly having a busy ride. First the conversation under the oak tree with Lord Riversleigh, now a full-scale quarrel with Mr Owen. Gregory hadn't been able to hear what had been said under the oak tree, but he knew what the argument with Owen had been about and he felt sorry for Charity. She might be too free with her tongue, and she certainly shouldn't have said what she did about Sir Humphrey, but Owen had had no business to come back at her like that. Any fool could guess how badly she felt about what Mr Mayfield had done—she didn't need her face rubbed in it. Gregory was glad to see Owen riding away. He was disappointed when he heard Charity call after him.

"Owen! Owen, wait a minute. It was my fault. If I hadn't abused Sir Humphrey you'd never have said it. I know that."

Owen came back to her. "That's no excuse," he said. "Just because you provoked me I should never…"

"Let's forget we ever had this conversation, shall we?" Charity asked, and held out her hand, smiling at him, though she couldn't quite hide the hurt in her eyes. "We've been friends for far too long to be on bad terms now." Strangely enough, she wasn't thinking about her plans to save Hazelhurst; she just didn't like being seriously at odds with someone she had played and bickered with since childhood.

Owen looked at her as if seeing her for the first time— perhaps he was. He'd known her for so long that he never really thought about her, or what she thought or felt. He'd taken her for granted. But now he was seeing a side of her he'd never even suspected, and he thought he liked it.

"You're a remarkable girl," he said slowly. "Lyddy wouldn't have forgiven me." Lydia was his sister.

"I'm not Lyddy." Charity smiled wryly. Lydia was the darling of the Leydon household, pampered and spoiled since birth. She was perfectly good-natured, but Charity had never had much in common with her.

"Come back to the house and I'll find you something to eat," Charity offered.

"Well, I must admit, I am *devilish* hungry," Owen confessed. "It seems such a long time since I last ate."

"It's *always* a long time since you last ate." Charity laughed. "Even if it was only five minutes ago!"

"No, that's not fair!" Owen declared. But from his new perspective he was thinking how well Charity knew him. He remembered all the times she had anticipated his wishes in the past, and how bravely she had bandaged up his leg with her petticoats when they had both been thirteen and he had fallen out of a tree and cut himself on a sharp stone. Perhaps his mother was right; perhaps it was time to start thinking about finding a wife.

Chapter Six

"My dear Mrs Mayfield, I came at once when Owen told me what had happened here last night. It must have been very distressing for you, but, Owen tells me, no harm done."

Sir Humphrey stepped briskly up to Mrs Mayfield as he spoke. He was a large, vigorous man in his middle fifties, and his devotion to both his sport and his wine could be clearly seen in his face and figure.

He was also the local magistrate, and he pursued his duties with a kind of casual diligence that served his neighbourhood remarkably well. Like most Sussex gentlemen, he paid no duty on the smuggled brandy in his cellar, and he knew as well as the next man when to look the other way, but for all that, his parish was remarkably well-governed. Charity particularly respected him for his ability to temper justice with compassion—though he always denied that he did any such thing. He was a man who knew his own worth and who valued his place in his community—but change made him nervous.

"Sir Humphrey, how kind of you to come!" Mrs Mayfield exclaimed. "I really wouldn't have had you put yourself to so much trouble."

"Nonsense, no trouble at all," Sir Humphrey declared, taking the seat Mrs Mayfield offered him. "Did you get a look at the scoundrel, m'dear?" he added, turning to Charity.

"I'm afraid not, Sir Humphrey," Charity replied. "It was dark and I was taken by surprise. I'm afraid I wouldn't be able to recognise him again."

"Pity," Sir Humphrey grunted. "I don't like to think of him getting away with this, but, if he didn't take anything and you can't recognise him, there's not much I can do."

"Oh, no, we quite understand," Charity assured him.

"I'm so looking forward to your party tomorrow night," Mrs Mayfield said. "It will be our last before we leave here. I shall be so glad of an opportunity to see everyone before we go."

"Hmph, yes." Sir Humphrey cleared his throat, looking uncomfortable. "It's a bad business, Mrs Mayfield. I don't say anything as to the cause of your leaving, but Lady Leydon and I shall be sorry to see you go. There've been Mayfields at Hazelhurst so long that it won't seem the same without you. If there's anything we can do, don't hesitate to ask."

"Thank you, it's so kind of you. Everyone has been very kind to us this last year." Mrs Mayfield smiled at Sir Humphrey. She hadn't caught his fleeting reference to her husband and, even if she had, she was spared some of Charity's distress because she divided the blame for what had happened between the Earl and Mr Canby.

Mrs Mayfield had conceived a violent dislike of the unknown Lord Ashbourne, but she saved her greatest ire for the unfortunate attorney. She blamed his negligence for their uncomfortable situation and, in the first few days after they had heard they must leave Hazelhurst, she had tried Charity's patience high by demanding they take action against him. Fortunately she had been diverted from the subject by the preparations for the move, and she hadn't returned to it.

"Owen particularly," Mrs Mayfield continued. "He was here only this afternoon, helping Charity with some of the arrangements. It's so complicated—I can't understand all these legal documents at all."

"Owen, helping! Well, well, I'm pleased to hear it. Not that he's got any experience. You should have asked me, Charity. I would have been glad to help." Sir Humphrey sounded slightly put out that Charity hadn't applied to *him* for assistance.

"You were my first thought," Charity assured him hastily. "And I know your advice would be invaluable. But I know how busy your magisterial duties keep you, sir, and how little time you have for your own affairs. I didn't want to trespass on your good will if I could get help from someone else, and, Owen being your son…"

"Well, you're a thoughtful young woman," said Sir Humphrey, puffing up with gratification in a way that reminded Charity irresistibly of Owen. There was a distinct likeness between father and son.

"But I'm here now, so if there's anything you'd like to ask me…"

"Thank you!" Charity tried to assume an expression of eager pleasure while her heart sank within her. "Oh…" she seemed to hesitate "…only if you're sure you have the time."

"All the time in the world for you, m'dear," Sir Humphrey assured her.

Despite the fact that she occasionally shocked him to his conventional core, the magistrate had always liked Charity. He thought she was a spunky little thing, and the day she'd tried to jump clear across the lily pond for a dare and climbed out covered in green weed and mud he'd laughed until tears had poured out of his eyes. Not that he necessarily regarded her wisdom as highly as he did her courage.

Charity saw the reminiscent gleam in his eyes and hurried into speech before he could comment once again on her childhood misdemeanours. That was the problem with being surrounded by people who'd seen you grow up—most of them still thought of you as the child you'd been ten years ago.

"If you'd like to come down to the library, Sir Humphrey," she said. "I have all the papers there."

"I'd be delighted, m'dear." Sir Humphrey stood up and bowed to Mrs Mayfield. "Excuse us, ma'am."

"Of course, so kind of you to help." Mrs Mayfield smiled brightly.

An hour later, feeling quite shattered, Charity led Sir Humphrey back upstairs again. She had not enjoyed the last sixty minutes and she hoped she wouldn't have to repeat them. It was not that Sir Humphrey's advice was bad—in fact, it was very good, just as she had known it would be. But he couldn't help commenting on her father's system—or lack of it—and regretting that there was no man to see to things properly.

Charity was grateful for his help, but she didn't like opening up her family affairs to the disapprobation of her neighbours, and she didn't intend to let it happen again. But she knew it was her fault: she shouldn't have used her need for advice as an excuse to get Owen to visit her. She should have guessed what would happen next.

"Well, I hope I've been of assistance," Sir Humphrey said as he sat down opposite Mrs Mayfield again. "Your late husband seems to have had a very peculiar way of doing things, ma'am. Not but the more recent records are in far better order. Still, it will be a relief to you, no doubt, when everything is sorted out and you're safely established in Horsham.''

''I shall be glad to be settled again,'' Mrs Mayfield admitted. ''Oh, Sir Humphrey! I met the new Lord Riversleigh this morning!'' she exclaimed, changing the subject completely.

''What did you make of him?'' Sir Humphrey asked cautiously.

''I thought he was a charming man. Not at all like his grandfather!'' Mrs Mayfield declared.

''No, by all accounts. I hear his *maternal* grandfather was a common tradesman! And apparently the new Lord is no better than… Well, there's no need to go into that! But it's a pity that such a fine old title should be brought to this!'' And Sir Humphrey shook his head disapprovingly.

Charity bit her lip in an effort to avoid saying something rude. She knew that Sir Humphrey didn't like change and hated any hint of social climbing, but she couldn't understand why both he and Owen should be so badly disposed towards a man they hadn't even met.

''Who told you about Lord Riversleigh, Sir Humphrey?'' she asked, trying to keep her voice friendly.

''Lord Travers. He's staying with us at the moment. Splendid fellow, marvellous horseman. He knows all about the new Lord,'' Sir Humphrey explained.

''Does he? What did he say?'' Charity asked.

''Oh, he told us how the grandfather—Pembroke, I believe his name was—started as a common apprentice. He'd no family or position; dare say he couldn't even read or write. No doubt a good enough man in his way, but rough, very rough. Not the kind of blood any man would want in the family,'' Sir Humphrey concluded, refraining from repeating some of the warmer stories Lord Travers had told him. He didn't think they were suitable for female ears.

"Lord Travers said that?" Charity said, resisting the urge to make a more heated reply.

She was beginning to feel extremely indignant on Jack's behalf, but it was clear that the slurs on his character and antecedents had not originated with the magistrate. Sir Humphrey was only repeating what he had been told, and it would do no good to be angry with him.

"Did Lord Travers say what the apprentice grandfather became, sir Humphrey?" she asked.

"No, I don't think so." Sir Humphrey frowned in an effort of memory. "No doubt he completed his apprenticeship and set up as a tradesman somewhere—if he could raise the capital. I wouldn't want any son of mine marrying a tradesman's daughter. Though by all accounts that must have been the least of Richard's crimes."

"Perhaps," said Charity slowly.

It seemed to her that there was a definite hint of vindictiveness in what Lord Travers had told Sir Humphrey. Apart from anything else, goldsmithing had always been one of the few trades in which it *was* possible for gentlemen to interest themselves. That was why so many French Huguenot refugees had links with the craft. Yet, despite his loquacity, Lord Travers didn't seem to have mentioned to the magistrate which trade Joseph Pembroke had been apprenticed in—or how he had developed his business. What other facts had Lord Travers misrepresented?

"Sir Humphrey!" she said suddenly. "Until a few days ago I'd always thought that Richard died more than thirty years ago. You've lived here all your life. Did *you* know Richard wasn't dead? Or, at least, that he didn't die until only seventeen years ago?"

"No-o-o." Sir Humphrey looked at her with a puzzled expression. "Now I come to think of it, I didn't. But I wasn't here at the time. My father had packed me off to

France to finish my education—and a dreadful place it was too.''

For a moment he was distracted from the subject in hand by his recollections of his time abroad. Like many Georgian gentlemen, Sir Humphrey had little love for the French and, when in his cups, he was quite likely to shout ''Hurrah for the roast beef of good old England''.

''Yes, but what do you remember about Richard?'' Charity reminded him.

''Oh, Richard,'' said Sir Humphrey, cut off before he could begin a diatribe against all foreigners. ''Not a lot. When I got back he was gone, name never to be mentioned again in Lord Riversleigh's presence. I wasn't much interested and it's a long time ago.''

''But did you think he was dead, or did you think he'd done something terrible?'' Charity persisted.

Sir Humphrey thought about it. ''Both!'' he said suddenly. ''I mean, I thought he was dead, but I was sure he'd disgraced the family. Not a savoury topic for discussing in the drawing-room. I dare say that this was why his name was never to be mentioned again.''

''But what was it he did that was so disgraceful?'' Charity asked, impatience finally creeping into her voice.

She was becoming increasingly annoyed by lack of substance in the magistrate's account. It seemed outrageous to her that Jack, his father and grandfather should all be condemned for sins or crimes which she was sure they hadn't committed, and which no one even seemed able to name.

''Damned if I know, m'dear,'' Sir Humphrey confessed. ''In fact now I come to think of it, young Richard always seemed devilish strait-laced to me. It just goes to show how you can be deceived in a man. Travers was telling me only last night...well, well, I beg your pardon, Mrs Mayfield, that's hardly a suitable story for your ears. But if this fellow is anything like his father I should be on your guard in his presence, that's all I can say.''

''I think I would have had more reason to be on my guard in the old Lord's presence than I have in this one's!'' said Mrs Mayfield unexpectedly. ''It seems most unjust to blame a man for the sins of his father. *Edward* never gave us any cause to doubt him, and his father was hardly a saint. Why should his cousin Jack be any different?''

''Well said, Mama!'' Charity exclaimed impetuously, and Mrs Mayfield blushed.

''You agree with Lady Leydon, then, that I should call on him and invite him to our party?'' Sir Humphrey asked.

''Certainly I do,'' said Mrs Mayfield firmly. ''It wouldn't be right to condemn him without even having met him. And *I* found him charming.''

''If that's your view, ma'am, I shall call upon him tomorrow morning,'' Sir Humphrey declared, despite his continuing personal misgivings. He took his leave of them soon after that, but he left Charity at least with a number of unanswered questions.

''Good morning, Mr Guthrie. How are you today?'' Charity asked as the land agent rode by.

She was sitting on the same gate which had caused all the trouble on the day of the hunt, and the land agent had been too engrossed in his thoughts to notice she was there until she spoke.

''Miss Charity! Don't you know better than to go startling a man like that?'' he reproved her. ''I've been worse. How about yourself?''

''I've been worse too,'' Charity replied. ''How do you like your new master? Isn't it a good thing he gave Jerry the lease?''

"A very good thing. And how did you know that?" Mr Guthrie looked at her suspiciously.

"I showed him the way to the Burdens'," Charity explained.

"Did you, indeed? I didn't think you'd met the man."

"Mr Guthrie! Haven't you been listening to the local gossip recently?" Charity looked shocked. "I've met him twice." She conveniently forgot the occasion when he had witnessed her quarrel with Owen over the gate.

"First he came to visit us with a message from Edward, only Mama was out," she continued unblushingly. "Then he was riding by on the way to the Burdens' and noticed me in the garden. Naturally I invited him in to meet Mama. He seems to be a great improvement on Harry."

She twirled the hazel twig she held in her hands as she spoke. With the blue sky behind her, and her hood thrown back carelessly from her dark curls, she looked the picture of innocence, but Mr Guthrie was not deceived.

"That's your opinion, is it?" he said drily.

"Certainly." Charity smiled at him ravishingly. Then she threw the twig away and jumped down from the gate. Mr Guthrie sighed ostentatiously and dismounted painfully.

"I'm too old for all this climbing on and off horses," he complained.

"I never asked you to get down," Charity pointed out.

"Mebbe not, but I'll get a crick in my neck if I try and talk to you from up there."

"How did you know I wanted to talk to you?" Charity asked, just as if she hadn't been sitting on the gate for the last forty-five minutes, waiting for the land agent to pass by. Mr Guthrie didn't deign to reply, and after a moment Charity laughed.

"I did want to ask you something," she admitted. "You

were here when Richard left. Why did Lord Riversleigh disown him? Did he do something dreadful?''

''I couldn't say. I was never admitted into his lordship's confidence,'' the land agent replied, his manner colder than usual when speaking to Charity.

''But you do *know*,'' said Charity, undaunted. ''After knowing the late Lord Riversleigh, and having met the new one, I can't believe it was anything to Richard's discredit, but that's what everyone will think—unless they know the truth.''

''I dare say that's what they'll think anyway,'' Guthrie replied. ''And why are you so concerned?''

''I don't know,'' said Charity, rather disconcerted to find herself blushing. ''But I don't think it's fair if people think badly of a man for something his father didn't even do,'' she added hastily as she met the land agent's shrewd gaze.

''No.'' Guthrie looked down at Charity thoughtfully. ''No, you wouldn't.'' He hesitated, and then seemed to make up his mind. ''You're quite right, of course,'' he said. ''Richard never did anything wrong. There was no scandal. That's the pity of it, the grievous pity. He wasn't like Harry. He fathered no bastards and ran up no debts he couldn't pay. He didn't cheat...'' The land agent caught himself up.

''Cheat!'' Charity exclaimed. ''Did Harry cheat?''

''That's another story, and nothing to do with Richard. Don't you go repeating it.'' Guthrie looked annoyed with himself. ''Where was I?''

''There was no scandal,'' Charity prompted him.

''No,'' said Guthrie. ''But Richard never could get on with his father. He was a man who couldn't abide to see things done badly, and he hated cruelty. I mind the time I was talking in West Street with him when we saw a horse struggling to pull a cart it couldn't shift because the wheels were locked. The idiot carter hadn't even bothered to get down and look. You should have heard what Richard said to the man.'' Guthrie smiled reminiscently.

''So what happened?'' Charity asked.

''Well, he didn't like his father's methods. He wanted improvements carried out at Riversleigh. He was a great believer in finding a better way of doing a job. Lord Riversleigh hated it—so did Harry. I think it was Harry who started that last quarrel; he always liked making trouble for Richard. I can't even remember what it was about—nothing important. But it was the last straw; Richard left that day and never returned. Lord Riversleigh gave orders that his name was never to be mentioned again. He was dead. I think Richard was glad to go. He'd given up any idea of trying his schemes at Riversleigh, and there was nothing else for him there—except his mother.''

''His mother!'' Charity exclaimed. ''What did she have to say about all this?''

''Very little. She was a quiet little woman, very much afraid of her husband. But she was brave enough to go with me in secret to see Richard in London. He couldn't come to her, you see. He'd sworn never to set foot on Riversleigh land again.''

''Good heavens!'' said Charity. ''What a terrible thing! Poor Lady Riversleigh. How could she bear it?''

''I don't think she could,'' said Guthrie sombrely. ''She died two years later. I've always believed it was grief that killed her.''

''Why did you stay?'' Charity demanded suddenly. ''Why did you work for that…that monster?''

''For Lady Riversleigh's sake at first. She trusted me to take her to Richard, d'y'see? And later…habit.'' The land agent shrugged.

Charity looked at him steadily for a moment. ''Habit?'' she said at last.

"Aye. And there was my wife: she came from these parts, she didn't want to leave. Besides…there were others who couldn't leave and I'd a foolish notion I ought to do my best for them." Guthrie looked half ashamed of his confession.

Charity smiled suddenly. "You're a good man," she said. "I'm glad I know you." She stood on tiptoe and kissed him on the cheek before he knew what she was about.

He flushed and mumbled with embarrassment.

"Did Richard meet his wife *after* he left Riversleigh?" Charity asked.

"Indeed he did. *She* never caused the breach with his father. It would be a wicked thing to suggest!" the land agent declared hotly, and from his immediate response Charity suspected he wasn't as unacquainted with the rumours as he might like her to imagine.

"I met her a couple of times. She was a lovely girl," he continued. "Half-French she was, and none the worse for it. Her grandfather on her mother's side was a Huguenot who'd come to England to escape persecution in his own land. She'd be much older now, of course. But I always thought Richard had done well for himself. Blood and birth don't count for everything, not by a long way."

"I never thought they did," Charity replied quietly. "Did Harry know Richard was married?"

"Oh, yes." Guthrie smiled grimly. "That's why he never married himself. It was his revenge on the old Lord. Lord Riversleigh dreaded the thought that Richard might one day inherit and Harry tormented him with it. He told me once that he'd wed the day the old man was finally in his grave—but not before."

"What a hideous pair!" Charity exclaimed. "Why did Harry hate his father so much?"

"That's a different story, and not one you need to know," Guthrie said. He gathered up the reins and prepared to climb up on his horse again. "As for the present Lord, I don't think you need worry about him. By all I can see, he's well able to take care of himself. I don't think a few unfounded rumours are going to upset him."

"You are pleased he's come, aren't you?" Charity said.

"Aye." Mr Guthrie settled himself more comfortably in the saddle. "Aye, I reckon it'll be a grand thing for Riversleigh. Mind, it's early days yet," he added with his customary caution. "Anything could happen. I'll be saying good day to you, Miss Charity. I have a great deal to do this morning."

"Of course, I didn't mean to hold you up," she smiled up at him. "Mr Guthrie, if anyone mentions the matter to you again, will you put them right?"

"Are you asking me to indulge in idle gossip?" the land agent asked austerely.

"No," she said quietly. "But so few people remember what really happened—even Sir Humphrey believes the rumours that Richard was disgraced. Don't you think his friends, those who remember him, have a duty to defend him?"

For a moment Guthrie stared down at her, then he said slowly, "Sometimes you're a very *daunting* young woman. Don't you think you've troubles enough of your own without taking up cudgels in defence of a stranger and a long-dead man?"

"Perhaps." She smiled wistfully, almost sadly. "But I'd like to think someone might do the same for me, or my family—if it was necessary."

"We do, my dear," said the land agent, speaking gruffly because he knew what people were saying about Mr Mayfield and he was distressed for Charity and her mother.

He couldn't tell her that he'd already defended them vigorously, because that would only confirm her obvious suspicions that her family was the subject of unkind gossip. But he could tell her that he'd defended Richard and perhaps, in the circumstances, that would do just as well.

"If you must know," he said, sounding as if he were speaking against his will, because that was what she'd expect, "if you must know, I've spoken out already against the lies I've heard about Richard. But the real scandalmongers lie outside my circle. I can't confront them."

"No, I know," Charity replied, thinking how it was Lord Travers who had played such a part in prejudicing Sir Humphrey against Jack Riversleigh and his father. "I'm sorry, Mr Guthrie," she continued. "I should have known you wouldn't stay silent."

The land agent smiled grimly to show he'd accepted her apology, and clicked his tongue at his horse.

"Well, if you've no further orders for me I'll be on my way," he said. "And mind you don't go startling any more travellers out of their wits this morning!"

Charity laughed and went back to the house, where she found Mr Canby and Lord Ashbourne's agent waiting for her in the library. She spent the rest of the morning making arrangements.

Chapter Seven

"I was so sorry to hear you must leave Hazelhurst," Mrs Carmichael said, patting Charity's hand comfortingly as they sat together on Lady Leydon's sofa. "It must have come as a terrible shock to you."

"It was a trifle...unexpected," Charity agreed steadily, and drew her hand away.

She wanted to say that it hadn't been a shock at all, that she and her mother had known all along that they were leaving Hazelhurst—but it would have been too obvious that she was lying. It was bad enough knowing that everyone was gossiping about her family, without giving them the added opportunity to talk pityingly about her futile attempts to cover up what had happened.

"You must have been so distressed," Mrs Carmichael continued. "I assure you, I felt for you and Mrs Mayfield when I heard the news. It's not even as if you have any other relatives to turn to; at least...doesn't Mrs Mayfield have a brother? I believe he came to visit you a few years ago. But perhaps he's back in India." She paused interrogatively.

"He did go back to India," Charity agreed calmly. "But I'm afraid he's dead now. In any case, we have received so much help from our friends, particularly Sir Humphrey, that we hardly feel our lack of relatives.''

She glanced around the crowded room as she spoke. She recognised nearly everybody at the supper-party; indeed, she had known many of them all her life. Normally she would have expected nothing but enjoyment from the evening, but tonight she was afraid that there were too many people present who, like Mrs Carmichael, would make it their business to pry into her affairs.

Charity knew that some of the questions she would be asked that evening would be prompted by genuine concern for her mother and herself, but she had no illusions about Mrs Carmichael's motives—and no hesitation at all in retaliating in kind.

''How is Mr Carmichael?'' she asked innocently, before Mrs Carmichael could frame another question. ''Is he not with you tonight? I was looking forward to seeing *all* our old friends before we leave the county.''

''I'm afraid he's not well,'' said Mrs Carmichael. She seemed slightly disconcerted by the turn of the conversation. ''Are you leaving the district? I'd heard you were moving to Horsham.''

''I'm so sorry to hear that,'' said Charity, addressing herself to the first part of her companion's reply and ignoring the second. ''When I met Mr Carmichael in the Carfax in Horsham a couple of weeks ago he seemed to be in excellent spirits. I do hope it's nothing serious?'' She looked at Mrs Carmichael earnestly.

''No, no,'' Mrs Carmichael replied hastily. ''A trifling indisposition—no more than that. I'm sure he'll be recovered by tomorrow, but it wouldn't have been wise for him to risk coming out in the cold night air.''

''No, of course not. But I'm so glad that it's not serious,'' Charity said brightly. ''You must know that Mr Carmichael has always been a great favourite of mine, he's such a friendly, genial man. He was *so* charming the last time we met, and very complimentary about my new hat. He became quite incoherent in his praise.''

She smiled blandly, though she felt a small bubble of amusement rising within her as she remembered *exactly* what the intoxicated Mr Carmichael had said. She didn't blame him in the least for his excesses; she thought she too might take comfort in the brandy bottle if she were married to Mrs Carmichael.

''Thank you,'' said Mrs Carmichael, her smile as insincere as her reply. ''He'll be delighted to know he made such a favourable impression on you; be sure I'll let him know what you said. But I believe you were telling me where you'll be moving to.''

''Was I?'' Charity frowned slightly; she was feeling a brief pang of sympathy for the hapless Mr Carmichael. ''I'd quite forgotten. How scatter-brained I am, to be sure. We're going to London, Mama and I—did I not tell you? Now that we can leave Hazelhurst there's nothing to keep us in Sussex any longer—we are free to live where we please. Ah, excuse me.'' She stood up as she spoke. ''I think Lady Leydon wants me. It's been so nice to see you again.'' She smiled politely and moved away before Mrs Carmichael could reply.

Well! said Mrs Carmichael to herself. Then, London? Who'd have thought it? She looked around for someone to whom she could pass on this interesting snippet of information.

Charity made her way quietly to Lady Leydon's side, smiling at her old friends and acquaintances as she passed between them, and occasionally pausing to exchange a few words. From her demeanour it would have been impossible to guess that she wasn't completely at ease, and only the faint shadows beneath her eyes hinted that she still hadn't caught up on the sleep she'd lost two nights previously.

The room was very hot, and brilliantly lit. There was an ornate chandelier hanging from the ceiling, a fierce fire blazing in the hearth and numerous candelabra standing on every free surface. There were even candles on the mantelpiece, their flickering flames reflected in the huge gilt-framed mirror that hung on the chimney breast.

Lady Leydon was standing beneath the mirror, fanning herself, and surveying her crowded room with satisfaction. She had never dared to hope that so many people would come to an out of season, out of town party, and she was savouring her triumph. It hadn't occurred to her that she owed a great deal of her party's success to the widespread curiosity about the new Lord Riversleigh. A curiosity which had only been increased by the rumours most people had heard about him, and by Sir Humphrey's ill-concealed doubts about the wisdom of inviting him.

Not that anyone had seriously believed that Jack wouldn't be present that evening, of course, and most people were anxious to meet him as soon as possible. Unfortunately he hadn't arrived yet and, as Charity threaded her way across the crowded floor towards Lady Leydon, she was aware of an atmosphere of thwarted curiosity. Life was imitating art, and the audience were getting restless as they waited for the principal actor in the latest local melodrama to appear.

Charity found it very distasteful, perhaps because she herself was experiencing at first hand what it was like to be an object of curiosity, and on at least one occasion she had been hard pressed to find a polite reply to a speculative remark made by one of her old friends.

She glanced around, noticing that her mother was deep in conversation with Lady Dalrymple, a dowager who lived to the north of Horsham. Then she reached Lady Leydon's side and smiled at her hostess.

"Ah, Charity!" Lady Leydon exclaimed with simple pleasure. "I wanted particularly to introduce you to Lord Travers. Lord Travers, this is my dear Miss Mayfield. Her family have always been our closest neighbours."

"Enchanted, Miss Mayfield!" Lord Travers bowed over Charity's hand with a flourish, but when he straightened up and smiled at her she thought the look in his eyes contained more appraisal than warmth.

It was as if he was assessing how useful she was to him, and had already decided that she would be of no use at all. She didn't like it, but it would have been discourteous to walk away so soon after they had been introduced, especially with Lady Leydon smiling so warmly at her, so she concentrated on attending to what Lord Travers was saying in such confidential tones.

Jack was late, but as soon as he arrived he knew he was the focus of everyone's attention. He also knew that a great deal of the interest was far from kindly, but he refused to allow it to disturb him.

Charity was standing near the wall, talking to Owen, when she first saw Lord Riversleigh. As usual he was dressed in black as a mark of respect for his grandfather, but she was immediately convinced that he was the most elegant man in the room. He was certainly the tallest, and he bowed over Lady Leydon's hand with the lazy grace which typified all his movements. His hostess was clearly delighted with him, and immediately took the opportunity to introduce him to her daughter, Lydia.

Charity watched surreptitiously, quite forgetting that Owen was standing beside her and paying no attention at all to what he was saying to her. She was too far away to hear what Lady Leydon was saying, but for a moment she was surprised that her hostess should respond so favourably to Jack—surprised, that was, because Lord Travers's conversation had been composed almost entirely of delicate but extremely damaging slanders against Lord Riversleigh.

From his description one would have supposed Jack not only to be a hardened rake, but also a man of dubious integrity in all matters of honour.

Charity had done her best to deny the stories, but Lord Travers had adopted a worldly air which was almost impossible for her to counteract. It was also very difficult for Charity to say too much without laying herself open to unwelcome questions.

On the whole, therefore, it was understandable that she should be momentarily startled by Lady Leydon's apparent willingness to introduce Lord Riversleigh to her daughter.

Then Charity realised that she was being foolish: one had only to meet Lord Riversleigh to realise at once that Lord Travers's insinuations could not possibly be true. Of course Lady Leydon had discounted the stories. She gave a faint sigh of relief and relaxed slightly, and it was only then that she discovered that in her first agitation she had gripped her fan so tightly that she had snapped one of its fragile sticks.

It was perhaps fortunate for her continued good opinion of her hostess that she didn't realise that Lady Leydon hadn't really been paying much attention to Lord Travers, and that most of what he had said had passed completely over her head. Lady Leydon, in fact, had been far more influenced in her opinions by what she had discovered from Lady Dalrymple—and Lady Dalrymple had made it very plain that Jack was an extremely wealthy man.

"So he's here, then," said Owen darkly, his eyes also on Lord Riversleigh. Unlike his mother, he continued to be more influenced by what he'd been told by another man, rather than by an old woman's foolish gossiping. "After what Lord Travers has told us I'm surprised he dares to show his face in public."

"And I'm surprised at you, Owen Leydon!" Charity rounded on him. "I hadn't spent more than two minutes with Lord Travers before realising he was a spiteful scandalmonger. He's making all the stories up! They have no basis in reality. He's a small-minded man; he'd hate to make a fool of himself in front of others. No doubt he did something stupid in Lord Riversleigh's presence and this is his notion of revenge!"

"How can you say such a thing about our guest?" Owen demanded. "Lord Travers..." He suddenly realised he had allowed his voice to rise, and broke off, continuing more quietly, but no less furiously, "Lord Travers is a *gentleman*, and a friend of my father, and you have as good as accused him of lying!"

"Not 'as good as', Owen," Charity corrected him, her eyes sparkling dangerously. "You know me better than that. I say he *is* lying. It would be interesting to know the real reason."

They were standing a little aside from the rest of the guests and no one had overheard what they'd said, but it was apparent to everyone that they were arguing. Mrs Carmichael was not the only one who began to edge closer in an attempt to find out what was going on.

"Not Lord Travers, Lord Riversleigh!" said Owen furiously. "What lies has *he* told you? How did *he* cozen his way into your favour? They say he has a way with the ladies. I think more must have happened on your ride together than you admit to!" He stopped, aghast at what he had said, and alarmed at the look in Charity's eyes.

Owen wasn't the only one to see Charity's expression

change. Everyone knew Owen Leydon and Charity May-field had been arguing with each other ever sine they had been children, and no one, not even Lady Leydon, took very much notice of their bickering. But this was different, and for the second time in two days Owen knew he had gone too far.

Charity didn't say anything; for a moment she just stared at him, her eyes dark in her pale face—then she walked away. She didn't exclaim and she didn't flounce, she acted as if she were quite alone in the room, and in the sudden silence the people simply parted before her. Even the musicians Sir Humphrey had engaged to add lustre to the occasion were aware that something was wrong, and paused briefly and discordantly in the middle of a tune.

Anger got Charity safely to her mother's side, then she realised what she had done and she nearly faltered, but pride took over, and she managed to smile at Mrs Mayfield, almost as if nothing had happened.

"Charity! Whatever did Owen say?" Mrs Mayfield asked anxiously.

"Nothing, Mama, don't worry. Would you like some lemonade?" Charity suddenly decided she couldn't bear to be questioned at that moment, and she seized at the first excuse she could think of to take her away from her mother's side.

"Yes, but…" Mrs Mayfield began. The hum of conversation had returned, and Lady Leydon had gestured urgently for the musicians to continue playing, but both Charity and Owen were receiving several surreptitious glances, and Charity knew that she had given the gossips something else to talk about.

"I'll get you some lemonade," she said, more curtly than usual, and stood up.

She was intercepted before she could reach the sideboard, or find a footman to serve her.

"Charity, I couldn't help noticing… I do hope Owen didn't offend you," Lady Leydon murmured anxiously.

"No. Please don't concern yourself." Lady Leydon was the last person Charity wanted to speak to, but she forced herself to relax and smile pleasantly to her hostess. "It was just a silly misunderstanding. I'm sorry if I distressed you; I didn't mean to disrupt the party."

"Owen can be too outspoken at times," Lady Leydon said. "I'm sure you know he doesn't mean anything by it. Please don't be annoyed."

"I'm not, really I'm not," Charity assured her, thinking that it was typical of Lady Leydon to be apologising for Owen without really knowing whether or not he was at fault. She was a quiet, nervous woman, often disconcerted by the more forthright, forceful characters of her husband and son.

"I was just going to fetch Mama some of your excellent lemonade," said Charity. "I believe you must have some secret ingredient which makes it so much more delicious than other people's. I always used to think so when I was a child."

"Thank you!" Lady Leydon exclaimed, glad that the conversation had moved on to a more innocuous topic. "You're quite right—however did you guess? It was my mother's recipe; she always insisted that one should put in half a teaspoon of…" She led Charity away, still talking about the best way of making lemonade.

"Do you know where Mr Edward Riversleigh is?" Mrs Carmichael asked. "It seems strange that he hasn't come back to Sussex. But perhaps the experience would be too painful for him—so soon after his grandfather's death,'' she finished with spurious innocence.

''I believe he's in Rome,'' Jack said calmly.

''Rome!'' Mrs Carmichael exclaimed, genuinely surprised. ''Whatever made him go there?'' She looked at Lord Riversleigh suspiciously.

''His interest in the architecture,'' said Jack with rather chilly politeness. ''He told me that he has always had a great desire to see it at first hand. I think he was looking forward to the opportunity.''

''Oh,'' said Mrs Carmichael. She was clearly not convinced. She undoubtedly suspected that Edward had gone away to nurse his grievances in private; or, even worse, that Jack had engineered Edward's absence deliberately in an attempt to remove a possible rival.

Jack sighed inwardly. He could make a fairly accurate guess at Mrs Carmichael's thoughts and he was annoyed—he disliked having his motives misconstrued—but he had no intention of justifying or explaining himself to her or anyone else. In any case, he had known that his unexpected arrival in Sussex would give rise to rumour and possibly suspicion, and he had thought that it would only be a matter of time before both died down.

What he hadn't expected was to discover that his own character, and those of his parents and his maternal grandfather, had been determinedly blackened. Jack still didn't know exactly what was being said—nobody repeated the stories to his face—but when he saw Lord Travers he knew who was behind the rumours.

He also knew that there were a number of people at the Leydons' that night who, out of consideration for his title or his wealth, were quite prepared to forgive him for his own supposed misdemeanours, for the trifling anomaly that his mother had been a tradesman's daughter, and even for the fact that his father had been anything from a cardsharp to a murderer—Lord Travers's stories were becoming increasingly lurid.

"Ah, Charity!" Mrs Carmichael reached out and caught Charity by the arm as she was trying to pass by with two glasses of lemonade. "Have you met Lord Riversleigh?"

"Yes, thank you." Charity extended her arms slightly so that the lemonade that had spilled when Mrs Carmichael jogged her arm didn't drip too badly on to her dress. "How do you do, my lord?"

"Excellently, thank you. May I hold that glass for you?" Jack said.

He took the glass from Charity, offered her a spotless linen handkerchief, and took the other glass while she wiped her hands.

"Oh, I'm sorry, I didn't know you were carrying anything," said Mrs Carmichael with an unconvincing show of concern. "I hope your dress isn't spoiled."

"No, not at all. But I'm afraid Lord Riversleigh's handkerchief is. Thank you, sir." Charity smiled at Jack.

"Lord Riversleigh tells me that *Mr* Riversleigh has gone to *Rome!*" Mrs Carmichael said, because it was to pass on that piece of news that she had stopped Charity in the first place, and she *never* allowed herself to be distracted from her purpose. Besides, everyone knew that Charity and Edward Riversleigh had been on very good terms.

"I know," Charity said immediately. "Mama and I received a letter from him only yesterday. He's enjoying himself immensely. He's always wanted to go there, you know." She smiled warmly at Mrs Carmichael. "But without Lord Riversleigh's generosity it would never have been possible. I believe he's written to you, also, my lord," she continued, turning to Jack. "But in case that letter goes astray he particularly asked us to tell you how very grateful he is to you. To be honest, I think he's rather relieved at the way things have turned out. He's finally got the chance to do what he's always wanted to do. Excuse me, but I promised Mama I'd fetch her some lemonade.'' She smiled impartially at Jack and Mrs Carmichael and went in search of Mrs Mayfield.

''A charming girl,'' said Mrs Carmichael, briefly distracted from her attempts to find out more about Edward Riversleigh by her desire to talk about Charity. ''But very headstrong. I'm afraid she takes after her father. I dare say you saw that argument she had with Owen Leydon earlier. I wouldn't want any daughter of mine to behave so forwardly in public. Mind you, I shouldn't say this, of course, but Owen could try the patience of a saint. But I expect Helena Mayfield was disappointed; I'm sure she'd like to see Charity settled comfortably. You've heard about their troubles, of course?'' But it was a rhetorical question, and Mrs Carmichael didn't wait for Jack to reply. ''It will be a sad day for us all when they leave Hazelhurst,'' she carried on. ''Have you met Lord Ashbourne, my lord? What's he like?''

''I have met him, but I'm afraid I'm not one of his intimates. Excuse me, ma'am,'' said Jack, and turned away abruptly before he was tempted to reply more forthrightly than he considered wise or desirable.

''Letter, Miss Mayfield?'' Lord Riversleigh asked. It was the first time he had had an opportunity to speak to Charity alone, and the evening was already well advanced.

She was standing near a window, unobtrusively pushing the curtain back slightly so that she could feel the cool air on her face. Using her other hand, she was fanning herself with her damaged fan with as much vigour as she considered compatible with decorum.

She blinked at Jack, briefly at a loss, yet suddenly feeling happier than she had done all evening. Then she smiled, that rare, open smile that seemed to distinguish her from almost anyone else Jack had ever met.

"Well, there might have been a letter," she said. "And if there had been that's exactly what Edward would have said, so I'm not going to feel guilty."

"But what possible reason could you have for thinking that Edward has any particular cause to be grateful to me?" Jack asked, something not quite a smile in his eyes.

"You told me the first day we met that he'd found a patron," Charity pointed out, returning his smile so delightfully that he felt his heart turn over. "I wondered at the time, but I had other things on my mind, so I didn't pursue it. But if you haven't made him, at the very least, a handsome allowance I shall be greatly surprised."

"I'd hate to disappoint you," Jack murmured. He was amused, but gratified by Charity's perception, and by the accuracy of her guess. In fact, Edward Riversleigh now had more financial security than he'd ever had before in his life, and arguably more than he would have had if he had actually inherited Riversleigh. He was very happy with the way things had turned out, though at first he had been somewhat bewildered by Jack's generosity.

"Are you always so quick to defend others?" Lord Riversleigh continued more seriously.

"That depends," Charity said vaguely, her mind on other things. "How much money did you lend Lord Travers?"

Jack gazed down at her in surprise. His anger had been growing throughout the evening, though he had concealed it very well. He wasn't a fool and, and though no one had said anything openly to him, it hadn't taken him long to get the gist of Lord Travers's slanders.

The slurs against his own character annoyed him, but the lies that were being circulated about his father outraged him—partly because they were so unfair, and partly because the breach between the late Lord Riversleigh and his second son made them too easy to believe.

He had been on the brink of challenging Lord Travers several times, but his inherent good sense had warned him that that was not the answer. A duel might well turn a difficult situation into a full-blown scandal. Besides, he had other, better ways of dealing with the man.

He had also known that not everyone would take the stories at face value, but so far no one had given any indication that they disbelieved Lord Travers, and he certainly hadn't expected anyone to see so clearly what lay behind his vindictiveness.

"I'm sorry," said Charity when Jack didn't say anything. "I'm afraid I spoke without thinking again. Please forget it."

"No, no, don't apologise." Jack suddenly realised he had been staring at her in silence for several seconds. "I was surprised, that's all. I hadn't thought anyone would guess."

"You did lend him money, then?"

"The bank did."

"I thought so," Charity said, pleased that her supposition had proved correct. "He looks the kind of extravagant man who'd get himself into debt. I told Owen I was sure he was taking revenge for his own stupidity on y...others," she amended hastily.

"You told Owen?" Jack echoed, an unreadable expression in his eyes. "Was *that* what your argument was about?"

"I think I ought to find Mama," said Charity. She suddenly seemed flustered. She closed her fan with a snap and tried to move away from the window. "It's getting late. We should be leaving soon."

"Miss Mayfield." Jack reached out to rest a detaining hand lightly on her arm.

Neither of them was prepared for the sudden surge of emotion which leapt between them as he touched her, and Charity almost gasped. She stared up into his face with wide, startled eyes, and it was only with an effort that Jack remembered what he had been intending to say.

"I know what's being said about my father, and since Travers is the Leydons' guest I'm sure Owen believes it. Did you defend me?" he asked in a calm voice which belied his inner feelings.

For a second he wondered if she'd heard what he'd said. Her gaze was fixed on his face, her lips slightly parted as if she was trying to understand…but then she looked down at her fan, half opening and closing it with hands that trembled slightly.

"I told Owen that Lord Travers must be lying," she said at last, her voice sounding muffled in her own ears, and her eyes still fixed on her fan. "I think he was annoyed because I'd insulted a guest in his house."

"I see," said Jack slowly. "Thank you." He looked down at her as if he were seeing her for the first time, quite forgetful of their surroundings.

"I am grateful to you, Charity; your good opinion means a great deal to me. But I would hate to think I'd been the cause of a breach between old friends. Please don't make things more difficult for yourself on my account."

"No, don't worry," said Charity, looking up at him once more.

He had used her name, but she had hardly noticed, she was so intensely aware of his unwavering gaze and of the depth of feeling in his voice. She wanted to look away—

but somehow she couldn't. Without knowing what she did she began to lean slightly towards him, and for a moment Jack was lost in the dark, luminous eyes. He lifted his hand to draw her closer to him—and suddenly remembered they were standing in a crowded room.

The realisation jolted him badly. Never before had he so nearly lost all sense of his surroundings. He stepped back abruptly, struggling to master his frustration at the self-imposed interruption, and searching for some way to steer the conversation back into safer channels.

For Charity there was a sense of confusion—and of something lost, or not quite found. One minute Jack was so close that he seemed to fill all her senses—the next he had moved away and was asking her politely whether she and her mother had made a final decision about where they were going to move to.

The change was so sudden that for a moment she felt quite bewildered, unable to comprehend what he had said, or frame a coherent reply. But then, once more, she could hear the voices and laughter of the other guests, and remembered where she was.

''Mama suggested that perhaps we ought to move to London,'' she said at last.

''London!'' Jack exclaimed. ''I'd thought you were planning to take lodgings in Horsham.''

''We were,'' Charity agreed, beginning to feel more like herself again. ''But I think perhaps Mama is right. There's nothing really to keep us in Sussex any more—and I believe that *she* might be happier in London. She likes to be surrounded by people and bustle. She hates it in the winter in Hazelhurst when the weather is bad and she doesn't see anyone.''

''Yes, I see,'' said Jack. ''And will you also be happier in London?''

"I…" Charity glanced up at him briefly and, as she saw the expression in his eyes, she began to feel her pulse quicken once more "…I hope so. Mama thinks…Mama suggests that I ask your advice. On where to live, I mean. It's so long since she was…and I only had one Season…" Her voice trailed away as she seemed to lose the sense of her explanation.

"I would be delighted to advise you," Jack replied in a hearty tone which was at a complete variance with the way he normally spoke—and with the way he felt.

He knew that he couldn't allow the refined torture of this very public conversation to continue much longer. He could sense the awakening responsiveness in Charity, and he knew that his own sudden retreat had confused her, but there was nothing he could do or say when at any moment he expected them to be interrupted by Owen, or Mrs Carmichael, or one of the other guests.

"May I fetch you some lemonade?" he asked abruptly; he didn't want to leave her but for her sake it would be better if they had some time apart to regain their composure.

"Lemonade?" Charity echoed, bewildered by the sudden change. "Oh, I… Yes, I am a trifle warm. Thank you." She started to fan herself again, watching as Jack threaded his way across the room.

Something had happened, something was different, but she wasn't quite sure…

"Charity, Charity!" The persistent repetition of her name recalled her attention and she turned reluctantly to find Owen standing beside her.

"I wanted to speak to you," he said, his manner a curious mixture of belligerence and sheepishness.

Chapter Eight

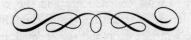

"Oh." Charity looked at Owen blankly. For a moment she had almost forgotten their quarrel. Then she remembered, and instantly decided that he must have sought her out to continue it—or to demand an apology. The idea of any prolonged conversation with him at that moment was so dreadful that she immediately decided her best course of action was to apologise straight away—anything to get rid of him.

"I'm sorry," she said, holding out her hand in a very fair imitation of her usual friendly manner. "It was unforgivable of me to make such a scene at your mother's party."

"No, no, it was all my fault," said Owen, taking her hand. He didn't think it had been, but Charity's ready apology disarmed him, and gave him a welcome opportunity to be magnanimous.

"I should have been more considerate," he said. "I know you're having a very difficult time at the moment. It's not surprising if you're feeling overwrought. I dare say there is so much on your mind that half the time you hardly know *what* you're saying. I should have made allowances. You look tired; come and sit down."

He drew her hand possessively through his arm as he spoke and led her to a sofa which had been pushed back against a wall. By now the party had turned into an impromptu dance, and the room seemed noisier and more crowded than ever. Charity felt quite dizzy as she watched the swirling dresses.

She wanted to send Owen away, but for some reason her wits seemed to have deserted her and she couldn't think how to do it. He was sitting beside her, but his voice sounded like a distant echo and she seemed unable to concentrate on what he was saying. On the other side of the room she could see that Jack had been waylaid by Lady Leydon and her daughter.

"Do you think it will be convenient for me to call on Mrs Mayfield tomorrow?" Owen asked earnestly.

"What? Oh, I dare say," Charity replied, leaning sideways slightly to get a better view and only half attending. Jack was laughing; what *could* Lydia be saying that was so amusing?

"Good. In the circumstances it seems best. Of course, if you had any close male relatives it would be different. Do you think Mrs Mayfield will be pleased to receive me?" Owen was looking flushed, and his earlier self-assurance seemed to have left him. He tugged at his neckcloth as he spoke.

"We're always pleased to see you," Charity said with automatic and uncomprehending politeness—she still wasn't listening properly. "And it's very kind of you to want to help, but I wouldn't like you to miss out on your hunting."

"Hunting!" He stared at her in disbelief. "Oh, I see. It's very kind of you to be so thoughtful, but in the circumstances I don't object."

"Oh, good," she said vaguely, starting to get up. "I think I'll just go…"

"Damn it all, Charity!" Owen seized her arm and wouldn't let her rise. "Don't you want to marry me?"

"What?" For a moment she gazed at his flushed face in disbelief, then it suddenly dawned on her what he must have been saying. "Oh, Owen, I'm sorry. I wasn't listening."

"No," said Owen, breathing heavily. "You've had a very trying time recently. I dare say it's all been too much for you. You'll feel better when you've had a good night's sleep. I'll escort you home."

"Yes… No! Wait a minute!" Charity exclaimed with an unexpected return to something like her normal manner. "Half an hour ago I didn't think we were on speaking terms; what on earth made you decide to ask me to marry you now?"

"I *was* very angry," Owen admitted, torn between gratification at this opportunity to explain his actions and exasperation at her lack of proper decorum. "But I shouldn't have been. I've been thinking, and I've realised that after the sheltered life you've led it's not reasonable to expect you to fully understand the ways of the world. I should have made allowances, but I'll be more tolerant in future, I promise." He squeezed her hand reassuringly. He seemed to have regained his confidence.

"Thank you," said Charity, gazing at him rather helplessly. She had suddenly realised that she didn't know what to do. For days she had been manoeuvring to bring this moment about, but now it had arrived all she felt was a sense of anticlimax and an overwhelming desire to laugh. Marriage to Owen!

Then she remembered Hazelhurst, the Burdens and

everyone else who depended on her. She couldn't let them down.

"You've made me very happy," she said resolutely, holding out her hand to Owen. "Mama will be delighted to receive you tomorrow. Do come as early as you can."

It had suddenly occurred to her that in order to get Owen's ring on her finger before the end of the month she was going to have to work very fast indeed.

"Yes, well, I think I'd better take you back to your mother now," he said; he still didn't feel entirely comfortable with the way things were turning out. "It's getting late—no doubt you'll be wanting to go home soon."

"Yes, I expect we will," Charity agreed, and allowed Owen to pull her to her feet.

Although she didn't realise it, he found her apparent docility very soothing, and his half-acknowledged doubts began to fade. He had had a very difficult few hours trying to reconcile his earlier decision to marry her with their sudden, disturbing quarrel. But in the end he had been able to resolve his inner conflict by concluding that Charity's actions had been prompted by an uncharacteristic nervous agitation.

It had been a great relief to him when he had realised that Charity's waywardness was caused partly by her upbringing, and partly by the lack of adequate male guidance in her life, because it was therefore curable.

As he shepherded her back to Mrs Mayfield he was even thinking complacently of what an excellent wife she would make—with a little gentle instruction from him.

"That reminds me," he said abruptly. "I know that your principles are too firm for you to be led easily astray, but I think, in future, it would be a good idea if you didn't have any more to do with Lord Riversleigh. I wasn't at all pleased to see you speaking to him just now, but I suppose if he accosted you you might find it difficult to excuse yourself.''

''How d—?'' Charity cut short her angry response just in time. An argument with Owen now would be fatal, but at the same time she realised she wasn't prepared to let him think he'd have the ruling of her in this marriage. Compromise was one thing, but her opinions and wishes were important and he must understand that.

''No, Owen,'' she said, making an effort to speak in a reasonable voice. ''I know you only have my best interests at heart, but I am not a fool and I cannot allow you to dictate who I speak to—or what I think. I'm sorry.''

''But when we are married you will naturally be guided by me.'' Owen frowned. ''It would be improper for you to flout my authority.'' He was thinking of his mother, who, to his certain knowledge, had never once disagreed with his father on any matter of significance.

''Of course I will be *guided* by you,'' said Charity. ''But I could never let you form my opinions for me.''

Owen looked at her, a hint of irritation in his expression. Then he remembered that she was over-tired and agitated, and decided to make allowances for her.

''You're very tired,'' he said. ''I'll have your carriage called for.''

Charity looked at him in exasperation. It seemed that Owen being tolerant could be even more annoying than Owen being dictatorial, but just now she didn't have the energy to argue.

From the other side of the room Jack watched them join Mrs Mayfield. He had finally extricated himself from Lady Leydon and Lydia and he had been about to return to Charity, but he had no wish to provoke another scene, and after a moment's indecision he decided to wait and continue their interrupted conversation in less public surroundings.

* * *

"Your luck seems to be quite out tonight, Travers," Sir Humphrey commented genially as he collected up the cards. "Shall we play another hand?"

"By all means," Lord Travers agreed shortly. "I'm out of practice, but I shan't be beaten again, I assure you." A faint crease in his forehead indicated that he was most unhappy at losing so heavily to a provincial squire, and he had every intention of drubbing Sir Humphrey soundly in the next game.

Sir Humphrey looked thoughtful as he shuffled the cards before dealing them again. He had been the perfect host all evening and now he was indulging himself with the pastime that, next to hunting, he enjoyed most. But he was becoming aware that, despite his surface urbanity, Lord Travers deeply resented losing. Most men hated being beaten, but Sir Humphrey thought there was something decidedly unsporting in Lord Travers's manner, and he was beginning to revise his opinion of his guest.

That didn't necessarily mean, however, that he was also revising his opinion of Jack Riversleigh. Sir Humphrey was still inclined to think that there could be no smoke without fire, and if Jack took after his paternal grandfather, the late Lord Riversleigh, then Lord Travers's innuendoes were more than justified.

Lord Travers picked up his cards and sorted them with brisk, irritable movements. He was annoyed to find that he had a very poor hand, and his annoyance showed in his face as he looked up at the man who had come to stand beside him at the card table.

Jack acknowledged Sir Humphrey courteously, but he spoke to Lord Travers.

"My lord." He nodded briefly in greeting. "It was an unexpected pleasure to see you here tonight. After our last meeting I was under the impression that you would be spending some time in Buckinghamshire. I trust you're in your customary good health.''

His voice was cool and unemotional and there was no warmth in his grey eyes as they rested on Lord Travers's face.

''Damn it, Riversleigh! I don't see what concern it is of yours if I chose to come into Sussex,'' Lord Travers burst out.

Sir Humphrey frowned; he was watching the encounter closely and there seemed to him to be something rather off-key about Lord Travers's response.

''No concern of mine at all,'' Jack agreed. He rested his hand lightly on the green baize surface of the card table and looked down at Lord Travers. ''But—I think you will agree—the same cannot be said for all your...activities.'' He smiled as he spoke, but the expression in his eyes was singularly cold.

''I don't know what you're talking about,'' Lord Travers blustered.

He was at a decided disadvantage. He had to crane his head back to meet Jack's gaze, and he could neither stand up nor push his chair back, because the card table was right in the corner of the room.

''Then perhaps you should try searching your memory,'' Jack said. He was speaking very quietly, yet his words had the sting and impact of a whiplash.

The colour drained out of Lord Travers's face. He looked afraid—and, indeed, he was afraid.

He was remembering—too late—a half-forgotten incident which had occurred nearly three years ago when a young, arrogant nobleman had set out to demonstrate his superiority over the goldsmith-banker's grandson. Lord Penwood had forced a quarrel on Jack Riversleigh, confident of his ability to defeat him with any weapon Jack chose. But it had been young Lord Penwood who had been wounded—even though he was generally considered to be a very fine swordsman—and he had later admitted, with commendable honesty, that it was only because of Jack's forbearance that he was alive at all.

Since then the two men had become friends, but, as Lord Travers stared into Jack's eyes, he knew that there was no possibility of such an outcome of the present occasion.

His eyes were locked with Jack's, he seemed unable to look away, and when he opened his mouth to speak he found he couldn't.

He ran his tongue nervously over his dry lips.

"I am speaking of certain *business* matters, my lord," Jack said at last. "I think—I really think—it is time we arranged a meeting. Shall we say tomorrow morning? Nine o'clock at Riversleigh?"

It took a moment for Lord Travers to comprehend what Jack had said. When he did his first reaction was one of overwhelming relief, which left him feeling weak and stupid. Then he remembered how much money he owed, and how far behind he was with the repayments, and he was filled with cold, dark foreboding.

Jack hadn't moved; he was still standing before Lord Travers, one eyebrow lifted, clearly waiting for a reply.

Lord Travers tried to speak, found that he couldn't and cleared his throat; then he tried again.

"Nine o'clock, at Riversleigh, I think you said," he croaked. He tired to smile, to put on a bold face, but he failed miserably. "It will be my pleasure, my lord."

Jack smiled sardonically; he was clearly not convinced. "I hope so," he said, and turned to take his leave of the dumbfounded Sir Humphrey.

* * *

Mrs Mayfield and Charity were taking their leave of Lady Leydon when Jack strolled up to join them, and as soon as he realised they were leaving he offered to escort them home—Hazelhurst lay almost directly between Leydon House and Riversleigh. Mrs Mayfield, still nursing her own matchmaking schemes for Charity, had no hesitation in warmly accepting his offer.

Charity herself had mixed feelings. When she had glanced up and seen Jack approaching she had experienced an instant upswell of happiness. But now, instead of looking forward to telling him that she had all but won their wager, she found herself strangely reluctant to mention the matter to him at all. In fact, for some inexplicable reason she felt more like bursting into tears than celebrating her forthcoming victory. She suddenly felt very tired and she longed for the peace and quiet of Hazelhurst.

Both Jack and Mrs Mayfield were aware of her mood, though neither of them fully understood the cause of it, and they both did their best to expedite their departure. Then they struck a hitch.

Owen hadn't been present when Jack had offered to escort the Mayfield ladies home, and when he found out he looked patently horrified, staring at Lord Riversleigh with such a mixture of hostility and suspicion before offering *his* services as escort that Mrs Mayfield began to feel uncharacteristically annoyed.

''It's very thoughtful of you, Owen,'' she said tartly, ''but there is really no need for you to put yourself to so much trouble. As Lord Riversleigh has said, he must pass by Hazelhurst on his way home anyway, and I'm sure he doesn't mind accompanying us—not that I think we really need an escort for such a short journey.''

''It's no trouble,'' Owen said obstinately. ''As for his

lordship, it would be much quicker for him to go across the fields by way of Bellow's farm. The moon is full—there would be no difficulty in doing so.''

"Possibly not," Jack agreed pleasantly, "but I'm still far too new to the district to be confident of my ability to pick my way across unfamiliar fields, even by moonlight. No, I think I must stick to the roads. But I'm sure, if you really think it necessary, Mrs Mayfield would be glad of your escort also," he finished diplomatically but untruthfully.

He could tell that Mrs Mayfield didn't really welcome the idea of Owen's presence—he didn't himself—but he could also see from the set of the young man's jaw that it would take a great deal to persuade him not to come. If Jack had been convinced of the necessity for doing so he might have made the attempt, but he had never been one to pursue an argument for argument's sake and, judging by Charity's expression, all she wanted was to get home as quickly as possible. He wondered what had caused her change of mood and hoped that he had not in any way been the cause of it.

In the end, despite Owen's hostility and Mrs Mayfield's lack of enthusiasm, the entire party set out together. As a compromise, it didn't really please anyone, but at least it satisfied Charity's increasingly obvious desire to go home.

The last farewells were said, the ladies were handed into the coach, the door was shut and the whole equipage rumbled off, with Owen and Lord Riversleigh riding alongside. Owen was stiff and very formal, Jack relaxed and faintly amused.

They didn't have far to go, and it wasn't long before the carriage passed through the main gates of Hazelhurst and began to trundle up the short driveway. Jack and Owen were riding a little way ahead, Owen determined at least to be the one to hand Charity down from the coach.

Jack glanced around appreciatively. The moonlight suited the beautiful old house, and he realised again what a wrench it would be for Charity to leave it. There had been Mayfields at Hazelhurst for so long. This house had been built by one of them nearly one hundred and thirty years before, and the family had been living in the same place for much longer than that.

So far that evening his thoughts had mainly been pre-occupied with Charity, but now he decided that he would do everything in his power to save the home she loved. He knew it would mean an encounter with Lord Ashbourne, and he was aware of a flicker of anticipation at the prospect because, despite his somewhat misleading words to Charity, he and the Earl were old opponents.

At that point he was roused from his thoughts by the sudden realisation that, although the curtains were drawn, the library window was slightly ajar. Was that carelessness on the part of the servants, or…?

The front door opened and two men ran out, their feet crunching on the gravel as they raced towards the shrubbery.

Instantly Jack touched his heels to the side of his horse and the bay sprang forward, riding down the men.

''Leydon!'' Jack shouted over his shoulder, because for a moment Owen had been too startled to do anything. But almost before Jack had called Owen had urged his horse into a gallop, his huntsman's instincts coming rapidly to the fore.

The man nearest Jack veered away, and Jack followed him. The other kept running straight to the shrubbery, with Owen hard on his heels.

The coachman hauled on the reins and the carriage juddered to a stop. The coachman had seen the men leave the house, and he didn't know whether his ladies would be safer in the carriage or under their own roof. If there were still intruders *inside* the house they would be better outside. He reached for the blunderbuss he always carried but never before had had occasion to use.

"Martin, what is it?" Charity put her head out of the window.

"Stay in the carriage please, miss," he said, his voice a mixture of excitement and apprehension.

Charity looked ahead. She was just in time to see Jack draw level with the running man. As he did so he sprang from the back of the speeding horse, and she felt a moment of sickening fear as both men went down.

Then Jack stood up, dragging his shaken captive to his feet and over to the carriage.

Charity realised she'd stopped breathing, and drew in a shaky breath. Then she remembered Owen—where was he?

"Charity! Charity!" Mrs Mayfield was tugging at her arm. "What's happening? Charity!"

"I don't know, Mama," Charity said briefly. "But I don't think it's anything to get alarmed about."

Jack searched his captive quickly, then he forced the man down on to his knees beside the carriage and ordered him to put his hands on his head.

"Watch him," he said briefly to the coachman, and turned back to the house, taking a pistol from his greatcoat pocket as he did so.

"Stay here, Mama," said Charity. Her earlier weariness forgotten, she opened the carriage door and jumped down on to the drive. Then she picked up her skirts and ran to Jack."

"Go back to the carriage," he said sharply. "I don't think there'll be anyone else in the house, but I can't be sure."

"It's my house," said Charity. "I won't get in the way."

She was slightly breathless, but quite calm, and very determined.

"Very well," said Jack after only the briefest hesitation. "But keep behind me."

He pushed open the front door and stepped into the house. The library door was open and a band of light fell across the floor of the otherwise darkened hall. There was a lantern on the library table, and several of the candles had been lit. It was only because the curtains had been drawn that the light hadn't shown from outside.

There was nobody in the hall, and Jack strode forward to pick up the lantern. Charity followed him into the library, but she didn't get much further than the door. She took one glance around and stopped dead, lifting her hands to her face.

The library was a shambles. All the desk drawers had been broken into and their contents upended on the floor, chairs had been overturned, and books pulled from the shelves.

"Oh, my God!" Charity whispered. "What were they looking for?"

"I don't know," Jack said briefly. "But this is clearly the room they were interested in. I'm sure there won't be anybody else in the house."

Nevertheless, he took the lantern and quickly checked the other rooms before returning to Charity.

She hadn't moved; she was still standing where he had left her, staring with horror at the chaos all around her.

"Here." Jack picked up one of the lighted candles and put it gently into Charity's hand. "Go and light some of the candles in the parlour, and I'll bring your mother in. She won't want to see this." Then he smiled at her reassuringly. "It's not as bad as it looks."

"No." Charity roused herself and walked mechanically out of the library, closing the door gently behind her.

Chapter Nine

When Jack got outside he found the coachman still covering the captured burglar with his blunderbuss, and Mrs Mayfield on the verge of hysterics inside the carriage. She'd tried to ask the coachman what was happening, but he'd been so overcome with the responsibility for guarding his prisoner that he had growled at her to get back inside the carriage and keep quiet.

Consequently Jack found her cowering inside the coach, almost afraid to move.

She jumped convulsively, and gave a muffled scream as Jack's head and shoulders, silhouetted by the moonlight, appeared at the window.

"Don't be alarmed, ma'am, it's only me," he said, his deep voice instantly recognisable. "You can come into the house now." He opened the coach door, let down the steps and helped her out.

"Is Charity all right?" she asked anxiously.

"Yes, ma'am," he replied reassuringly. "The situation seemed more alarming than it was. You're quite safe."

He offered her the support of his arm and escorted her into the house. He'd deliberately gone to the door on the opposite side of the carriage to where the prisoner still knelt, and Mrs Mayfield didn't see him. Jack paused briefly at the door of the parlour, pleased to see that in the short time he'd been gone Charity had already made the room seem comfortably welcoming; then Mrs Mayfield saw her daughter and ran towards her.

Charity was feeling more normal. She had pulled herself together when Jack had gone out to get Mrs Mayfield and not only had she lit most of the candles, but she'd also kindled the fire in the hearth and sent Charles to fetch some brandy.

The servants had been told not to wait up for their mistresses' return from the party, and until they'd heard all the commotion outside they had not realised they had had housebreakers.

Charles, who'd appeared with his breeches and his coat hastily pulled on over his nightshirt, was somewhat inclined to exclaim at the peculiar goings on. But Charity had cut him short and sent him away to find some brandy. She thought it might calm her mother's nerves.

"Oh, Charity! What's happening?" Mrs Mayfield cried, throwing out her arms to her daughter.

"Nothing dreadful, Mama," Charity said reassuringly. For some reason which she didn't full understand, she felt quite calm. There had been a moment when she had first seen the damage that had been done when she'd felt really distressed, but somehow the sight of Jack's tall figure behind her mother seemed immensely comforting.

"Come and sit down by the fire," she said soothingly to Mrs Mayfield. "Charles is going to bring you some brandy. There's nothing to worry about, is there, my lord?" As she spoke she gently persuaded Mrs Mayfield to sit down, and held her mother's cold hands reassuringly in hers.

"Nothing at all," he replied calmly. "I'm afraid you've

had intruders again, Mrs Mayfield. But I've checked thoroughly and there's no one here now. You're quite safe.''

''Oh, thank you.'' Mrs Mayfield sighed with relief. As Jack had suspected, the fear of strangers in her house was of more immediate concern to her than the possibility that anything might have been stolen. ''I'm sure if you say so it must be true, my lord. Thank goodness you were here. I don't know what we'd have done without you.''

''I think Miss Mayfield would probably have managed,'' he said, a half-smile in his eyes as he looked down at Charity.

She was feeling torn between admiration and exasperation at the ease and speed with which he had allayed Mrs Mayfield's fears. Two nights ago, when the intruders had first appeared, Charity had had to dedicate several hours to achieving the same effect.

''Charles is your manservant, I take it,'' Jack said, without acknowledging that he'd seen or understood Charity's look. ''When he comes back, could you send him out to me, Miss Mayfield? Excuse me, ma'am.''

He went back outside and surveyed the moonlit scene before him. The coachman was still grimly guarding the prisoner, and Jack's horse was standing with the reins hanging, near the edge of the shrubbery. Owen was nowhere to be seen.

Jack whistled quietly, and his horse pricked up his ears and began to walk sedately towards him, nuzzling him in the hope of a reward. Jack spoke quietly to him and picked up the reins, tying them to one of the thick stems of ivy that climbed the outside wall of the house. Then he went over to the carriage.

''Well done,'' he said to the coachman. ''You've done excellently. You can leave the prisoner to me now. Take the carriage round to the stables and then come back for my horse.''

''Yes, sir.'' The coachman laid down his blunderbuss with relief and swelled with pride at Jack's words. He hadn't seen much of the new lord, but he'd already come to the conclusion that Jack's praise was worth having. He immediately decided to give Jack's horse the best possible care.

''All right, you can stand up now,'' Jack said to his prisoner as the coach rumbled away. ''But don't try anything. I have a pistol, and if I have to I'll use it. Do you understand?''

''Y-y-y-y-yes,'' said the man, speaking for the first time, just as Charles arrived.

''Is that him, my lord?'' Charles asked darkly, his hands doubled into fists. ''Only let me show him what he gets for breaking into a ladies' establishment.'' He took a determined step towards the man as he spoke.

''Later, perhaps,'' said Jack coolly. ''I want to ask him some questions first. If he doesn't answer to my satisfaction, I may well allow you to teach him better manners.'' His words were intended for the prisoner's benefit—not Charles's. Fear might induce the man to speak more quickly, and more truthfully, than might otherwise have been the case.

There were sounds of movement coming from the shrubbery, and Jack turned towards them, his pistol once more in his hand, though he suspected it was nothing more alarming than Owen's return.

His supposition proved quite correct. Owen emerged into the moonlight, minus his hat and muttering under his breath. He was leading a strange horse, but he'd lost his quarry and he wasn't in a good mood. He looked down at Jack balefully.

"He got away," he said, somewhat obviously. "They had horses tied up on the other side of the shrubbery. I followed him as far as I could, but I lost him behind the three-acre woods. It would have been a different story if I'd had my hounds with me." He eyed Jack belligerently, as if blaming him for this omission.

"I'm sure it would," said Jack mildly. "And at least you've brought the second horse back. Now we can be certain there were only two of them. Let Charles take the horses round to the stables and we can go into the house and question this fellow." He indicated his prisoner.

Owen hesitated. He could find no real fault with the plan, but he never liked being told what to do at the best of times, and when it was Jack Riversleigh making the suggestion Owen was inclined to disagree on principle.

"What do we need to question him for?" he demanded. "We know what he was doing. We caught him in the act."

"True, but there are one or two unusual circumstances that need explaining," Jack replied. "Of course, if you're not interested in being present when I question him…" He left the words hanging and, after a rather significant pause, Owen jumped down from his horse and handed the reins to Charles.

"My father should be present," he said. "He'd know the best way of going about this."

"I'm sure he would," Jack agreed. "But it's very late, and I don't think there's any need to trouble Sir Humphrey tonight. You can fetch him in the morning. In the meantime, I don't think we'll do any harm if we question the prisoner now. We'll take him into the library."

It was very cold in Charity's bedroom and, by the time she'd undressed and put on her nightgown, she was shivering slightly. She slid quickly into bed and pulled the covers up under her chin, thinking about the events of the evening.

Jack had managed everything so smoothly that there had been very little disruption to the household, but Charity could hardly repress a shudder when she thought of what might have happened. It would have been bad enough to have come home to find they'd been burgled, but it would have been worse if they'd actually disturbed the house-breakers at their work!

Jack had questioned the man he had caught, but the prisoner seemed to be somewhat slow-witted, and that, combined with the fact that he had a very bad stammer, had made it very difficult to make sense of anything he said.

Owen had quickly come to the conclusion that the whole exercise was a waste of time, and had left Jack to get on with it alone while he went to see Charity. He'd intended to reassure her, but neither Charity nor Mrs Mayfield had seemed to need much reassurance, and Mrs Mayfield had completely exasperated him by her obvious confidence in Lord Riversleigh's ability to manage the whole affair.

Owen's temper was even more uncertain than usual because his failure to catch the second intruder had piqued his pride. He had seemed to feel the need to justify his failure, and he'd explained several times that he had been at a great disadvantage because he'd had to chase *his* man through the shrubbery. Things would have been different if his quarry had stuck to the open drive, as Lord Riversleigh's had done.

Charity had agreed mendaciously with everything Owen said, though inwardly she continued unshaken in the opinion that a few shrubs wouldn't have made any difference to *Jack's* chances of success.

But Owen had slowly talked himself into a better mood; and when Jack finally joined them in the parlour he had been able to greet him with a reasonable level of politeness, though certainly not warmly.

With Mrs Mayfield's permission, Jack had suggested that they lock the burglar in the cellar for the rest of the night, with Charles to guard him, and in the morning Owen should fetch his father to arrange for the disposal of the man. In the meantime, though he didn't anticipate there would be any further disturbances, he suggested that both he and Owen remain at Hazelhurst for the night.

Mrs Mayfield had greeted his suggestion with delighted relief and immediately asked Charity to organise rooms for their unexpected guests. Owen was less delighted by the notion that Jack would be staying under the same roof as Charity, but consoled himself with the thought that his own presence would surely prevent the notorious Lord Riversleigh from doing anything improper.

These knotty problems having been solved, it hadn't been long before the entire household, with the exception of Charles, had retired for what was left of the night.

Charity smiled to herself in the dark. She was aware of a profound sense of relief that, for once, she wasn't solely responsible for the well-being of everyone at Hazelhurst. The idea that there was someone she could rely on was an unusual but far from unwelcome sensation.

She turned over and prepared to go to sleep. Then she remembered the library. There were still books and papers strewn all over the floor, and tomorrow she had another meeting with Lord Ashbourne's agent. She sighed. She could always offer the excuse that they'd been burgled, but for her own sake she wanted matters settled as quickly as possible.

Besides, Sir Humphrey would want to know if anything had been taken, and how could she tell if she hadn't checked? She pushed back the bedclothes and sat up, wondering why Jack hadn't suggested she check to see if anything was missing. Then she decided that he probably hadn't wanted to distress her any further that evening.

She put on her slippers and robe, wrapped a shawl around her shoulders for good measure, and tiptoed quietly downstairs. She didn't want to disturb anyone else.

There was a light shining beneath the library door and she supposed they must have forgotten to put out the candles, but when she opened it she saw Jack sitting in a chair before the fire, a glass of brandy in his hand.

He turned his head quickly as the door opened and stood up when he saw Charity.

"Is something wrong?" he asked.

"No, no. I just came down to…" She looked past him and her eyes widened. "You've tidied up already!" she exclaimed.

She never doubted that it had been Jack who'd collected up all the papers and put them in neat piles on the desk.

"Only very roughly," he said apologetically. "I think I've put most things in a reasonably logical order, though I can't guarantee you'll be able to find everything first time. But I thought you might find it less distressing if you didn't have to scramble on the floor for everything tomorrow. It's not pleasant having your belongings mishandled in such a way."

"No." It was true. Charity had been dreading sorting out the mess—that was partly why she had got up in the night to do it, rather than waiting until the next day. She felt her eyes fill with unexpected tears.

"Thank you," she whispered.

"Come and sit by the fire," Jack suggested. He knew he probably ought to persuade her to go back to bed, but he suspected she needed to talk about what had happened—at least, that was what he told himself. But the truth was, he was too pleased to see her to send her away.

"Thank you." Charity sat down, hugging her shawl about her. "I still don't understand what they wanted," she said, glancing around. "I mean, as far as I can tell, nothing has been taken—and what were they looking for in the *library?* There weren't any valuable papers in the desk—only farm and household accounts!"

"No," said Jack. "That's the puzzle that's been keeping me awake. Your book-keeping is excellent, by the way. I'd have no hesitation in offering you employment—should you ever want it." He grinned at her.

"You really mean it!" Charity exclaimed, quite startled by his praise.

"Of course." The smile warmed his eyes. "I never joke about such *serious* matters."

"Now you're laughing at me," Charity said uncertainly. "No."

He was teasing her, but there was nothing insincere about the expression in his steady grey eyes, and Charity suddenly felt quite breathless. She looked away, feeling the colour rising in her cheeks.

"May I offer you some of your own excellent brandy, Miss Mayfield?" Jack asked with humorous formality. "There doesn't seem to be much else in the way of refreshment."

"Yes, please," said Charity, rather glad that he'd changed the subject. "I don't drink it as a general rule, but it is good, isn't it? It comes directly from France."

"I thought perhaps it did," said Jack, sounding amused. "I don't suppose you happen to know what kind of arrangements my grandfather had with the smugglers, do you?"

"Gentlemen," Charity corrected him, smiling. "In Sussex they're known as the gentlemen. Mr Guthrie will take care of it for you.''

''Will he, indeed? A man of many parts, I perceive.'' Jack offered Charity a glass of brandy.

''Oh, he doesn't do any smuggling himself,'' Charity assured him, taking the glass. ''But he knows *everyone*. He's lived here a very long time, you know.''

''Yes, I do,'' Lord Riversleigh said more seriously. The land agent was almost the only person he'd met since he'd come into Sussex who could remember his father, and that alone recommended him to Jack.

Charity looked at him curiously. He was gazing down at the fire with unfocused eyes, and she wondered what he was thinking, what memories her words might have triggered. But she didn't ask. She was warm and relaxed, and in his company the silence didn't worry her.

She tucked her feet up beneath her, settled herself comfortably back against the wing of the chair, and took a sip of the brandy. Though neither of them realised it, they made an incongruous pair as they sat before the hearth.

Jack was still wearing the formal, very elegant clothes he had worn to the Leydons' rout. The black velvet of his coat glowed in the firelight and, despite all his exertions, the crisp white lace at his wrists remained as unsullied as it had been when he had dressed for the party—yet nobody could have mistaken him for a fop. Even in repose, he possessed an unmistakable aura of determination and power.

Charity, on the other hand, was entirely and blissfully relaxed. Earlier that evening she had been as elegant as Jack, dressed in hoops and silk, with a fashionable train on the back of her dress—but no one could curl up in front of the fire in such a gown.

Now, in her simple nightdress and robe, with her dark

curls falling back around her shoulders and her feet tucked up beneath her in the large wing chair, she was far more comfortable. It never occurred to her that there was anything shocking about her presence in the library in such a state of undress—perhaps because she felt so much at ease in Jack's company.

He didn't say anything for some time—he was still apparently thinking—but the continuing silence didn't worry her. She sipped her brandy now and then and gazed into the fire, watching the dancing orange flames with unfocused eyes, until at last it became too much of an effort even to lift the glass, and she rested it on the arm of the chair. She was neither quite asleep nor quite awake, but she was overwhelmed by a delightful languor which made even the thought of rousing herself unthinkable.

The glass began to tilt as her hold on it relaxed, and Jack reached out and took it gently from her.

"You should go back to bed," he said. "You can't go to sleep here. At least…you could, of course, but you'd be more comfortable in bed."

"I'm not going to sleep," Charity said drowsily, because she felt too pleasantly tired to move. "What are you thinking about?"

Jack grinned, well aware that she was simply trying to delay the need to get up. "You're not awake enough to listen to me, even if I tell you," he said. "Come on, stand up."

He took her hand and tried to pull her gently to her feet.

Charity didn't move; she simply let him pull at her arm. Her feet were still tucked up beside her and, until she chose to set them down on the floor again, it wasn't really possible for Jack to get her to stand up.

She looked up at him, a faint challenge in her eyes. She was too close to sleep to be self-conscious, and she was vaguely curious to know what he'd do next—but mostly she simply wanted to stay where she was.

"You'll be cold when the fire goes out," Jack said.

Charity glanced at the grate. "It won't go out just yet," she replied.

Jack looked down at her, a half-smile in his eyes. She'd woken up slightly, but not enough to retreat behind the barrier of reserve she usually erected around herself, and there was a humorous gleam in her eyes as she returned his gaze.

He was still holding her hand, though he was no longer trying to pull her to her feet. The moment stretched out and, as Charity gazed up at Jack, she felt her heart begin to beat faster. His clasp on her hand tightened, and the expression in his eyes changed. He wasn't laughing anymore, and the intensity of his steady gaze nearly hypnotised her. No one had ever looked at her that way before.

Very gently he began to draw her towards him, and this time she didn't resist. Almost without knowing what she was doing, she let her feet drop to the floor and stood up.

Her gaze was still locked with his and for an instant longer she remained unaware of anything but the look in his eyes. Then he put his free hand on her waist and she gasped as his touch sent tremors rippling through her body. He let his hand track very gently around the belt of her robe until it reached the small of her back, and as she felt herself begin to tremble anew he bent his head and kissed her parted lips.

For a moment surprise and confusion held her motionless, but then, as his lips continued to caress hers, the rigidity melted from her body and without realising what she was doing she slid her arms about his neck and pressed herself even closer against him. At some point she had closed her eyes, and now she was lost in a world in which touch was the most important sense. She could feel his arms around her, and she could feel and taste his lips on hers, and nothing else mattered.

Her responsiveness heightened Jack's desire even further, and he too began to lose all sense of his surroundings. Her shawl had long since fallen unheeded to the floor and now, somehow, her robe had become unbelted. His hand slipped within, and through the thin fabric of her nightdress he touched her breast.

Charity opened her eyes, but she didn't pull away, and there was a curious mixture of trust, wonderment and desire in her expression as Jack briefly cupped her breast in his hand before once more holding her tightly against him.

The first shock of surprise at what was happening to her had passed, yet if anything she now felt more intensely aware of everything Jack did than she had before—and more able to savour the pleasure of it. She let her head fall back as he kissed the base of her throat, her own hand caressing the nape of his neck while he began to undo the fastenings of her nightgown.

Then two of the candles, which had been burning for some hours, suddenly guttered and went out almost simultaneously, and Jack looked up, finally recalled to time and place.

His right hand was still beneath Charity's robe, pressing her to him, and he moved his other hand gently to cup her head. At that moment it was more than he could bear to let her go or put her away from him, but he also knew that he couldn't continue as he had been.

Even his experience at the party hadn't prepared him for the way Charity now dominated his thoughts and feelings, and he was shaken to realise what an effect she could have on him—was still having on him. It was only with the greatest difficulty that he resisted the temptation to kiss her again. But, however great the pleasure of this moment, Charity deserved more than this: a wedding and a bridal night to remember—with no regrets to plague her in the morning.

The moment's respite gave Charity time to think, though at first she was aware only of the rapid beating of her heart, and an overwhelming regret that Jack was no longer kissing her.

"I'm sorry," said Jack rather hoarsely, and with an effort he let her go and stepped back. "I didn't intend... I think it would be best if you went back upstairs."

He hadn't intended the words to come out so harshly, but he also hadn't realised how hard it would be to move away from her—or how hard he would find it to crush down his desire for her—and he was too disturbed to frame an elegant speech.

"Sorry!" Charity's eyes flew to his face, suddenly convinced that in some way he had found her wanting and was sending her...

Of course! Well-bred young ladies didn't...

Horror filled her as she remembered what had happened between them, and she blushed crimson and turned her back on him, unable to lift her eyes to what she imagined must be his disapproving gaze.

"No, I'm sorry," she replied, her voice sounding muffled and uncertain. "I don't... I'm not usually... I didn't mean to offend you with my lack of propriety."

"Offend *me!*" Jack exclaimed, relief and amazement mingling in his voice. When she'd turned her back on him he'd been afraid that her action had been prompted with disgust at *his* behaviour.

"You haven't offended me! It was I who took advantage of you."

Despite his earlier resolution, he couldn't help taking a

step towards her as he spoke and slipping his hands around her waist.

Instinctively she leant back against him, and his hold on her tightened, one hand lifting to caress her breast, and she felt fresh thrills of pleasure course through her.

"You have nothing to be sorry about," he murmured, his lips brushing her hair.

She closed her eyes and smiled, her hand instinctively covering his at her waist as he bent his head lower and kissed her just below her ear. Her momentary embarrassment was forgotten as fresh ripples of delight radiated from the spot his lips were touching, and she almost felt she no longer had the strength to stand without his support. Without conscious thought she began to turn in his arms to face him...

And then she remembered Owen.

This time she gasped with horror—not pleasure—and Jack felt the change in her immediately.

"What is it?"

"Nothing." With an effort Charity pulled herself out of his arms and moved away from him.

"I— Oh, dear, the candles have gone out," she said, speaking at random.

"Charity, what is it?" Jack looked at her, a slight frown of anxiety in his eyes. Her unexpected change of mood had thrown him off balance.

"Nothing," she said again. "I must have been more tired than I thought." She laughed uncertainly and tried to fasten her robe with hands that trembled uncontrollably.

She was betrothed to Owen! Only that evening she had agreed to marry him and urged him to speak to her mother as soon as possible, yet here she was, a scant few hours later, letting—encouraging—another man to make love to her!

How could she have been such a fool? How could she not have known that this was where her friendship with Jack was leading—was where she wanted it to lead? All the signs had been there, at the party, and earlier—she just hadn't understood them.

But what did Jack really want from her? She began to feel cold as she remembered that he hadn't said anything to indicate his intentions towards her. He had apologised for his behaviour, but he hadn't excused it on the grounds of love, and she began to realise how little she knew about him. He had said once that he had no immediate plans to marry: was that because there was no one he cared for—or was it that he did have an agreement with a lady, though for some reason the wedding had been delayed?

He was standing in front of her now and, as she stared up at him with huge, frightened eyes, he put aside her cold hands and carefully fastened her robe. Then he picked up the discarded shawl and put it back round her shoulders.

"What's wrong?" he asked gently. "You look as if you've seen a ghost. Have I frightened you? I didn't mean to."

"No," she whispered. It was true, he hadn't frightened her, though perhaps she had frightened herself with the intensity of her response to him.

"It's just…so much has happened that it's… I think I'm just confused."

"Yes, yes, I know," he said quietly, almost ruefully. "Can I help?"

For a moment Charity stared at him, but for once her famous outspokenness failed her and she couldn't bring herself to ask the one thing she most wanted to know— what did he feel for her? And did she really want to hear the answer anyway? All her customary self-confidence had deserted her and she felt that if he told her he didn't love her she wouldn't be able to bear it—because she loved him.

But he had no plans for marriage—he had said so. It would be better not to hear the worst tonight, not when she was so tired and so confused. Tomorrow she would be strong, tomorrow she would be able to face anything—but not tonight.

"No, no, I don't think so, thank you," she said at last, and knew that now she ought to leave. But she couldn't quite bring herself to do so.

In the morning Owen would ask her mother for her hand in marriage, Mrs Mayfield would consent and Jack would congratulate them.

There would be no more private conversations then, no more rides and no more comfortable evenings by the fire. The thought was so terrible that tears welled up in her eyes. She was so tired and so overwrought by everything that had happened to her in that very crowded evening that it didn't occur to her that she was being foolish.

Jack didn't know exactly what lay behind her sudden distress, but he guessed how she felt far more accurately than she realised. He had still not entirely recovered himself from the fire of their embrace, yet not only was he more experienced, but he had also been partially prepared for it by the strength of his response to her earlier at the party. It wasn't surprising that Charity should find herself overwhelmed by such powerful and unaccustomed feelings. She needed some time to recover and Jack knew he must give it to her.

But it would do no good to send her to bed just yet, he told himself, she wouldn't sleep; but he was honest enough to admit to himself that he didn't want to part from her with so much unsettled between them. He wanted to banish the haunted expression from her face—and he wanted to rekindle the warmth he had seen glowing in her eyes only minutes before. No, he couldn't send her to bed yet.

"Come, sit down," he said, and gently guided her back to the chair she had occupied before. "Would you like some more brandy?"

"Thank you." She took the glass from him and held it cupped in cold hands as she watched him kick the dying fire back into life. Circumstances had gone beyond her control and she felt an odd sense of unreality as she waited for him to speak.

Jack looked down at her ruefully, finally realising that there was nothing he could say to her tonight that would help. Too much had happened to her too quickly, and now she was too tired to understand—perhaps too tired even to feel anything.

"You must go to bed," he said, reluctantly accepting the situation. "I'll take you upstairs."

"No, no, I can manage. Thank you."

A brief resurgence of pride and independence brought Charity to her feet. If he wanted to get rid of her she could at least leave with dignity. She took a couple of steps towards the door, and suddenly the question which had been hovering on the edge of her thoughts for some time rose unbidden and unexpectedly to the surface of her mind.

"Why were you still sitting here after you'd tidied up?" she demanded, both sounding and looking far more like herself. "You said it was a puzzle. Is there something you haven't told me—do you *know* what the burglars were looking for?"

For a moment Jack looked at her, then he smiled faintly. He hadn't intended to mention his suspicions tonight, but if she was actually asking…

"I don't know exactly," he replied. "But I have a pretty good idea of what they think they were looking for."

Chapter Ten

"But what was it?" Charity asked.

"Treasure," said Jack simply.

"Treasure!" she exclaimed. "In our *library!* You must be mistaken. There's no treasure here!"

"Possibly not," replied Jack equably, "but the thieves certainly think there is."

"Good heavens!" said Charity blankly.

"Don't worry about it now," Jack said. "I shouldn't have said anything about it to you when you're so tired. Go to bed; I'll tell you in the morning."

"Certainly not," said Charity indignantly, and now she sounded just like her old self. "It's my library. I want to hear exactly what the man told you. Treasure at Hazelhurst! He must be mad! Or—are you sure you understood him properly? Owen said he was incomprehensible."

"He certainly wasn't the most articulate man I've ever spoken to," Jack agreed. "And he'd obviously had the fear of God—or the Devil—put into him by his master. But some things he said were plain enough. He didn't know what the treasure was, and he didn't know why they were searching here—but they were definitely looking for something in the library. Something they had to find before the end of February.''

''Good God! They must be crazy!'' Charity declared again. ''There's nothing here but books and ledgers. Perhaps they've got the wrong house. I mean…'' She looked around at the dimly lit library, shadows from the firelight flickering on the walls and the bookshelves. ''There's nothing here,'' she said again.

''You may be right,'' said Jack. ''But I think it bears investigation. There are one or two things about what he said, and about what else has happened here recently, that…'' He paused abruptly and held up a warning hand as Charity looked at him questioningly.

In the silence she heard the creak of wooden floorboards outside and felt a sudden flare of alarm as she wondered wildly whether the prisoner had overcome Charles and was escaping—or was it the master thief returning for his apprentice?

Then she remembered Jack was there and her fear subsided. She turned to him for guidance.

Jack was looking at the door, one hand in his pocket, the other still holding his brandy glass.

There was a moment of silence—then the door burst open and Owen plunged into the library, a poker upheld in his hand.

He lowered it slowly as he saw them, and Charity watched the look of astonishment on his face change to one of outrage as he took in her presence.

''Charity!'' He goggled at her for a moment, then he looked at Jack, his expression redolent with suspicion.

''Ah, Leydon,'' said Jack smoothly. ''I hope I didn't wake you. I'm afraid I must have made more noise than I intended when I was putting the furniture back in its place. Miss Mayfield has already come down to investigate.''

"Putting the furniture back?" Owen said disbelievingly.

"I'm afraid I have an obsession with tidiness," Jack explained, straight-faced. "The thought of a disorderly room can keep me awake all night."

"Really?" Owen looked at Jack as if he were mad, and Charity had to restrain a sudden urge to laugh, though at the same time she was on tenterhooks in case either man said anything to arouse the other's suspicions—they both had good reason to suppose they occupied a privileged position in her affections.

"Oh, yes," said Jack, blandly enlarging upon his theme. "I've been known to drive servants mad with my insistence that everything *has* its place and that everything is kept *in* its place. But I assure you there's no cause for alarm. It's quite safe to return to bed; I'll do my best not to disturb you again. Indeed, as soon as I've put these books back on their shelves, I shall feel able to retire myself."

"I see," said Owen, for once almost lost for words, though he retained sufficient presence of mind to feel scornful of what he considered to be a very unmanly—almost housewifely—weakness.

Jack's lips twitched slightly, but he didn't say anything, and Owen was so disconcerted that he started to turn away without continuing the conversation.

Then he remembered that Charity was still in the library—and wearing only her nightdress!

Owen's conventional soul was horrified and he swung back to face Jack, new suspicion dawning in his eyes.

"There's no need for Charity to help you tidy up," he said, so belligerently that Charity felt a flicker of alarm.

"None at all," Jack agreed calmly, taking the wind out of Owen's sails.

"Come, Charity, I'll escort you back upstairs." Owen held out a masterful hand, trying to regain the initiative.

"For heaven's sake! Owen!" Charity exclaimed, exasperation at his high-handedness overriding her anxiety that he might provoke a scene. "I'm quite capable of finding my way upstairs in my own house. Do go back to bed!"

"I'm not leaving you downstairs alone," said Owen magnificently, ignoring Jack.

"But I'm not alone," Charity pointed out. "Besides, there's something I want to ask Lord Riversleigh. Do go to bed, Owen. I won't stay up much longer, I assure you."

"I'll wait," said Owen stubbornly.

Charity sighed in exasperation and glanced at Jack. His wooden expression was belied by the twinkle in his eye, but he clearly wasn't going to give her any help. If she didn't want to include Owen in a discussion about real or imaginary treasure she was going to have to submit gracefully.

She frowned, and walked over to the door Owen was holding open for her. Just before she went through it she looked back at Jack, and he grinned at her. Indignation flared in her eyes and she turned her head away, walking upstairs with great dignity.

Jack closed the door that Owen had neglected to shut and leant back against it. Then he looked around the library, though he was actually thinking about Charity. It still hadn't occurred to him that she might actually have succeeded in getting herself betrothed to Owen when he so obviously infuriated her at every turn, and Jack was hoping that he would have an opportunity to talk to her again in the morning. But first he had other things to do and, after a moment or two, he pushed himself away from the door and headed towards the section of shelving where the first intruder had been standing when Charity had surprised him.

The sun was high in the sky when Charity woke the next morning. Despite her weariness the previous evening, sleep hadn't come quickly and even when she had fallen asleep she'd been restless and uneasy. It had only been just before dawn that she had at last fallen into a profound and deep sleep, and for once she'd overslept badly.

The pale winter sun was streaming in through the curtains, which despite the horrified protests of her mother and the maids, she never allowed to be closed. If she turned her head she could see the tops of the trees outlined against the sky. If she moved her head she could make the pictures through the window shift from one leaded glass pane to another. As a child it had been a game she had played with herself. Does the holly branch look better through this glass pane or that one? She turned her head experimentally. This one, she decided. A perfect picture in a perfect frame.

What had happened last night? Now the sun was shining it was hard to believe that the interlude in the firelit library could be anything more than a dream. But Charity knew it wasn't. Even now she could feel her body begin to glow anew with the remembered ecstasy of his touch. What *had* happened? What did he want from her—and what did she want from him?

She thought of her coolly laid plans to marry first Edward, and then Owen. There had never been any question of love. She liked Edward and she was fond of Owen, but marriage to either would be a practical arrangement to meet practical needs—and she'd always thought that that was what she wanted. Now she knew that it wasn't—and she didn't know what to do.

She felt reluctant to get up and go downstairs to face either Jack or Owen. She was still too uncertain of her feelings—or Jack's—and today was the day Owen was going to ask Mrs Mayfield for permission to marry her!

For one craven minute she thought about claiming she

was unwell and staying in bed. But that would have been cowardly and Charity never turned her back on a challenge—even when she was hungry. It suddenly occurred to her that she was, in fact, extremely hungry. She got up and dressed quickly. Things always look better after breakfast, she thought, and for the first time wondered why she'd been left undisturbed for so long. Normally she was up before the maids to go to the dairy and plan the day ahead.

She hurried downstairs and found her mother at breakfast.

"Hello, dear, do you feel more rested now?" Mrs Mayfield asked placidly. "Lord Riversleigh thought you looked tired last night and suggested you be allowed to sleep in. I must say, I thought myself you were looking very weary. It must be the worry of all the arrangements—not to mention the excitement of having burglars."

"Burglars!" Charity's first flush of embarrassment at the mention of Jack's name was forgotten as she suddenly remembered what Jack had said about treasure. In the light of day the notion seemed even more fantastic than it had the previous night, yet she realised now that Jack had been quite serious when he had spoken about it.

"Where is Lord Riversleigh?" she asked urgently, hardly noticing her mother's unusual complacency.

"He's a very nice man, isn't he?" said Mrs Mayfield. "So thoughtful, and very reliable in a crisis. I'm sure all the rumours about him are just spite."

"Yes, Mama."

Charity blushed uncomfortably. She didn't want to think about all Jack's good qualities now—it made her nervous. She preferred to concentrate on the probably apocryphal treasure.

"Where is he?" she asked again, interrupting her mother.

"I was saying to Lady Dalrymple only yesterday…" Mrs Mayfield broke off and looked at Charity in mild surprise, though inwardly she was delighted by her daughter's impatience to seek out Jack.

"He went to ask one of the stable-lads to take a message to Riversleigh," she said.

Charity turned and hurried out of the room, but at the doorway she checked and swung round to face her mother.

"And where's Owen?" she asked suspiciously, suddenly afraid that he might already have declared himself to her mother.

"He's already on his way to fetch Sir Humphrey." Mrs Mayfield dipped another piece of toast into her tea.

"Good." Her mind relieved of one of its cares, Charity hurried off to find Jack.

She came face to face with him, re-entering the house through a side-door, and stopped suddenly. For the first time she felt shy in his presence, and she didn't know what to say.

He was standing with his back to the light and for a moment she couldn't see his expression. Then he turned slightly and smiled, and she felt quite breathless.

"You said something about treasure last night," she said somewhat incoherently, knowing she was blushing and hoping she didn't look as foolish and unsure of herself as she felt.

"So I did." Jack closed the outer door and came towards her. For an instant he was standing beside her, looming over her, then he moved past her and opened the door of the back parlour—politely holding it for her.

"If you have a moment, Miss Mayfield, I think there are a few things we ought to discuss before Sir Humphrey gets here."

Miss Mayfield? He'd called her Miss Mayfield. Last night he'd called her Charity. What did it mean?

"Yes, of course," she said sedately, and went into the parlour.

"What did…?" she began as he was closing the door—and stopped mid-sentence as for the first time she realised that there was an aura of suppressed excitement about him.

"You don't mean you found something?" she demanded.

Jack laughed. "How did you know?" he asked. "I meant to surprise you."

"You have!" said Charity emphatically. "Good heavens! What is it? Show me!"

"Here." Jack took a beautifully made box from his pocket and handed it to her, watching her expression as she opened it.

There was a jewel inside, but a jewel unlike any she had ever seen before. It was an oval pendant of gold, set with diamonds and three blood-red rubies, and it looked as beautiful and perfect as the day it had been made.

Almost without thinking, Charity went over to the window, and in the better light the precious stones seemed to take on new life.

Jack reached past her and picked up the jewel. He opened it carefully and handed it back to her, taking the jewel case from her as he did so.

She took the pendant in her hands, almost afraid to touch it, and saw that it was in fact a locket, containing the most exquisite miniature portrait she had ever seen. It was a picture of a lady, painted against a brilliant blue background and dressed in the style of the Elizabethans. Her glowing hair was drawn back from her face, there was a ruff around her neck, and roses on her breast.

Charity gasped, because it was almost as if the lady were

alive. She seemed to be looking straight into Charity's eyes and she was smiling with a joyous happiness which was almost painful to behold.

"I believe it's by Nicholas Hilliard," said Jack quietly; he'd been watching Charity's expression. "He was a miniaturist during Elizabeth's reign. He painted many pictures of the Queen, some of them placed in jewelled settings every bit as magnificent as this one, but he painted other people as well."

"I've never seen anything like it," Charity murmured. "Hilliard? I've heard of him, of course, but I never guessed that *this* was what he could do. An engraving of a dead Queen in a book doesn't prepare you for this glorious colour. It's so *beautiful*."

She couldn't take her eyes away from the picture; she was entranced by its beauty and by the exquisite detail of a portrait barely more than two inches long. How could there be so much life in something so small?

"He was a goldsmith," said Jack quietly. "The definition of craftsmanship was wider in those days. He probably didn't make that jewelled setting himself, but he *could* have done. A goldsmith, a jeweller, and a painter."

Something in Jack's voice caught Charity's attention and she looked up at him.

"You're a goldsmith too, aren't you?" she said. "Not just a banker. Could you do this?"

"I'm not a genius," he replied.

"But you'd like to?"

"Would I?" he said musingly. He took the pendant from her and held it up. "Perhaps I would, but I have little time for such things now. And fashions change—this isn't what I'd seek to make. He was a genius, but in many ways he was still painting in the medieval tradition. You can't see it in these close portraits, but he had no idea of perspective!''

"I haven't either," said Charity. "Edward explained it to me, and I understand the theory, but every time I try to put into practice it goes all wrong.''

She sounded so aggrieved that Jack laughed, and that made her laugh.

"You should make time," she said more soberly, laying her hand on his arm. "We all have so little time to do what we really want. That's what I used to think about Edward; I used to worry about him. I'm so glad that things have turned out for him as they have. I'd hate to think that..."

"I'm not unhappy." Jack looked down at her, and covered her hand with his. "I still spend time in the workshop, I still make things—one day I may even create a masterpiece." He smiled self-deprecatingly as he spoke. "But I have a responsibility to the partnership not to neglect our banking interests, and I enjoy that also. You should understand, after all, what I do is not so very different from what you've been trying to do here at Hazelhurst.''

Charity looked at him searchingly. She was concerned about him, and because she wasn't thinking about herself her self-consciousness had completely vanished.

"Yes, I see," she said at last. "But you'll get busier, everyone always gets busier. You must be careful that one day all your time doesn't get eaten up by your business.''

"Some people might say that was a good thing." Jack smiled. "You've never seen an example of my work!''

"I don't need to," she replied, and for the first time she became aware of his hand on hers. She blushed and drew her hand away.

"What are we going to do about that?" she asked, nodding towards the jewel, and trying to speak normally, though suddenly her heart was racing. "And now I come to think of it, where did you find it? And how did it get there?"

"In the library." Jack took the case out of his pocket and handed it to Charity. He too had been affected by their touch, but he had himself well in hand this morning.

"I *know* that," Charity replied exasperatedly as she opened the box and held it for him to replace the pendant.

"Well, considering that you thought the whole idea was nonsense…" he said tantalisingly.

"I was wrong, I admit it," Charity said hastily. "Where did you find it?"

"There was a concealed cavity in the wall behind the bookcases," Jack explained. "Once I'd taken all the books off the shelves I discovered a mechanism for swinging the entire bookcase away from the wall. It's on hinges, you see, but the design and the weight of the books usually disguise the fact. And, even when I'd done that, the hiding-place wasn't obvious. But it's easier to find something if you have a rough idea of what you're looking for, so it didn't take long."

"But what was it doing there in the first place? And how did those thieves know about it?" Charity demanded.

"I'd like to know the answers to those questions too," Jack admitted. "I'm assuming that you have no idea of its existence?"

"None at all!" she replied emphatically.

"And your father…?"

"He never said… I'm sure… No," she finished decisively. "He didn't know. He was never any good at keeping secrets, and he was always in need of money for one scheme or the other. I don't think over the years, he would have been able to resist…" She stopped as she suddenly realised what she was saying was hardly flattering to Mr Mayfield.

''That's what I thought,'' said Jack calmly. ''Even if your father had never before had any occasion to sell the locket, he might have considered doing so when the future of Hazelhurst was at stake—but he obviously never mentioned the matter to your lawyer. Besides, there is other evidence to suggest he knew nothing of its existence.''

For a moment Jack tapped thoughtfully on the pendant's case, which he was still holding in his hands. He made no attempt to explain himself, and Charity frowned, not quite sure what he was getting at, but before she had an opportunity to ask any questions he spoke again.

''It would be very interesting to know where the pendant came from—but I think there's a far more pressing problem that we ought to tackle first, don't you?''

He looked at Charity, his eyebrow slightly lifted, and she gazed back, not immediately sure what he meant, but pleased that he seemed to value her opinions; then she understood.

''The thief!'' she exclaimed. ''He's tried twice already—he'll be back. Of course he'll be back. And this time we must catch him. What are we going to do?''

''I've been thinking about that,'' said Jack, ''and I'm not sure you're going to like what I suggest, but we probably haven't got much time now before Sir Humphrey arrives—''

''What is it?'' Charity interrupted.

''Do you want to tell anyone what we've found?''

Charity thought about it quickly. ''No,'' she said at last. ''I will, of course, but at the moment there are too many other things to worry about, and I don't want Mama to be any more alarmed than she already is. Besides, apart from anything else, I'm expecting to see Lord Ashbourne's agent this morning.''

''Really?'' Jack said thoughtfully. ''Perhaps it would be

better if… Well, we can decide that later. What I *was* going
to suggest was that you and your mother go and visit the
Leydons for a few days. They won't be surprised if you
don't feel comfortable here any more—not after two break-
ins—and particularly since you'll be leaving here soon anyway."

"Leave?" Charity exclaimed. "Run away? This is our
house! We're not going anywhere—not until we have to—
and certainly not because we're *afraid!* How *can* you think
I'd agree to such a thing?"

"I didn't," said Jack. "I knew you'd argue about it. But
we haven't got time, and the situation is too serious, for
you to be offended by my high-handedness. If you're determined to quarrel with me it would be better if you postponed it until *after* you're settled with the Leydons and
we've caught the thief."

"Postponed…" Charity glared at him. "You've already
arranged it, haven't you?"

"I mentioned the idea to Owen, and your mother," he
admitted. Then, "Don't, Charity!" He'd seen the look of
fury in her eyes and seized her shoulders before she had a
chance to say any of the outraged words hovering on her
tongue.

"I've seen you lose your temper before," he said. "But,
believe me, now is *not* the time. I don't know whether the
thief has been frightened away or not, but we need him—
and not only to bring him to justice. So I'm not just sending
you away to keep you out of danger, but to encourage the
thief to think that with you gone the house will be less well
guarded. With any luck he'll try again—and this time we'll
have him." He paused, but Charity didn't say anything;
she simply looked at him.

"That's why I agree with you about not telling Sir Humphrey," he said more quietly. "We must make the thief

think that we still don't know what he's looking for—that we think it was an ordinary burglary. If he knows we've found it he won't go back to the library—''

''He'll try to take it from whoever's got it!'' Charity interrupted. ''What are we going to do with it?''

''I was going to suggest you leave it in my care,'' Jack replied. ''I'll give you a receipt for it. It doesn't really matter where it is as long as no one knows it's been found.''

''No, of course it doesn't.'' Charity sighed with relief. ''For a moment I thought…what else have you arranged?''

''I've sent for my man Alan. He's intelligent and quite capable of independent action. You can tell your people that he's here to help with the move. If they think it's odd you can always imply that it's my fault, that I'm being embarrassingly over-attentive. It does happen.'' There was a question in his eyes as he spoke, but Charity didn't see it.

''I can deal with the servants,'' she said. ''I take it you won't be staying here all the time.''

''No, I must go back to Riversleigh. But I'll return later, after dark, before the moon has risen. I think it should be possible for Alan to let me into the house without either your servants or the thief knowing I'm here.''

''But you can't keep on doing that,'' Charity protested. ''Are you sure—?''

''I think Sir Humphrey has arrived,'' Jack interrupted her. ''I doubt if I will have to do it many times. In fact, if we don't catch the thief tonight or tomorrow I shall be very surprised—he'll have to make his move within two weeks. We must greet Sir Humphrey.''

''Why so soon? And what's this?'' Charity asked as he handed her something and at the same time took her arm and pulled her towards the door.

"The receipt. Keep it carefully. I'll explain *why* the first chance I get, but Sir Humphrey is already harbouring enough suspicions about me, without giving him any more grounds for disapproval by keeping him waiting," Jack said. "Particularly when we're going to such lengths to make everything seem normal."

"Yes, all right." Charity went with him unresistingly. "But you can come and visit me at the Leydons' and explain then."

"Very well. But I've already got Lord Travers waiting for me at Riversleigh. I must deal with him first."

"Lord Travers! What's *he* doing there?" she stopped dead.

"Charity! Later!" Jack took a deep breath. "I'll explain later," he said. "Now, come *on!*"

"Yes, my lord," she said obediently.

Chapter Eleven

The Leydon coach jolted across the uneven road surface, and Charity braced her feet firmly to prevent her from being thrown against her mother. Mrs Mayfield was sitting beside her, and Tabitha, the maid, sat opposite. They'd asked Mrs Wendle, the housekeeper, if she also wanted to come. But she'd refused, ostensibly on the grounds that she had too much to do, but really because she couldn't abide the Leydons' housekeeper and had no intention of spending even one night under the same roof as her.

The ladies in the coach formed the first part of a cavalcade; behind them rode Owen and Sir Humphrey on horseback, with the captured burglar under guard. The unfortunate thief was to be taken to Horsham gaol, but the first part of the journey was the same for all of them.

Once again Sir Humphrey had demonstrated why he was such a good magistrate. He might dislike change and react badly to innovation but, faced with a straightforward situation, he was usually able to respond in a straightforward manner. He believed that the Mayfields had been the victims of commonplace burglary and he had dealt with the matter appropriately.

But Charity, who had asked as a favour to be present

when Sir Humphrey initially interviewed the captured intruder, thought that he had failed to pick up some of the
things the prisoner said. Of course, that could be because
she already knew what the man was hinting at but, on the
whole, she was glad that Jack had been the first person to
question him.

She thought about Jack now, and then about Owen. The
next few days were going to be very awkward. Owen was
showing increasing signs of possessiveness, which was
only natural—considering he thought she was betrothed to
him. It was going to be very difficult telling him that she
didn't want to marry him when she was a guest under his
roof, but she knew that she had to.

And she was going to lose her wager with Jack. Was she
pleased or sad about that? She began to feel disturbed by
the trend of her thoughts and tried to concentrate instead
on the pendant. Perhaps they could use that to save Hazelhurst. Perhaps they could—

There was a shot, and the carriage swayed as the horses
plunged.

A voice outside the carriage roared a command for
everyone to stand still—and then there was silence, disturbed only by the sound of the restless horses.

"If you stand still, you're safe. If anyone moves, I'll kill
them."

From inside the carriage Charity couldn't see who was
speaking. But the voice came from one side, and slightly
towards the rear of the coach. Sir Humphrey's coachman
could do nothing—the horses were too restless for him to
concentrate on anything but controlling them. And though
she thought Owen and Sir Humphrey had their mounts under better control, Charity guessed that they were too well
covered to make any move against the man with the voice.

Her first thought was that this must be an attack by a

highwayman, but then she heard the attacker ordering the release of the prisoner—and she knew it was the master thief.

Tabitha was looking grim, but beneath the fixed line of her mouth Charity detected fear, and Mrs Mayfield looked terrified. Charity was too worried to be afraid. This wasn't a normal highwayman—he had no interest in the valuables of the party he held up; he simply wanted his henchman back. They were safe in the coach. It was Owen and Sir Humphrey who were in danger—Owen and Sir Humphrey who might try to prevent the seizure of their prisoner and end up being killed.

Charity put a comforting hand on Mrs Mayfield's wrist, then she edged forward cautiously in an attempt to look through the window. But Mrs Mayfield caught her arm and pulled her back, terrified that Charity might show herself and be hurt.

"You won't get away with this," she heard Sir Humphrey say, his voice shaking with rage.

"I already have, you fool," replied the mocking voice of the thief, and she clenched her fists in angry helplessness, only half aware that it was the voice of a gentleman.

"Quickly, Luke! Mount the spare horse I've brought." That was the thief to the prisoner.

He was in a hurry; of course he was in a hurry. One man against so many. He held the advantage only so long as the situation didn't change. A chance traveller, a moment's distraction and he would be lost. A chance—that was all Owen and Sir Humphrey needed. Charity looked desperately around, trying to think of a way of giving it to them. Should she scream, distract the thief just long enough for the Leydons to arm themselves?

Then she remembered how her father had died and she grew cold. The best laid plans went wrong—and would the

Leydons really be able to deal with the thief, or would she kill them with her good intentions?

She sat still and afraid, and willed the man to go without hurting anyone.

Then it happened. A sudden movement, a shot—and a roar of rage and despair from Sir Humphrey.

There was a pistol in one of the pockets of the coach—like most men, Sir Humphrey preferred to travel armed. Charity wrenched herself free of Mrs Mayfield's grip and seized it. Then she opened the door and almost fell out of the carriage on to the side of the road.

One quick glance around and she saw that Owen was down, blood already spreading across his shoulder, and the two thieves were galloping across the fields—getting further away with every passing second.

Charity was filled with a cold, unaccustomed fury. She lifted the pistol, aimed it at the nearest man, steadied it with both hands—and fired.

The second thief fell forward, but he stayed on his horse, and the first thief slowed in his headlong chase to pick up the trailing reins and lead his companion to safety.

Charity's hands were shaking as she dropped the pistol, but, though she was afraid of what she would find, she didn't hesitate as she ran to Owen's side.

He wasn't dead. The bullet had entered his shoulder and she thought nothing vital had been hit. But blood was pouring from the wound and she knew that if something wasn't done quickly he would bleed to death.

Sir Humphrey was in a state of shock. He'd almost fallen from his horse and he was kneeling at Owen's side, but he'd done nothing to stop the bleeding. If it had been anyone else who'd been hurt he'd probably have dealt with the situation—but it was his son, and for a moment he was paralysed with despair.

Charity dropped down beside Owen on the cold ground and opened his coat. The amount of blood he'd lost horrified her, and she had nothing to staunch the flow but her hands.

Owen wasn't a slight man, but she hauled him up against her and pressed her hand against his wound, desperately trying to slow the loss of blood.

"Open the cases and get me some linen!" she ordered. "Sir Humphrey! Now!" She didn't recognise the sound of her own voice, but it roused Sir Humphrey.

He stood up and staggered towards the boot of the carriage, while the men who had been guarding the prisoner stood around and looked on in horror.

"Will this help, miss?" One of them offered her his scarf and she seized it gratefully.

"Yes, yes. Now, help me get his coat off. We must tie up the wound as tightly as possible," she commanded.

To her relief the guard was willing and obeyed her instructions implicitly, though she didn't know what he would have done if she hadn't been there. It wasn't so much that the men were stupid, it was just that they were as bewildered and horrified as Sir Humphrey by what had happened. Given time, they would have taken the appropriate action—but Owen didn't have time.

Sir Humphrey had brought the linen and Charity contrived a makeshift bandage. She still had to keep her hand pressed tightly into the wound, but she thought that it would now be safe to transport Owen back to Leydon House. She was about to give orders to move him when she heard the sound of hoof-beats.

She looked up and she saw Jack.

He'd heard the shots as he'd been riding to Riversleigh and had come as fast as he could, estimating their location from the sound they had made. He had paused only once, just before he'd nearly reached the carriage, because he too remembered how Charity's father had died and he didn't want to precipitate a similar tragedy. But even from a distance it was clear that the highwaymen were no longer present, and he had urged the bay into one last burst of speed.

He left the saddle while the horse was still running, and three paces brought him to Charity's side.

Charity stared up at him with huge dark eyes, and in them he read not only relief, but also an absolute conviction that he would be able to deal with the situation. Her confidence in him was absurdly gratifying—but he did no more than smile reassuringly at her and lay his hand briefly on her shoulder, before turning his attention to Owen.

"Good," he said. "You've bound him up well. I don't think he's losing much blood now. We'll get him into the carriage."

As he spoke he lifted Owen gently in his arms and stood up. Owen was still unconscious and his head lolled distressingly against Jack's shoulder. Charity reached up to support it and to keep her hands pressed against the bandages, hurrying along beside Jack.

"Get in. I'll hand him in so that you can support him," said Jack.

"Yes, of course. Oh, Mama!" Mrs Mayfield had fainted and Tabitha was trying to revive her. "I'm sorry, Tabitha," said Charity firmly as the maid shuddered at the sight of Owen, "but you're just going to have to support Mama in the corner of the coach, and if she wakes up, comfort her. I'm ready," she said to Jack.

It wasn't easy lifting an unconscious man into the carriage, but Jack managed it with the minimum of fuss, lying Owen across the entire width of the seat with his head and shoulders supported in Charity's arms. There was no help for it but to bend his legs, but the drive to Leydon House was a short one.

Jack emerged from the carriage and ordered the coachman to drive on. Then he turned to Sir Humphrey, who was beginning to recover his wits.

"I think he'll be all right, sir," he said gently. "It's his shoulder only that's hurt. With proper care he'll soon be hunting again."

"Yes, yes, yes," said Sir Humphrey eagerly. "For a moment there I was quite…but it's not serious. All that blood, but it's not…I must stay with him." He made a move as if he was about to climb into the carriage, but Jack restrained him. He didn't know whether it would be better for Sir Humphrey if he travelled in the coach, but he was sure it would be easier for Charity if he didn't.

"I think it would be better if you went straight home," he said. "A bed and dressings must be prepared for Owen, and you must warn Lady Leydon. It will be very distressing for her. I think she'll need your support more than Owen does right now."

"My wife?" Sir Humphrey looked dazed.

"Yes. You wouldn't want anyone else to tell her, would you?" Jack said. He beckoned to one of the guards as Sir Humphrey turned away.

"Go with Sir Humphrey," he said. "Make sure that there will be a bed, bandages and warm water waiting when the coach arrives. Do you understand?"

"Yes, sir." Like the others, the man felt better now that someone had taken charge. He hurried after Sir Humphrey, and Jack heard him say encouragingly to his master, "Come along, sir. We mustn't delay. We must get there before the coach does so there's time to get everything ready."

The carriage was still lumbering along, jolting over each

rut, getting slowly further and further away. The remaining guards were still standing in an untidy circle around Jack, waiting to be told what to do.

Before he said anything he whistled, and the bay gelding came back to him. He took up the reins thankfully, glad that he had devoted so much time to training the animal, and looked around at his companions.

"You," he said, indicating the guard who had originally offered Charity his scarf, "do you know where the surgeon is to be found?"

"Yes, sir," the man answered immediately.

"Good; take my horse and fetch him. Don't delay, but don't lame the horse either—it'll take longer if you do."

"Yes, sir." The guard mounted the horse and set off down the road. Jack watched him critically for a moment. It wasn't just that he was worried about his horse. He was genuinely concerned that an accident might delay the arrival of the doctor. But, if not a master horseman, at least the man appeared to be an adequate rider, and Jack turned his attention to other matters.

"How many men held you up?" he asked the two remaining guards.

"One, sir."

"Who fired the shots?"

"The highwayman." The guards looked bewildered.

"There were three shots," said Jack. "The first was a warning shot?" He looked at the men interrogatively, and they nodded. "Who fired the second—Mr Leydon?"

"No, sir. The more talkative guard shook his head. "He tried to get to his pistol, but he never had a chance. That was the shot that hit him."

"I see. So who fired the third shot?"

The two guards looked at each other. Until that moment they'd hardly been aware that there had been three shots.

They'd been so shocked by the sight of Owen's lifeless body that they'd been only dimly aware of what Charity had done.

"It must have been Miss Mayfield," said the first guard disbelievingly at last. "There was a shot from beside the carriage, and when I looked up I saw that one of the highwaymen had been hit. It couldn't have been anyone else; it must have been Miss Mayfield. But I don't…"

"That's all," said Jack. "One last thing. Did the man give any sign that he wanted to rob the coach? Or was he only interested in rescuing the prisoner?"

"He never said anything about the coach," said the guard definitely.

"Thank you. Go back to Leydon House now," said Jack.

The two men nodded respectfully and set off across the fields, following the same route that Sir Humphrey had taken earlier. It was only the coach that had to stick to the rutted, winding road.

Jack looked thoughtfully after them for a moment, then he turned and set off after the coach. He was on foot now, but the coachman was forced to drive so slowly over the bad road that it wasn't difficult for Jack to catch up.

Charity stood in the Leydons' drawing-room, resting her head against the cool glass of the window-pane. She was alone. Mrs Mayfield was resting in the comforting presence of Tabitha and the Leydons' housekeeper, and Lady Leydon was with Owen.

Mrs Mayfield had been inclined to be hysterical, but Lady Leydon had been remarkably self-possessed. She was one of those retiring women who could always rise to the occasion when there was genuine crisis—and she had the doctor's assurance that her son was not fatally injured. Charity suspected, rather guiltily, that once Lady Leydon had recovered from her initial shock she had even been able to find some compensations in the situation. For the first time in years one of her children was dependent on her again, and Lady Leydon was feeling a renewed sense of purpose.

The door opened, and Charity turned to see Jack. She felt a sudden urge of relief at the sight of him, still so calm and assured after all the terrible things that had happened.

"How is Sir Humphrey?" she asked, not entirely able to conceal her anxiety.

"Much better." Jack crossed to her side. "The doctor has convinced him that Owen will survive, and now he's putting all his energies into raising a hue and cry against the attacker. By the time Sir Humphrey has finished I doubt if there'll be a magistrate or a constable this side of London who doesn't know what happened."

Charity smiled uncertainly. "I can imagine," she said. "And I dare say you encouraged him."

"I did," Jack admitted. "He's doing something constructive—and it might flush out our man."

"Perhaps," said Charity. She was trying to be sensible and rational, but it was difficult. There had been no time for her to give way to her feelings earlier, but, now that her whole attention was not devoted to the task of keeping Owen alive, she felt weak and tearful.

"You saved his life," said Jack quietly. "Sir Humphrey knows that—the doctor told him. He's very grateful. You were very brave."

"I was terrified," Charity whispered, and the tears she had been holding back so doggedly ever since she had at last been relieved of the responsibility for Owen finally overcame her.

Her head was lowered and she didn't see Jack come towards her; she only felt him take her in his arms. For a moment she tensed, then she relaxed and leant against him, feeling the gentle touch of his hand against her hair. She would have fallen without his support and Jack knew it, and his arms tightened about her.

He had loved her before, and now his love and respect for her had grown beyond all measure. It was only the inappropriateness of the moment which prevented him from speaking—or was it really the memory of the haunted, almost horrified expression he had seen in her eyes when she had pulled away from him the previous evening? Something had certainly upset her, and now, in the cold light of morning, he was increasingly afraid that it might have been his own unrestrained ardour which had appalled her. One thing was certain—he never wanted to see that look in her eyes again.

Charity had never felt so comfortable, or so safe, but after a moment she forced herself to step away and look up at Jack. His hands were still resting on her waist, he hadn't let her go, though he was no longer holding her so closely, and she could only bring herself to meet his eyes very briefly.

"I'm sorry, I didn't mean to be so foolish," she murmured. She was confused and unsure of his intent, and in the back of her mind the illogical fear lingered that there might be some other woman. No *immediate* plans for marriage, he had said...

"Foolish is not the word I'd have used," Jack replied, his voice deeper than ever. "If you don't feel afraid—how can you be brave?"

Charity looked up at that, this time meeting his gaze steadily.

"I shot a man," she said.

"I know."

"I was so angry that I wanted to kill him, but now..."

She broke away from Jack and went to stand by the window, staring out at the tree-studded lawn.

"My father taught me to shoot," she said. "I wanted to learn, but when it came to it I hated killing things. Sometimes it's necessary, but…" She sighed.

"Did you see him fall from his horse?" Jack asked.

"No." Charity remembered how the man had fallen forward, but he'd still been riding.

"Then perhaps you didn't kill him. Owen was shot and he'll recover—but he would be dead if you hadn't acted so quickly. What you did was difficult, but in the circumstances it was necessary." Jack put his hands on her shoulders. "It's always easy to say what should or shouldn't be done—much harder to be the person who has to do it." Jack turned her round to face him.

"No one else showed much presence of mind," he said. "You should be proud of yourself—I am."

"*Proud of me?*" There was a note of almost disbelief in Charity's voice. She had been expecting…what? Horror? Shock at her unladylike behaviour? It was one thing to nurse the wounded, but quite another to fire upon their assailants. Mrs Mayfield still didn't know what she had done, and Charity was dreading the moment when she found out.

"Of course," he said.

Charity looked at him searchingly, still not quite sure that he meant it, but then she saw from his eyes that he did, and she felt a sudden, overwhelming happiness that he should have such a good opinion of her.

The moment lengthened and neither of them spoke. The urge to pull Charity back into his arms was very strong, but Jack resisted it. He was convinced he had upset her the previous evening, and she meant too much to him to risk distressing her again, particularly after all the other events of the morning. She was trying hard to hide it, but he knew she was still feeling shocked by what had happened.

"Come and sit down," he said, guiding her to a chair.

"I *am* being foolish," Charity said with a weak attempt at humour. "Whenever I think Mama's upset I always make her sit down too."

"Possibly," said Jack doubtfully. "But in this instance I think it would be more honest if I admitted that I'm trying to make myself useful. You don't *have* to sit down, of course—but I'll feel better if you do. That way I can deceive myself into thinking I've done something constructive too."

Charity blinked at him. He smiled back at her, the expression in his grey eyes kind and self-deprecating, and at last she felt the final vestiges of the horror caused by the events of the morning fade into oblivion.

"Thank you," she said. "You came to the rescue again. I don't think I have ever been so happy to see anyone in my life. I was feeling quite desperate!" She held out her hand impulsively as she spoke.

"You'd left me very little to do," he replied, taking her hand. "But I'm glad if my presence expedited matters. Now," he added more briskly, "we must decide what to do next."

"The pendant!" Charity exclaimed. "Is it still in your pocket?"

"Yes, I've got it." Jack sat down opposite her. "And I think our original scheme is still a good one. Your highwayman was interested in only rescuing his henchman; that could be because he's a devoted master—or it could be because he was afraid he'd talk. Either way it seems to indicate that he doesn't know we've found what he's looking for. If he did know he might have wanted to search the coach."

"Oh, my God!" said Charity. "You mustn't carry it around with you any more—it's not safe!"

"Yes, it is. He doesn't know I've got it," Jack reminded her, feeling ridiculously pleased by her obvious concern for his welfare.

"But even so…" Charity wasn't convinced.

"I'll put it somewhere secure as soon as I can," he reassured her.

"But that won't make any difference if he finds out you've got it, or that you've had it," she protested. "Even if you tell him you haven't got it now, he won't believe you; he'll—"

"Charity!" Jack interrupted firmly. "The pendant and I are both quite safe and will continue to be so. He doesn't know I've got it, and he won't find out. And, even if he does, I'm forewarned of his intentions, which gives me the advantage."

"Yes," said Charity. "Yes, I suppose it does."

"Good. Now, as soon as I've taken my leave of Sir Humphrey, I must return to Riversleigh, and then I'll go back to Hazelhurst. I don't know if the thief will come tonight or not, but, judging by the speed with which he acted this morning, I wouldn't be surprised. We won't underestimate him again."

"We?" said Charity with a flash of spirit. "I thought you'd already decided that I was to be relegated to the role of nervous female in this whole affair?"

But inwardly she felt her heart begin to sing. Would he really be doing all this on her behalf if he felt no more for her than simple friendship? Of course he would! He was too much a gentleman not to offer his help to anyone who needed it. All the same…

"Now you're trying to provoke me," said Jack. "You

know perfectly well that that was *not* what I thought—even before you went out of your way to prove me wrong!''

''I *didn't*...'' Charity began indignantly, and then relaxed as she saw that he was teasing her. ''I thought of creating a disturbance,'' she admitted. ''Anything to give Owen or Sir Humphrey an opportunity to turn the tables— but then I remembered all the things that could go wrong and I decided to sit quietly and pray that the man would leave without hurting anybody. I wish he had.''

''Yes, I know,'' said Jack. ''I never thought you'd do anything foolish.''

''I've done a great many foolish things,'' said Charity. ''But not at a time like that—at least, I hope not.''

As she finished speaking the door opened, and they turned their heads to see Sir Humphrey entering the room.

''I've been thinking,'' he announced without preamble, ''and it seems to me that there's something damned fishy going on.''

Chapter Twelve

"In what way, sir?" asked Jack mildly, standing up at the magistrate's approach.

"That attack on the coach," said Sir Humphrey, so intent on his train of thought that he'd barely registered Charity's presence. "Didn't occur to me before, but damned risky business! And for what? To save a stuttering idiot! And why? That's what I'd like to know. You don't want to believe any of that nonsense about honour among thieves," he added, glaring at Jack belligerently.

"I don't," said Jack.

"No, well…quite," said Sir Humphrey. He'd been about to argue the point, and now he was feeling somewhat disconcerted.

"But what do you think we should make of it?" asked Jack.

Charity glanced at him doubtfully. She was afraid Jack was making fun of the squire and she didn't approve of it. But there was nothing in Jack's expression or in his tone of voice to suggest he was secretly mocking Sir Humphrey, and in fact he was simply curious to hear the magistrate's opinion.

"I don't know," Sir Humphrey replied honestly. "It

doesn't make sense to me. Nothing that idiot said made sense. But the hold-up isn't the only odd thing. There are the two break-ins as well. Thieves don't usually go back to the same place twice—not in my experience, at any rate. And I think we can assume that the man who rescued our prisoner *was* one of the thieves from last night."

Jack nodded. Sir Humphrey's summing up of the situation might be slightly disjointed, but it was far from inaccurate. On the whole, Jack was inclined to think that the magistrate deserved to know the truth—as far as he and Charity knew it themselves—but he was reluctant to say anything without Charity's agreement.

He glanced at her, a question in his eyes, and when she nodded imperceptibly he said to Sir Humphrey, "We think there may be a great deal more to the affair than just a simple burglary."

"You mean, you *know* something?" Sir Humphrey demanded. "What do you know?"

"Nothing very concrete," Charity intervened suddenly.

She was prepared to tell the magistrate about Jack's original suspicions, but she still didn't want him to know that they'd actually found the pendant. She couldn't overcome the belief that Jack would be in danger if anyone knew the jewel was in his possession, and she wasn't prepared to let anyone else in on that secret.

"Well, come on! Come on! Either you know something or you don't," Sir Humphrey said, looking from one to the other impatiently.

"Perhaps, since Miss Mayfield is so closely involved, it would be better if she explained," Jack replied, his relaxed expression belied by the intent look in his eyes as they rested on Charity's face.

He wasn't quite sure why she was equivocating, but he had every faith in her good sense, and he had no objection to following her lead—at least until he knew what was in her mind.

"Well?" Sir Humphrey stared at her.

"We didn't say anything at first because it seemed such a foolish idea," Charity said composedly. "But when Lord Riversleigh questioned the thief last night the man said certain things that seemed to suggest he was looking for treasure—and in our library!"

"Well! I'll be damned!" said Sir Humphrey after a moment. "Treasure, you say? In the library! Good God!"

"Lord Riversleigh mentioned the matter to me," Charity continued when Sir Humphrey seemed to have recovered from his initial astonishment. "And of course I said the whole thing was nonsense. But..." she paused ruefully "...we were talking about it just now before you came in and, if it's true—that they really believe there's treasure in our library, I mean—it might help to explain what's happened. The return of the thieves to the same place, and the desperate rescue of the captured man. The first man might have been afraid in case the prisoner gave any information away, so he wanted to rescue him before he could talk."

"But good God! Treasure in your *library!*" Sir Humphrey wasn't really listening to her any more; he was still trying to grapple with the outlandish suggestion about treasure.

"The important point is not whether there is any treasure, but whether the thieves believe there is," Jack said smoothly.

It was now clear to him that Charity wanted to conceal the discovery of the pendant and, although he hadn't guessed her true reason for doing so, he was inclined to think it was a good idea.

The callous attack on Owen had made Jack more determined than ever to catch the master thief, and the thief would be far more likely to make a third attempt on the library if he didn't know the pendant had been found. It wasn't that Jack didn't trust Sir Humphrey, it was just that the fewer people who knew, the less likely the information was to leak out.

"Yes, you're quite right, of course," said Sir Humphrey. "But what an *incredible* notion. I wonder where they can have got it from?"

"I'm rather curious about that myself," Jack admitted.

"Most unaccountable—treasure, indeed," said Sir Humphrey. "We're not used to all this excitement, are we, Charity?"

"No, sir," Charity smiled at him. "Actually, I think I could do with a great deal less."

"So could I." The magistrate's smile faded. "When I saw Owen…" His words trailed away and his expression clouded as he remembered the painful events of the morning.

He had submerged his grief and worry in a flurry of magisterial activity, and then his attention had been diverted by his sudden suspicion that there was something odd about the whole affair—but beneath his impatience and his bluster there was genuine fear and concern for his son.

"Owen's very strong," said Charity gently, taking the magistrate's hand. "And nothing vital was hit. You know the doctor said it won't be long before he gets his strength back. Please don't worry."

Sir Humphrey blinked, and then focused his gaze on her face.

"You're a good girl," he said, patting her hand. "I haven't thanked you yet, m'dear, and I know you saved him. I wasn't much help to you. But it shook me, do you see? I wasn't expecting it, and when I saw him lying there…" He stopped and dashed a hand across his eyes.

He was still standing—somehow it hadn't occurred to him yet to sit down, or to invite Jack to do so—and now Charity stood on tiptoe and kissed his cheek.

"Owen's safe now," she said. "And Lady Leydon will make sure he gets better quickly. Everything will soon be back to normal."

"I hope so." Sir Humphrey sighed. "Well," he continued more briskly, "what are we going to do about catching the scoundrels? My dear..." it suddenly occurred to him that he'd shown remarkably little consideration for Charity's sensibilities "...don't you think you ought to go and lie down? After all you've been through, I wouldn't like to cause you any more distress."

"I think it would probably be a good idea if Miss Mayfield stayed," Jack said quickly before Charity could reply. "After all, it is her family home that seems to be at the heart of the puzzle. If you feel up to it," he added blandly to Charity.

"Certainly." She returned his quizzical look with dignity.

"Of course she's up to it," said Sir Humphrey inconsistently, but with great good humour. "I've never yet known Charity overset by anything."

"Thank you," she replied, slightly overwhelmed by this tribute.

"Good," said Jack firmly, and in what he hoped was a decisive manner. He could see that unless they were careful they were going to end up completely side-tracked from the main issue. "But to return to the matter in hand..."

"Catching the thieves," said Sir Humphrey. "I have a piece of information which may be helpful. Apparently one of the thieves—the prisoner, I think—was shot while they were riding away. That should make it easier to find them. A wounded man is harder to hide than a fit one. I don't know who shot him,'' he added, frowning. ''When I questioned them the men were quite clear that one of the villains had been wounded, but none of them seemed to know who had fired the shot. Most odd. It certainly wasn't me. I would have remembered.''

Jack didn't say anything. He hadn't given the men any instructions to keep quiet on the subject and he suspected that either they'd simply found the idea of Charity firing the pistol too remarkable to be believable—or else they'd decided not to say anything to protect her from embarrassment. They all knew her and it was quite likely that they didn't want to make trouble for her.

''It was me,'' said Charity awkwardly, after a brief pause.

''You?'' Sir Humphrey looked at her incredulously.

''I was angry.'' She looked at him anxiously. She still hadn't quite come to terms with what she had done, and she was afraid he would think badly of her.

''Well, well.'' He gazed at her with narrowed eyes, almost as if he was seeing her for the first time.

Somehow he hadn't really been surprised that she had dealt with Owen's injury so competently—but it did surprise him that she had the determination to respond so decisively to their attackers.

Sir Humphrey was always inclined to create comfortable mental images of the people he knew and, when they did something which didn't fit the character he had created for them, he would often ignore the implications of their action. The habit was too deeply ingrained for him ever to lose it, but, for a moment at least, he did become aware of an aspect of Charity's character which he had never before fully appreciated. For a moment his reaction was uncertain. Did he approve of her determination—or disapprove of her reckless and unladylike behaviour? But he was usually gen-

erous in his judgement of others, and not the man to let
knowledge of his own failings sour his opinion of others.

"Well done, my dear," he said heartily. "You had more
courage and presence of mind than any of us."

"You mean, you approve?" Charity was surprised.

"Well, it's not quite the conduct I'd expect from a young
girl—but courage and quick wits are very important qualities to have," Sir Humphrey declared. "It's a pity you're
not a man."

Charity blinked, and then opened her mouth indignantly.

"I'm not sure that I'd agree with you on that point,"
said Jack hastily, frowning at Charity slightly. "But I think
we are in danger of becoming side-tracked here. May I be
so bold as to suggest that we all sit down, and consider the
matter in hand sensibly?"

There was no doubt that his last few words had been
directed specifically at Charity, and she closed her mouth
and simmered quietly.

"My dear fellow, of course. I'm so sorry. Do sit down,"
Sir Humphrey exclaimed, dismayed that he should have
proved so inhospitable a host. "Would you like some bur-
gundy, claret, brandy—tea…?" He remembered Charity's
presence.

She started to laugh. "Sir Humphrey, you hate tea," she
said.

"No, no, my dear," he assured her. "I confess, I'm not
as fond of it as you ladies seem to be, but…"

The door crashed open and Lord Travers strode into the
room, angrily stripping off his riding gloves.

"I have spent hours cooling my heels waiting for that
jumped-up jackanapes and I'm damned if I'll wait any
longer. *I'm* not answerable to any misbeggoten son of a…"
He stopped dead, the colour draining from his face as he
saw Jack.

Jack stood up slowly.

"You were saying?" he said. There was no expression on his face, but his eyes were cold, and his voice was quiet and dangerous.

"Nothing." Lord Travers stared transfixed at Jack.

"What were you saying?" Jack repeated implacably.

"I...I believe my remarks were not addressed to you, my lord." Lord Travers finally regained the power of speech, and even attempted a casual laugh—but his effort failed dismally.

"Nevertheless, I suggest you retract them," said Jack. "You would be most unwise to rely any further on my forbearance."

He paused. There was something terrible in the silent intensity of his manner and, in the silence that followed his words, the only sound to be heard was Lord Travers's uneven breathing.

"I...I must have been misinformed," said Lord Travers breathlessly.

"Misinformed?" Jack's eyes narrowed. "Then you have been discussing the matter with others?"

"I...I mean, I was mistaken," Lord Travers stammered, seeing another trap opening before him. Later he would writhe with self-reproach at his craven response but now, as he felt the full force of Jack's anger and contempt, he did not even think of trying to save face. Lord Travers was deeply afraid, and he would have abased himself before Jack if doing so would have preserved him from Jack's revenge.

"You *were* mistaken," said Jack. "Don't ever doubt it."

"N-no."

"Good. And no doubt in future you will remember that I do not care to have my affairs discussed in public."

"Y-yes, my lord." Lord Travers looked so wretched that

Charity was almost inclined to feel sorry for him. But then she remembered how prejudicial his slanders could have proved to Jack's acceptance by his new neighbours, and she no longer felt any sympathy for Lord Travers. The gossiping lord was not only a fool who gave no thought to the ultimate consequences of his actions, but he was also a coward at heart, with all the instincts of a bully. He neither could nor would repeat his slanders to their victim, and his fear of Jack reduced him to grovelling imbecility.

For a moment longer Jack continued to look steadily at Lord Travers, then he seemed satisfied, and some of the tension left him.

"I sent you a message that I would be delayed," he said. "Unfortunately the delay proved to be greater than I had expected. It is no longer convenient for me to see you now. We will postpone our meeting until a future—but not too far distant—date. There are several things we must discuss."

"Yes, my lord." Lord Travers bowed jerkily and turned to Sir Humphrey.

"Sir Humphrey, I have so much enjoyed my stay, but, I regret, I must...that is, I have urgent affairs...so sorry...very pleasant time...apologies to Lady Leydon...excellent hunting...and must leave at once." Lord Travers backed out of the room, still talking.

"Well!" said Sir Humphrey, taking a deep breath. "What the *devil* did you do to him?"

"Nothing in particular." The sparks of cold diamond fire had left Jack's eyes, and now his expression was as mild and faintly humorous as always. "I believe you were about to offer us some tea," he said.

"In a minute," said Sir Humphrey with uncharacteristic inhospitality. "Now, there has been something odd going on between you and Travers ever since you arrived, and I want to get to the bottom of it. Travers is—was—a guest in my house. I have a right to know.''

''There's nothing to discuss,'' said Jack pleasantly. ''Lord Travers made certain…unfounded allegations, which you have since heard him retract. That's all there is to it.''

''Yes, but—'' Sir Humphrey began doubtfully.

''Oh, for heaven's sake!'' Charity interrupted, quite out of patience with both of them. ''Lord Travers borrowed money from Jack's—I mean, Lord Riversleigh's bank, but because he's a mean-spirited man he resented having to put himself at such a disadvantage. I dare say telling all those lies made him feel powerful and important—he's too stupid to realise the consequences until too late. Now he's gone scurrying home, to try to persuade himself that it never happened—at least…''

She looked at Jack, suddenly concerned. ''You don't think he'll try to take his revenge in a more…more devious way, do you?''

''Waylay me in a dark alley?'' Jack asked. ''No, I don't think he'll do that. Words are his chosen weapon, and I don't think he'll deviate from his custom.''

''But, all the same, I think you should be careful,'' Charity insisted.

''That *blackguard!*'' Sir Humphrey burst out, paying no attention to Charity.

It was true he'd already begun to have doubts concerning the truth of the rumours about Jack, and the events of the morning had completely driven his earlier suspicions out of his mind. Nevertheless, it was still a very unpleasant shock to discover exactly what kind of man had been enjoying his hospitality.

''My lord,'' said Sir Humphrey with stiff formality, ''I owe you an apology. I believed what Travers said and now

I see that I have been guilty of gross injustice. I trust that you will forgive me.''

Jack smiled and held out his hand. ''You didn't know me,'' he said. ''There was no injustice.''

''That's generous—''

''I think you mentioned tea earlier,'' Jack interrupted. ''I think perhaps Miss Mayfield…''

''Of course, of course.'' Sir Humphrey relieved his feelings by tugging at the bell-pull so vigorously that Charity was half afraid he was going to yank it down.

She glanced at Jack and saw the amusement in his eyes and had to look away before she started to laugh.

''Well, you'll live, but you'll be no good to me for weeks.'' The master thief dried his hands on a rough towel and looked down at his henchman irritably.

''I-I-I'm s-s-sorry, s-sir,'' the man stammered wretchedly.

''You should be,'' Ralph Gideon replied curtly. ''Were you questioned?''

''Y-y-y—''

''Did you say anything?'' Gideon interrupted sharply.

''N-n-n-no, sir!'' The man lay on his uncomfortable bed and looked up at his master fearfully. He really didn't think he had said anything, but he was afraid of Gideon.

''I hope you didn't. Dear God! I shall be glad to be out of this place.'' Gideon had been about to ask some more questions, but he was suddenly recalled to a sense of his surroundings by the aggravating bite of a flea, and instead he looked round the cheap inn room in some disgust. Then he turned his attention back to his servant.

''Remember, if anyone questions you, we were attacked by footpads on Horsham Common. It happens all the time, I'm told. Do you know who shot you?''

"N-n-n..." At the time Luke had been too preoccupied to turn and look, and now he didn't understand the gleam in his master's eyes.

"It was the girl," said Gideon softly. "She was the one who foiled me the first time. When this business is over, I think I shall turn my attention to taming her."

For a moment he gazed into space, contemplating some vision of his own, then he recollected himself and tossed the towel on to the floor.

"Go to sleep," he said abruptly. "I have work to do." He opened the chamber door and went downstairs, and Luke heard him calling for the innkeeper's daughter to bring him ale.

Charity opened the door quietly and crept over to where Lady Leydon was sitting beside the bed on which Owen lay. He appeared to be sleeping comfortably, and his mother was sewing with an expression which was almost peaceful.

She glanced up at Charity but, though she smiled, it was clear that her thoughts were elsewhere. She was remembering the long-distant days when she had been the most important person in Owen's life. Not like now, when all too often his affection was tempered with impatience and even irritability. He was becoming increasingly like his father and, though Lady Leydon knew how important she was to Sir Humphrey's comfort, she also knew he was very unlikely to tell her so—or to think she needed telling. The magistrate might be prepared to allow *Charity* a certain latitude in her opinions and actions, but he would have thought it a very strange thing if his wife had been equally independent.

"How is Owen?" Charity asked in an undertone.

"Sleeping. He woke earlier, and I was able to give him some broth," Lady Leydon replied.

He'd also asked after Charity, but Lady Leydon didn't mention that. She would lose Owen again soon enough when he was no longer dependent on her, she had no intention of doing anything to bring that situation about more quickly than necessary.

"I'm so glad," said Charity impulsively. "I was worried earlier—but I was just being foolish. With you to look after him, he'll soon be well again."

"Yes," said Lady Leydon baldly.

It was unusual for her to be so abrupt, even curt, and for a moment Charity was afraid Lady Leydon blamed her for Owen's injury. She didn't know what to say. She couldn't apologise for something that hadn't been her fault, nor could she say that Owen had been shot because of his own hasty temper.

"I shall be sorry to leave Sussex," she said instead. "You have been such good neighbours to us all these years. I know this isn't the last time we shall be seeing each other, but I did want to thank you for all your kindness to Mama and me."

"But you won't be far away," Lady Leydon said slightly more cordially.

"Far enough," Charity replied, surprised that Mrs Carmichael had obviously failed to pass on this piece of information to Lady Leydon. "We're moving to London, did you not know?"

"I thought you were going to Horsham!" Lady Leydon exclaimed.

"That was our first plan," Charity admitted, "but Mama never really cared for it. We're going to London instead. We're in the middle of making the arrangements now."

Even as she spoke she wondered why she was telling

Lady Leydon all this. With the discovery of the pendant it might not be necessary for them to move at all.

But perhaps she was telling Owen's mother that she was leaving Sussex because she couldn't tell Owen that she wasn't going to marry him. She had never regretted anything so much as she regretted her folly at the party the previous evening. She should never have encouraged Owen to believe they were as good as betrothed, and now, with Owen sick, there was nothing she could do to put her mistake right. She must wait until Owen recovered—and hope that he wouldn't be too disappointed.

Perhaps the gentlemanly thing to do would be to go through with the marriage—but Charity was too honest to contemplate such a course. In the past she had always believed that love was not necessarily essential for a successful marriage, but now she knew that, for her at least, it was. She wanted Jack, and if she couldn't have him she didn't want anyone.

"London!" Lady Leydon exclaimed, interrupting Charity's thoughts. "I had no idea. We'll all miss you so much—I know Owen will," she added significantly.

"Thank you. It will be sad for us too," Charity replied sedately, trying not to look self-conscious. "But you know how Owen and I are always arguing. You'll be able to have some peace for a change!"

"No such thing," Lady Leydon assured her, but there was a warmth in her expression which had been lacking previously. She had suspected that there was more between Owen and Charity than either had admitted and, though she didn't dislike Charity, she was relieved that her suspicions had apparently been unfounded.

"You must come back and visit us whenever you feel homesick for your old haunts," she offered generously.

"Thank you. And when we are settled in London you

must come and visit us,'' Charity replied, though inwardly she hoped the suggestion would never come to anything. She was grateful that the undercurrent of tension that had seemed to exist between Lady Leydon and herself had disappeared—but she had no desire to pursue their friendship. It would be too awkward.

There seemed to be very little more to be said and so, with one last look at Owen's recumbent form, she took her leave of Lady Leydon and returned to her bedchamber.

It was nearly dark, and Mrs Mayfield was still resting after the upsets of the day, but Charity sat quietly in her room, knowing that Sir Humphrey and Lord Riversleigh were already on their way to Hazelhurst, ready to lay the trap for the master thief.

When they had finally managed to discuss the problem of trapping the thief Sir Humphrey had insisted that he take part in the scheme. Jack had tried to dissuade him, pointing out that if too many people were involved the thief was more likely to become suspicious and perhaps not even come.

But Sir Humphrey would not agree to remain behind. He had invoked his authority both as a Justice of the Peace and as the father of one of the thief's victims—and Jack had made no further attempt to exclude him. He would have felt happier without the magistrate's presence, but in all fairness he could not deny Sir Humphrey's right to be involved.

With that decided, they had laid their plans quickly, the only further matter of slight dissension being the number of men they took with them—Sir Humphrey wanted four; Jack didn't want any. In the end they compromised on two, but Jack was beginning to despair of how they would get so many men into the house unobserved.

He was certain that the thief would be watching the house, if not all day then at least for an hour or two before he made another attempt to enter it. It was for that reason that Jack wanted his party to arrive in the late afternoon before dark. There was a possibility that the thief wouldn't be watching the house during the day, especially since he already had the problem of finding somewhere to take his wounded confederate.

But if he didn't return that evening he would certainly be back the next—if he didn't come during the day. It was unlikely—even with the house apparently unoccupied by its owners, there were still several people about—but it was possible. That was why Jack had arranged for his own servant to be present while he himself was absent. He could rely on Alan to react quickly and effectively during an emergency—unlike Charles, who invariably needed guidance in any unfamiliar situation.

Charity had listened to the discussions quietly. She had made one or two suggestions as to how they could best enter the house unobserved, but apart from that she had taken no part in the arrangements. She had seemed rather withdrawn, but she couldn't help smiling at the enthusiasm Sir Humphrey displayed for the plan.

"Well, we've some time yet before we must leave," Sir Humphrey had declared at last. "How about a game of piquet while we wait, Riversleigh?"

"Certainly," Jack had smiled.

"Good, good. I'll just go and set things in motion, then we can play a quick hand or two." Sir Humphrey's eyes had lit up in anticipation as he had hurried off to order his servants to be in readiness later in the afternoon.

It was then, when she had been left briefly alone with Jack, that Charity had spoken. And it was that moment which she remembered now as she sat on the edge of her bed in the gathering darkness at the end of the short winter day.

"You will be careful, won't you? Sir Humphrey is sometimes too impulsive," she had said.

"I will act as a restraining influence," Jack had replied lightly.

"It's important," she had insisted. "He's a ruthless man, this thief. He'll hurt you if he has to—perhaps even if he doesn't. And it's my house you're defending. If anything happens to any of you—I will feel responsible."

"That's nonsense," Jack had said firmly, a slight frown creasing his forehead as he looked at her. "You aren't responsible for what he does—or for us. Don't ever think it."

"I'm not sure I agree, but, anyway, do be careful," Charity had repeated as she had heard Sir Humphrey returning.

She remembered her words now, and she couldn't rid herself of the feeling that she *was* responsible, and that she should be at Hazelhurst. If her father had been alive he would have been waiting with Jack and Sir Humphrey. It was her home and they were her friends—she should be there.

She came to a decision and stood up briskly. It wasn't difficult to leave the house without being observed, and once outside she made her way quickly to the stables.

Chapter Thirteen

The house was dark and still. The candles had been extinguished and the fires banked. The doors were bolted and the windows locked, and the only movement in the library came from the gentle billowing of curtains caught in the gentle draught from the closed casement. Upstairs the servants slept; downstairs the only sound came from the ivy leaves brushing against the windows—but six silent men were waiting for the thief.

Only Alan, Lord Riversleigh's manservant, had known that Jack would be returning, and he had let Jack and his party in at a side-door while the rest of the household was at supper. It would have been relatively easy at that point to conceal their presence in the house, but both Sir Humphrey and Jack had agreed that such excessive secrecy was probably not advisable.

Jack in particular was anxious to avoid the kind of chaos which might arise if there was a disturbance and the rest of the household was unaware of his and Sir Humphrey's presence. At the very least there would be some confusion, but it would be far worse if the thief managed to escape because the men who should have been defending the house were tripping each other up in the dark.

So they had spoken to Charles and Mrs Wendle. The alarmed housekeeper had agreed to remain in her room until she was told it was safe to come out, but Charles had been determined to join the others, and now he was waiting in the parlour with Alan and the two men Sir Humphrey had brought.

Only Jack and the magistrate waited in the library. Jack had been firm on that point and, on reflection, Sir Humphrey had agreed with him. After all, he had brought his men to guard his anticipated prisoner—not get in his way while he was catching the villain.

But they had been waiting a long time in the dark, and Sir Humphrey, never the most patient of men, was beginning to get restive.

"Riversleigh," he hissed, "why don't we open a window a little bit? It might encourage the scoundrel."

"I don't think so," Jack replied in a low voice which gave no hint of the exasperation he felt. "It would make the trap too obvious. Our man is not a fool."

The magistrate sighed, because he knew Jack was right, and shifted uncomfortably. He found such inactivity more trying than a hard day in the saddle. In the darkened library all he could see were shadows. If he hadn't known that Riversleigh was waiting on the other side of the room he would have been convinced he was alone. How was it possible for a man to be so still, and so silent? Apart from that one comment, Jack had made no sound since they had begun their vigil.

Sir Humphrey became aware of how noisily he seemed to be breathing. He tried to breathe more quietly, taking shallow, careful breaths, but it didn't seem to help. He was making less noise, but he was also becoming extremely self-conscious about the whole mechanical process of breathing and increasingly desperate to gulp in a huge lungful of air. With an enormous effort of self-discipline he did no such thing, and instead his tortured imagination became obsessed with the notion that his lungs were like bellows. He put his hand on his chest to feel the rise and fall of his ribs and found himself becoming more and more fascinated by his flight of fancy. What a remarkable creature a man was, how admirably designed, how exquisitely made—how loud.

Riversleigh didn't seem to be having similar difficulties, Sir Humphrey thought resentfully. Perhaps he'd solved the problem by not breathing at all—he was certainly making no more noise than a dead man. The magistrate was just about to enquire about his companion's welfare when all thoughts of lungs and bellows were driven completely out of his head.

He plunged to his feet, his hand reaching instinctively for the hilt of his sword as a woman's scream splintered the silence.

She was outside, desperate with terror and, even as Sir Humphrey listened, the sound of her screams began to recede. She was being carried away.

"Good God! The villain's attacking a woman!" Sir Humphrey burst out. "Come on, Riversleigh!" he shouted and dived towards the door, nearly colliding with the horrified men who'd erupted from the parlour.

The woman's despairing screams could still be heard. She was being carried further away, but the intensity of her fear was as palpable as if she'd been standing beside them.

Sir Humphrey tugged at the bolts on the front door, the others crowding behind him. Alan looked at his master for guidance and Jack nodded. Then the door was open and they burst out on to the drive, running across the gravel towards the despairing cries of the woman.

At that moment she gave one last, panic-stricken

scream—and all was silent. Sir Humphrey checked for a moment, horrified by the dreadful implications of that silence—then he forced himself to run even faster. But already the younger men were overtaking him, forging their way through the shrubbery.

Then they were all gone, the distant sounds of their running feet only emphasising the silence of the empty and deserted house.

A man stepped out from behind the holly tree and ran lightly towards the house. In one hand he carried a shuttered lantern—in the other a pistol.

The front door was still ajar and he pushed it gently open and stepped cautiously inside. He listened carefully, but no sound came to him from within the unguarded house and he moved quickly into the library.

He could no longer be certain that the booty he sought was still there, but he had no intention of abandoning his search while there was a possibility that it might be. He knew his servant had been questioned, and the fact that a trap had been laid for him at Hazelhurst seemed to indicate that his opponents had guessed something at least of what he was doing. But he was hoping they'd either failed to understand, or else discounted his servant's story as nonsense. If they *had* found the pendant he would have to approach the problem differently.

He dropped the pistol into his pocket, removed the shutters from the lantern and held it up to look at the bookshelves. Nothing seemed to have changed. The books were still on the shelves and there was no indication that anything had been moved—or that anyone had been searching here.

He felt an inward surge of relief and set the lantern down on the desk. He knew he would have to work quickly, but he knew what he was looking for; there should be time.

He reached up to lift down a handful of books, and a voice behind him said, "You're wasting your time, Gideon. It's not there any more."

For a moment the thief froze, disbelief suspending his actions. Then he spun round, his hand reaching for his pocket—and heard the sharp click as Jack cocked his pistol.

"I'll kill you if you make another move," he said pleasantly, and the thief believed him.

"Damn you!" he said viciously. "Meddling, impertinent…"

Jack smiled. "Until you walked in and unshuttered the lantern I had no idea it was you," he said quietly. "It was quite as much a surprise to me as my presence must be to you. But I'm not sorry. One day you were bound to fail—and I'm glad I'm here to see it. Put your hands in the air and turn round."

"And if I don't?" Insolent blue eyes locked with cold grey eyes in an unspoken contest of will. The tension between the two men was almost visible in its intensity.

"If you don't I will put a bullet through your leg," said Jack."

Gideon stared at him for a second longer, but the steady grey eyes were implacable, and he knew that if he didn't obey Jack would do exactly as he'd said.

The thief turned round slowly, cursing himself. He'd known that Riversleigh was in the neighbourhood, he'd even heard the rumours and laughed scornfully at the credulous Sussex yokels. But it had never occurred to him that *he* would have to deal with Jack before he was through. He should have questioned his servant more closely.

He felt Riversleigh come up behind him and take the pistol from his pocket, but he made no attempt to retaliate. Some men might drop their guard when they believed their mastery of the situation was complete—but not Jack; no, certainly not, Jack, not after what had happened before.

Gideon was aware of a grudging flicker of respect—the same respect he'd first had for Jack nearly sixteen years ago when they'd both been schoolboys, and Jack the younger of the two. He frowned; the memory of what had happened all those years ago had sparked an idea for escape. He was no longer interested in searching for the pendant, only in saving his own life. If he hadn't gone by the time the others returned he would almost certainly hang for what he had done.

"May I turn round?" he said.

"Yes." The pistol in Jack's hand didn't waver, but he was curious to know more of his opponent. It had been half a lifetime since they had last encountered each other, but all the old animosity still existed between them.

"Are you going to keep me covered with that pistol like a common criminal until your friends return?" Gideon asked insolently. "I am a gentleman."

"No, you are a thief," said Jack. "A thief, a liar and possibly even a murderer. I wish I could say that you've improved since last we met—but I can't."

"When last we met I proved conclusively that a moneylender's son is no match for a true gentleman," Gideon replied arrogantly.

Jack smiled. "Is that what you proved?" he said quietly. "My recollection of the affair is somewhat different."

"Of course it is," Gideon agreed. "No loser can bear to remember honestly how he came to be defeated!" He paused, watching Jack closely. "I could do it again," he continued softly. "You and I both know that. That's why you're hiding behind that pistol until your friends can come and tie me up. Because if we met with our swords as gentlemen—you wouldn't stand a chance."

The scorn in his voice would have roused a marble statue to fury, but the only indication that Jack had heard was a slight narrowing of his eyes as he looked at Gideon.

Then he laughed. ''No,'' he said. ''Not this time.''

For a moment Gideon thought he'd failed, that he'd have no opportunity to cross swords with Jack, but then he saw the look in Jack's eyes and knew that he'd have his fight after all.

But not because of anything he'd said. His words hadn't roused Jack to blind fury, only to cold and calculating anger. Perhaps he'd even wanted the fight and Gideon's words had only furnished him with the excuse he'd needed.

Gideon had no lack of faith in his own ability, but the unexpected thought chilled him, and for the first time he began to wonder whether his plan would be successful.

''Push back the desk,'' said Jack. ''And the chairs.''

''Are you afraid you'll trip over them?'' Gideon taunted, but he did as Jack said. He had no desire to fall over furniture in the half-light either.

''Draw your sword,'' said Jack.

They met in the centre of the room, barely saluting each other before their blades tangled. Both men were intent on their opponent; neither of them knew they were no longer alone.

Charity had been standing in the hall, listening to what they said and trying to make sense of it. But now she stood in the doorway, watching them fight by the flickering light of the lantern.

She could see Gideon's face and his expression chilled her. He would kill Jack if he could, even though he only needed to disable him to escape.

She was terrified. She had never known that such fear could exist. Her thoughts were so paralysed that she did not even berate herself for not having intervened sooner. She could only watch—and pray.

She couldn't see what was happening properly. Jack's back was towards her, and she was afraid to move into his line of vision in case her presence distracted him. But she had to know what was happening.

She'd been clutching convulsively at the door-frame, but now she released it and began to edge along the wall into the corner of the library. She was still behind Jack, but now she could see more.

The blades moved so fast that she could never have described the encounter, but she had a sense that neither of the two men had fully committed himself to the attack. They were waiting, watching, trying to discover the other's weaknesses.

The swords gleamed dully in the inadequate light, and Charity began to feel dizzy and confused, uncertain of what was happening—or of who was winning.

Gideon lunged, his movements so fluid that his sword seemed like an extension of his arm. Jack parried and Charity heard the sickening slither of steel. She saw that his sleeve had been torn, and she began to feel as if she were suffocating.

This could not go on. The pace had quickened, both men were fighting hard now, and Jack was beginning to press the attack. Gideon's blade missed him by less than half an inch and Charity closed her eyes.

Then she opened them resolutely. She must not be afraid and she must not flinch, because if Jack fell—God forbid— then it would be up to her.

Before she had left Leydon House she had spent several minutes debating the wisdom of bringing a pistol. She could not forget that she had already shot one man—she didn't think she ever would—and she never wanted to repeat the experience. But, though she had been sorely tempted to come unarmed, in the end it had seemed to her that to do so would not be to show common sense—but simply to surrender to her fear. So she had taken one of Sir Humphrey's duelling pistols from his study.

She had never really thought she'd need it, but now she took it out with shaking hands and pointed it at Gideon. She mustn't tremble—she *must not* tremble! She blocked out all other thoughts and kept the pistol levelled at the thief. Her concentration was complete and her hands were steady. Whatever happened, there would be no escape for Gideon now.

Gideon didn't even know Charity was there. His breath was coming in short sharp gasps and the sweat was trickling into his eyes, but he didn't dare to wipe it away. There was nothing casual about this encounter and he was growing desperate.

He was running out of time. Soon the other men would be back, and if he didn't finish Jack soon he would be caught like a rat—so he fought like a rat. But he couldn't find an opening. Whatever he tried, Jack anticipated it. It seemed as if he were surrounded by an impenetrable barrier of steel.

At last! Gideon thought he saw an opportunity. He lunged forward, fully committed to his attack—and realised too late that it was a trick. He staggered back, his sword falling from his nerveless hand as Jack's blade penetrated his right shoulder.

He was lying on the shabby carpet, dizzy and sick, and Jack towered over him. Gideon blinked and tried to clear his head. He saw the tip of Jack's sword, slowly dripping blood, then he looked up and met Jack's quizzical eyes.

"You should have killed me," he gasped.

"No doubt you deserve it," Jack replied mildly; he was

breathing heavily, but he wasn't winded. "But you can't answer questions if you're dead."

"You calculating bast..." Gideon tried to struggle up, fury in his eyes, but he was too dizzy, and in too much pain, and he finally lost consciousness.

Jack looked down at him thoughtfully, shaking his head a little. Then he wiped his sword and sheathed it, before kneeling down beside Gideon. It was only then, as Charity made a slight sound, that he turned and discovered her presence.

She was still holding the pistol before her, though she'd lowered it so that it was pointed at the ground. She was deathly pale, and when she looked at Jack her eyes hardly focused; it was almost as if she didn't recognise him. It had taken so much effort for her to block Jack out of her thoughts and concentrate only on Gideon that now she was finding it equally difficult to return to normal.

Jack stood up and crossed swiftly to her side. Her hold on the pistol was so fierce that it was only with difficulty that he took it from her and laid it on the desk.

"Charity, it's all right now," he said.

She looked at him uncomprehendingly, her eyes dark with remembered fear and reaction, and he put his hands on her shoulders.

"Charity! It's over!" He shook her slightly.

She stared at him a moment longer, then her eyes cleared and she began to tremble.

"Oh, my God!" She put both hands up to cover her face and leant against him.

He put his arms round her and she began to cry.

Jack drew her closer, speaking in a low, soothing voice— but knowing she wasn't listening to him. She needed time to recover, and he gave it to her. Perhaps he needed some time himself. It had been a hard fight, made harder by the fact that he had never wanted to kill Gideon. In that respect, Gideon had always held the advantage; because Jack had had his own reasons for fighting, and the death of Gideon was not the victory he sought.

At last Charity became aware of where she was. She could feel the touch of Jack's hand on her hair, and the warmth of his body against hers as he continued to support most of her weight. She felt his lips brush her hair, and felt a renewed flutter in her breast, but this time it wasn't caused by fear.

"Charity," he said softly.

She looked up, shyly, but quite openly.

"You shouldn't have come," he said. "It was a crazy thing to do."

"I had to," she said simply. "It's my house; besides—"

"Riversleigh! Where the devil are you, man?" roared Sir Humphrey from outside.

There was the sound of running footsteps on the gravel and the next minute Alan burst into the house, followed by Charles.

"Sir, where...?" Alan checked on the threshold of the library, stunned by the evidence of violence before him.

"Ah, Alan," said Jack calmly, guiding Charity to a chair. "You must learn to be less impetuous. Now you're here, you can bind up my...victim. It would be most inconvenient if he bled to death!"

"Yes, sir." The manservant hastened to obey, rather crestfallen at Jack's remark, but when he saw Gideon he swung round in surprise. "Sir! It's..."

"I know," said Jack quietly. "I want him alive, Alan."

For a moment their eyes met and held, then Alan looked down. "Yes, sir."

Jack smiled faintly. "Where's Sir Humphrey?" he asked.

"He's coming, my lord," Charles replied, dragging his eyes from Gideon's recumbent form. "We caught a *woman*."

"Yes, I thought you might," said Jack. "I think you'd better fetch some linen and some warm water."

"You mean, you knew it was a trick?" Alan demanded, looking up from Gideon and quite forgetting himself in his indignation. "Why didn't you stop us...sir?" he added as an afterthought.

"Of course he couldn't stop you," Charity said. She wasn't fully recovered, but she was more than capable of holding up her end of any conversation. In fact, for some reason she felt better than she had done for a long time. "It was only because you all ran out that *he*," she nodded at Gideon, "came in. And that was the whole point."

Jack glanced at her, amusement in his eyes. Once again she had proved herself to be far from lacking in wit, and there were a number of questions he wanted to ask her— but now was not the time.

Sir Humphrey arrived, followed by the other two men, dragging a girl between them. She was struggling half-heartedly, but they had no difficulty in restraining her.

"Where are you taking me?" she demanded. "You ain't got no right to do this to me. I ain't done nothing wrong."

"Well, you may be correct," Jack agreed, apparently unconvinced. "I'll leave it up to Sir Humphrey to decide that point. In the meantime you might tell us why you were creating such a disturbance."

"*He* told me to do it." She jerked her head at Gideon. "He told me it was for a joke, and I'd earn some money if I did it well. Doesn't look as if I'm going to get paid now, does it?"

"No, I think not," said Jack. "In fact, it has been an extremely unprofitable evening for you, hasn't it? In the circumstances, I think the best way for you to help yourself will be for you to help us—don't you, Sir Humphrey?''

''Yes,'' the magistrate grunted. Strictly speaking, he should have been the one conducting this interrogation, but he didn't object to Jack's taking charge. He'd already seen Gideon and he knew now that he had been tricked. He was angry with himself, but he was too fair-minded to resent Jack for having been less gullible.

''You mean, you'll let me go if I answer your questions?'' the girl demanded.

''Possibly.'' Jack made no promises, but on the whole the girl thought it would probably be wisest to do as he wanted.

''How did you meet our friend?'' he asked.

''He was staying at my father's inn.''

''Alone?''

''No, he had a servant with him. The man's hurt.'' The girl looked at Jack with appraising eyes. ''Is that what you wanted to know?''

''How badly?'' Jack ignored her question.

''Bad enough to be laid up in bed, but he won't die,'' she replied scornfully.

''Did he explain how he'd been hurt?'' Jack asked.

''Footpads, *he* said.'' Once more she was referring to Gideon. ''He said they were held up on Horsham Common.'' The girl watched Jack suspiciously.

''And you believed him?''

''Why shouldn't I?'' she demanded belligerently. ''It happens all the time.''

Jack smiled. ''Is the wounded man still at the inn?'' he asked.

''Was when I left. Where would he be going?''

''Where indeed?'' Jack murmured. ''How long have they been at the inn?''

"A week, maybe a little longer. Can I go now?"

"No. Tonight you stay here. In the morning you can show us the way to your father's inn." Jack looked at Sir Humphrey as he spoke, and the magistrate nodded.

"Have you any other questions you wish to ask, my lord?" he asked.

Jack shook his head. Sir Humphrey smiled grimly and turned to the two men who were still standing on either side of the girl.

"Take her to the kitchen and guard her," he ordered. "What are we going to do with him?" he added, looking at Gideon, who was now being tended by both Alan and Charles.

"He'd better stay here," said Charity firmly. "There's no point in moving him. Beside, he's got to answer some questions, and the quicker he's able to do so, the better."

"Quite, quite." Sir Humphrey nodded his agreement. Then he looked at her as if he was registering her presence for the first time. "What the devil—?"

"Is there a bed ready for Gideon?" Jack interrupted, addressing himself to Charles.

"No, sir," the man answered; he seemed rather puzzled. "We didn't know he was coming."

There was a moment of silence as the assembled company absorbed this piece of information.

"Come on, Charles, I'll tell you what I want you to do," said Charity at last.

She was grateful that Jack had intervened before Sir Humphrey could begin interrogating *her,* but she couldn't help thinking he was amusing himself at their expense. There was certainly a distinctly humourous glint in his eyes as he briefly met her gaze.

Chapter Fourteen

Jack and Sir Humphrey were playing cards in the library when Charity finally rejoined them. She had arranged rooms for everyone who needed them, and supervised the bandaging of Gideon's wound. In fact, for someone who wasn't even supposed to be there, she thought she'd been very useful.

Jack looked up and smiled as she came into the room. Sir Humphrey looked up too, but he frowned.

"Now, miss," he began, "perhaps you'll explain exactly what you're doing here."

"It's my house," she said, just as she had done earlier to Jack.

"It's your mother's house, or it is until the end of February," said Sir Humphrey precisely. "And, in any case, you had no business interfering in such a matter. Good God, girl! You might have been hurt. It might have been you we heard screaming! How would I have faced Mrs Mayfield then?"

"But it wasn't me," said Charity calmly. "Sir Humphrey, if someone had told you Leydon House was about to be burgled, would you have stayed behind and let someone else protect it for you?"

"The case is entirely different," Sir Humphrey protested. He'd intended to give Charity a good scold, but somehow the conversation wasn't going as he'd planned. "If you were my daughter…" he began.

She laughed. "I dare say you're glad I'm not," she said.

"No, m'dear," he said unexpectedly. "I would have been very happy to have had you as a daughter." He put down his cards and stood up.

"I'll talk to you in the morning, Riversleigh," he said to Jack. "We must go and see the man at the inn, and we must also decide what we're going to do about the fellow we've got upstairs. There are one or two things I don't understand…and I wonder…" he frowned, looking around the library "…perhaps we did ought to see if there's anything here. No doubt it's nonsense, but after all this it would be a pity if we missed something."

Jack glanced at Charity, but she was looking uncharacteristically subdued—stunned, even. And she certainly didn't show any signs of wanting to enter the conversation.

"You're quite right, sir, we should discuss it," he said, and stood up, offering Sir Humphrey his hand.

"We achieved a lot tonight," he said. "I enjoyed working with you."

Sir Humphrey flushed. "I'm not sure I was much help, or only by accident," he replied. "But it's been a pleasure. You're a man after my own heart, my lord. It was a lucky day for all of us when you inherited Riversleigh." He shook Jack's hand vigorously.

"Thank you, Sir Humphrey." Jack smiled. "I had my doubts at first. I was bred to be a banker, not a baron. But I think it will work out."

"I'm sure of it," the magistrate replied emphatically. "I'm sure of it. Goodnight, m'dear." He glanced at Charity.

"Oh, goodnight, Sir Humphrey." She roused herself to reply. "Thank you for your help."

"No thanks necessary," said Sir Humphrey earnestly. "I'll be indebted to you for the rest of my life. I'll always be at your service."

He took her hand in both of his for a moment, then he nodded to Jack and left the library. A few seconds later they heard him stub his toe against the bottom stair and swear under his breath. Then he climbed the stairs and the library was silent again.

Charity stood up uncertainly, not sure whether she should stay—or go to bed. She couldn't forget that on the previous evening Jack had seemed so anxious for her to leave. She glanced at him shyly and saw that, although he was smiling at her, there was an uncharacteristic gravity in his expression. Suddenly she was afraid of what he would say.

"I must go…" She started to move towards the door.

"Not yet." He was still some distance away from her, but his voice stopped her almost as effectively as his touch might have done.

She turned slowly, looking up at him with surprised and almost fearful eyes.

"How long were you waiting outside?" he asked.

She blinked; that had been the last thing she'd expected him to say and for a moment she could hardly frame a coherent reply.

"Oh, a couple of hours, I think," she said at last.

"You must have been cold." He had come to stand right in front of her and now she had to tip her head back to meet his eyes.

"Not really," she murmured. "I had my cloak, there's no frost…"

"You shouldn't have come." He lifted a hand to brush a stray tendril of hair from her face, and she saw that his grey eyes were darker than usual. "Sir Humphrey was right. It could have been you we heard screaming, and if it had been…"

For the first time, Jack's voice faltered, and at last Charity realised that it was retrospective fear for her that had briefly quenched his customary humour.

The past twenty-four hours had been filled with so much anxiety and worry that her sudden insight left her feeling quite weak with happiness. She had hoped that she was important to Jack—and now she could see in his eyes that she was. It was true she still didn't understand everything he had said, or done—and, most of all, she still didn't understand why he had seemed so anxious to be rid of her on the previous evening—but at last she could no longer doubt that he cared deeply for her.

With no other thought than the need to reassure him that she had come to no harm, she reached out to touch the velvet of his coat, and smiled up at him.

"There was no need to be afraid for me," she murmured. "It was not I who deliberately put myself into danger. Why *did* you do it?"

Jack didn't answer; he might not even have heard the question. His whole awareness was dominated by the way she had reached out to him, so naturally and unself-consciously. Could she—would she—have done that if he had frightened her on the previous night?

He remembered the relief he had seen in her eyes when he'd arrived after Owen had been shot, and her absolute confidence that he would know how to deal with the situation. And he remembered how she had allowed him to take her in his arms to comfort her after she had seen him fight Gideon. There had been no indication then that she did not welcome his presence—or his touch. So why had she seemed so horrified when she had wrenched herself out of his arms last night?

She was standing only inches away from him and he desperately wanted to crush her against him—yet he was afraid that if he did so he would see the expression in her eyes change to fear or disgust.

"Last night…" he began, and saw the colour flood into her cheeks at his words.

She dropped her arms awkwardly to her sides and moved away from him, afraid of what he might say. "I love you, but I'm already committed to someone else"—would that be it? Could she bear to hear it?

"I didn't mean to frighten you," he said, half lifting a hand towards her and then letting it fall. "You must know that the last thing I'd ever want to do is hurt you… I don't think I shall easily forget the look of horror in your eyes," he finished, his manner far less assured than usual.

"Frighten me!" Charity turned back to him in amazement. "You didn't frighten me. I told you so at the time— I think." To be honest, she wasn't entirely sure what they had said to each other; her memories were rather confused.

"But you seemed so appalled!" he protested, relief and excitement flaring through him as he began to realise he might have been mistaken in her feelings.

"Did I?" She sighed, and glanced down for a moment, then looked up and met his eyes. "Perhaps I did, but not because of anything you'd done. It was just a tri-fle…unexpected. You didn't frighten me," she said again, very earnestly.

Very soon she would have to tell him about Owen, but not yet, not while so much else was still unsettled between them.

"Unexpected?" Jack repeated softly, reassured as much by her manner and the glow in her eyes as by her words.

"It was certainly that. After all, despite your very flattering proposal, when I first came into Sussex I had no intention of getting married."

His hands were on her waist and he began to draw her towards him.

"And now?" Charity whispered, his words thrilling her almost as much as his touch. Did he mean…?

"Now I think it's a pity I didn't know you better when you first put the question." He paused, smiling down at her, his eyes filled with a gentle, teasing light. "I might have given you a different answer," he said.

"Might?" she questioned gently.

"Well…" for a moment longer he continued to tease her, then his expression changed, and she saw a new light blazing in his eyes "…if I had known you better," he said, "I would have pre-empted your proposal with one of my own."

She smiled, joy filling her at his words.

"I'm so glad," she murmured and, as he bent his head to kiss her, she closed her eyes and gave herself up shamelessly to his embrace.

He had lost his earlier unaccustomed hesitancy, and she could feel the strength in his arms as he held her against him, claiming her for his own—now and forever.

Then he relaxed slightly, without releasing her, and let his hand glide leisurely down her spine from the nape of her neck to the small of her back. Even through the fabric of her riding habit his touch could ignite a fire deep within her soul, and she clung more tightly to him, feeling his lips on her cheek, her eyelids and her hair. She was lost in a world in which only they existed, and when he put his hand up to the lace at her throat she made no protest. He held her slightly away from him and slowly unbuttoned first her jacket, and then her waistcoat. Then he paused, a question in his eyes, and Charity smiled and drew his head down to hers again.

"I wasn't afraid, I'm not afraid," she murmured, her lips moving delightfully against his.

For a moment longer Jack made no effort to restrain his desire, but then he lifted his head and drew back slightly, though his hands still rested on either side of her waist, within the folds of her waistcoat.

Charity sighed; she was still feeling dazed with passion, yet it took only an instant for her to read the intention in his eyes, and regret and relief mingled within her as she finally understood what had prompted some of his actions on the previous night.

"Now you're going to send me to bed," she predicted. "It's not…I mean, I don't…" she blushed and glanced down, then looked up again, an expression of shy, almost rueful humour in her eyes.

"People have been telling me for years that I'm unlady-like," she said, "but I never knew before how true it was! Last night you were being a gentleman, but I thought…"

Her voice trailed away, but Jack had understood and a wave of relief washed over him as he realised that one more misunderstanding had been cleared up.

He smiled. "That particular aspect of the situation hadn't occurred to me," he admitted. "But, if you must know, you make it very difficult for me to be…a gentleman. You see?"

As he spoke his hands drifted higher until they were resting just below her breasts and, instinctively, Charity leant towards him—then she leant back again.

"I shouldn't… Oh, dear, am I too forward?" she asked, with such a comical look of anxiety on her face that he nearly laughed.

But he had heard the anxiety in her voice, and he chose instead to reassure her.

"No." He drew her towards him until their bodies were just touching, in subtle, tantalising proximity. "Sincerity in your dealings with others is always a virtue—you could never lose my respect because you don't play conventional games."

"Sincerity?" she murmured as he kissed her again. He was still holding her no closer than he had been a moment before, but the feel of his lips on hers, and the delicate tracery of his hands beneath her waistcoat, along her sides and across her back, filled her with trembling, shimmering pleasure.

It was hard to pull away, but she knew that she had to. She had to tell Jack about Owen. It never occurred to her that she might terminate her engagement without Jack's ever knowing about it. She had to tell the truth, and she had to tell him now. She should probably have told him sooner.

She stepped reluctantly away from him and, when he tried to take her back into his arms, she braced her hands against his chest, holding him off.

"Wait, there's something I have to tell you," she said. "It's not...I mean, I'm going to do something about it as soon as I can, but..."

"What is it?" Jack's smile faded as he saw the expression in Charity's eyes.

"Owen thinks I'm betrothed to him," she said baldly.

For a moment there was silence as Jack stared at her in disbelief.

"Good God!" he said at last. "I never thought you'd bring it off!"

"You mean, you don't mind?" Charity gasped in confusion and broke away from him.

"Well, yes, actually," he said quietly, and from his voice she knew she had shaken him more than he wanted to admit. "I hadn't thought… When did it happen?"

"At the party," she said sadly, regretting more than ever what had happened. He had said earlier that hurting her was the last thing he ever wanted to do—and now it seemed that it was she who had hurt him. "I didn't even understand what Owen was asking at first!" she continued. "I wasn't really listening—it was just after you'd gone to get me some lemonade. I wasn't really…" She broke off, looking at Jack. "Something had happened, hadn't it?" she said.

"To me, certainly," he replied, his calm manner not entirely hiding his underlying tension. "I nearly kissed you in front of all the other guests! You were—you are so…" He smiled almost apologetically at her. "I had to leave you," he said. "I'd have caused another scandal if I hadn't! But that was when Owen asked you?"

"I was trying to make him go away," she said. "I didn't want to talk to him just then—but I realised what he was asking, and it was what I'd said I was going to do, so…"

"So you went ahead and did it," Jack finished for her.

The first stab of pain he'd felt when she'd told him what she'd done was easing. He couldn't blame her for feeling bewildered by everything that had happened, and in the circumstances it wasn't surprising that she'd stuck to her original plan when everything else must have seemed so uncertain and confusing.

"I knew I'd made a mistake almost immediately," she said quickly. "Please believe me. I was going to tell him this morning, but he was gone before I woke up, and after that…" She sighed as she remembered what had happened to Owen. "Oh, I do hope he'll be all right."

"He will be," said Jack quietly.

He no longer sounded upset, but it suddenly occurred to

Charity that perhaps, once again, she had been less than tactful.

"I didn't mean…" She looked at him anxiously. "It's just that I've known Owen so long. I don't…"

"No, I know." He smiled at her. "Mind you, if it had been Edward you'd accidentally found yourself betrothed to I might have been less understanding."

"Edward!" she exclaimed. "Why…?" Then her lips curved deliciously and she smiled up into his eyes. "Jealous, my lord? You can't be jealous of Edward."

She was standing very close to him and she lifted her hands and laid them against his chest. She had done the same thing before, to hold him off, but now she let her hands slide sensuously across the black velvet of his coat until they were linked behind his head.

"He *was* your first choice of husband," Jack pointed out, resisting the urge to put his arms around her.

"True," Charity admitted. "But in the past few days what I'm looking for in a husband seems to have changed. I used to be so sensible too," she added. "It's a sad fact that you've turned me into a heedless and frivolous woman."

As she spoke she leant against him, pressing her slim body against his until his resolution began to disintegrate. He let her draw his head down until their lips met, and lost himself in the passion of their kiss, his hands moulding her against him.

Then he sighed and held her away from him.

"This will not do," he said.

"You're not going to send me to bed!" she protested.

"I don't want to, but I've got to get some sleep too," he pointed out mildly. "Besides, I'm afraid this business isn't over yet, and we'll need our wits about us when we question Gideon in the morning. So I really think—"

"Gideon!" Charity exclaimed, the other events of the evening suddenly recalled to her mind. "Of course, that's what I was going to ask you! How could I have forgotten? How do you come to know the thief? And why did you fight him?" she demanded, ignoring Jack's smile at the first part of what she said. "You didn't have to. All you had to do was wait for the others, but instead you let him goad you into nearly getting yourself killed!"

"No, that's not quite what happened." With an effort Jack put Charity away from him, and guided her to a chair. Then he sat on the edge of the table, one foot braced on the floor, the other swinging freely. He felt almost bereft now that she was no longer in his arms, but rational conversation wasn't really possible when they were too close to each other.

"It's what it looked like." Charity looked at him squarely, puzzlement and something like disapproval in her eyes.

At the memory of what had happened, the fear she had felt at the time rose within her, chilling her and making her almost angry with him. It seemed so wanton to have deliberately put himself into danger.

"You think I let my temper get the better of me?" he asked, sensing her change of mood. "That I fought him to prove myself because he had belittled me?"

"N-no. I don't know," she stammered, startled by the momentary, uncharacteristic harshness in his voice.

"I'm sorry." The tension left him and he smiled crookedly. "And, in a way, perhaps you're right. But it was the end of something—not the beginning."

"I don't understand."

"We attended the same school once, a long time ago," Jack explained. He was gazing into the fire, remembering, and Charity suspected that, for the moment, he had almost forgotten her presence.

"He's two years older than I am, and at that age two years makes a lot of difference."

"What happened?"

"We fought a duel."

"At school! How old were you?"

"I was fourteen, he was sixteen. He won."

"But why? For God's sake!" Charity exclaimed. "They can't have permitted duelling at school!"

"No, of course not. It was…unusual, even at Westminster." Sudden amusement flared in Jack's eyes, and just as quickly died.

"It's a simple story," he said. "It happened because one of the masters temporarily had a large supply of money in his quarters with which he intended to buy a home for himself and his mother. His elder brother had inherited the family home, you see, and his wife didn't want her mother-in-law living with her."

A log collapsed, hissing in the hearth, and Jack went over to tend the fire.

"Nobody knew he had the money," he said as he stood up. "Except Gideon. I don't know how Gideon found out, but he has a way of hearing things. He stole it."

"Then what happened?" Charity demanded; she was watching Jack intently.

"One of the servants was blamed. There was evidence against him. That was Gideon's doing. He always liked to cover his bets. But I didn't believe it." Jack's smile was slightly twisted. "And, being young and impetuous, I thought it was up to me to do something about it. Besides, I had no proof, so no one would have believed my accusations."

"But what about the money?" Charity asked. "If Gideon had it, the servant couldn't have had it. So how could they prove he'd taken it?''

"It was assumed he had a confederate," Jack explained. "They were going to hang him. And the master didn't have his money, and his mother didn't have a home. So I confronted Gideon. I knew where the money was by then, but I had a misplaced notion that he deserved a chance to put right what he'd done. After all, he was supposed to be a gentleman—he'd taunted me with the fact often enough.''

He moved restlessly over to the table and swept up the cards that were still lying where they'd been left in the middle of the game Sir Humphrey had interrupted earlier.

Charity watched him riffle through the cards, shuffling them with quick movements. She didn't think he was aware of what he was doing; he was just giving himself time to think before he carried on with his story.

She was beginning to see the obstacles he must have encountered all through his life. He was the grandson of both a baron and a man who had begun life as penniless apprentice, but he did not completely belong to the world of either. Perhaps there was nowhere he felt entirely at home.

Gideon had mocked Jack for being a money-lender's son, and he must have been referring to Richard, who had chosen to become a banker rather than continue to live at odds with the late Lord Riversleigh. Jack was proud of his father, she knew that, but he must have been hearing such damning comments for most of his life.

She began to understand why he had been so sympathetic to her own fear of gossip, and to see why he had been so moved by her defence of him at the Leydons' rout. He too must have spent a great deal of his life defending himself against the unkind or unfounded judgements of others, and there must have been times when he had held to his principles at considerable cost to himself.

It did not occur to Charity that she had done the same; she was too preoccupied by her sudden increased understanding of Jack.

"You confronted Gideon," she prompted gently when he showed no sign of continuing.

"Yes." He put the cards down on the table and turned back to face her. In the flickering candle-light she could see his expression was tense.

"He chose to assume I'd challenge him. Naturally he accepted. And, since I'd issued the challenge, he had the choice of weapon. He chose swords."

"So you fought," said Charity. It was a statement, not a question. Even if he hadn't said as much earlier she would have had no doubt of it.

"I thought he was going to kill me," said Jack. "I don't know if he intended to or not, but in the end he just put his sword through my side and stood laughing at me. That was all."

"No, it wasn't," said Charity. "What happened about the master and his money and the servant?"

"Oh, yes." Jack roused himself from his rather painful recollections. "Well, Gideon and I were discovered before he had time to leave. There was no scandal—too many of the people concerned wanted to hush up what had happened. But before I completely lost consciousness I was able to say where the money was, and who had taken it. I was ill for several days—the wound became infected—but when I finally regained my senses I found that Gideon had been sent down and the servant exonerated. I left school at the same time to take up my apprenticeship. I don't think anyone was sorry to see me go."

"They should have been," said Charity. "Particularly the servant and the master."

"I think they were both grateful," said Jack. "Alan certainly was—he insisted on coming with me."

"Alan!" Charity exclaimed. "Good heavens!"

Jack smiled. "There's a happy ending for you," he said.

"I should say so!" she agreed. "And for you?"

"And for me." Jack frowned thoughtfully. "For a long time I thought I hated Gideon, then I realised it was myself I was angry with. I haven't seen him for years—I didn't know he was in Sussex. But when I saw him tonight I wanted the chance to re-fight the duel. I'm a fool, you see." He looked at her steadily. "I had to prove to myself that I was no longer afraid of him, that he is no longer better than I am."

"He never was," said Charity. "He was just older than you—older and unscrupulous."

"Don't you think I should have known that, and let it rest?" Jack asked. "It would have been the sensible thing to do, and I would have saved you a lot of anxiety!"

It would be a long time before he forgot the look in her eyes when he'd turned and discovered she'd seen the duel.

"It might not have been the right thing," she replied. "And now it really is over. Sometimes it's not enough just to know; we have to prove it to ourselves. You wouldn't believe the number of trees I've fallen out of, and the number of ponds I've fallen into, to prove I can do what I say I can. Owen used to dare me," she explained.

"Yes, I think you two would make a fatal combination," Jack agreed. "Climbing trees is one thing; marriage is another!"

"I know I made a mistake, but I feel badly enough about it as it is!" she exclaimed. "You don't have to rub it in."

He raised his eyebrow, a distinct gleam in his grey eyes.

"And I still don't really know who Gideon is," she said hastily before he could speak. "He must have a name and a family. What are they going to say when they find out he's going to be on trial for his life? What is it?"

Jack was looking at her with a strange expression on his face.

"No, you don't know, do you?" he said slowly. "And, what with one thing and another, I haven't thought to mention it. His name won't mean much to you—it's Ralph Gideon. But you might be interested to learn that he's Lord Ashbourne's nephew."

Chapter Fifteen

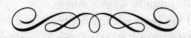

"He's awake," said Charity. "We can talk to him now."

It was morning, and Sir Humphrey and Jack were just finishing their breakfast when she came to tell them that Gideon was conscious.

He had been left all night in the care of Alan and one of Sir Humphrey's men, though in fact he hadn't been in a condition to escape. But Jack knew Gideon was both cunning and vicious, and he had no intention of underestimating him.

"We?" Sir Humphrey frowned. "I really don't think it's appropriate for you to be present, m'dear."

"No, but I'm going to be," she replied inflexibly. "This matter concerns me more closely than anyone, and I want to know what he's doing here, and what part Lord Ashbourne has played in the whole affair."

Sir Humphrey stared at her worriedly. There was something implacable in her determination. He was becoming more aware than ever of her uncommon strength of will, and it almost frightened him. He didn't know what she would do next.

"I don't think it will do any harm if she's present," said

Jack quietly. "And she certainly has a right to be. Shall we go up?"

He opened the door for the others and held it as they passed out of the room. Sir Humphrey looked up at him anxiously and he nodded reassuringly.

Gideon's eyes were closed when they entered the room in which he lay, but there was a crease of pain in his forehead, and he certainly wasn't asleep.

He turned his head at their approach and his expression was hostile. He wasn't going to answer questions willingly; perhaps he wasn't going to answer them at all.

"Hiding behind a woman's skirts," he sneered, and Sir Humphrey started forward angrily.

Jack caught him by the arm and held him back.

"How did you know there was something in the library?" he asked almost pleasantly.

"I had a dream," Gideon replied insolently.

Jack smiled. "So did I," he said. "It told me you're going to hang."

Gideon's eyes narrowed. He had certainly committed enough capital offences for that to be the case, but he still thought he could evade the rope.

"No, I won't," he said. "Do you think my uncle is going to let me hang? He has the ear of the King. Even if I'm convicted, I'll be pardoned."

Sir Humphrey opened his mouth to speak. It was his son that Gideon had nearly murdered, and he was angry. Then he felt Jack's grip on his arm tighten and he suddenly decided to leave the questioning to Riversleigh.

"Perhaps you *might* be pardoned, even acquitted," Jack said calmly. "But only if you survive long enough to stand your trial. And there are so many misfortunes that can befall a man—particularly when he's already injured. The wound may become infected, or you may fall and open it again. It's so easy to bleed to death.''

Gideon stared at him, understanding dawning in his angry eyes.

''You wouldn't *dare!*''

Jack smiled coldly and Gideon began to feel doubtful. He knew that neither Jack nor Alan had any cause to love him—perhaps Jack really would carry out his threat.

''If I answer your questions, will you tell my uncle where I am?'' he demanded.

''I think that could be arranged,'' Jack agreed.

''What do you want to know?''

''What made you think there was something hidden in the library?''

''I found some papers in my uncle's desk. He should have locked them up, but on one occasion he was interrupted before he could. He doesn't know I saw them.''

''I don't suppose you'd be here if he did,'' said Jack. ''What did the papers say?''

''They were notes Uncle made. I think he'd taken them from a diary. That didn't interest me. I was only concerned with finding the pendant. It was there, wasn't it?'' He looked at Jack.

''Why did you want it?'' Jack asked, ignoring Sir Humphrey's amazed gasp.

''Because it's worth a fortune, you fool,'' Gideon said savagely.

''But, when you realised there was a trap set for you last night, you must have suspected it had already been found. You took a risk; you must have wanted it badly,'' Jack said.

''That's none of your business,'' Gideon replied sullenly.

''It wasn't. It is now,'' said Jack implacably. ''Anything you do is my business now.''

The two men stared at each other, they might have been alone, for all the notice either of them took of Charity and Sir Humphrey. The balance of power had changed, but their mutual dislike remained unaltered.

"Perhaps it was because you wanted a bartering point with Lord Ashbourne," Jack suggested. "I'd heard he'd finally had the good sense to disown you. But everyone knows he collects such things."

Charity looked at him sharply. She didn't entirely understand what was happening, but it was becoming clear to her that Lord Ashbourne lay at the back of everything that had happened.

"What *does* Lord Ashbourne want?" she demanded harshly. "Why were those notes in his desk in the first place?"

Gideon turned his head on the pillow and looked at her.

"He wants the pendant," he said softly. "Any way he can get it. He nearly cheated your fool of a father out of a fortune he didn't even know he possessed! But if it hadn't been for *him*," Gideon looked at Jack with hatred, "*I* would have got there first."

Charity's eyes burned with fierce indignation and anger. She was standing on the opposite side of the bed to the others and, as she took a step towards Gideon, Sir Humphrey tried to intervene.

"M'dear, I think this is a matter…"

She looked up at him and as he met her gaze he faltered into silence.

"What did he do to Papa?" she said, her voice low and dangerous.

"You don't think my uncle normally demeans himself by playing cards with country bumpkins, do you?" Gideon said scornfully. "As I said before, your father was a fool."

"Gideon!" The sound of Jack's voice was so compelling that both Gideon and Charity were startled.

Gideon turned his head towards Jack and began to regret the petty revenge he had taken on Charity. At that moment he was convinced that Jack was going to carry out his earlier threat, and he was afraid.

"Be careful," said Jack with dangerous softness. "Be very careful."

Beads of sweat stood out on Gideon's brow and upper lip, and his mouth was so dry that he couldn't speak.

"So, let us be clear," said Jack, after a moment. "Lord Ashbourne tried to trick Mr Mayfield out of possession of the pendant—and you tried to get hold of it first so that you could use it to force your uncle to acknowledge you again. Have I that correctly?"

Gideon nodded, unable to say a word.

"You'll hang, Gideon. In the circumstances, I don't think your uncle is going to lift a finger for you."

"But the scandal," Gideon croaked. That was how he'd always escaped the consequences of his actions in the past, right from the moment when he'd almost killed Jack. Lord Ashbourne didn't care for scandal.

"We'll see," said Jack. "Alan!" He summoned his servant. "Watch him!"

"Yes, sir." Alan looked at Gideon with dislike.

"Charity," said Jack quietly. She looked at him as if she didn't know who he was, but when he held out his hand imperatively she walked over to him and allowed him to guide her out of the room.

Sir Humphrey, still too staggered to think of anything to say, followed them downstairs.

"We must send someone to the inn to see the wounded servant", Jack said as he closed the library door.

"What? Good God! I'd quite forgotten the fellow! What a head you have," Sir Humphrey exclaimed.

"I don't think what we've just heard has come as such a surprise to me as it has to you," Jack said apologetically. "I've had my suspicions for some time. Though I admit I hadn't guessed that Gideon was involved."

He was looking at Charity as he spoke. She seemed to be in a daze, and he knew that she had not been prepared. He took her hand and led her to a chair. She sat down obediently, but she hardly seemed to know that she wasn't alone. Her whole awareness was taken up by the sudden and unexpected knowledge that her father had been cheated out of Hazelhurst—and out of an inheritance he hadn't known he had.

Until that moment she had felt more exasperation than sympathy for the situation in which her father had found himself. She had been angry with Mr Mayfield for what she had seen as his folly. But now she knew he had been the victim of another man's duplicity, and the full force of her rage and dislike was directed towards Lord Ashbourne. *He* had caused all the misery and pain her family had suffered in the last year.

"Suspicions!" Sir Humphrey was still preoccupied by what they had learnt from Gideon, and by the amazing notion that Jack seemed to have anticipated it. "And a pendant? You said you'd found a pendant?"

"The night before last. It was hidden in a cavity behind the bookshelves. It's by Hilliard," Jack said, his eyes still on Charity.

But Sir Humphrey had never heard of the miniaturist and he didn't care who the pendant was by.

"You mean that, when we were discussing it yesterday, you knew all the time that there was really treasure here?" he demanded.

"It was my fault," said Charity distantly. She was looking pale and almost unnaturally calm. "When Jack first showed it to me I didn't want to tell anyone until I'd decided what to do with it."

"And then events rather overtook us," Jack continued. "I'm sorry, Sir Humphrey."

"Well, I'm not sure that I blame you," the magistrate confessed. "All this is beyond my experience. I wouldn't have taken that stuttering fool's ramblings seriously. Is that when you first started to be suspicious?"

"That's when my initial nebulous doubts were confirmed," Jack replied. "And it was also the point at which it became obvious that Lord Ashbourne must be involved in some way."

Charity looked up at that. "You mean, you *knew* he was behind everything?" she said. "Why didn't you tell me?"

"I did try, at least once," Jack said. "But we were interrupted and the subject never arose again."

"I don't understand," she said. "When did you try to tell me?"

"It was after I'd first shown you the pendant," Jack explained. "We were discussing my plan to trap the thief and I said we wouldn't have to wait long, that he'd have to make his move within the next two weeks. I was just about to tell you why when Sir Humphrey arrived."

"I still don't see…" She frowned; she didn't seem to be thinking as clearly as usual.

Jack took her hand.

"In two weeks, in less than two weeks' time now, Hazelhurst will belong to Lord Ashbourne," he said gently. "The stuttering thief said they had to find the pendant— only he called it the treasure—quickly, within that time period. But that amount of haste could only be necessary if the new owner knew what they were looking for. They had to find it before he arrived.''

''I see.'' She took a deep breath. ''I've been a fool.''

For a moment she frowned distantly into the fire; then she stood up in sudden decision.

''I'm going to London,'' she announced. ''I thought when we caught the thief this business would be ended, but it isn't. Gideon was only a distraction; Lord Ashbourne is the real villain. I'm going to confront him.''

''But you can't...'' Sir Humphrey began, confused and appalled by the speed at which events were overtaking him. ''Wait!''

Charity was already on her way to the door when Jack seized her arm and swung her round to face him.

''What are you going to say to the Earl when you meet him?'' he demanded.

''I'm going to tell him what we know. I'm going to ask him why he did it—and I'm going to make sure he never does anything like this again. Ever.''

Charity's eyes burned with a greater rage and a more implacable sense of purpose than she had ever before felt. She was impatient of restraint and she tried to pull her arm away from Jack's grasp in her haste to start for London.

''How?'' Jack put his hands on her shoulders and almost shook her. ''How are you going to make sure he never does it again? The law can't help you—I don't think the Earl has done anything illegal. So what are you going to do— shoot him?''

He had had a horrifying vision of Charity turning up at Lord Ashbourne's house, armed with a pistol and bent on vengeance. He had never seen her so angry. ''Then you'll be the one to hang,'' he finished harshly.

''What do you mean, he didn't do anything illegal?''

Charity demanded. "He cheated Papa. He *stole* Hazel-hurst."

"It's not as simple as that. Gideon was lying to you."

"I don't understand." She stared up at him. The immediacy of her rage had passed, but not her determination. "Are you saying that Lord Ashbourne isn't responsible? You just said he was."

"He is." He met her eyes squarely. They had both forgotten Sir Humphrey's presence. "What he did was immoral—but not illegal. And I don't think you really understand what he *did* do. You think he lured your father into a card game and then cheated him out of a fortune, and ultimately out of his home, don't you?" His eyes bored relentlessly down into hers. "But there's one thing I'm certain of," he continued, "the Earl never cheated in a card game."

"Gideon said he did. Why shouldn't I believe him?" Charity was beginning to feel confused, almost suspicious. She didn't understand why Jack seemed to be defending Lord Ashbourne. She'd expected him to support her, to feel the same outrage that she felt—why was he protecting the Earl?

"Why shouldn't I believe Gideon?" she said again.

"Because he was trying to hurt you," Jack said.

He was desperately trying to make Charity understand what he thought had happened, but he was still haunted by the vision of what she might do if he failed, and in his anxiety for her he was neither as gentle nor as conciliatory as he might have been.

"He had to tell us nearly the truth—he was too afraid of me not to do so. But you spoiled all his plans and he wanted revenge—so he twisted the story just enough so that it would still be believable, but so that it would also cause you the maximum amount of pain. It would amuse him to set you and Ashbourne at each other's throats.''

For a moment there was silence in the library. Then Charity lifted Jack's hands from her shoulders and stepped away from him, deliberately distancing herself from him, and Jack felt a stab of pain at the coldness in her voice.

''Then what do you think did happen?'' she asked.

''I think Lord Ashbourne knew about the pendant, and I think he might well have flattered your father into playing cards with him to get it,'' Jack replied. ''But he didn't cheat. The Earl is a devious, and in many ways an unscrupulous man—but he has his own peculiar code of honour, and he would never cheat. It wouldn't accord with his own image of himself.''

''I don't see that what you have said makes any difference at all,'' Charity said inflexibly. ''I don't care whether he cheated or not. It seems to me that everything that has happened to us has been the Earl's fault. I don't care whether what he did was legal or not. He's not going to get away with it.''

''I didn't say he should get away with it,'' Jack replied. ''I said you should know what you're blaming him for— and what he isn't guilty of.''

Charity looked at him sharply and Jack gave a twisted half-smile in response. He knew she wouldn't welcome what he was about to say, he knew he might even alienate her completely—but he was still afraid of what she might do.

He was also certain that in the long run it would be far better if she didn't persist in blinding herself to some of the more distressing aspects of the situation, though later he wondered if he should have given her more time before he said anything.

''What do you mean?'' Charity demanded, and now there was an underlying hostility in her tone.

For the first time it had dawned on her that Jack and Lord Ashbourne came from the same world—and that they'd known each other for years. What a fool she was! All the time she had been thinking of the Earl as the outsider in her world—but that wasn't how it was. It was *she* who was the outsider in Jack's and Lord Ashbourne's world! No wonder Jack was defending the Earl.

If Jack had known what she was thinking he might have approached the situation differently—but he didn't; and he was still trying to prepare Charity for what she would have to face if she confronted Lord Ashbourne.

''I believe you can blame the Earl for encouraging your father to play cards with him,'' he said slowly. ''But not for forcing him to do so. You can also blame him for having done so with a secret ulterior motive. And you can blame him for having continued the game until Mr Mayfield was twenty thousand pounds in debt—there was always something slightly odd about the fact that your father lost almost exactly the same sum as his estate was worth.''

That was one of the things which had always seemed strange to Jack, even before he had suspected there was anything more sinister behind the debt.

''But you can't blame Lord Ashbourne for not having given your father enough time to repay his debt—he gave him a whole year,'' he continued, even though he knew that Charity might not accept what he was saying. ''Perhaps the Earl thought that by doing so he was giving your father a fair chance to recover himself. Nor can you blame him for Gideon's presence, the Earl certainly wouldn't have permitted that if he'd known anything about it—and, most important of all, you can't blame him for your father's death,'' he finished more gently, because he thought it was that belief which lay at the root of Charity's distress.

She stood, shocked and still. Jack's words washing over her like icy water. She knew he was right about Gideon; the Earl would have been as much a victim of his nephew as she and her mother would have been if Gideon had been successful.

But she couldn't be as dispassionate as Jack apparently was about what the Earl had done. And Mr Mayfield had died so quickly after that bitter card game that in her mind the two events were inextricably linked. She couldn't rid herself of the notion that her father must have been feeling desperately unhappy, despairing even, when he died. Lord Ashbourne might not have caused Mr Mayfield's death, but he was certainly responsible for the distress he must have been feeling at the time.

Jack was watching her closely and he saw the hardening of her purpose in her eyes. She still intended to confront the Earl, and to do so half armed, because she still hadn't accepted one basic, unpleasant fact.

There was one last thing for him to say. He knew that if he did so not only would he hurt her, but she might also never forgive him for it. But he also knew that there were others involved who would be less considerate, and he wanted her to be prepared.

''Your father must always have had a choice,'' he said gently. ''No one, not even the Earl, can force a man to play cards with him against his will.''

To Jack, that was the key to the whole affair. What he believed Lord Ashbourne to have done was immoral, devious and dishonest. But everything he knew about the Earl convinced him that Lord Ashbourne had neither cheated, nor forced Mr Mayfield to play cards with him. So Charity's father must have had a choice—and he had made the wrong one. He was not blameless for what had happened to his family. No man needed to gamble with his home.

But Charity didn't want to hear that: it hurt too much—and it was too close to the truth.

"Why do you keep defending the Earl?" she demanded. She was flushed and breathing rather quickly. "Is he your friend? Yes, of course, he must be. How else could you claim to know so much about him?"

"Charity..." Jack began. He was appalled at the hostility in her eyes.

"I dare say you knew all along what was happening," Charity swept on, ignoring his attempt to speak to her indignation and fury. It was difficult to know whether she really believed what she was saying, but in her own pain and distress she lashed out as hard as she could at Jack.

"No wonder you found everything so amusing, such *country bumpkins* as we are. I dare say his lordship will be very grateful to you for rescuing his pendant—and all the time I thought you were keeping it safe for me. Well, you haven't won yet, my lord. I want it back. You haven't had time to go home; you must still have it."

She held out her hand imperatively.

Jack was very pale, but he didn't say anything. He simply put his hand in his pocket and drew out the box which contained the pendant.

Charity took it and opened it. Jack smiled, rather bitterly, at that.

"It's still there," he said, not angrily, because he wasn't angry. It was too easy for him to understand why she thought as she did—but it still hurt him.

"I had no intention of stealing it—or of delivering it into any hands but yours," he said.

Charity looked up, and for a moment her eyes met his—then she looked away again. Her anger had passed now, but she felt drained and confused. The ground seemed to be shifting beneath her feet, and she turned with relief to Sir Humphrey, who was always the same, and who hated change.

"Will you look after this for me?" she asked. "I don't want to take it to London—something might happen to it."

"Of course, my dear," he said instantly. "But I think you're doing Riversleigh an injustice."

The magistrate hadn't entirely followed everything that had happened, and he wasn't sure if he approved of everything Jack had said—but he also thought Charity had been less than fair.

"Am I?" she looked at Sir Humphrey bleakly. "I don't feel certain of anything any more. Perhaps things will seem clearer when I've seen Lord Ashbourne."

"You can't go to London on your own," said Sir Humphrey gruffly, knowing he'd never be able to persuade her not to go at all. "If you're determined to go I'll come with you."

"Oh, Sir Humphrey!" Charity exclaimed. She could feel tears pricking at the back of her eyes at this evidence of friendship. The magistrate disliked travelling and hated going outside his own county. "Thank you so much, but please don't come," she said. "You know how much you dislike London—and you won't want to leave Owen now. I shall be quite all right."

"My dear, I can't—" Sir Humphrey began.

"I'll escort you to town," said Jack quietly. "You and your mother can come as guests of my mother."

"No," said Charity flatly. "Mama isn't to know anything about this business. You must promise, both of you, not to tell her."

She looked from one man to the other.

Sir Humphrey sighed.

"Very well, my dear," he said.

She looked at Jack.

"And you," she said.

"You have my word," he replied steadily.

"I don't see how it's going to be managed, though," Sir Humphrey protested. "You can't go rushing off to London on your own, or even in Riversleigh's company, without starting a lot of gossip. What's your mother going to say? I really think you ought to let someone go in your stead."

"No," said Charity. "I want to hear the truth for myself, then perhaps things will begin to make sense again."

She was dangerously close to tears; only a supreme effort of will made it possible for her to speak so calmly.

"I don't think there'll be any great difficulty, Leydon," said Jack quickly.

He was still very pale, but his concern now was for Charity. He could feel her distress as if it was his own and he wanted to bring the discussion to an end as soon as possible in the hope that, if something was decided, Charity would begin to feel better.

"We can say that my mother has invited Charity and Mrs Mayfield to visit her, but, since Mrs Mayfield doesn't feel up to travelling at the moment, Charity is to go on ahead—to arrange things. Most people know the Mayfields are planning to move to London; I don't think the news will be too surprising."

"But what about Mrs Mayfield?" Sir Humphrey asked. "Won't she think it odd?"

"Not necessarily." Jack's lips twisted in a wry smile. He was well aware of Mrs Mayfield's matrimonial designs for her daughter, and fairly sure that she wouldn't have any objection to Charity visiting Mrs Riversleigh. "I believe it was her idea that Charity should ask my advice on where they ought to live in London," he said to Sir Humphrey.

"The only problem may be to convince her that she doesn't feel up to the journey at the moment—and I'm sure Charity can manage that."

"Oh, yes," said Charity distantly; she seemed to have dissociated herself from the conversation now. "She hates travelling more than Sir Humphrey. I'll just have to tell her that there's been a lot of rain between here and London. When can we leave?"

"Now, if you like," said Jack calmly. "But it would cause less comment if we set off tomorrow morning. There are several things that need to be arranged."

Charity looked at him and he wondered if she suspected him of deliberately trying to hinder her efforts to see Lord Ashbourne, but if she did, she didn't say anything.

"I must go and speak to Mrs Wendle," she said. "Then I'm going back to Leydon House."

She went out, closing the door behind her, and Jack drew in a deep, slightly ragged breath.

"I take it that that blackguard *isn't* your friend?" said Sir Humphrey quietly.

"No." Jack sat down on the edge of the table. "No, he's no friend of mine."

"Why didn't you tell her?" Sir Humphrey demanded. "Why did you make it sound as if you were protecting him? It was bad enough for her to hear what she did about her father, without it sounding as if her…friends are on the side of her enemy."

The magistrate hadn't been blind to the growing intimacy between Charity and the new Lord Riversleigh; that was partly why he found Jack's attitude so difficult to understand.

"You think I shouldn't have rammed it down her throat that her father shared responsibility for what happened?" Jack said. "You're right, of course. But you don't know the Earl. You have to see things clearly when you deal with him—otherwise he manipulates everything to his own advantage. If Charity marches in and accuses the Earl of forcing Mayfield to play cards with him—or of cheating—the first thing Ashbourne will hit her with is the fact that Mayfield *didn't* have to play. That he was a fool to be flattered by a great man's praise!''

Jack caught himself up. There was no point in justifying what he'd said. He'd been motivated by fear for Charity more than anything else, but he knew he'd handled the situation badly. Ironically, he suspected that if he had cared less he would have done better.

''It's a complicated situation,'' he said more quietly. ''The Mayfields still owe the Earl twenty thousand pounds, and I think the law will favour Ashbourne.''

''But good God, man!'' Sir Humphrey burst out. ''Even if he didn't cheat, he will have obtained Hazelhurst under false pretences—and now we know—''

''As far as we're aware, there were no witnesses to what happened at that card game,'' Jack interrupted. ''And by the time they came to sign the agreement everything seemed to be in order—Mayfield's lawyer certainly thinks so. So do I. I saw the agreement the night this place was burgled and I tidied up for Charity. Ashbourne was very clever; there's no mention of a gambling debt in the agreement—the courts are notoriously reluctant to enforce gambling debts. The agreement merely mentions a loan for a non-specified purpose secured against Hazelhurst. We might be able to overturn it—but it would be a long and costly legal battle.''

''Then they're still going to lose Hazelhurst!'' the magistrate exclaimed, quite horrified by the idea.

''Unless we do something to avert the inevitable,'' said Jack grimly. ''That's what I was trying to explain to Charity, though I'm afraid I didn't do it very well. Righteous anger is a very poor weapon when you're dealing with a man like the Earl.''

"Good God," said Sir Humphrey blankly. "Do you have a better one?"

Jack looked thoughtfully into the fire, and drummed his fingers against the edge of the table.

"I think I may be able to lay my hands on one," he said at last. "This isn't the first time I've had dealings with the Earl. Besides," he glanced up, with the first glint of real humour in his eyes that morning since they'd spoken to Gideon, "I don't imagine any of us care for the idea of having the Earl for our neighbour."

"I should say not!" the magistrate exclaimed. "I hadn't thought of that. He may not be a cheat—to be honest, Mayfield was such a poor card-player that he probably didn't need to be—but he certainly doesn't sound like the kind of man *I'd* care to welcome into the area!"

"I didn't think he would be," Jack murmured, and looked up as Charity came back into the room.

She was still very pale, but quite composed.

"Shall we go?" she asked, looking at Sir Humphrey.

He hesitated for a moment. He wanted to help her in any way he could, but it was in his mind that it would be better if he left her alone with Jack in the hope that they settle their differences.

"I'd be glad to escort you, my dear," he said at last. "But I'm afraid my duty obliges me to go to the inn to see the other scoundrel involved in the house-breaking. I'm sure Riversleigh will be pleased to accompany you."

He took her hand.

"I'm sure everything will turn out all right in the end," he said gruffly. "If there's any way I can help, don't hesitate to ask. And don't fear that I won't keep your mother, and the pendant, safe.''

''Thank you.'' She smiled at him, her eyes glistening.

He squeezed her hand warmly and hurried out of the room, leaving Charity alone with Jack.

''Are you ready to go?'' he asked quietly.

''In a minute.'' She turned away from him and went to stand looking out of the window.

''I'm sorry,'' she said, without looking at him. ''I had no right to accuse you of complicity with Lord Ashbourne.''

''Charity!'' He came towards her.

''No! Don't touch me.'' She turned to face him. ''I believe that you're not working with the Earl—if you had been there would have been no need for you to show me the pendant at all.''

She saw the sudden leap in his eyes and smiled without much humour.

''But there are still too many things I don't understand,'' she said. ''You're a stranger from a world that's foreign to me, a world where all kinds of despicable tricks seem to be acceptable as long as you don't actually break some peculiar code of honour—and I'm not sure I want any part of it. Take me to London, my lord. I accept your help so far because I have to—but after that...''

She didn't finish what she was saying. Instead she walked over to the door, turning to look back at Jack with her hand resting on the door-handle.

''I'm ready to go now,'' she said.

Chapter Sixteen

The carriage jolted uncomfortably towards London, and Charity closed her eyes and tried to sleep. She was tired—she had had so little undisturbed sleep over the past few days—but she couldn't close her mind to the terrible thoughts that tormented her.

She couldn't stop thinking about her father and what he must have felt when he'd realised he had lost everything—and that led her to think about Lord Ashbourne. She had never hated anyone in her life before, but she had no doubt that she hated the Earl. She knew she could never rest until she had confronted him, and all through the long carriage ride she rehearsed again and again what she would say to him. Only now and then did her thoughts wander away to other, less compelling matters.

Sometimes, as she braced her feet against the jolting of the carriage, she found herself thinking about Jack. It was a painful exercise, in some ways more painful than her thoughts about her father. She had trusted Jack, and relied on him—now she realised she hardly knew him.

She couldn't understand why he hadn't condemned Lord Ashbourne more strongly for what he had done. He had taken the news so calmly, almost dispassionately. Did he not find Lord Ashbourne's actions shocking? Did he even *admire* the Earl for his cunning?

She shied away from the thought, resolutely putting Jack out of her mind. He was riding beside the carriage, escorting her to London, but she had hardly acknowledged his presence since their departure that morning. At the back of her mind she was dimly aware that he was trying to help her, but she was too confused and too bewildered to make any attempt to understand his point of view. She didn't know what he wanted her to do, but she was afraid that if she listened to him she might be diverted from her purpose—and that would have been a betrayal of her father.

They'd been travelling some time and she wanted to open her eyes and see where they were. She wanted to look at the passing countryside in the hope that the changing scenery would take her mind off her problems; but Tabitha was sitting opposite her and Charity knew that if she opened her eyes the maid would begin talking to her. She couldn't bear the idea of conversation, so she kept her eyes resolutely shut and remembered instead her meeting with Owen the previous afternoon.

"Charity!" Owen exclaimed delightedly.

He looked up at her as she stood beside the bed. A band of pale afternoon sunlight illuminated her face, and he thought she had never looked more beautiful. He didn't notice the shadows in her eyes or her pallor—he was too pleased to see her.

"How are you?" she asked, and smiled at him with something of an effort.

"I'll be on my feet in no time," he declared. "Sit down, sit down."

She obeyed, folding her hands demurely in her lap, though inwardly she felt anything but calm.

"I was hoping you'd come before," said Owen. "I asked for you. I know you saved my life. I wanted to thank you."

"I did what I could," Charity replied. "I'm thankful that it was enough."

"And you shot one of the ruffians," said Owen with satisfaction. Sir Humphrey had told him that, though he still didn't know everything else that had happened at Hazelhurst since he had been confined to his sick-bed.

"Mind, I'm not sure that I like the notion of you having anything to do with guns, but in the circumstances you did well. Not like me. I don't seem to be able to do anything right at the moment," he added bitterly. "I hear Riversleigh came to the rescue again."

"He heard the shots," said Charity.

"He's always in the right place at the right time," said Owen, "but he won't always have the advantage on his side."

"I don't think he does now," said Charity, surprising herself because she wasn't feeling particularly in sympathy with Jack and she hadn't expected she'd have any urge to defend him.

"What do you mean?" Owen looked at her suspiciously, but she didn't reply.

She didn't know how to explain that, whatever else Owen might lack, he had always possessed the one advantage denied to Jack. Owen wasn't rich and he wasn't particularly clever, but he was the squire's son and, from birth, his place in his small world had always been accepted unquestioningly by himself, and by everyone around him.

By contrast, as Charity thought about Jack, she realised his world must always have been a more complicated place, and she was aware of a fugitive notion that perhaps, to survive in a complicated world, it might be necessary to be a complicated person. But then she dismissed the idea. She had other, more important things to think about than Lord Riversleigh.

"Charity!"

At the sound of Owen's voice she recollected herself and smiled at him.

"I'm glad you're feeling better. But you always did have a very strong constitution. It would be very hard to kill you, I think."

Owen looked pleased.

"We're a tough lot, the Leydons," he declared. "We always breed true. When we're married—"

"Owen!"

He looked at her in surprise. "I know I haven't spoken to your mother yet, but as soon as I'm able to stand on my feet I will. I'm sure she won't object. There's no need for you to be anxious."

"I'm not," said Charity with a hint of her old tartness, but it wasn't fair to be annoyed with Owen. This whole dreadful misunderstanding was entirely her fault.

"Owen, I'm sorry…" she began. But then, because she wanted there to be no doubt of what she was telling him, she said simply, "I can't marry you."

"What?"

"When you proposed to me at the party I was…flattered, but I was also confused," she said steadily, trying to make her rejection of him as painless as she could. "I was surprised, and I didn't know what to say—so I said yes. But I shouldn't have done. It was very wrong of me. I'm sorry."

"You mean, you don't *want* to marry me?"

"No. I don't think we'd suit. I'm sorry," she said again.

For a moment he didn't say anything, he just lay staring up at the ceiling. There was an unreadable expression on his face and Charity didn't know what to do.

She didn't know whether he'd accepted what she'd said, whether she'd hurt him, or whether he was angry with her. She didn't know if she should say anything else, or if she should allow the silence to lengthen until he broke it himself.

In the tree outside the window a crow began to make its harsh cry, and Charity thought it sounded as desolate as she felt. So many birds sang in the summer, but the sound of the crow always reminded Charity of winter.

"It's him, isn't it?" Owen said at last, still not looking at her.

"No, it's me," she replied quietly, knowing that he was referring to Jack Riversleigh.

Owen turned his head at that, frowning. "You?"

"We wouldn't suit, Owen. Think how many arguments we've had in the past few days. We would spend the rest of our lives quarrelling. I don't want that."

"No, we won't," he said. "It's true you're headstrong, and not always very…sensible. But one must make allowances for your circumstances. I'm sure things will be different when we're married."

"You mean, I'll change and become more biddable, less opinionated?" she asked, smiling faintly. "But I don't want to change, Owen. I like the way I am."

He looked puzzled; he was very fond of her, but he didn't really understand her. The very qualities in her which he admired when they led to her saving his life distressed him when they resulted in a clash of wills between them. He wanted part of Charity, but not all of her, and he didn't see that that wasn't possible.

"I'm sorry, I can't stay any longer," she said. "I'm going to London tomorrow. I have to get ready."

"London?" He stared at her with renewed suspicion. He couldn't rid himself of the notion that somehow Lord Riversleigh had something to do with Charity's change of heart.

"Mama and I are going to move to London," she said calmly. "Mrs Riversleigh has invited us both to stay with her while we find somewhere to live. It will be easier to make arrangements if we're on the spot. Unfortunately, Mama doesn't feel up to the journey yet, so I'm going on ahead. I hope I'll be able to have everything arranged by the time she arrives."

"You're going to London on your own!" Owen was outraged. "Whatever can you be thinking of? Headstrong! Heedless! It's most improper behaviour!"

"No, it's just practical," said Charity. "I have always made all the arrangements. There's no reason why I should cease to do so, just because we're moving elsewhere."

"I suppose *he'll* be going with you?" Owen said sullenly.

"Lord Riversleigh has business of his own to attend to in London. He has kindly agreed to escort Tabitha and me," she said flatly. "Goodbye, Owen."

Charity sighed, wishing her parting with Owen had been more amicable. Owen still didn't like Jack—perhaps he never would—and it must have been difficult for him to hear that she was going to London in Lord Riversleigh's company.

The carriage was turning off the road. She felt the altered motion and opened her eyes, looking out of the window. They were stopping at an inn. It was time to change the horses and eat a quick meal before they continued their journey.

The door was opened, the steps let down, and Jack held out his hand to assist her. She hesitated for a moment, then she put her cold hand in his and let him help her out.

"Thank you," she said, her voice polite but very cold.

"Charity…" he began, still holding her hand in his.

"Will we be stopping here long?" she asked, drawing her hand away.

He looked at her steadily for a moment, knowing that she was deliberately distancing herself from him.

"No," he replied at last, reluctantly accepting the situation, even though he had a strong desire to take her in his arms and shake her until her eyes lost their blank, desolate expression and sparked instead with indignation.

"No, we won't be staying here long, Charity, but if you come into the inn you can rest for a while, and they'll give you something to eat." He offered her his arm.

"I'm not tired," she said, but she took his arm. It was the only friendly gesture she had made and she would have been surprised if she had known how much comfort Jack took in it.

It was late afternoon by the time they arrived in London, and Charity was exhausted and Tabitha sick. Normally Charity would have been fascinated by the sights and sounds of the metropolis because, though Mr Mayfield had come to town regularly, this was only her second visit. But now she didn't care.

Somehow she had imagined that they would go straight to Lord Ashbourne and she was vaguely surprised when she realised that in fact Jack was escorting her into his mother's house.

He guided her gently into the elegantly yet comfortably furnished drawing-room. Outside it was cold and dark, and for the first time in days it had come on to rain, but inside the house the candles had been lit and the fire crackled welcomingly.

Charity was too tired to feel anything but faint relief at

her arrival, but she made an effort to smile as she saw a dark, plumpish woman stand up to greet her. She had no quarrel with her hostess, however mixed her feelings about her son.

"Miss Mayfield! I was so pleased when Jack told me you and your mother would be visiting us," Mrs Riversleigh exclaimed. "I'm only sorry that your mother didn't feel she could face the journey yet. You must be exhausted. Come and sit down."

Mrs Riversleigh was shocked by Charity's exhausted and haunted appearance, but no sign of her feelings could be detected from her voice. Instead she took Charity's hand and led her to a chair by the fire.

"Thank you." Charity's smile was a mere vestige of its usual self. It hadn't yet occurred to her to wonder how Mrs Riversleigh had known she was coming, though in fact Jack had sent a messenger on ahead, warning his mother of their arrival.

"I'm sorry." She roused herself with an effort. "You must think it very rude of me to arrive unannounced like this."

"No, of course not," Mrs Riversleigh replied firmly. She was a kind woman and, even if she hadn't known Jack wanted her to welcome Charity, she would still have greeted her warmly. "But you must still be very shaken from the coach. Let me take you up to your room so that you can rest. Or are you hungry?" she added as an after-thought. "I can never eat when I first get out of a carriage, so I always assume that no one else can, but I know it's not the case with everyone. Would you like something to eat first?"

"No, no, thank you." Unintentionally, Charity's expression indicated that the thought of food at that moment was as nauseating to her as it obviously was to Mrs Riversleigh after a long journey.

"Come, then." Mrs Riversleigh took Charity upstairs herself and saw that she was settled in a very pretty room before she left her alone.

"Would you like me to send some food up to you later? Or will you come down?" she asked as she opened the door.

"Oh, no, I'll come down," Charity said quickly. "I'm sure I'll be more myself soon, it's just that, at the moment, every time I close my eyes I have the foolish notion that I'm still being tossed about in the coach." She smiled apologetically, a distinctly self-deprecating expression in her eyes, and Mrs Riversleigh felt herself warming to her unexpected guest.

She closed the door quietly and went down to join Jack.

"That poor girl looks quite exhausted," she said as she sat down in her favourite wing chair. "Why have you brought her to London?"

"She has some family business to attend to," Jack replied mildly, though his voice sounded slightly strained. "Where's Fanny?"

"She's gone to dinner with the Markhams. When I received your note I sent my apologies. I thought you would want me to be here when you arrived."

"I did. But I'm sorry to spoil your evening." Jack sat down in a straight-backed chair, sideways to the table, and selected an apple from the fruit bowl.

"You haven't," said Mrs Riversleigh calmly. "The Markhams are very nice people, and Fanny is fond of Lucinda—but an evening in their company bores me to distraction! This promises to be much more interesting."

Jack had been peeling his apple, but he looked up at that, an unforced gleam of amusement in his eyes that pleased his mother. She wasn't unaware of the tension which filled him, and it both puzzled and slightly concerned her.

"You are quite reprehensible," he said. "Sometimes I blush for you."

"No, you don't. You agree with me," she replied.

"Touché." He flung up his hand and laughed.

"What is this all about, Jack?" she asked more seriously. "Miss Mayfield looks as if she's seen a ghost."

"I think, in a way, she has," he said. "No, I can't tell you any more. I think you must ask Charity if you want to know anything else."

"Certainly not," said Mrs Riversleigh firmly. "I don't know her!"

"Not yet," said Jack. He smiled faintly. "It doesn't usually take long to get to know Charity. She may ask your advice on finding a house in London," he added more briskly. "I don't think it's likely; she's got a lot of other things on her mind at the moment. But that *is* the ostensible reason for her visit. So, if she does…"

"If she does I'll give her all the help I can," said Mrs Riversleigh.

"Thank you," Jack said. "Now, I must send a message to Lord Ashbourne." He stood up and went over to an elegant bureau.

"Lord Ashbourne! Is he involved in this business?" Mrs Riversleigh exclaimed.

Jack nodded.

"I don't like the man," said Mrs Riversleigh firmly.

"You're prejudiced," he responded lightly.

"Of course I am," she replied. "His nephew nearly killed you!" She saw a flicker of something in Jack's eyes and a sudden suspicion flared within her.

"Have you seen Ralph Gideon recently?" she demanded.

He folded his note, addressed and sealed it before he replied.

"We ran into each other the night before last," he said as he pulled on the bell rope for a footman to take his letter to Lord Ashbourne.

"And?"

"He is now nursing a wound in his shoulder."

"You're a fool," she said with conviction."

"Yes, I probably am," he agreed reflectively.

Charity sat quietly in a comfortable chair. She hadn't wanted to lie on the bed—she felt too vulnerable in that position. Her eyes were closed and her mind finally empty of almost all thought. It had been impossible for her to remain at the same fever pitch of emotion with which she had begun the day, and by the time she had arrived at the house she had felt quite numb, and drained of all emotion.

But she was resilient, and the time on her own had helped her. After a while she began to feel more like herself. She knew she wouldn't be seeing Lord Ashbourne that evening, and she owed it to her hostess to make some effort to be a charming guest. She didn't want to see or speak to Jack, but it would be rude to hide in her room, or allow her own troubles to worry others—particularly when she had virtually forced her presence on Mrs Riversleigh.

She went over to the mirror and gasped at her appearance. She looked terrible—her hair was falling down, there was a smudge of grime on her cheek, and her dress was creased and dusty. She could never go downstairs like that.

She glanced at the bell rope nervously; despite her earlier attention, she already knew she was staying in a far grander house than any she had previously visited, and she wasn't quite sure what would happen if she pulled it, but she needed Tabitha's help—if Tabitha was well enough.

She took a deep breath, and resolutely tugged at the rope. Within an astonishingly short space of time a shy maid appeared. She asked for Tabitha, but Tabitha was apparently quite unwell—in fact, she was groaning on a bed, but the maid didn't tell Charity that.

"May I help you, miss?" she asked.

Charity looked at her doubtfully for a second, then she nodded decisively. It took nearly forty-five minutes to repair the ravages of the journey, but when they had finished the maid stood back admiringly.

"You're beautiful, miss," she said shyly.

Charity stared critically at herself in the mirror. Her dark curls shone and the activity had brought a glow to her cheeks, but the beautiful eyes looking back at her seemed tired and sad.

She sighed.

"You're flattering me," she said. "But thank you anyway." She took a deep breath. "I must go downstairs," she said, "but I wasn't really attending when Mrs Riversleigh brought me up here. I'm not sure if I can remember the way back."

"I'll show you, miss," said the maid eagerly.

She really did think Charity was beautiful, and she was quite charmed by her kind manner. Mrs Riversleigh was very kind too, but until that moment the maid had been inclined to think that such considerate ladies were rare.

Charity paused in the doorway. She felt shy, and a little confused, because Jack and Mrs Riversleigh had been joined by another man she didn't recognise.

"I'm sorry," she said hesitantly. "I hope I haven't kept you waiting."

"Not at all," Mrs Riversleigh replied warmly, walking over to her with a stiff rustle of silk. "As soon as I knew you were coming I had dinner set back. It was quite easy, and not at all inconvenient,'' she added reassuringly as she saw that Charity was looking guilty.

''Come and let me introduce you to Matthew.'' She took Charity's arm and led her over to the other man.

Charity followed obediently but, as she did so, she couldn't resist the impulse to look across at Jack. He was watching her quietly. There was no humour in his eyes—only a question, and something that was not quite an apology.

''This is Matthew Dawson,'' said Mrs Riversleigh, unconsciously recalling Charity's attention. ''He was my father's partner; now he is Jack's. Matthew, this is Miss Mayfield.''

He was a spare man, not above middle height, with stooped shoulders. He was clearly bashful in strange company, but his eyes were shrewd and kind, and Charity found herself warming to him.

He sat next to her at dinner, but, though he replied when she spoke to him, he introduced no new topics of conversation himself. He only felt at ease with his craftsman peers, with his apprentices and with the people close to him that he had known for years. Elegant young ladies—to him, Charity was an extremely elegant and self-assured young lady—made him nervous and uncomfortable. He couldn't imagine that anything he had to say would interest her.

Jack said very little, and Mrs Riversleigh was frankly curious. She knew there was an undercurrent of tension between Charity and Jack and she wanted to know what Charity meant to her son but, though he might have told her if she'd asked, she hadn't chosen to do so. She had never pried into her children's affairs and, on the whole, they had rewarded her tact by being frankly open with her. She was afraid that this time, it might be different, but she knew that she could only wait, and hope that in the end she would find out what was happening.

When the meal was over she took Charity back to the drawing-room, leaving Jack and Matthew to their wine.

"Would you like some tea?" she asked as they sat down. "There's no knowing how long those two will sit over an empty table. It's not that they're heavy drinkers, you understand. It's just that when they start talking about their craft they forget all sense of time!"

Charity smiled. "Lord Riversleigh told me about Mr Dawson," she said. "I think he must be a very clever man—and a very nice one."

"Yes, he is." Mrs Riversleigh was slightly surprised.

She knew that Matthew did not always appear at his best in unfamiliar company. It was not everyone who could see beyond the monosyllabic and awkward replies to the talented and sensitive man he really was. She felt a growing respect for Charity, which increased when Charity said, "You must think it very rude of me to invite myself like this; I don't normally behave so badly. Well…" she paused ruefully "…perhaps I do."

"You seem troubled," said Mrs Riversleigh, because she wanted Charity to feel that she could confide in her, but she didn't want her to think that she was being vulgarly curious.

"Yes," said Charity, "but it's so complicated that I just don't know how to explain. Didn't Ja…Lord Riversleigh tell you anything about it?"

"No. I don't think he felt it was his place to do so," said Mrs Riversleigh. "He would never betray another's confidence."

"No." Charity looked at her hostess rather strangely. "No, he wouldn't."

She remembered the other confidences he hadn't betrayed. He could have made her the target for every gossip in Sussex if he'd chosen to do so—but he hadn't. He had been very kind to her; perhaps she was doing him an injustice—but *why* had he defended Lord Ashbourne?

"I don't think it's a secret," she said at last as she realised Mrs Riversleigh was waiting for her to continue. "I'm afraid I've been treating it like one, but that's only because it feels so much like a nightmare. Does that make sense?"

"We don't always want to talk about the things that upset us most," said Mrs Riversleigh gently. "Sometimes it helps. But sometimes when we're confused, and people ask questions we can't answer—because we don't know the answers—we just end up feeling more confused."

Charity looked at her gratefully. "Yes," she said. "That's how I feel. Do you mind if I don't explain now? I promise I will later."

"There's no hurry," said Mrs Riversleigh, and looked up as Jack and Matthew came into the room. For once Jack had had no desire to linger over the dining table, discussing their craft, and he had made the move to rejoin the ladies long before Matthew had felt ready to do so. Matthew would have been quite happy if he'd never gone back into the drawing-room.

Charity saw his hesitation and guessed how he must be feeling. It would be a kindness not to embarrass him further by trying to engage him in conversation, but she didn't want to talk to Jack, nor even to Mrs Riversleigh. Jack confused her and, although she liked her hostess, she couldn't feel entirely at ease with her while there was still so much unexplained between them.

Matthew was the only one present who offered no threat, only the challenge of setting him at his ease. To Charity the combination was irresistible, and she took a cup of tea from Mrs Riversleigh and gave it to Matthew, sitting down beside him as she did so. It had occurred to her that the best way to draw him out must be to ask him about his work, and that was what she proceeded to do.

Matthew looked rather alarmed at her approach. But when she was neither patronising nor flirtatious he began to feel more at ease. And when she asked if it had been he who'd made the beautiful silver gilt teapot, and seemed genuinely interested in his reply, he became quite talkative.

Mrs Riversleigh appeared to be concentrating on her embroidery, but in fact she was watching them in some amusement. Even after forty years, Matthew was as enthusiastic about his craft as he had been as a new apprentice. Given the opportunity, he could talk well and at length about what he'd made in the past—and he was always full of his plans for future work.

He described the processes of casting, soldering and annealing to Charity; explained the difference between embossing, chasing and engraving, and even upended the contents of the tea caddy on to the silver tea-tray so that he could show her how he'd finished it.

Charity had begun to talk to him partly because she really was interested, and partly to take her mind off her other problems. But it wasn't long before she became quite engrossed in what he was telling her. She'd always enjoyed the company of people who were good at something and, once he'd lost his initial self-consciousness, Matthew was able to bring his stories and descriptions to life.

"Of course, that was the salvar Hogarth engraved for us," he said at one point.

"Hogarth!" she exclaimed.

"He began life as an engraver," Jack explained, looking up briefly from what he was doing. "I don't think Matthew has ever forgiven him for his fall from grace to become a mere painter!"

"Well, I can see the merit in his pictures too," Matthew admitted. "But it was a sad loss to the trade." And he continued with his description of the early days of the business, when Joseph Pembroke had realised that he would never have a son to succeed him and had taken Matthew into partnership.

Jack didn't interrupt any more. Early in the conversation he had taken some paper from the bureau and begun to sketch Charity and Matthew as they sat talking. Mrs Riversleigh knew what he was doing, but neither of the other two did.

His movements were quick and deft and, when he at last put down his pencil, Mrs Riversleigh got up and went to stand at his shoulder to look at the finished sketch.

Jack was a very fair artist, but Mrs Riversleigh had always believed that he drew best those people that he knew best—and those people that he loved. He was as close to Matthew as he had been to his father and she wasn't surprised to see how well he'd caught the silversmith's likeness. But she had to restrain a gasp when she looked at his picture of Charity, and she knew then that at least one of her unspoken questions had been answered. The girl on the paper was as vibrant and full of life as the girl talking to Matthew. Jack had surpassed himself.

"It's very good," she said softly.

"It is, isn't it?" he looked at the sketch almost as if he was surprised that it should be so.

"What is it?" Charity glanced up, momentarily distracted from her discussion with Matthew.

Jack passed her the sketch, and she looked at it for a long moment without saying anything. Then at last, with her eyes still on the picture Jack had drawn of her, and apparently quite irrelevantly, she said, "When can I see the Earl?"

''Tomorrow morning. I've arranged a meeting.''

''Good.'' For almost a full minute Charity continued to look at the sketch, and Mrs Riversleigh wondered what she saw in it.

''It's very good,'' she said quietly as she finally handed it back to Jack. ''It's not often one sees oneself through someone else's eyes. Thank you.''

For a moment her gaze locked with Jack's, almost as if she was seeking the answer to her question. Then she stood up.

''I'm sorry, I hope you'll excuse me,'' she said to Mrs Riversleigh. ''But it's getting quite late and I'm afraid I'm very tired.''

''You've had a tiring day,'' said Mrs Riversleigh. ''I hope you'll sleep well.''

''Thank you.'' Charity smiled briefly, and went quickly out of the room.

Chapter Seventeen

"Yes, Bolton?" Lord Ashbourne was sitting at the table, his head bent over the letter he was writing, and he didn't look up at the servant's approach.

"Lord Riversleigh has arrived, my lord."

"Show him into the library. You may tell him I will join him shortly." The Earl's pen continued to travel unhurriedly over the paper as he spoke.

"Yes, my lord. There is a *lady* with Lord Riversleigh, my lord."

"A lady?" Lord Ashbourne finally looked up. "Did she give a name?"

"No, my lord."

"I see." A hint of curiosity gleamed in the Earl's eyes, but he didn't say anything further on the subject. "Provide them with refreshment, Bolton. The lady may care for some tea, perhaps." He dipped his pen in the ink and completed his unfinished sentence.

It was twenty minutes later when Lord Ashbourne finally joined his guests in the library, and they were twenty very difficult minutes for Charity. She suspected, though she couldn't be sure, that the Earl was making them wait to display his own consequence, and she began to feel angry.

''It's not you he's slighting,'' said Jack softly. ''Don't let it agitate you. I didn't tell him in my note I was bringing anyone with me and, although he certainly knows you're here now, I'm fairly sure he doesn't know who you are. It's *me* he's trying to provoke. I asked for this meeting, which means that I probably want something from him, and that made it almost inevitable he'd keep me waiting.''

''Doesn't that anger you?'' Charity demanded; she couldn't understand how Jack could be so calm in the face of such an insult.

''It might if I allowed it to,'' Jack replied quietly. ''But it would be a waste of energy—and a victory for the Earl. It's better not to let yourself be side-tracked from your purpose.''

He had tried to explain this to Charity before, but without much success and, despite his calm demeanour, he was in fact unusually tense. It was not his forthcoming meeting with Lord Ashbourne which worried him, but how Charity would react in what was bound to be a difficult situation. He had tried to prepare her for the meeting, but she had been unresponsive and distant. She was afraid of being misled, or of having her purpose blunted, and she was determined to deal with Lord Ashbourne on her own terms.

''Riversleigh, my dear fellow. How delightful to see you again. I'm sorry to have kept you waiting.'' The Earl strolled into the room, calm and unhurried.

''Not at all,'' Jack replied politely, standing at the Earl's approach. ''It was kind of you to grant us an interview at such short notice.''

''Us?'' Lord Ashbourne queried courteously. ''I believe I have not previously had the pleasure of meeting your charming companion.''

He turned to Charity as he spoke, and she saw the slightly appraising look in his eyes as he smiled at her.

"No, I don't think you have," said Jack. "This is Miss Charity Mayfield."

Lord Ashbourne clearly hadn't expected that, but he was too sophisticated to show his surprise openly.

"My dear Miss Mayfield," he said, after only a moment's hesitation. "I am delighted to meet you. I was...very sorry to hear of your father's death. He was a remarkable man."

"Thank you." Charity's voice was as cold as the hand she allowed the Earl to kiss, but she was containing her fury very well.

She didn't know Lord Ashbourne and she was sure he was mocking her. It was only Jack, watching his host carefully, who thought there was something odd in the Earl's manner. The Earl was doing his best to conceal it, but Jack was convinced that he had been thrown off balance by Charity's presence.

"I'm all the more delighted to make your acquaintance because my agent has been so impressed by your remarkable grasp of business," said Lord Ashbourne urbanely. "Do, please, sit down again."

He gestured towards a comfortable chair before the fire.

"I hope things are proceeding to your satisfaction," he continued. "Is there any way in which I may be of assistance—or have you come to pay your father's debt?" His voice was almost languid in its lack of emphasis.

"No, my lord," said Charity.

She ignored the chair he offered and sat at the table, her hands clasped tensely before her.

"I've come to ask you why you tricked my father into losing Hazelhurst to you," she said baldly.

"Tricked?" There was a hint of contempt in the Earl's voice now, though the expression in his eyes was quite unreadable. "My dear young lady, there was no trick. Mayfield and I simply amused ourselves with a few hands of piquet. Unfortunately your father lost rather heavily.''

''Ashbourne!'' said Jack suddenly before Charity could speak, and the Earl swung round to face him. ''It may save time at this point if I tell you that we know that your meeting with Mr Mayfield was not entirely...accidental,'' Jack continued quietly.

He didn't think this was a situation in which there was anything to be gained by fencing, and the quicker they reached some kind of understanding, the better.

''Do you, indeed?'' said the Earl, his attention now entirely directed at Jack, almost as if he found Jack easier to deal with than Charity. ''May I ask why?''

Jack glanced briefly at Charity, but she seemed surprisingly reluctant to speak, so he continued with the explanation himself.

''Two nights ago I had the misfortune to encounter Ralph Gideon,'' he said. ''He was just about to make his third attempt to ransack the library at Hazelhurst.'' He saw the look of sharp understanding spring into the Earl's eyes, and smiled grimly.

''Quite. Perhaps I should inform you that during his brief stay in Sussex he has not only helped a prisoner to escape from the custody of the local magistrate, but also shot that same magistrate's son in the process.''

''Dead?'' Lord Ashbourne asked sharply.

''No. But only because Miss Mayfield was on hand to administer immediate assistance,'' Jack replied.

The Earl glanced at Charity, a frown in his eyes.

''A most unpleasant experience,'' he said. ''I'm sorry that any relative of mine should have caused you such distress.''

''Sorry!'' Charity burst out, forgetting her previous intentions as she impetuously rejoined the conversation.

Her unusual silence until that moment had been prompted by the sudden realisation that she might find it more instructive to listen than to speak. It had finally dawned on her in those painful minutes while she had been waiting for the Earl to appear that she was even more anxious to know how Jack would deal with the situation than she was to find out what had happened to her father. And she was afraid that, if *she* took the lead in questioning Lord Ashbourne, she might never find out what Jack really felt about the Earl. Nevertheless, it was impossible for her to remain silent for long.

"It wasn't Gideon who tried to cheat my father out of everything he possessed—and it's not Gideon who is responsible for all the misery my family has suffered this past year!" she exclaimed. She was breathing quickly, her eyes burning with anger and dislike.

"Lord Riversleigh says you did nothing illegal," she continued, her voice quieter now and more compelling than any scream of outrage. "I'm not sure I believe him. But even if he's right—how do you justify what you've done to us?"

Her eyes were locked with the Earl's.

"I'm not sure I know what you think I *have* done," he said at last, his voice stripped of all expression.

"You wanted the pendant, the jewel by Hilliard," she said. "I don't know how you knew it was in the house, and it's not important. But you didn't go to my father like a gentleman and tell him it was there—or offer to buy it. Instead you tricked him into playing cards with you, and into losing so much money that the only way he *could* repay the debt would be by selling Hazelhurst—and then you agreed to take our home in lieu of cash. Isn't that what you did?"

She was leaning forward, her arms resting on the table,

her eyes blazing with fury. She had forgotten Jack; she had forgotten everything but the man sitting before her who had caused so much pain to so many people.

For a moment there was silence. The Earl was looking at Charity, a curious expression on his face.

"Broadly speaking, you're quite correct," he said at last, and some of the tension left Charity.

"You consider such conduct unforgivable," he said softly. "No doubt you're right, but having admitted my guilt so readily, perhaps I might be permitted to say a couple of things in my own defence."

Charity didn't answer, and after a moment Jack said, "You're the only witness to what happened, Ashbourne. I think it would be best if you told us everything."

"Will you believe what I say?" the Earl asked.

"Perhaps." The two men looked steadily at each other for a moment, then Lord Ashbourne turned to Charity. "I didn't cheat," he said. "Please understand that. Whatever else I might have done, I have never cheated at cards in my life. I would scorn to do so!"

"You sound very grand," she replied quietly, meeting his gaze with her honest brown eyes. "No doubt you are very grand. But beneath the fine speeches and the fine clothes you're still only a man, and you can never be any more than that—only less."

The Earl drew in a deep, slightly uneven breath and turned away to lean his arm on the mantelpiece.

"I tried to buy Hazelhurst first," he said after a moment. He was staring down into the fire, not looking at Charity. "Through an agent, of course. Your father wouldn't sell, even though I offered nearly half as much again as it's worth. After that I really had no choice but to pursue other methods."

''You could have told him the truth,'' said Charity inflexibly.

''That did not occur to me,'' Lord Ashbourne glanced up briefly, ''although at first I did wonder whether he knew about the pendant—but he didn't. Certain things he said made that plain. But you mustn't think I lied to him—lying, like cheating, is something I never do. I simply didn't tell him all the facts.'' He paused, but Charity didn't comment.

''Well, I don't suppose you're interested in my personal foibles,'' he continued, turning back to face her. ''I arranged for a chance meeting; I believed he was flattered when I invited him back here; he was certainly quite willing to play cards with me—unfortunately for him, his skill was not equal to his ambition.''

Charity bent her head and closed her eyes. The Earl's words could have been an epitaph for Mr Mayfield's life. It hurt her to think that he should have exposed himself to the scorn and ridicule of a man like Lord Ashbourne.

''He was a very brave man,'' said the Earl quietly. ''At first he wasn't aware of how much he'd lost, and when he realised he couldn't afford to pay what he owed he tried to win his money back. He didn't, of course, but I stopped the game when the debt equalled the value of the property. There was no need to continue any longer.''

''Should I be grateful for that?'' asked Charity bitterly.

''No,'' said the Earl. ''But when he left me I did think he would seek out the man who'd tried to buy Hazelhurst and take up his offer. If he had done he would have had ten thousand pounds in hand.''

''Would you still have bought it?'' Charity asked incredulously. ''Even when there was no longer any need?''

''I didn't want to have to wait a year before looking for the pendant,'' Lord Ashbourne replied.

"Why *did* you give him that year?" Jack asked suddenly.

"I really cannot say," the Earl said, and, whatever his earlier feelings might have been, his mask of indifference was now firmly back in place. "No doubt I had a reason at the time, but I cannot recall it now."

"Then it seems to me you're in danger of being convicted by your own boasts," said Jack.

Lord Ashbourne frowned, then he realised what Jack meant.

"The truth then, if you must have it," he said, a sharper note in his voice. "I won twenty thousand pounds from Mayfield that night. But even when he knew he was ruined he continued to act with dignity and courtesy. I had expected him to be distraught, angry, even suspicious, but he wasn't. I have done many things in my life, but I have never destroyed a man before—and then heard him thank me for giving him a pleasant evening. I told you he was a brave man."

Charity looked away, tears in her eyes. The Earl was the last person she had ever expected to praise her father, and she was thrown off balance. Everything had seemed so simple before; now it was becoming so complicated.

"I still wanted the pendant," said Lord Ashbourne. "But Mayfield deserved a chance to recover—he'd earned it. So I gave him a year. I expected him to sell Hazelhurst to the interested buyer. But when he didn't I thought he'd found another way to pay the debt."

"He was dead," Charity whispered.

"Yes, I know that now. I didn't know it then. I didn't find out until your lawyer contacted me a couple of weeks ago." Lord Ashbourne walked over to stand before Charity.

"I'm sorry," he said.

Charity turned her head away.

"You didn't make any effort to find out *how* he was going to raise the money?" Jack asked.

"No." The Earl looked down at Charity's averted face, then went back to stand by the fireplace. "The cards had been dealt. It was up to Mayfield how he played them."

"An unlucky metaphor, don't you think?" Jack said, an edge to his voice.

"Yes. I apologize. At the time I had no desire to interfere any further. I regret that now. Had I done so I would have discovered that Mayfield was dead—and that you had apparently no knowledge of his agreement with me."

"I found out two and a half weeks ago," Charity said. She was looking pale and stressed, but she was quite calm.

"You are very like your father," said the Earl slowly.

"How can you say you regret not knowing my father was dead?" Charity demanded, ignoring his comment. "Are you trying to suggest it would have made any difference? You have known for more than two weeks that neither Mama or I knew we would have to leave Hazelhurst by the end of this month, but you have done *nothing* to ease our distress. Your words are empty. You still wanted the pendant and you didn't care how much suffering you caused as long as you got it!"

The Earl winced.

"Yes," he said. "I wanted the pendant; I still do. But I wouldn't have kept Hazelhurst as well. A couple of days and I would have had the jewel. Then perhaps an error would have been found in the agreement. Or perhaps I would have discovered that Mayfield had already repaid me and I hadn't been informed because of an inefficient underling." He shrugged. "I wouldn't have kept Hazelhurst," he said again.

"Do you expect me to believe you?" Charity asked.

"My dear, you can believe what you like," he replied

tartly. He'd finished abasing himself. "Would you care for some more tea?"

"No, thank you." Charity frowned slightly; she didn't understand the Earl.

Lord Ashbourne turned to Jack.

"I was surprised to see you involved in this business, Riversleigh," he said. "But I recall now, you have land in Sussex, have you not?"

"Hazelhurst and Riversleigh share a common boundary," Jack replied. "Naturally I'm delighted to assist Miss Mayfield in this matter in any way I can."

"Naturally." The Earl smiled faintly. "I trust Ralph was equally gratified to renew his acquaintance with *you?*"

"Not demonstrably," Jack replied.

"You surprise me. Where is he?"

"In the custody of Sir Humphrey Leydon. He believes you'll use your influence on his behalf."

"Does he?" The Earl's expression was inscrutable. "I wonder why?"

"To avoid a scandal," Jack suggested.

He was more relaxed now. They had already discovered most of what they wished to know, and there were only two more matters he wanted to raise. He had no interest in what the Earl decided to do about his nephew.

"To avoid a scandal," the Earl repeated. "In the circumstances, it seems an inadequate reason. It's a pity you didn't kill him, Riversleigh. Think how much trouble you would have saved everyone."

"How did you know they'd fought?" Charity demanded, suddenly re-entering the conversation.

"I didn't," said the Earl calmly. "But in view of their last meeting…"

"Of more interest to me," said Jack, who had no desire

to discuss the past, ''is how the pendant came to be in the library in the first place. And how you found out about it.''

''Yes, I imagine you would like to know that,'' said Lord Ashbourne. ''Is it beautiful, Riversleigh? Was it worth all that abortive trouble I took?''

''It is beautiful,'' said Jack quietly. ''But I don't think it's worth the distress it's caused. No inanimate object is worth so much pain.''

There was an edge to his voice, and Charity looked up at him quickly—but Jack was looking at the Earl.

''A predictable response,'' said Lord Ashbourne. ''I have no desire to waste my time describing how I discovered the existence of a jewel which I failed to obtain possession of. If you're interested you can read its history for yourself in the Duke of Faversham's diary.''

He walked across the room and unlocked a bureau with a key he took from his waistcoat pocket. There were a number of papers in the desk, but he ignored these, taking up instead two leather-bound volumes, which he put on the table in front of Charity.

''A present, my dear,'' he said. ''You may read all about the origins of the pendant and how it came to be in your family at your leisure. There is just one other matter.''

He returned to the bureau and locked it carefully before turning back to look at both Jack and Charity.

''The ownership of Hazelhurst,'' he said. ''You have the pendant, my dear. And, by catching my nephew, Riversleigh has dragged my family into a very unpleasant scandal. In the circumstances, I think it only fair that I should recoup some of my losses. After all, your father—or his heirs—still owe me twenty thousand pounds.''

Charity gasped.

''You said you didn't want Hazelhurst!'' she exclaimed.

''I don't,'' said the Earl blandly. ''I want the pendant.

Of course, if you'd care to exchange possession of one for the other…but, failing that—'' he'd seen the immediate refusal in Charity's eyes—I'll settle either for ownership of Hazelhurst or for twenty thousand pounds. I'm sure Riversleigh will have no trouble in raising such a sum.''

"You are despicable!" Charity burst out, her first reaction simply one of horror as she realised that Lord Ashbourne meant to enforce the debt.

Then she absorbed the implications of his last words and she began to feel angry instead. How *dared* he suggest that she would leave the management of her affairs in someone else's hands—or allow someone else to pay the debt for her?

"I am quite capable…" she began, and felt Jack put his hand on her shoulder "…of managing…" she continued.

Jack tightened his grasp imperatively, and she knew he wanted her to remain silent. In fact, he was *ordering* her to remain silent! The arrogance of it outraged her; nevertheless, she obeyed his unspoken command. Partly because she didn't want to quarrel with him in front of the Earl, and partly because she knew that, apart from righteous indignation, she herself had very little with which to counter the Earl's ultimatum.

Lord Ashbourne was looking at Jack and there was something curious, almost expectant in his expression.

"It would be no trouble at all to raise such a sum," said Jack pleasantly. "On the scale of things, twenty thousand pounds is hardly an enormous investment."

He dropped his hand from Charity's shoulder and moved to one side so that he faced the Earl with no barrier between them. He was quite at his ease—he seemed almost amused.

"I have often encountered men who will invest far more than that if they believe the returns will be high enough," he continued conversationally. "Of course, some ventures are more risky than others. I heard only this morning that Mark Horwood and Adam Kaye have finally found a third investor for their East Indian venture. It must have been a great relief to my friend Horwood. They've been held up for weeks because Adam Kaye is so particular about who he'll do business with. I hope nothing goes wrong for them this time. I'm sure you share my hope.''

Jack smiled blandly at Lord Ashbourne, and the Earl looked back, an unreadable glint in his eye. Then he unlocked the bureau once more and took out one of the documents it contained.

As Charity watched, quite bemused, he wrote quickly on the paper, dusted it with sand, and handed it to Jack.

"Satisfied, my lord?" he asked softly.

"I think so.'' Jack scanned the paper quickly. "Yes, definitely.''

He passed the document to Charity and she saw with bewilderment that the debt had been cancelled. For some reason which she didn't understand, Lord Ashbourne had suddenly renounced all claim to both Hazelhurst and the twenty thousand pounds.

"Well,'' Jack turned back to the Earl, "that seems to settle things nicely. I don't believe we need take up any more of your time, my lord. Thank you.''

"It's always a pleasure to do business with you,'' Lord Ashbourne replied, inclining his head ironically.

Jack smiled, and picked up the two volumes of the diary that Lord Ashbourne had given to Charity.

"Shall we go?'' he asked her quietly.

They completed the journey back to the Riversleighs' house in almost complete silence. A great deal had happened in a very short space of time, and Charity was still trying to make sense of it. She didn't know what she had been expecting the Earl to be like, or what she had expected him to do, but nothing in her imaginings had prepared her for such an outcome to their meeting.

Jack sensed her preoccupation and made no attempt to intrude upon it. Charity had been anticipating disaster for so long that he thought she probably needed time to come to terms with the fact that the whole unhappy business was finally finished with. Soon she would realise that Hazelhurst was hers once more, and then they would be able to get on with their lives. He still had one very important question to ask her.

He took her into the drawing-room on their return, and Charity went immediately to sit by the fire, perched on the edge of her seat, her hands clasped tensely in her lap.

Jack glanced at her, frowning slightly; he didn't entirely understand her mood. He was about to speak to her, then thought better of it and opened the diaries Lord Ashbourne had given them instead. He meant to see if he could find the passage explaining the presence of the pendant so that he could read it to Charity.

He flipped through a few pages in growing bewilderment then, as understanding dawned, he closed the book and started to laugh.

"What is it?" Charity demanded, looking up at him with an almost hostile expression in her eyes.

"Do you remember Gideon told us he'd found *notes* his uncle had made on the diary?" Jack asked, still obviously amused by something. "I should have remembered that. There was a reason—the diary itself is written in a sort of code. Quite unintelligible unless you know the key."

"*What?*" Charity leapt to her feet and went to look. "How can you laugh?" she exclaimed when she saw he was right. "It's not funny."

"It is in a way," said Jack. "The Earl isn't the man to allow himself to be outmanoeuvred on every account."

"You *like* him, don't you?" Charity demanded, her pent-up feelings finding an outlet in the accusation. "After everything he's done, you *like* him! Perhaps you even *admire* him!"

"No." The humour had died out of Jack's eyes. "I don't like him, and I don't admire him either—the Earl is not an admirable man. But I do respect him."

"*Respect* him! More than you respect me, it appears!" Charity's eyes flashed indignantly. The anger she had been feeling ever since he had bidden her to silence in Lord Ashbourne's house overflowed, and now she hardly stopped to consider what she was saying.

"You certainly seemed quite happy to do business with him, regardless of my wishes on the matter," she said hotly. "How *dare* you interfere in my affairs? How *dare* you pay my debts for me? You had no right!"

"No right?" Jack tossed the diary down on to the table with a thud as he, too, finally lost his temper. "How dare you talk of rights to *me?*" he said, his voice throbbing with anger. He thought he'd been very patient, but now he was thoroughly roused by what he considered to be her unreasonableness.

"In the past two days you've judged me and condemned me for actions which you don't understand, and without once asking me to explain why I've done what I have," he said, his anger no less terrible because it was tightly controlled. "I've been very patient—I know things have been hard for you—but after all my efforts on your behalf I'm damned if I'll stand here and have my generosity flung back in my face! You've got Hazelhurst *back.* That's what you wanted, isn't it? Whatever your feelings about me, you might have the grace to show a little gratitude."

"Why should I be grateful?" Charity blazed back, all the anger she had felt at her father and Lord Ashbourne finding an outlet in her quarrel with Jack. "I never asked for your help. I never asked for you to step forward in that lordly manner and take over as if you were some kind of king or god. Hazelhurst belonged to my family; it was ours to keep or lose. My father wouldn't have wanted you to give it back to him in that charitably gracious manner—and nor do I!"

Her heart was pounding and she was breathing very quickly, but she met Jack's eyes squarely. Part of her was horrified at what she had done and afraid of Jack's reaction—but on the whole she was too furious to care what he said.

Whatever else he might or might not have done, he had had no right to take over the management of her affairs without even consulting her. It was obvious to Charity that he must have known even before they had arrived at Lord Ashbourne's house how he would deal with the Earl's threat to keep Hazelhurst, yet he hadn't once mentioned the matter to her.

"Hazelhurst is not yours to refuse," said Jack coldly, though his eyes sparked dangerously. "It belongs to your mother. But there is certainly no reason why it should remain in your family if you don't want it—you may transfer its ownership into my name. After all, the fact that I was not obliged to spend any money does not alter the fact that I was instrumental in wiping out the debt which preserved the property from Lord Ashbourne."

"Give it to you?" Charity gasped, paling.

"Certainly." The heat had gone out of Jack's anger, but there was no softening in his expression as he met Charity's eyes. "It would make a very useful addition to the Riversleigh estate," he said. "And I hate to think I'd done anything to offend the obviously inordinate family pride of the Mayfields! No doubt it would be possible for you to have the tenancy of the place. Would you like to come into my study so that we can discuss the arrangements?'' He began to move towards the door as he spoke.

''I'm not going to be your *tenant!*'' Charity was starting to feel confused and, in her bewilderment, she clung to her anger rather like a losing gambler clung to the cards that were failing him. ''Is *this* the way you made your fortune?'' she demanded, trying to turn the argument back on to Jack.

''No,'' he said, looking at her sardonically. ''It's not often I end the morning twenty thousand pounds richer than I began it in exchange for absolutely nothing—or for no more than the price of a little gossip. You accused me of being arrogant, Charity; I dare say you're right, but in your own way so are you.''

She stood quite still, staring at him almost as if she had been petrified. She tried to rekindle her anger, but it was gone. She was alone in the middle of the room. He was still standing there, still watching her, but he had gone beyond her reach. She had driven him away. She still didn't understand him, but she had denied him the opportunity to explain before, and now she didn't know if he ever would.

He was looking at her coldly; there was no warmth in his eyes, no softening. There was so much she wanted to ask him—but it was too late.

A servant came softly into the room and hesitated, sensing the tension.

''Yes, James?'' said Jack without turning his head.

''Mr Sedgewick wishes to speak to you, sir,'' said the servant respectfully. ''He says it's urgent.''

''Tell him to wait,'' said Jack curtly.

''No, don't,'' said Charity. ''I'm sure you should speak to him now.''

She smiled uncertainly, but she was glad of the interruption; she was too confused, she needed more time to think.

''Very well,'' said Jack after a moment. ''Where is he, James?''

''In the book-room, sir.''

''Thank you.'' Jack glanced once more at Charity, then he left the drawing-room quickly, closing the door quietly behind him.

Chapter Eighteen

Charity let out her breath in a long, shaky sigh and sat down limply at the table, dropping her head into her hands. She couldn't remember ever having felt more confused or more miserable in her whole life.

She loved Jack. For two days she had been trying to pretend that she didn't care, that everything she had felt when she was in his arms meant nothing—but she knew now that she had been deceiving herself. She loved him, whatever he'd done and whatever he was. To be at odds with him was the worst fate she could imagine—yet she still didn't understand him.

Less than five minutes ago she had condemned him for his arrogance, but she knew that the real cause of her distress wasn't his high-handedness—it was her underlying fear that in some strange way he shared Lord Ashbourne's peculiar code of honour. She had once accused him of defending Lord Ashbourne and, although she was now certain that the two men were not friends, she still couldn't blind herself to the fact that Jack had openly admitted to respecting the Earl.

Was that all, or did he also emulate the Earl's methods? She didn't know exactly how Jack had persuaded Lord

Ashbourne to give up Hazelhurst, but she knew no money had changed hands, and she was fairly sure that the Earl had been blackmailed in some way. Did Jack always use such methods? What kind of man had she fallen in love with?

She lifted her head from her hands and, in a vain attempt to distract herself, she began randomly to turn over the unreadable pages of the Duke of Faversham's diary. For a moment she almost thought of trying to decode it herself, but she didn't really care what was in it. It wasn't the past that interested her—it was the future.

She stood up restlessly and took a turn about the room, wondering what she should do now. It was raining outside, a bleak February day, in tune with her mood. She wanted to go out, but there was nowhere to go. She had nothing to read and nothing to do.

Then she heard voices in the hall outside, exclaiming against the damp, and in a moment or two Mrs Riversleigh came briskly into the room.

"Miss Mayfield, back already!" Mrs Riversleigh exclaimed. "I hope you missed the worst of the rain. Fanny was caught out in it and got quite drenched. She's had to go up and change."

"We were back before it started," Charity said, smiling with something of an effort. "I hope your trip was successful."

Mrs Riversleigh and Fanny had been shopping.

"I'm glad to say we got most of what we went for," Mrs Riversleigh replied. "I do *not* enjoy shopping, particularly in February, but we both needed new gowns. What about you—has your morning been successful?"

She glanced shrewdly at Charity as she spoke, then turned her attention to warming her hands at the fire.

She hadn't failed to notice the slightly distracted look in

Charity's eyes and she was afraid that the interview with Lord Ashbourne must have gone badly.

"Successful?" Charity repeated distantly.

She was thinking of her quarrel with Jack—there was nothing to boast of in that. But then she cast her mind further back to the meeting with Lord Ashbourne, and it suddenly occurred to her that it had indeed been a successful morning.

Hazelhurst was hers again!

Before Mrs Riversleigh's surprised eyes Charity suddenly seemed to lighten up. The dejected young woman of thirty seconds ago vanished, to be replaced by a glowing girl who could hardly prevent herself from dancing around the room in her excitement.

"Yes!" she cried, stretching out her arms in her delight. "I've got Hazelhurst back! I've got Hazelhurst *back!* I don't know why, but until this moment I never really…I'm sorry." She stopped in mid-sentence and looked at Mrs Riversleigh contritely. "You don't even know what I'm talking about."

Mrs Riversleigh smiled. "It doesn't matter," she said. "I'm just pleased to see you so happy. You looked so sad last night that I was worried about you—I know Jack was too."

"Jack?" Charity looked at Mrs Riversleigh quickly, almost doubtfully.

"Of course," said Mrs Riversleigh calmly. "Now, tell me about Hazelhurst. Is that your home? How did it come about that you had to get it back?"

"My father used it to secure a debt," said Charity, and without more ado she told Mrs Riversleigh the whole story.

"Good heavens!" Mrs Riversleigh exclaimed when Charity had finished. "What a terrible business. No wonder you looked so haunted last night. But you seem to have dealt with it all very well. Your mother must be proud of you.''

''She doesn't know much about it,'' Charity admitted. ''I couldn't bring myself to tell her. I'll have to, of course, but I just couldn't face… The last year has been very difficult for her,'' she added quickly, in case it sounded as if she was criticising Mrs Mayfield.

''Yes, I remember how hard it was when my husband died,'' said Mrs Riversleigh quietly. ''I'm sure you must have been a great comfort to her. I know how much I relied on Jack in that first, difficult year. He was only thirteen, and of course my father was still alive then, but Jack still insisted on taking on many of my husband's responsibilities.''

''You must be very proud of him,'' said Charity softly.

It was clear to her that, whatever methods Jack might adopt when he was dealing with outsiders, he would never let down those he cared for. But then, hadn't she always known that? Why else had she been able to accuse him of collusion with the Earl in one breath and in the next accept his escort to London?

Mrs Riversleigh smiled.

''Yes, I am,'' she said. ''But he hates it if he thinks I've been praising him to others, so perhaps I'd better not say any more. Tell me instead, what do you mean to do, now that you've got Hazelhurst back?''

''Do?'' Charity blinked at her hostess.

Mrs Riversleigh's brief comments about Jack had given her a great deal to think about, but it would be rude to appear distracted when her hostess had been so kind.

''I suppose I'll put into practice all those plans I thought I'd have to abandon,'' she said slowly. ''We've increased our yield quite considerably over the last few years and I have hopes that, with…'' she stopped, smiling. ''I'm sure you're not really interested in such things," she said guiltily. "I know I can become quite boring on the subject if I have even half an opportunity."

"I'm not bored," said Mrs Riversleigh, encouraging Charity to continue. It was true that she wasn't particularly interested in the best time to plant wheat in the Weald, but she was fascinated by Charity's obvious knowledge and enthusiasm.

It wasn't often that Charity was given such an opportunity to talk about something which was so close to her heart and, despite her preoccupation, she soon found herself describing some of the innovations she had introduced.

"Of course," she said at one point, "things don't always happen as I intend. Even Sam Burden has a tendency to prefer the old ways, and our other tenant, and many of the farm-workers, are completely resistant to change. But I usually get what I want in the end."

"How?" asked Mrs Riversleigh curiously.

Charity laughed mischievously. "On at least one occasion by proposing an enormous change I didn't want at all," she said. "By the time Sam had managed to persuade me it wasn't a good idea he was so grateful that he agreed to make the change I *really* wanted as a concession to sweeten my defeat on the larger issue." She smiled reminiscently. "I suppose I should feel guilty about my underhand methods," she continued, "but I know for a fact he's done the same to me. It's almost…" Her voice trailed off.

"Almost what?" Mrs Riversleigh prompted her.

Charity was sitting still, staring into space as if she'd been stunned.

"Almost a game," she said distantly.

Jack wasn't like Lord Ashbourne! Why hadn't she seen it before? Of course he respected the Earl's cunning—only a fool underestimated his enemy. Perhaps he even found pleasure in outwitting Lord Ashbourne, as she had enjoyed outmanoeuvring Sam Burden. But he had never approved of the Earl's motives—or his methods.

For the first time she remembered the moment when Lord Ashbourne had asked whether the pendant had been worth all his trouble—and she could hear Jack's reply just as clearly and unambiguously as if he were speaking to her at that very moment.

"No inanimate object is worth so much pain."

She could even remember what the Earl had said next. "A predictable response." He had known Jack better than she had. She had been so wrong.

The revelation was blinding in its force. She leapt to her feet, forgetful of Mrs Riversleigh's presence in her urgency to speak to Jack.

She had to tell him that she did understand. She had to apologise for all her doubts, for her rudeness and her coldness—and she had to thank him for what he'd done for her.

She turned to the door, but she had taken no more than two steps towards it before it opened and a servant came in.

"His lordship's compliments, miss," he said respectfully to Charity. "And would you be kind enough to join him in the library?"

"Oh, yes!"

She picked up her skirts, almost as if she intended to run—and belatedly remembered Mrs Riversleigh.

"I'm sorry, do excuse me," she said incoherently, and left the room so quickly that her hostess had no chance to reply.

"Thank you, James." Mrs Riversleigh dismissed the footman and picked up her embroidery, smiling to herself.

"Jack!"

Charity burst through the library door, every bit as impetuously as she had once burst through the library door at

Hazelhurst when she had thought it was Edward who was waiting for her.

And, just as she had on that occasion, she stopped short, uncertain of how to go on. Now she was in Jack's presence she felt shy and unsure of herself. He looked so stern. How could she ever explain she had been wrong?

He had indeed been looking unusually serious when she had opened the door, but now, at the sight of her breathless arrival, his expression softened.

"You never know what's going to be on the other side of the door, do you?" he said, and moved past her to close it.

She revolved slowly so that she could continue to look at him.

"I'm sorry I summoned you in such an arrogant manner," he said without irony, "but I wanted to speak to you alone. I should not—"

"Jack!" she interrupted. I…" She glanced up at him and saw that he was looking down at her intently. He was making her feel nervous, but she was determined to tell him what she had been thinking. "I came to thank you," she said simply. "And to tell you I'm sorry for all the dreadful things I said. I know they weren't true. You were right, I didn't understand, and I wouldn't let you explain. I'm sorry."

She looked up at him quite frankly, making no attempt to excuse herself, though in her eyes he could see her longing that he accept her apology.

"I wouldn't blame you if you're still angry with me," she said quietly when he didn't immediately reply. "I accused you of some terrible things. I even demanded the pendant back as if I thought you were a thief! And you still helped me. I don't deserve it, I know, but I am grateful for

everything, you've done—and for giving Hazelhurst back
to me.'' She paused, but when he still didn't say anything
she added rather desperately, ''Please say something!''

For one more long minute Jack didn't reply, then he let
out his breath in a long sigh and smiled crookedly at her.

''Do you always apologise so devastatingly?'' he asked,
and Charity could see the relief in his eyes.

''Oh, Jack,'' she said. ''I was so unkind; I wish—''

''You don't have to apologise,'' he interrupted, taking
her in his arms. ''And you don't have to be grateful to me.
I did what I thought was best, but you were right earlier—
I didn't consult you, and I didn't explain.''

''But I should have trusted you,'' Charity whispered. It
would be a long time before she forgave herself for her
doubts.

''I wonder,'' he said slowly.

He was still holding her, his hands resting lightly on her
waist, but for the moment he made no move to draw her
any closer.

''Perhaps I don't deserve your good opinion,'' he said
at last. ''Charity, I want you more than I've ever wanted
anything in my life, but I can't offer myself to you under
false pretences. Sooner or later you would know me for a
fraud—and sooner or later I would hurt you. If you come
to me it must be because you see me as I am—not as you
would like me to be.''

She looked up at him seriously. She could feel the tension in his arms, and see it in his expression—and she knew
that, whatever it was he wanted to say to her, he wasn't
finding it easy.

''What are you telling me, Jack?'' she asked quietly.

''You made me angry when you accused me of liking—
or even of admiring—the Earl,'' he answered steadily.

"You came too close to the truth, you see. I don't like him—but I do like dealing with him. Owen and Sir Humphrey get their sport from chasing a fox through the fields; I get mine from pitting my wits against men like Ashbourne. I get less muddy, but in some ways I take more risks."

He sighed, gazing down into her luminous brown eyes. She was too honest and too forthright, and he wasn't sure if she would ever be able to understand him.

"I'm a devious man," he said. "Perhaps even more devious than the Earl, though my aims are different. I'm not proud of myself, but I can't change."

Charity tipped her head on one side. From her expression it was hard to tell what she was thinking.

"Did you blackmail Lord Ashbourne into giving me Hazelhurst?" she asked curiously, but without any particular suggestion of condemnation in her voice.

Jack hesitated.

"Yes," he said at last, rather reluctantly. He was afraid she would disapprove. "That is to say, I had information which I knew he would be very unwilling for me to repeat."

"That's not a proper explanation," said Charity firmly. "What information?"

"You heard me tell him that Horwood and Kaye had finally found a third investor?" Jack asked, wondering what she was thinking. He had never expected that she would be able to hide her thoughts so well. "Well, that's Ashbourne, although they don't know it," he continued, feeling very much as if he were on trial. "He's using an agent as usual, and if Adam Kaye finds out before he signs the final agreements he'll withdraw. He hates the Earl. But it should be a very profitable partnership—for all three men."

"What about poor Mr Kaye?" Charity asked, continuing her interrogation. "Shouldn't you warn him?"

"The Earl won't cheat his partners—he'll just taunt them for failing to discover his involvement. Besides, Kaye had just as much chance of finding out as I had—and I'm not responsible for protecting *his* interests," said Jack.

He might also have pointed out that Adam Kaye was both bigoted and unpopular, but he really was trying to avoid giving Charity a false impression of his character.

She gazed up at him thoughtfully, and for a moment he was afraid of what she would say—but then, at last, he saw the growing twinkle in her eyes.

"One day I must tell you how I persuaded Sir Humphrey to sell my father the five-acre field," she said reflectively. "I still don't think Sir Humphrey knows I had anything to do with it."

She began to laugh at his startled expression and looped her arms around his neck.

"We have more in common than you think," she murmured, stretching up to kiss him lightly on the chin.

For a moment longer he continued to stare down at her; then his expression relaxed.

"You little devil!" he exclaimed. "You..." Words failed him, and he silenced her laughter with his kiss.

There had been so much doubt and so much misunderstanding that it was bliss for Charity to feel his arms around her again, and to taste his lips on hers. He was holding her to him fiercely, possessively, as if he never intended to release her again, and she surrendered joyously to his embrace.

"You're quite shameless!" he murmured, brushing his lips against her hair. "There I was, laying my soul bare to you, fearing at any second your disapproval or rejection—and all the time you were laughing at me!"

"I wasn't!" She lifted her head indignantly. "But I thought I'd better find out everything I wanted to know before I told you how I felt. I might not have remembered to ask later."

Her indignation dissolved into a wickedly tantalising smile, and she ran her finger lightly along the line of his jaw.

"No, I don't think that's exactly what you thought," he replied, an answering gleam of humour in his grey eyes. "Are you sure you weren't getting your own back for my arrogance earlier?"

She shook her head, setting her dark curls dancing.

"No," she said quietly. "I finally understood how you must feel about Lord Ashbourne just before I came to see you. That's what I was so anxious to tell you—that I *did* understand how it was possible for you to respect him. But when you started to explain…my good opinion seemed to mean so much to you—and *that* meant so much to *me*."

Jack gazed down at her, wonder and love in his eyes.

"Charity…" he began, but there were no words to describe what he was feeling. "I love you," he said simply.

Her hands were resting on his shoulders, and he took one in his own hand, kissing it almost reverently, then turned it over, kissing her palm, and the deep lace ruffles of her sleeve fell back to above the elbow. His lips followed, caressing the soft skin of her inner arm, tantalising, soothing and exciting her.

She sighed and leant against him, weak with desire and pleasure as she felt him kiss her throat. Then he bent lower, his lips teasing and exciting her as he pushed down the lace of her bodice and kissed the hollow between her breasts.

She caught her breath and clung to him, longing to feel him even closer.

Jack lifted his head and looked down at her; with one

arm he was supporting her, with the other hand he started to stroke the nape of her neck. A ripple of pure delight coursed through her and she leant back against his arm, her dark eyes languid with love and desire.

"Did you speak to Owen?" he asked quietly.

"Mmm? Oh, yes," she said, only half listening, and admiring the straight line of his nose.

"What did he say?"

"Who?"

"Owen!" Jack began to laugh softly, his customary good humour completely restored. "Do concentrate, Charity! I'm about to propose to you. Mind you," he added thoughtfully as he saw that she was still not giving his *words* her full attention, "you do seem to make a habit of letting your thoughts wander at crucial moments like this. In the circumstances, perhaps it would be better if…"

Instead of completing what he was saying he suddenly swept her up in his arms and glanced quickly round the room.

"Jack!" she exclaimed. "What on earth…?"

"I'm not having you wriggle out of this betrothal on the grounds that you didn't understand what I was asking until it was too late!" he declared, and carried her over to a chair.

"There, sit here, and pay careful attention to what I'm about to say to you," he said firmly, stepping back and looking down at her. "And while you're about it you can confirm that you really have told Owen you're not going to marry him."

"Of course I have." She folded her arms demurely in her lap and laughed up at him.

"Good. Now, then, Miss Mayfield—" he began briskly, only the faintest twitch of his lips indicating his own amusement.

"You mean you're not going to get down on your knees?" she interrupted in a disappointed voice.

Jack paused and appeared to think about it. "One knee, if you insist," he said at last. "Both knees—definitely not. Most undignified."

"Oh, I beg your pardon. It was a slip of the tongue. Of course I only meant one knee," she replied graciously.

Jack grinned. "In that case…" he began, but before he could continue the door opened and a servant came in.

"A letter for the lady, my lord," said James discreetly. "No reply is expected."

"Thank you," said Jack calmly. "Leave it on the table, please."

He waited until the footman had turned to go, and then he raised his eyebrow at Charity, who had suddenly been overcome with amusement.

"I'm sorry," she gasped as the door closed behind James, "but I was just imagining…"

"I dare say," said Jack austerely, going to pick up the letter, "but such merriment—" He broke off abruptly, his eyes narrowing as he read the direction on the outside.

"What is it?" Charity asked.

"I'm not sure," he replied slowly. "But I think you'd better open it." He passed it to her and watched her changing expressions as she read it.

My dear Miss Mayfield,

No doubt you will be surprised to receive a letter from me; no doubt, also, you will be sceptical of the contents. I would be disappointed in you if it were otherwise. As I said when we met, you are very like your father in your courage and your composure, but in one respect at least you are immeasurably his superior. If Mayfield had been blessed with your wit, and your clear-sightedness, I would feel less guilt for what I did a year ago. But Mayfield was not my opponent—he was my dupe. A brave, heroic, generous dupe. I will avoid such men in future—they make me uncomfortable.

But you, my dear, are different. I have no doubt that we shall meet again, and when we do I want no unfinished business lying between us. I fear I'll need all my wits to survive that encounter—and guilt is a bad companion.

So…I enclose the key to decoding the Duke's diaries and, to appease your immediate curiosity and to save you the need to read through the entire two volumes, I also enclose a brief resumé of the pendant's history. Thus I feel I have discharged my obligations to you—and to Riversleigh.

Until our next meeting, I remain,

your faithful servant,
Justin Ashbourne.

By the time Charity had finished the letter she was a prey to so many conflicting emotions that she didn't know what to say. She handed it to Jack without a word and waited for him to speak.

''The man's incorrigible!'' he exclaimed as he came to the end.

He glanced at Charity to see what she was thinking.

''He didn't want Hazelhurst, you know,'' he added more quietly. ''By the time you went to see him I think his conscience had given him a lot of trouble. All he wanted was the opportunity *not* to take it—and he was expecting me to give it to him.''

''So you did,'' said Charity, smiling at him. ''I suppose

he would have felt as if he was losing face if he'd just given it back to me.''

''I think so,'' said Jack. ''What does he say about the pendant?''

Charity scanned the second sheet quickly.

''It's a portrait of the fifth Duchess of Faversham, painted just after her marriage in 1578,'' she said at last, paraphrasing Lord Ashbourne's more elegant sentences. ''It was given by her son, the sixth Duke—the one who wrote the diary—to Thomas Mayfield in 1639 as a reward for his extraordinary loyalty to the Duke's son. Of course!'' she interrupted herself. ''Thomas was the man who built Hazelhurst. I wonder if he actually built the house to hide the pendant?''

''That was always a strong possibility,'' Jack agreed, not at all surprised at what she'd told him. ''I've suspected from the first that Thomas must have had something to do with it. You never did see where the jewel was hidden, but it certainly seemed to me that the hiding-place was an integral part of the house, and you told me on our very first meeting that Thomas had built it. You also told me that he'd died fighting in the Civil War only a few years later, and that might have been when the knowledge of the jewel was lost to your family. What's the matter?''

Charity was staring at him in amazement.

''You mean you guessed all that the minute you found the pendant?'' she exclaimed.

''Not immediately,'' he said apologetically as he realised that she wasn't entirely pleased. ''But you must admit, the man who built the house did have the best opportunity for installing such an elaborate hiding-place. Anyway, I still don't know why he was given the jewel. I'm waiting for you to enlighten me.''

''But why didn't you tell me?'' Charity demanded, ignoring the last part of his comment, and obviously feeling torn between admiration and annoyance. "And, now I come to think about it, this isn't the first time you haven't told me all you know."

"Yes, I'm very sorry," said Jack hastily, because he didn't want to be side-tracked into an argument. "I won't do it again. But you must admit, I didn't have much opportunity to tell you—besides, it was really only supposition. Until the Earl sent you that letter there was nothing to confirm my suspicions. Now, are you going to tell me why the Duke gave Thomas the pendant?"

Charity looked at him consideringly for a moment, as if debating whether he deserved to be told, but then she glanced back at the letter.

"Well," she said slowly, "according to Lord Ashbourne's interpretation of the diary, the Duke's son was not entirely…sane. He suffered from periods of great melancholy, interspersed with periods of frenzied activity. He must have caused his father great distress and eventually Thomas was the only loyal friend he had left. In the end, there was a fire in which the Duke's son died and, because the Duke's only surviving heir was a nephew he didn't like, he gave the pendant to Thomas instead. Thomas must have told him of the hiding-place he'd devised for it, and the Duke wrote that down in his diary too."

"Very careless," Jack commented. "To write it down, I mean. But I dare say he didn't think anyone would be able to read what he'd written, or that the knowledge of the pendant, would be lost to your family. If the knowledge hadn't been lost, of course, your father would probably have guessed what Lord Ashbourne was trying to do, and none of this would have happened. The only question now is how the Earl came to have possession of the diary, but I dare say that's one thing he'll never tell us."

"No," said Charity slowly. "You know, it's just occurred to me that if it hadn't been for Lord Ashbourne—and Gideon, especially Gideon—we would never have known about the pendant. So at least one good thing has come out of this whole business."

"Only one?" Jack asked, taking her back into his arms.

Charity looked puzzled, and then she laughed.

"Lord Ashbourne didn't have anything to do with you inheriting Riversleigh," she pointed out. "And if you hadn't we would probably never have met."

"True," said Jack. "And that reminds me of something far more important. In less than two weeks' time you are going to owe me ten guineas! I hope you don't intend to renege on our bargain!"

For a moment Charity stared at him in confusion, then realised that he was talking about their wager.

"But I am *betrothed*," she protested half-heartedly.

"Not sufficient. As I recall, the wager was specifically as to whether you would be *married* by the end of February," Jack pointed out.

"Oh, dear." Charity gazed at him helplessly for a moment; then she started to laugh as she remembered something. "I haven't actually got any money," she said. "I was so preoccupied when we left Sussex that I never thought to bring any. Will you take an IOU?"

"If you wish, but are you sure you can't think of a better solution to the problem than that?" Jack asked, wickedly teasing her with his eyes. "I'm sure Lord Ashbourne would be disappointed in you."

"I don't… We couldn't!" Charity gasped as enlightenment suddenly dawned. "We *can't* get married in such a rush. What will everybody say?"

"Congratulations?" Jack suggested. "I'm sure your

mother will be delighted. She's been viewing me as a prospective son-in-law ever since we met.''

''Mama has?'' Charity exclaimed. ''She never said anything.''

''No, it's a constant source of amazement to me that such a tactful woman could have produced such an outspoken daughter,'' said Jack, his eyes gleaming humorously as he saw the sudden flare of indignation in hers. ''I do not, however, feel this is the moment to discuss your mother.''

He smiled down at her and she felt her heart turn over.

''Are you, or are you not going to consent to win ten guineas from me?'' he asked.

Charity gazed up at him consideringly for perhaps three seconds, then an answering smile lit her face.

''I would be delighted to do so,'' she replied.

* * * * *

The Rake
by
Georgina Devon

Georgina Devon has a Bachelor of Arts degree in Social Sciences with a concentration in history. Her interest in England began when the United States Air Force stationed her at RAF Woodbridge, near Ipswich in East Anglia. This is also where she met her husband who flew fighter aircraft for the United States. She began writing when she left the Air Force. Her husband's military career moved the family every two to three years and she wanted a career she could take with her anywhere in the world. Today, she and her husband live in Tucson, Arizona, with their teenage daughter, two dogs and a cockatiel.

Chapter One

The morning sun barely peeked through the thick overhang of tree limbs. Green Park was still deserted at this time of morning. Not even the servants were about.

'Miss Juliet, you can no' be doing this,' Ferguson Coachman said sternly, his voice breaking the morning quiet.

Juliet Smythe-Clyde looked up between her thick cinnamon eyelashes while wiggling her toes in the too-large Hessians she had commandeered from her younger brother's wardrobe. She stamped her foot to try and better settle the heel. 'Rather this than for Papa to fight the Satanic Duke.'

The tall, spare coachman, his grey whiskers bristling about a narrow face, frowned. 'The master is a grown man. You are a slip of a girl and should no' be fighting his battles.'

'Enough,' Juliet said, slipping off the coat that

fitted her brother like a second skin and herself like a too-large nightrobe. 'Take this and fold it carefully. You know Harry will have an apoplexy if it gets wrinkled.'

Ferguson snorted, but carefully laid the coat on the seat of the dilapidated coach. Hobson, the butler, who was as round as he was majestic, presented the box holding two duelling pistols to his young mistress. Juliet reached for the one on the bottom.

That one is primed and ready to go, miss,' Hobson said. 'I saw to it myself.'

Out of perversity, Juliet took the top one.

'That too is ready,' Hobson said, allowing himself a knowing smile which quickly disappeared. 'Stop this now, Miss Ju, while there is still time.'

Ferguson came to stand beside his crony, the two having become fast comrades despite the disparity in their stations. 'Have I no' been telling her the same since this began? She will no' listen to either of us.'

'I have to do this,' Juliet said, her voice cracking as the fear she had been holding at bay threatened to spill out of control. 'Someone must protect Papa from this latest folly.'

'Someone should no' be you, lass,' Ferguson retorted, his brogue thickening with anger and anxiety. 'You did no' tell the master to marry that doxy.'

'I promised Mama to care for Papa,' she whispered, the memory of her mother's dying request tightening her stomach. Mama was dead barely a year, yet Juliet remembered as if it had happened yesterday.

Mama had lain on the daybed in the morning room, the pale sunlight giving false colour to her shrunken cheeks. The illness that had eaten at her and kept her in constant pain had shrivelled her body and made Juliet secretly glad the end was near. She could not bear to see her beloved mama suffer so.

When Mama had beckoned her closer and begged her to care for Papa—flighty, irresponsible Papa—Juliet had promised. There had been nothing else she could do. She would have done anything to ease Mama's suffering. Anything. And someone had to watch over Papa once Mama was gone. Everyone knew that.

She sighed. She had not been able to keep Papa from marrying Mrs Winters, but she could keep him from throwing his life away for the woman. Surely not even the Duke of Brabourne would shoot to kill a young man who was only taking the place of the original dueller—would he?

Besides which, the Duke was at fault. Not she or Papa. The Duke was the one who had seduced another man's wife. As the one in error, he should delope. It was the honourable thing to do.

Juliet straightened her shoulders and sighted down the barrel of the pistol. At least growing up in the country had taught her something. She could shoot with the best of them, although Brabourne was said to be as deadly with a gun as he was with a sword and just as cold-hearted with either.

The sound of horses' hooves drew her attention. Three men stopped under a large oak some distance from Juliet's little group. All were dressed in great-coats and shiny Hessians with beaver hats perched rakishly atop their heads. She knew all by reputation and one by sight.

Dressed in man's garb, she had paid a very late-night visit to Lord Ravensford, one of Brabourne' seconds, four days before to tell him there was a change in plans. The duel needed to be moved forward. His lordship, too surprised by a puppy visiting him uninvited, had agreed to the change without argument, although his bronze brows had been raised in sardonic amusement during the entire conversation.

The other two men she had never seen. Lord Perth was said to be a rogue who went his own way, regardless of Society's rules. She guessed him to be the one who stood beside the bronze-haired Lord Ravensford. They were much of a height. She spared them little interest for they were not the person she was here to fight.

The third man jumped to the ground with a wiry grace that spoke of strength. She had heard the Duke was not only a rake but a Corinthian of the first stare. He was tall and lean, and when he shrugged out of his greatcoat and navy jacket, she noted his shoulders were broad in their stark white shirt, and his hips were narrow in their close-fitting breeches. His hair was as black as some said his heart was. His nose was a commanding jut of authority. She had heard his eyes were a deep blue, inherited from an Irish ancestor.

A *frisson* of something akin to fear, yet much more delicious, skittered down her spine. She turned away.

She gulped a deep breath of the cold air and wiped her damp palms along the sides of her breeches. For seconds she stared sightlessly at nothing and wondered if she would survive this encounter. It was a weakness she had not allowed herself before. She did not allow it for long now, either.

Lord Ravensford headed their way.

The rising sun glinted on his hair, making it look bright as a new-minted penny. There was a twinkle in his hazel eyes and a dimple in his square chin. He was a very fine-looking man.

'Well, puppy, where is Smythe-Clyde? You said he is the one who wanted this earlier meeting.'

Juliet felt a dull flush spread up her face only to recede. 'He…' she forced strength into her voice '…he is sick. Too sick to leave his bed. But honour demands that he meet Brabourne. So, as his second, I am taking his place.' She looked defiantly at Ravensford.

Ravensford glanced from her to the servants. A hint of disapproval tinged his words. 'Where is the other second? And where is the surgeon?'

'There is no other second, and Ferguson—' she gestured to the coachman '—is as good as any surgeon.'

'Havey-cavey.' Ravensford's gaze bored into Juliet. 'You are only a boy. There is not a chance that Brabourne will meet you. If Smythe-Clyde is too scared to follow through with this, then let him accept the dishonour.'

Juliet's hands clenched. 'I assure you, my lord, that my...that Smythe-Clyde is not afraid to meet the Duke. He is ill. Rather than draw this affair out, I am empowered to meet the Duke in Smythe-Clyde's place.'

Ravensford shook his head. 'I will pass on your words, but I doubt they will change anything.'

Without further discussion, the Earl turned away. Juliet sagged.

'Just as it should be,' Hobson said with smug satisfaction. 'Not even the greatest rakehell in all England would meet a mere boy on the field of honour. Especially when the quarrel is with another.'

Juliet had known from the beginning that the entire thing was far-fetched and likely to fail, but she'd had to try. Even now, as she saw Ravensford talk to the Duke, who looked her way, she knew she had to do something. Papa still intended to meet the

Duke at the original time, two days hence. Keeping Papa from coming here then was the next hurdle Juliet intended to face—after today's duel. One thing at a time, she always told herself. Anything could be accomplished if you did it one step at a time.

Even from this distance, Juliet could see a scowl mar the Duke's dark looks. The light breeze seemed to carry his words.

'Smythe-Clyde is a coward and I refuse to meet his stand-in.'

Panic shot through Juliet as the Duke turned from Ravensford and reached for the coat he had just discarded. She grabbed up one of the duelling pistols, aimed and fired. The noise was loud in the still morning. Splinters of wood exploded from the side of the oak nearest Brabourne. Her adversary spun around to face her.

Her bravado and the closeness of the shot froze her to the ground. Not even the Duke's advance towards her released her paralysed muscles. With the only part of her mind that still seemed to function, Juliet noted the liquid power of his body as he neared her. He stopped a scant foot from her shaking body and razed her with the coldest blue eyes she had ever seen.

'You are either an excellent shot or very lucky. I don't know who you are, or why you feel compelled to stand in for Smythe-Clyde, but the meeting between you and I is now personal. Whatever happens between us will have no bearing on the other. Do you understand me?'

His voice was as hard as his look, and yet the deep timbre did something to her insides that could only be described as exciting. Surely she was not going to fall under the legendary charms of one of England's greatest rakes? She had to wound him severely enough to keep him from meeting Papa, not swoon at his feet.

Juliet raised her chin up higher. 'I understand perfectly.'

'Good. Perth is going after a surgeon. We will wait upon their return to continue.'

Panic shot through Juliet. A surgeon would be fine if the Duke were the one injured. If she were, a surgeon would be a disaster.

'We do not need a sawbones, your Grace.'

His full bottom lip curved into a smile that was anything but friendly, yet did unnameable things to Juliet's breathing. 'You will need one, be sure of that.'

She blanched. 'Th…then Ferguson will do. He is better than anyone to be found in London.'

Brabourne's gaze flicked to the servant and back to Juliet. 'Your coachman.'

She nodded.

'Then it is on your head.'

He strode away before Juliet could respond. She

stared after him. He walked with a loose-limbed grace that flowed from his shoulders down to his narrow hips. She began to understand how her stepmother had succumbed to him. Even she, an innocent in spite of her three-and-twenty years, would be hard pressed to resist him if he pursued her. Not that he would. Not in a millenium. Not before today and especially not after today. Still, there was something incredibly attractive about him.

'Miss Juliet,' Hobson said, breaking into her ridiculous thoughts, 'best you use the gun I first recommended. It is bad luck to use the one already shot.'

'And I need all the luck I can get,' she murmured.

Ferguson stepped forward. 'Now, you remember what I said?'

She nodded. 'We meet, turn our backs to one another and walk twenty paces. Pivot and fire.'

She nodded again, worry gnawing at her nerves. Her jaw wanted to clench and her legs wanted to run away. Her stomach twisted into a knot and, if she had eaten anything before coming here she would be vomiting. Did men feel this way? She knew Brabourne did not.

'Now, Miss Juliet,' Hobson said softly.

Glancing at him, she saw the anxiety he felt for her. It made her hands shake more.

She did not look at the coachman, knowing she

would see the same fear in his eyes. Better to walk boldly forward and meet whatever fate held for her.

The pistol at her side, Juliet moved towards the approaching Duke. His black hair was tied back in a queue a style that was no longer in fashion, but then he was a rule unto himself. One strand had broken free. He ignored it, his attention on her.

Earlier she had seen and felt only the overwhelming sense of power he exuded…now she saw details. His brows winged over eyes the shade of indigo from which tiny lines radiated out, speaking of dissipation and long nights. The late-night growth of whiskers was black against his pale skin. His jaw was a firm line that belied the relaxed set of his shoulders.

He gave her a curt nod, and she knew it was time to turn and begin pacing. One, two…nineteen, twenty.

Juliet spun around, bringing her arm up as she moved. The pistol felt heavy and awkward. In spite of all her practice and determination, she wavered. It was one thing to plan on shooting a man. It was an entirely different thing to do so.

Brabourne had no such reservations.

A shot rang out in the still, quiet air. Juliet experienced a moment of surprise, followed by excruciating pain in her right shoulder. She crumbled to the ground, her pistol falling from unresponsive fingers.

He had shot her.

She brought her left hand up to the wound. Her fingers came away sticky. The metallic tang of blood pinched her nose. She felt herself losing consciousness and wondered if she would die.

'Here, here.' Ferguson fell to his knees beside her and waved smelling salts under her nose. 'This is no' the time to be passing out.'

Juliet nodded feebly. 'No. I have never fainted in my life. I shan't do so now.'

'That's my lass,' Ferguson said, probing gently at the wound.

A jolt like lightning twisted through Juliet. 'Ahh—that hurts,' she gasped.

Ferguson grunted. 'It will hurt much more before it gets better. The ball is lodged between muscle and bone. It must come out. You will be a while getting well.'

She gazed at him, knowing what he said and what it meant, but not wanting to believe him. 'How will I keep this from Papa? I cannot stay in my room unattended even for a day. He will need me. The staff will need me.'

Hobson was on her other side. 'You should have thought of those things before starting this hare-brained escapade, miss.'

'I thought he would delope,' she said softly, wincing as Ferguson probed deeper. 'He…' She gasped as fresh pain seared her. 'He is the one at fault, not Papa. Not me.'

Dark spots danced in her vision. 'The smelling salts,' she whispered.

The two servants exchanged glances. Better to let her faint. She would not feel the pain.

'Is something vital severed?' the Duke of Brabourne said from where he had stopped to watch the situation. 'If the puppy had maintained a side profile instead of squaring completely around, the ball would have grazed the flesh of his upper arm. I did not shoot to kill him.'

'Thank you for that, your Grace,' Hobson said, never taking his attention off Juliet.

'Don't thank me for something I did for myself. If the boy dies, I must flee to the Continent,' Brabourne said. 'That does not suit my plans at the moment.'

Ferguson snorted in disgust.

'You understand perfectly,' Brabourne said. 'Now, what is the prognosis?'

'He's lost a fair amount of blood, and I do no' ken if I can get the ball out here. I can stop most of the bleeding.'

Ravensford, who had come up, looked down. 'You had better get the lad home, then. We will send the surgeon to your direction.'

Juliet listened to the men talking, their words seeming to come through a long tunnel, but at the mention of going home she forced her eyes open. 'Ca…cannot go home. No surgeon. No one know.'

The effort to talk made her feel even more light-headed. She tried to sit up, but found she could not.

'Do no' fash yerself, lad,' Ferguson said. He pressed a makeshift bandage to the wound, trying to staunch the flow of blood.

'What did he mean, not go home?' Ravensford asked.

Hobson, who had gone to the carriage for the laudanum he had packed just in case, returned and said, 'Just that, my lord. The lad cannot go home.'

Brabourne eyed the butler. 'Surely you jest. What type of family does the boy have that he cannot go home?'

Hobson stoically met the Duke's gaze. 'The young master cannot go to the London house in this condition. We will convey him to the country estate.'

Juliet tightened her grip on the butler's hand. 'I must be bandaged so none will know. I cannot stay from home long. You know that.'

Ferguson, tried beyond his patience, said, 'You will do as we tell you.'

Juliet frowned. 'I will do as I must.'

'How far away is the estate?' Brabourne asked.

'Half a day, your Grace,' Hobson said.

'That is much too far, Brabourne,' Ravensford said quietly. 'The wound does not look fatal now, but the continued loss of blood could make it so.' He met his friend's gaze. 'You cannot afford that. Only six months ago you nearly did away with Williams in a sword fight. Prinny will not be so lenient with you if this boy dies.'

Brabourne smoothed one winged brow. 'You must take the puppy to his London house. There is nothing else to be done.'

Ferguson paused in his ministrations to look up at the Duke. 'I will no' do that, your Grace. The lad is right in saying that no one must know what has happened.'

Brabourne looked hard at the servant and spoke softly. 'Are you telling me no?'

Ferguson swallowed hard. 'Yes, your Grace, that be what I'm telling you.'

'And you?' Brabourne pinned Hobson with his gaze.

The butler's ruddy complexion blanched. 'I must stand by Ferguson, your Grace.'

Brabourne looked at Ravensford. The Earl shrugged.

'What is the boy's secret?' Brabourne demanded.

The two servants looked long at one another. Hobson made the Duke a bow. 'The young master met you today without anyone knowing, except us. Lord Smythe-Clyde still plans on meeting you in two days. Master Ju was hoping that by duelling with you today you would consider it finished and not be here when his lordship comes.'

'Stupid.' Brabourne shook his head.

'Misguided,' Ravensford murmured.

Juliet groaned as much from having her plan revealed and hearing how inadequate it sounded when spoken as from pain. Everyone's attention snapped back to her.

'Enough,' Ferguson said. 'Hobson, help me carry the young master to the carriage. We must be on our way if we hope to get him to Richmond before he has lost too much blood.'

'Ravensford?' Brabourne looked at his friend.

Ravensford put one well-manicured hand up as though to ward off a blow. 'Not me, Brabourne. Nowhere does it say a second's duty is to house a wounded opponent.'

Brabourne's lips thinned before forming a small smile. 'As usual, Ravensford, you are correct. I suppose if I don't want the boy to die on me I shall have to make arrangements for his shelter. It is apparent his servants are misguided in their loyalty.' He turned to the men who were in the process of depositing the youth in the coach. 'Take the boy to my town house.' He cast a wicked glance at his friend. 'Ravensford will direct the surgeon to my address.'

Ravensford made a mocking bow. The two servants exchanged horrified looks. Their charge lay limply on the cushions, having passed out when lifted.

'Is something amiss?' Brabourne enquired at his haughtiest.

Ferguson climbed out of the coach and made the Duke a bow. 'Nothing, your Grace. If you will give me directions, we will go there immediately. But we have no need of a surgeon. A clean knife, hot water and plenty of bandages will be enough.'

'Be sure you do not need help before turning it away,' Brabourne said quietly. 'I do not intend to have the boy die.'

'Neither do I, your Grace.' Ferguson stood his ground in spite of the discomfort that had him twisting his hands.

'Then follow me,' Brabourne ordered.

Minutes later, he, Ravensford and Perth cantered from the shelter of the trees, the lumbering coach close behind.

'I hope you do not live to regret this day's work,' Ravensford said.

'So do I, my friend.' Brabourne cast one last look over his shoulder. 'So do I.'

Chapter Two

Sebastian FitzPatrick, Duke of Brabourne, frowned down at his unwanted guest. The boy's milk-white skin was covered in cinnamon freckles. Hair the colour of a sunset tangled around the sweep of cheekbone and curve of brow. There was a tight look around the eyes, as though the youth were in pain even though he slept. He probably was. It had taken time and considerable digging to extract the ball. He had lost a fair amount of blood during the ordeal and would be weak for some time.

A chair scraped behind Sebastian. 'Can I be helpin', your Grace?'

Sebastian glanced back at the coachman whose head had been nodding seconds before. Ferguson was the man's name. 'Has your master regained consciousness?'

'No, your Grace.'

'Have you eaten or had any sleep?'

'No, your Grace.'

'Then do so.'

'Beggin' your pardon, your Grace, but I must stay with the master.'

'One of my servants will do as well. Now go.' Sebastian returned his scrutiny to the boy.

He was as frail as a willow and with a hint of lavender about him, a strange scent for a man. Full lips the colour of pomegranates gave him an effeminate air. And yet the youth had fought him in a duel. He had put his life at stake for another person. Sebastian would not do so, and was sure he did not know anyone who would, with a few exceptions— Ravensford and Perth. Perhaps that was the fascination this boy had over him, the reason he found himself in this room gazing down at a person he did not even know. He reached out to touch the boy's brow.

The servant cleared his throat.

Sebastian's hand dropped to his side. 'Haven't you gone yet?' he asked without turning around.

'I can no' be leavin' my charge…your Grace.'

Irritation chewed at Sebastian. 'I told you that one of my servants will stand watch.'

The servant made a sound very much like choking. 'Beggin' yer pardon, your Grace, but I canna trust the young master to someone unknown.'

Sebastian lowered his voice to a silky thread. 'You are stubborn and forthright for a servant.' The coachman stood his ground even though his gaze lowered deferentially. 'Then I shall stay with your charge. Surely that will meet your requirement.' In the silence that followed, Sebastian heard the man gulp.

'I must no' leave his side.'

'Are you afraid I will do something to your precious charge? I have plenty of vices, but I assure you that molesting boys is not one of them.'

Ferguson whitened, but spoke around his obvious discomfort. 'I am well aware of your Grace's pastimes.'

His patience suddenly gone, Sebastian spun around. *'Get out now.'* Still the servant hesitated. Sebastian wondered what kind of master the boy must be to engender such loyalty in his people. 'If you do not leave, I shall have you thrown bodily from the room. When your master awakens, I wish to speak privately with him. In the meantime, I will watch him and have my housekeeper provide anything needed. I don't want him dead any more than you do.'

Still the servant stayed. Sebastian strode to the fireplace and reached for the velvet cord above the mantel.

'Ferguson…' a weak voice came from the bed '…do as his Grace says. I will be all right.'

'I'll no' be leavin' you with the likes of his Grace.'

This loyalty was vastly interesting, but Sebastian was not known for his patience. 'Get out now, before I finish what I started and have my footmen throw you out.'

The boy struggled to sit and the servant rushed to his side. 'No, you should no' be doing this.' The coachman fussed like a mother hen.

'Go,' the boy said. 'If the Duke wanted to hurt me, he would have…' He took laboured breaths, his cheeks flushing and then paling. 'He would have aimed to kill.'

'You ken why I can no' leave,' Ferguson muttered under his breath.

Sebastian had excellent hearing, but said nothing. There was something amiss here, and he was beginning to see what it might be. There was a delicacy to the youth's wrist when he lifted it to pat the servant's gnarled hand. Sebastian's mouth twisted. He was a fool not to have seen it earlier, but the puppy's bravery had blinded him.

The boy whispered, 'You will only make him more suspicious by insisting.' Raising his voice, the youth said, 'Now go. You may come back as soon as his Grace is done questioning me. Please.'

Ferguson gave the Duke a threatening look, but did as ordered. The door closed behind the servant with a defiant snap.

Sebastian noted the dark circles under the girl's gold-flecked hazel eyes, for girl she was. Now that he knew, it was obvious. He was a connoisseur of women and knew that her lashes, the colour of honey sable and just as thick as that fine fur, would be the envy of any courtesan. As would the lush, burnt red curls that lay like flames on the pillow. For a moment he wondered if her temper matched her hair and if her passion matched her determination. It would be interesting to find out—but not now.

'Why are you impersonating a boy?' he asked without preamble.

She paled even more, but her voice was defiant. 'You are addled from too much dissipation, your Grace.'

He smiled slowly, his gaze running boldly over her, enjoying her bravado. 'Not at the moment. Now that I look beyond your dress…and actions, it is obvious you are a woman.' He ignored her snort. 'Probably with your breasts bound and the borrowed finery of a male family member. Since I have never had your acquaintance foisted on me, you haven't been presented to Society, although you speak and carry yourself like Quality. I would imagine you have lived your life in the country and have only recently come to town.'

She stared baldly at him. For a long moment, Sebastian thought she would continue to deny her true gender.

With a sigh of weariness, she sank back into the pillow. 'But, how...? You did not suspect before...?'

Sebastian smiled, a rare one of enjoyment that softened the hard angles of his face. He reached for the hand nearest him, realised it was on her wounded side before touching her and stretched across her instead. He caught her fingers even as she started to slide them under the covers.

Leaning over her, he brought her captured hand towards him, but not so near as to force her on to her wounded shoulder. He turned the palm up.

'Your skin is soft as velvet and unblemished. Your nails are short but well cared for. No sun has touched you to toughen or darken your complexion.' One by one, he examined her fingers. 'Long and elegant. A lady's hands. Certainly not those of a man.'

With that inherent need to charm and seduce that made him the successful rake he was, he brought her hand to his lips. She yanked back as though bitten. He let her go.

'Why did you meet me?'

She met his eyes openly even as her body sagged visibly with exhaustion. 'I had to. Someone had to stand up to you.' Her voice was weak, but a thread of determination ran through it.

Sebastian found himself taken aback by her vehemence. 'Stand up to me?'

The hand of her wounded arm lay flaccid. Her

other hand clenched the fine linen sheet. 'You are a libertine and a dangerous, amoral man in a position of power that has allowed you to do as you pleased.'

A glint of admiration for her courage lit his eyes, only to be doused by an emotion Sebastian had long ago decided would not rule him. She spoke only the truth. 'And what of it? I am not the only one of my ilk.'

'I know,' she muttered. 'But you are the only one of your kind to impact on my family.'

'Ah,' he said mildly, his reactions once more under control. 'Your family. What is Smythe-Clyde to you? An uncle, cousin, father?'

Her skin, which he had thought pale as milk, took on the translucent clarity of the moon. With the right clothing she would be a beauty; a very unusual one, but a beauty none the less. Beautiful women intrigued him—for a while.

She turned away from him. Her chest laboured. 'It is none of your business.'

'A lover, perhaps?'

Her head whipped back and there was such anger in her that he found his interest increasing. When one could have anything one wanted, a challenge was not to be ignored. Particularly one with such possibilities.

'You are perverted,' she breathed.

He pulled the nearest chair to the edge of the bed and lounged back into it. 'No, merely curious.'

He found himself fascinated by the way colour played across her cheeks, only to flee and return again later. Her lips compressed into a thin line, then opened like a fine rose when heated by the sun.

She sighed. 'It is none of your business, and I am too tired to continue arguing with you.'

He could see by the deepening of lines around her eyes and mouth that she spoke the truth. 'This is a delicious game we play, my sweet, but you are right, you have not the strength for it.'

Her face tightened. The angle of cheek and jaw sharpened. But she said nothing.

He studied her a while longer. 'I can always make enquiries about Smythe-Clyde's family. I assure you it will not take my secretary long to find out more.'

Her body stiffened. 'Why are you doing this?'

'Because you are a mystery, and mysteries beg to be solved.'

'A mystery. Something to entertain you, not a person.'

He nodded his head in curt acceptance of her hit. 'Exactly. What is Smythe-Clyde to you?'

Her chin lifted. 'My father. Now will you leave me alone?'

The answer was not what he had expected. 'For now.'

Not only was the girl foolhardy, she was reckless. As the daughter of a baron, she would be completely ruined if word of her escapade got out. Well-brought-up young ladies did not even know about duelling, let alone participate in one. Worse, if rumour reached the *ton* that she was in his house, in one of his beds, Society would try to force him to marry her. The girl had to go.

Long minutes went by as they met each other's gaze. The clock on the mantel chimed eight. A knock on the door signalled interruption.

He rose with languid grace and crossed to the closed curtains of the window before saying, 'Enter.'

Juliet sagged in relief when Ferguson entered carrying a tray. Exhaustion, pain and fear ate at her. What would Brabourne do now that he knew she was a woman? Would he denounce her to the world?

She glanced over to see him watching her with a brooding intensity that did nothing to calm her frayed nerves. He was dressed for evening. Perhaps Almack's, although she doubted that he frequented that very respectable Marriage Mart. More likely he was headed out to one of his clubs, to be followed by dalliance with one of his many female companions. At least this time it would not be with her stepmother.

Still, he was the most handsome man she had ever seen. The perfect cut of his black coat showed broad shoulders to advantage. Black pantaloons hugged narrow hips, and white stockings revealed impeccable calves. His cravat was tied in what she assumed was the Brabourne Soirée, an arrangement her younger brother had yet to be successful duplicating, although Harry tried repeatedly. But all Brabourne's sartorial elegance was nothing compared to the man himself.

He took her breath away. Or, more probably, she told herself, it was her wound making her think air was in short supply. His unfashionably long hair waved over his collar like a raven's wing, moving with every step he took. His eyes were brilliantly blue and penetrating. Too penetrating, she thought, as a blush heated her flesh. And his mouth. She had only seen lips like his on the marble face of a Greek god. His male beauty—for there was really no other word to describe how he looked—was marred only by a look of bored dissipation that hovered around his eyes and mouth.

She was more than thankful he had no interest in her, for she did not think she could resist him if he wanted her. Better for all of them if she left immediately. Ferguson would see to it. He should have taken her to her father's country house in the first place.

'Here, young master,' Ferguson said, setting the tray down on the table near the bed.

The scent of chicken broth made Juliet's mouth water. She tried to sit up, but after a feeble attempt fell back. The exertion made her voice a thin reed.

'There is no need for the pretence, Ferguson. His Grace knows I am a woman.'

Ferguson's hand, with a spoon of broth, paused halfway between bowl and patient. He cast the Duke a fulminating look.

'Don't worry,' the Duke drawled, 'I will resist the urge to ravish her. But you had best see to it that no one else realises her deception.' His eyes gleamed wickedly. 'I cannot control everyone who works for me.'

'Yes, your Grace,' Ferguson said, frowning down at Juliet. 'I will have the lass out of here before anyone is the wiser.'

'That would be best,' her reluctant host said, going to the door. He looked back at her once, then left. The door closed softly behind him.

Tension Juliet hadn't felt rushed out, and she sank further into the softness of the feather bed. 'As soon as I've eaten we must leave.'

Ferguson nodded. 'Hobson will be back shortly to see how you do, lass. I will fetch the coach while he is here.'

Tenderly, he propped her up on the full pillows and helped her eat the broth. Juliet was glad of his help since her hand refused to be steady. When she finished her head fell back.

'I am so tired, Ferguson. I think I will sleep. Waken me when Hobson arrives.'

'Yes, lass.' He poured a generous portion of laudanum into a glass and added water to blunt the bitter taste of the medicine. 'Take this. It will help ye sleep and ease the discomfort.'

Ju smiled weakly. 'I do not need it to sleep, but it would be nice to have less pain.' She swallowed the concoction with a grimace.

Ferguson settled her comfortably, noting that she fell asleep before he reached his chair. She was a good, brave lass. Headstrong and not much accomplished in feminine things, but a good girl.

Sebastian lifted his hand and a waiter rushed over. 'Another bottle of port.'

'Immediately, your Grace.' The servant hurried away.

'This is our sixth bottle,' Ravensford said. He tunnelled long, white fingers through his thick red hair. He had a smile and a way about him that could charm the chemise off a doxy without a penny changing hands.

'Then we are four behind,' Jason Beaumair, Earl of Perth, said. He was wickedly handsome, with the blackest eyes set in a narrow face, which was framed in equally black hair frosted at the temples and forehead. A scar ran from his right eyebrow to the corner of his mouth. It was said he had received it in a duel over another man's wife.

Sebastian gazed at his friends. If Jonathan, Marquis of Langston, were here, they would be complete. But Langston had married the famous actress, Samantha Davidson, and was an infrequent visitor to White's now.

'We need one more for whist,' Sebastian said, pouring from the newly arrived bottle of port.

A flurry of words, followed by the thud of a table hitting the floor, drew Sebastian's attention. A boy—or young man—was wrestling his way into the room. The youth had a narrow face and carrot-red hair. His hazel eyes were wild and angry. Freckles marched across his prominent nose, looking as though a cook had sprinkled nutmeg on his skin.

His gaze came to rest on Sebastian. Fierce satisfaction curled the boy's lips into a snarl. 'Release me!' he demanded, twisting out of a servant's grasp. He strode to Sebastian's table.

Sebastian took in the look of the cub and knew instantly who he was related to. In a bored tone, he said, 'A Smythe-Clyde.'

'Harold Jacob Smythe-Clyde.' The boy stood defiantly, hands on hips.

Sebastian groaned inwardly. First the chit and now this. And all because of Emily Winters. The former Mrs Winters was getting the cut direct the next time he had the misfortune to meet her, and the girl was leaving as soon as he returned home.

He propped one well-shod foot on the table and lounged back to look up at Harold Jacob Smythe-Clyde. 'You are not invited to join us,' he drawled.

The boy drew himself up. 'I did not come to game with scum such as yourself…your Grace.'

Sebastian raised one dark brow. He sensed both Ravensford and Perth tensing. To ease them he waved one languid white hand. 'Then begone. You are a bore.'

'And you, sir, are a libertine, a rake and a seducer of innocent women.' The furious words fell into a dearth of sound. Red rose up the boy's cheeks and spread to his ears. But he held his ground.

The tic at Sebastian's right eye started. He focused on the cut of his shoe. 'You tread dangerous ground,' he said softly.

'I challenge you to a duel. Weapons of your choosing.' If the boy's voice trembled, it was barely noticeable.

'I do not stoop to duel with halfwits.' Sebastian reached for his glass and took a long drink of the strong wine. This family was becoming unacceptable.

'You, your Grace, are a bastard. I know how you—'

In one smooth movement, Sebastian rose to his feet. He planted a facer on the boy that knocked the cub to the floor. 'No one calls me a bastard,' he said quietly, dangerously. 'Now get out of here before I run you through where you stand.'

He poured out the remainder of the bottle and downed it in one long swallow. 'It is time we left,' he said, his gaze sweeping over his friends. 'White's has lost its exclusivity.'

Before the boy could get to his feet, Sebastian and his friends left. The hour was early yet, and St James's was crowded with people.

'Another puppy after your blood,' Perth said in his dark, deep voice. 'Smythe-Clyde must have been busy in his youth.'

'My understanding,' Ravensford said, swinging his gold-tipped cane nonchalantly, 'is that the baron has only one son.' He smiled at Sebastian. 'And you just laid him out with an upper cut that Jackson himself would have admired.'

Sebastian settled his beaver hat at a devilish angle. 'That is high praise coming from someone Jackson cannot defeat in the ring.' He glanced around. 'But enough. Shall we head for Annabell's? There is more to life than wine and gaming.'

'So true,' Perth drawled, falling into step. 'There is wine, gaming and women.'

'Particularly women,' Ravensford said with a devilish gleam in his eyes.

Chapter Three

In the small hours of the morning, Sebastian strolled into the room where his unwelcome guest stayed. The two servants hovered around the bed, muttering direly. The Duke did not like the tension he sensed.

'What is the matter?' Sebastian asked, striding to the group.

Hobson looked up, his round face creased with worry. 'Miss Juliet is worse.'

Sebastian looked at the patient. Her face was flushed. The nightshirt he had loaned her lay damply against her neck and shoulder. Her hands fluttered like trapped butterflies. Irritation mingled with concern, making his brows dip inward.

'Is her wound inflamed?'

Ferguson looked up from where he was gently taking the bandage off. 'I believe so, your Grace.'

The skin where the ball had entered was swollen and red, with streaks of crimson starting to form.

Her eyes opened and their sparkling gaze alighted on Sebastian.

'Brabourne,' she muttered, the words slurred but recognisable. 'A man's nemesis and a woman's heart's desire.' She giggled, only to end in a gasp of pain as Ferguson tried to clean the seeping wound. 'Blast! Must you be so clumsy?' she gasped.

They were the last coherent words she said as Hobson tipped a glass of water and laudanum down her throat.

'I need to make a poultice,' Ferguson said, laying aside the cloth he had used to sponge her shoulder. He looked at the Duke.

Sebastian almost sighed as he felt the noose of involvement tightening around his neck. It was obvious the chit could not be moved. 'And what do you expect from me?'

'You are supposed to have one of the best stables in the country, your Grace. I am sure your head groom has what I need.'

'You mean to put the same poultice on your mistress that you would use for a horse?'

Ferguson shrugged. 'It works for four-legged creatures. Why not two-legged ones?'

Sebastian had no better suggestion since they would not allow a doctor, which he thoroughly agreed with now that he knew the circumstances. 'Go and tell Jenkins that you have my permission to use whatever you need.'

The one servant left and, with a resignation that tightened his gut, Sebastian turned to the other. 'And what do you need?'

Hobson glanced up. 'More cool water would help, your Grace. Miss Juliet is raging hot; no matter how much I sponge her, she only seems to burn the more.'

Sebastian moved to the bellpull over the mantel only to stop before summoning a servant. His brooding glance settled on the girl. With her flushed cheeks and swollen lips, no one could mistake her for anything but what she was. If someone were still so unobservant as to think she was male, the swell of her breasts under the shirt and single sheet would be enough to enlighten them. One of the first things she had done after he had pierced her disguise had been to remove the binding from her breasts so she could breathe better and lie more comfortably.

This situation was becoming more and more complicated. The very last thing he needed was for word of his unwanted guest's real identity to leak out. At three and thirty, Sebastian had no intentions of marrying someone not of his choosing. Not even if some foolish chit's reputation depended upon him wedding her.

Nor did he want the world to know he had shot a woman. It was bad enough that he knew. Damn her for putting him in this dishonourable position.

He pulled the bell and moved quickly into the

hall. A footman appeared instantly, impeccably dressed in the Duke's black and green colours.

'Fetch Mrs Burroughs,' Sebastian instructed.

The young man's eyes widened, but he bowed and left.

Sebastian had a rule that servants who worked during the day would not be expected to work at night. That went particularly for his housekeeper and butler, whom he knew laboured fourteen and sixteen hours a day. Never before had he summoned Mrs Burroughs from her bed. He did not intend ever to do so again.

He stepped back into the sickroom. Mrs Burroughs would knock, and he did not intend for anyone else to hear their discussion.

Juliet Smythe-Clyde looked no better. Hobson's worried frown was deeper. 'Ferguson knows what he's about,' the butler mumbled, as though to reassure himself.

'If he does not, then we are going to have problems,' Sebastian stated. 'I have no intentions of fleeing to the Continent. Nor do I intend for anyone to discover your mistress's whereabouts.'

A discreet knock stopped the butler from saying whatever was on the tip of his tongue. Instead he turned back to his charge.

Sebastian crossed to the door and asked, 'Mrs Burroughs?'

'Yes, m'lord.'

He let her in, quickly closing the door behind her. 'We have a problem.'

She looked from him to the bed. Her iron-coloured brows shot up, wrinkling her forehead into a dozen creases. Her mouth puckered in dismay and then disapproval. ''Twould seem we do, *your Grace.*' Her emphasis on his title told him more clearly than words that she was shocked and unhappy with the situation.

He looked at the old woman who had started service with his father over thirty-two years ago. She had been his nanny. When he'd inherited the title, he had retired his parents' housekeeper and appointed Mrs Burroughs. She was not a woman who would have taken well to retirement.

'You are the only person I can trust with this information. We must nurse her until she is able to be moved. And no one must find out.'

She snorted. 'I would hope my husband can be trusted with this, your Grace. 'Twill take more than the three of us here to give the girl round-the-clock care. I have a house to run, I'm sure this gentleman here has duties, and you have all of London to carouse through.'

The disapproval in her voice when she described his activities was softened by the affection in her brown eyes. She did not like the life he led, but she cared for him.

Hobson, realising that Mrs Burroughs had a sensible head on her shoulders, moved closer. 'I am the butler to Miss Juliet's father and I cannot be gone much.'

Her knowing gaze went from Hobson to the girl. 'A secret. Well, his Grace was always one for getting into scrapes.'

Ferguson's return from the stables saved Sebastian from needing to comment. There were times he regretted making his nanny his housekeeper.

Ferguson set about applying the poultice.

Late the next afternoon, Sebastian sat at table breaking his fast. Soon he would have to take up his post with the patient. Ferguson had returned to Smythe-Clyde's house after rebandaging the shoulder. Hobson had stayed until Mrs Burroughs could find time in the late morning hours. Burroughs had been in and out. From the surreptitious glances the footman was sending his way, Sebastian knew the servants wondered what was going on.

'Your Grace.' One of the footmen bowed and presented a silver tray on which lay a white calling card with the corner bent.

Sebastian picked it up and read the name Harold Jacob Smythe-Clyde, his unwelcome charge's brother. 'I am not at home.'

'Yes, my lord.'

Minutes later, the sound of a raised voice reached

Sebastian. It was followed by the closing of the front door. This family was nothing but trouble.

With a sigh, Sebastian rose. How had he let himself get into this predicament? He was a man who had always considered his own comforts first.

First it had been to keep the girl's servants from taking her into the country and possibly threatening her life. Then it had been because she was too sick to be moved.

In an unconscious gesture, he smoothed his left eyebrow with one finger. Now he allowed the chit to stay here because she needed to regain some strength before returning home. In her present condition it would not be long before someone realised she was hurt. Then the duel would come out, and her stay here. That would ruin her. Her courage intrigued him and he did not want to see her pay for it. Too few people of his acquaintance had her strength.

In spite of all that, respectable young women of the *ton* did not spend nights under any man's roof, let alone his. His reputation as a rake did not bear scrutiny. Even he, as immune as he was to Society's dictates, would be hard pressed to refuse marriage if it were ever discovered that the girl had spent several nights under his roof. She had to leave. Soon.

In the meantime, he would amuse himself at Tattersall's. There was a fine filly that had caught his eye last week. Spirited and headstrong, the horse reminded him of his unwanted guest. At least with the animal he could determine whether he wanted her in his stable.

Juliet roused from a nightmare where Papa duelled with Brabourne and was hit. Moisture beaded her brow and her night shirt clung to her skin. Why was she so hot?

Where was she?

The sound of someone lightly snoring caught her attention. A long, lithe man sprawled in one of two chairs, his legs spread out and seeming to go on for ever. A wave of dark hair shadowed his sallow cheeks and gave him a demonic cast.

Memory returned.

She rolled to one side and pushed up with her good arm. Pain shot through her bad shoulder. She gasped and squeezed her eyes shut against unwanted tears.

'What the deuce are you about?'

She turned her head and stared straight up at him. Without her hearing him he had come to the bed. His black brows were drawn and his blue eyes shot sparks.

'I am trying to sit up,' she said peevishly, wishing she did not hurt so much. 'Why else would I be twisting around?'

'Whining does not become you,' he stated baldly,

the lines between his brows easing. 'Let me help you or you will undo all the good work your coachman has done.'

Without waiting for her reply, he reached down and hooked a hand under each of her arms and hauled her up on to the pillows. Another gasp of pain escaped her and once more tears welled in her eyes. She told herself that her blurred vision gave her the impression his face held contrition. There was no doubt in her mind that he found her a nuisance rather than someone he might be concerned over.

Long moments passed and his hands stayed on her. His warmth flowed into her, increasing her fever and making her pulse jump. No man had ever touched her so intimately. Juliet looked up at him and felt herself blushing.

He finally released her. 'Is that better?' he asked, his voice hoarse as though he had a cold.

She nodded. Strange sensations coursed through her body, and for a weak moment she wished he would touch her again. She was a fool.

'Would you like some water?'

'Yes,' she muttered. 'Please. I am so hot. It is like a furnace in here.'

He poured the liquid and held it to her lips. 'You are feverish. The wound is inflamed and Ferguson has been treating it with horse poultices.'

Juliet chuckled. 'That is very like him. Has it helped?'

He set the empty glass on a stand. 'It seems so. This is the first time since last night that you have been awake and coherent at the same time.'

Her eyes widened. 'Surely you jest?'

'Not about this.' He turned away and fetched the chair he had been sprawled in. He set it near the bed and sank into its thick leather cushions.

'I suppose not,' she said, looking away from his intense perusal. 'I cannot suppose I am the kind of woman you would choose to be in one of your beds.' As soon as the words were out, she realised how provocative they were. 'I...I did not mean that the way it sounded.'

He raised one brow. 'You did not? How disappointing.'

She had thought herself warm before, but now she flamed.

A slow smile cut a line into his cheek. It was seductive in the intensity it gave to his face, as though he were truly interested in her as a woman. Part of her wanted to melt. A larger part wanted to run. He was a dangerous man for a woman to be around.

'I am sure there are many women eager to share one of your beds and that none of them would be here from wounds.' The words came out like an accusation instead of the reasonable statement of fact she had intended. He was a disturbing man.

'True, but then they would be boring. You, I'd wager, are never boring.'

She had a sense that he was flirting with her. She looked away from his unsettling scrutiny and her fingers plucked at the sheet without her being aware of what she did.

'Anyone can be boring,' she finally whispered.

'So I have generally found,' he replied drily. 'But then no other woman has ever fought me in a duel. Nor has any other woman told me she could not go home and then convinced me to let her stay in mine. Why wouldn't your family help hide your condition?'

The abrupt change of subject surprised her. It was as though he had been trying to trick her into answering him, but there was no secret. 'Harry would have. Poor Papa would have run to his new wife and expected her to handle everything. I don't trust my stepmother. Everything she does is designed to further her own ends. She would be furious.'

'Because you fought a duel or because you tried to take your father's place?'

'Both.'

'Would she have hit you?' His eyes darkened as he waited for her answer. 'Would your father?'

'No,' she squeaked, shocked that he could even think such a thing. 'Papa has never hit us. Mama was always the one to discipline us. She or our nurse, and later our governess and tutor. My stepmother would not dare.'

His mouth tightened. 'Did you see much of your mother?'

A soft smile of memory lit Juliet's face. 'Yes. Always. Mama was a curate's daughter, and she believed children were a gift to be treasured.'

'A nice fancy,' he said, bitterness making the words hard and brittle.

No emotion showed on his face. It was as though he had shut his real self behind a mask. The urge to ask him why was great, but Juliet hesitated. He was not a man who invited closeness or questions about himself.

He stood so sharply that his chair tottered on its back legs before settling down. He paced to the fireplace, grabbed the poker and jabbed viciously at the already roaring fire.

Juliet saw pain in the tense set of his shoulders. The longing to comfort him was great, but she sensed that to say something would only make him draw further into himself. Instead, she waited quietly for him to make the next overture. She did not wait long.

He put the poker back and strode to the bed, where he grabbed the chair and repositioned it in its original place. 'I will send Mrs Burroughs to help you change into a fresh shirt. But first tell me why your father's anger kept you from going home when you knew he would not punish you.'

She smiled ruefully. He would not give confidences, but he expected them of others. Still, it would do no harm. 'I could not have kept my condition hidden from Papa. When he found out, he would have been angry with me because he would have been hurt that I felt he needed to be protected. That I did not trust him to take care of himself. Although everyone will tell you that he cannot.'

'A grown man cannot take care of himself?' the Duke asked in disbelief. 'I think you exaggerate.'

'Not about Papa. He can find his way anywhere in the country, but he is forever becoming lost here in London. Just as he will misplace every one of the twelve pairs of glasses I have got for him. Or reach his hand into a lion's cage because he is curious about what the creature will do.' She gave a long-suffering sigh.

The Duke chuckled. 'A handful.'

'Always. At first I was thrilled that he was re-marrying, even though it was not yet a year after Mama's death. But then...' She clamped her mouth shut on the words. In a falsely brisk voice, she stated, 'But that is neither here nor there. You are right, your Grace. A clean nightshirt would be most welcome.'

He made her a mocking bow before leaving. She had no doubt he knew exactly what she had stopped herself from saying. After all, he was the man her stepmother was having an affair with. He would know the woman. Just the thought made her chest tighten, and the wound she had nearly forgotten started to ache anew.

How long would it take her to learn to protect herself against his charm? Probably for ever, said a tiny voice she wanted to ignore.

Sebastian sprawled across the large leather wingback, his right leg indecorously thrown over the chair's arm. He swung his foot, the evening pump catching the firelight. He twirled the half-full glass of whisky before taking a long swallow. The liquor burned down his throat. He smiled grimly. The savageness of the liquid matched the emotions running through him.

'Damned uncivilised drink,' he muttered, taking another gulp. He would probably consume the entire decanter. He had got a taste for it from his friend Jonathan, Marquis of Langston, who had learned about it from his younger brother, Lord Alastair St Simon.

The chit had to go. The only thing worse than having her continued presence in his home would be to have her die while occupying one of his beds. She had already been here two days and was on her second night. But she was out of danger, or nearly so. And she was a distraction.

He emptied his glass.

A knock caught his attention as he rose to pour more whisky. 'Who is it?' he demanded, moving to his desk and emptying the contents of the decanter into his glass.

'Your Grace,' Burroughs, the butler, intoned, entering the room and closing the door behind himself. His long, rather bulbous nose rose several inches, a pose Sebastian knew the man assumed when his sensibilities were affronted.

'There is a *person* to see you.'

Sebastian raised one black brow. 'A *person*?'

Burroughs puffed up his ample girth. 'A woman…as your Grace very well knows.'

Which one of his lady-friends would be so lost to propriety as to visit him here? Sebastian neither cared nor knew. He drank the whisky in one gulp. 'Tell her I am not at home.'

Burroughs bowed, a smile of approval making his round face glow. 'My pleasure, your Grace.'

Sebastian set the empty glass on the corner of his desk and decided it was time for bed. Most of London was asleep, and only his irritation at having his home pose a threat to his peace of mind had kept him up this late.

Sounds of a scuffle barely preceded the library door bursting open. A woman dressed in black strode into the room followed by a harassed Burroughs.

'Your Grace,' she murmured breathlessly, 'I have something of the utmost importance to discuss with you.'

Sebastian was good at remembering faces and voices. He recognised his intruder and frowned. She was the reason he was in this bramblebath. He waved away Burroughs, who hovered behind her. The only way he could evict Mrs Winters—now Lady Smythe-Clyde—would be to have her bodily carried from the room. The hair rising on the nape of his neck told him to listen to her first.

Not until Burroughs closed the door behind himself did Sebastian offer her a seat. He propped one hip on the edge of his desk and looked down at her. 'It is very late to be making a social call, Lady Smythe-Clyde.'

She pushed back the hood of her cape and untied the strings at the throat. The heavy taffeta slipped from her shoulders to billow around her lap and spill down the back of her chair. Her pale blonde curls framed a heart-shaped face with eyes the colour of a fine spring sky. Many poems had been written about the beauty of her cupid's bow mouth. Her evening dress was daringly low, even for a married woman, and showed an almost childlike figure. Sebastian knew the heart of a courtesan beat under the small bosom. But why was she here? He had already refused her overtures.

She smiled endearingly up at him. 'Please, your

Grace, do call me Emily. We shall soon be well acquainted.'

'Shall we?' he murmured, wondering what her game was and knowing it boded no good for him or the girl upstairs. He knew the former Mrs Winters from old. She had been as shocking in her flaunting of conventions as she was as Lady Smythe-Clyde. The rest of their conversation would likely be just as vulgar.

She threw back her head and laughed, a tinkling sound that was her signature. Slowly, her eyes only slightly narrowed, she lowered her head and smiled at him. 'Very well indeed. Do you know where my stepdaughter is?'

Sebastian kept his gaze on her even as the warmth provided by the whisky evaporated. 'Your stepdaughter? Do you have one?'

Her lips parted in a languid smile. 'Really, your Grace, there is no need for games between us.'

Sebastian put both palms on the desk and leaned backward. 'Isn't there? There is nothing between you and I, yet you are the reason your new husband challenged me to a duel.'

She leaned forward, showing the dark valley between her breasts. 'But there could be…'

Sebastian studied her, wondering how far she would go in her pursuit of him. Women flocked to him for his wealth and power. Usually, however, they took 'no' as just that. This woman had been pursuing him for the past month.

In a mildly curious voice, he asked, 'Why are you so persistent? You have an older husband who is titled and reasonably wealthy. Isn't that enough, considering where you started life?'

An angry scowl marred her childish beauty before she smoothed her brow with an index finger. 'My husband is not the Duke of Brabourne, one of the most influential men in the realm.' She paused for effect and flicked her small pink tongue along her bottom lip. 'Nor is he renowned as the best lover in England, a man all women find irresistible—in and out of bed.'

Sebastian's gut tightened. He dipped his head to her in mocking acknowledgement of her statement.

His father had never thought of him as more than a means to pass on the title. His mother had never thought of him at all, her own lovers being legendary and all-consuming.

In an attempt to be more than a title and money, he had taught himself to be a lover. He had made himself into a man women remembered, and if it was by giving them more pleasure than any thought possible, then so be it. They would remember him as more than a wealthy Duke, an object of advancement. They would remember him as a man.

But not this woman. He had not even kissed her,

and she had already caused him more problems than any of his numerous mistresses put together.

He smiled, a cold stretching of his sensual lips. 'Lady Smythe-Clyde, I would never presume to enter a dalliance with a married woman.'

Her own smile was equally frigid. 'You would do whatever you damn well pleased, and we both know it.'

'Ah, the gloves are off,' he murmured.

'As will be more than that,' she countered, 'if you know what is good for your future.'

'Are you threatening me?' he asked, his voice silky.

She smoothed the satin of her skirt, the action drawing attention to the fine lines of her thighs, her gaze never leaving his face. 'Nothing so dramatic. Merely offering not to divulge some information my lady's maid was so obliging as to find out for me.'

He did not need an explanation. Somehow, even with all his efforts to keep Juliet Smythe-Clyde's presence in his house secret, one of the servants had found out and spread the information. Eventually the news would spread to other homes of the *ton*. And quickly.

Whether he agreed to the dalliance being proposed or refused, the result would be the same. Juliet Smythe-Clyde was ruined.

'Just why exactly are you pursuing me?' he wondered. 'There are plenty of other men who would be eager to accept what you offer. And,' he added in an aside, 'I have it on good authority that some of them are very good in bed.'

She rose and sauntered to him. Running her index finger down his shirt, she watched him through thick blonde lashes. 'But none of them are you. You are rich and powerful…and appealing. You can raise me in the eyes of the *ton*. My husband cannot. He is a mere baron, and an old, fat one at that. He has no fire.' Her eyes took on a sultry gleam. 'And I desire you.'

Sebastian's lip curled. 'If you are so quick to cheat on him, then perhaps you should not have married him.'

Her tinkling laugh rang out as she stood on tiptoe and lightly kissed him. 'Do not come the naïve with me. You, of all people, know about women marrying men and then having *cicisbeos*.'

Sebastian stiffened, her words like ice sliding down his spine. Anger immediately followed—an anger so intense it would have melted any amount of ice.

'Out.' He spoke softly, but the menace of his posture clearly conveyed itself. 'Out before I wring your very lovely neck.'

The former Mrs Winters rose abruptly. Her fingers shook as she tied her cape around her shoulders. Still, she met his unyielding gaze without flinching.

'Do not take long to make up your mind, *Brabourne*. I am not a patient woman.'

He watched her sweep from the room, the heavy scent of jasmine lingering. Yes, he knew about women who cheated on their husbands. No matter what the repercussions, he would not be the one to help her cuckold Smythe-Clyde. Dallying with married women was one vice he did not have.

Chapter Four

Juliet woke from a laudanum-induced slumber. Her shoulder throbbed and her eyes felt gummed over. Her mouth was filled with cotton, or so it seemed.

A brace of candles flickered on the mantel, their golden light illuminating a chair and table. The Duke lounged in what she thought of as his favourite piece of furniture, one hand holding a wine glass. She must have made a noise because he turned to look at her.

'I see you are finally awake. Ferguson must have overdone the laudanum last time.'

He rose and moved to the bed. She watched him in fascination. Perhaps it was her illness, but it seemed that he became more intriguing each time she woke. No wonder women flocked to him.

He put a cool hand on her forehead, and she jerked. He gazed quizzically down at her, a small smile curving his sensual lips. He was very aware of his effect on her.

'You are not as warm as earlier. Ferguson's poultice works. A good thing. You are going home to-night.'

'Going home?' she echoed, feeling stupid, but still reacting to his touch.

He nodded. 'There has been a new development and it is best that you leave. I am sending Mrs Burroughs with you. She will keep people from bothering you and provide the perfect alibi.'

'Alibi?' It was the remnants of the drug making her sound so dull.

The cold hauteur she associated with him returned, making his eyes resemble ice. 'Yes, alibi. Ferguson will drive you up to your home this evening and you will alight from your own carriage with Mrs Burroughs. Everyone will be told you had to make an emergency trip to visit your old nanny. Ferguson says she lives close enough that the excuse is plausible.

Juliet nodded, beginning to understand. 'But I cannot return in your nightshirt or Harry's clothes.'

'Do you think we are such poor conspirators?'

'Why don't I have my own maid, then?' she asked archly.

He stared at her for a moment. 'Why indeed? Let me think.' After a pause, he added, 'She was out running an errand for you when word of your old nanny's plight reached you. You did not have time to wait for the servant's return, you were so fearful of what might happen if you delayed.'

'And I paid Mrs Burroughs out of my pin money?'

'What else?' he countered, a devastating smile playing over his lips. 'Don't tell me your Papa keeps you on a short lead, for I shan't believe it. If he did so, you would never have been able to sneak off and meet me for the duel without someone finding out.'

'True,' she muttered. 'Neither Papa nor Emily care much what I do. Harry does, but he is too intrigued by his first visit to London to pay much attention to me. And since I run the household, it is easy to do as I please.'

'Exactly,' he stated.

She shook her head, amazed at his ingenuity and correct reading of her situation, and instantly regretted it. Her ears rang and dizziness made her close her eyes.

'Are you all right?' he asked, a tinge of anxiety in his voice.

She managed a tight smile. 'Yes. I have no intention of staying here longer and causing you further trouble.' She took several deep, slow breaths before opening her eyes. 'Did Hobson manage to get some of my clothes?'

'Yes. Your servants are loyal to foolhardiness,'

he said curtly, disapproval obvious in the stiffness of his shoulders.

Her smile came again, softer. 'They have always been there to help. Mama used to say she would not accomplish half of what she did if not for them. They came with her when she married Papa. Hobson was a footman then, and Ferguson a stable boy.'

'Old family retainers. That explains a lot.'

A soft knock was followed by Mrs Burroughs' appearance. 'Your Grace. Miss.' She billowed into the room, her arms full of clothing. 'Now, you must leave,' she said to Brabourne, 'while I help Miss Juliet dress. I will let you know when to return.'

The Duke made a sardonic bow and left.

Mrs Burroughs helped Juliet sit up with pillows propping her back. From then on everything was agony, and it was only stubbornness that kept Juliet from fainting. She was going home. No longer would she be beholden to the man she had tried to shoot.

Juliet woke to the scents of lavender and lilac. She had to be in her own room because she always kept bowls of the dry flowers and fresh when they were in season. She stretched and winced. Her shoulder hurt.

Everything came back in a rush. The duel, the wound, the Duke. The last thing she remembered was him kissing her hand as he helped her into the carriage. The arrival home and her getting to her room were a blur.

She forced herself to a sitting position and stopped. Her head spun, and it was all she could do not to collapse back on to the pillows. She would have to move more slowly.

After what seemed an eternity the room stopped twirling. She swallowed, her tongue feeling swollen and dry. A little water would be nice. A glance at the bedside table showed a pitcher and glass. Careful not to set off another dizzy spell, she poured the liquid and drank it down. It tasted like ambrosia.

Only now did she notice that she was dressed in her favourite nightrail. She looked around, noting the shades of lilac and lavender in drapes, carpet and bed-covering. Being in her own room provided a sense of comfort and security that she had not realised she was missing until now. It was wonderful.

A knock alerted her instants before the door opened. A short, robust lady with a grey bun and iron-straight eyebrows slipped in, quickly closing the door behind herself. Mrs Burroughs. She held a silver tray from which came the smell of hot chocolate and toast. Juliet stared as the woman set the tray on a table by the fire.

'Thank you, Mrs Burroughs. I feel as weak as a newborn pup.'

'I've just the thing, then, Miss Juliet,' the housekeeper said, a twinkle in her brown eyes. 'I see you are much better, just as Ferguson said you would be. 'Tis a good thing you hired me as your lady's maid for the last several days while you went to visit your old nanny. Bless the lady's heart, being so sick and all that she needed you immediately and left you no time to notify your father. Unfortunately, your note did not arrive till today.'

The Duke had thought of everything.

She crossed to the bed and put a sturdy arm around Juliet's waist and helped her to a chair. Juliet sank like a rock on to the lavender silk cushion of her favourite chair. She was so tired.

'How long will you be staying? It seems that I am not up to snuff yet.'

Mrs Burroughs smiled gently. 'As long as needed. I have already had the devil of a time keeping your own maid out. The only thing that has saved us is the fact that you hired the girl here in London and she has no loyalty to you. Now, take some hot chocolate and toast. You need plenty of nourishment to regain your strength.' She frowned as Juliet sipped the drink. 'I would give you some laudanum, for I know your shoulder pains you a great deal, but you will need all your wits about you today.'

Juliet sighed. 'So true. Emily will very likely be here at any moment, demanding to know why I took off like I did.'

'Tut, tut, child. We will get through this.'

Juliet nibbled a triangle of toast, her dry mouth

making it difficult to swallow. 'How long exactly was I at Lord Brabourne's? I seem to remember him saying two or three days.'

'Two nights and three days.'

Two nights and three days. Papa. The duel. She turned an anxious gaze to the other woman. 'What about Papa? Did he meet the Duke? Did Brabourne shoot him?'

'They met,' Mrs Burroughs said softly.

'Why was I not told?' Juliet demanded, trying to push herself up and failing.

'There, there. The Duke felt it was better that you not know. He did not want the worry causing a relapse.'

'It must have been while I was drugged with laudanum.'

Mrs Burroughs rearranged the pillow behind Juliet's back. 'It was, but everything is fine now. The Duke's bullet went wide and your Papa shot into the ground. No one was hurt.'

Juliet sagged in relief and a shiver of aftershock shook her. 'Then my foolishness accomplished something.'

'More than you know, child,' Mrs Burroughs murmured, a strange look on her face. 'But you are trembling. Where do you keep your robe?' Mrs Burroughs fetched it and put it around Juliet's shoulders.

Juliet huddled into the warmth of her lilac robe

as another thought erupted. 'He could have shot Papa, but did not. Why? Is he admitting that he dallied with my stepmother?'

Fierceness toughened Mrs Burroughs's features. 'His Grace saved your Papa a nasty wound. That is not admitting anything. The Duke would never become involved with a married woman. Never.'

Juliet glanced at the older woman, surprised by her vehemence. It seemed that Brabourne also commanded loyalty. Juliet took a gulp of too-hot chocolate and choked. 'Ahh!'

Mrs Burroughs was instantly solicitous, her ire of seconds before forgotten. 'Are you all right?' Juliet nodded and wiped the tears of pain away with one hand. 'Are you always so impetuous? If so, the two of you will make quite a pair.'

Juliet put the china cup down on to the saucer with such force the chocolate sloshed over the edges. She stared at the woman and wondered if her hearing had been impaired by her injury.

'Whatever are you talking about?'

'You are stubborn like him, too.'

'Are we still discussing Brabourne?' Juliet asked with an underlying chill in her voice.

Mrs Burroughs sighed. 'You do not like him. Well, that is understandable. He does not have a good reputation, and he goes his own way and the devil take the hindmost. And he is arrogant.' She moved to the bed and straightened the cover but, even with her back to Juliet her words were clear. 'He came into his title young. Much too young. And he had a disappointment that made him bitter and hard. But he's good and honourable at heart.' She sighed again, her ample bosom rising and falling like a tidal wave. 'He just needs a situation to make him act good and honourable.' She turned to face Juliet and pinned her with intense brown eyes. 'You are that situation.'

Juliet's eyes widened, and her head jerked back at the force of the other woman's look and words. 'Me? are you mad?'

'No.' She leaned down to Juliet, her face serious and her voice lowered so that Juliet had to strain to hear. 'We tried to keep your presence in his Grace's home secret. We did everything we could think of, but somehow it leaked out. We made up the story of your whereabouts for your family and we will stick to it, but the rumours of where you really were will be circulating about the *ton* before long.'

Juliet shrank into her robe, thankful for its warmth as a chill of foreboding moved through her body. 'I am ruined.'

Mrs Burroughs nodded, sympathy softening the tightness around her mouth. 'His Grace must marry you, as he will soon realise.'

Juliet stared at nothing, not paying attention to Mrs Burroughs. 'Ruined—and I have not even been presented to the *ton*. I shall never dance at Almack's or have a coming-out ball. All the things I have missed because Papa was busy in the country and then Mama was ill.'

'His Grace will see that you have all those things.'

'Well,' Juliet said, still in her own world, 'I do not need those things.' Her chin notched up and she squared her shoulders. 'They are all fripperies that mean nothing and accomplish nothing. I shall tour the cultural sights here and then return home to Wood Hall where I belong.'

'We shall see. We shall see,' Mrs Burroughs muttered. 'Now, be a good girl and eat up your toast and drink every drop of that hot chocolate. You need everything we can get into you so that you regain your strength.'

Juliet obediently finished her repast. Daintily wiping her mouth, she canted her head to better see the other woman. 'But you can forget this harebrained idea of yours concerning Brabourne. I shall never marry a man of his ilk.'

Mrs Burroughs's lips parted but, before she could speak her mind the door to the room slammed open. The former Mrs Winters, now Lady Smythe-Clyde, stormed inside. Her fair hair curled around her dainty face, and a light white muslin Empire dress flowed around her colt-like limbs. Juliet could understand why her papa had married the woman.

Lady Smythe-Clyde thrust out a clenched fist, a sheet of paper crumpled in her fingers. 'See this?

This is a note to your father. Me. You. From the Duchess of Richmond, saying she is truly sorry, but she rescinds our invitation to her ball.' Her fair face was mottled in anger. 'Because of you. You. Do you hear me?' Her voice rose into a shrill demand.

'I imagine the entire household can hear you, Emily,' Juliet said drily, using the other woman's Christian name. 'You may go,' she added to Mrs Burroughs. 'And thank you.'

The housekeeper hustled out.

'All my work. All my careful planning and it is all coming to naught,' Emily fumed as she paced the floor.

'I know this is a great disappointment to you, after all your plans and hard work to present me to Society.' Juliet managed to keep a tone of sympathy in her voice, even though she knew the other woman had merely used her as a reason for her pursuit of the *ton*.

Emily stopped in her tracks and a curl of contempt marred her otherwise perfect mouth. 'Let us lay off this game-playing, Juliet, for I am prodigiously tired of it. Bringing you out was to be my introduction to Polite Society; now, through your ill-judged stay in the Duke of Brabourne's house, you have put paid to everything I have worked so hard to achieve.'

Juliet suppressed a jolt of shock. How did Emily know? Surely the rumours had not reached here yet?

'How can you say that? I have been with my old nurse.'

Emily's lips curled. 'Save that twaddle for others. I know the truth.'

Juliet eyed the other woman but said nothing, waiting to see what would happen. There were times when she managed not to react. Few, but occasionally.

'Oh, yes.' Emily moved to the fireplace and threw the paper into the flames. 'In fact, it was I who let slip the secret of your whereabouts.'

Juliet gasped, all her careful control slipping. 'You? Why? If I am ruined, then everything you have done to enter Society is in vain.'

A cruel light hardened the other woman's eyes. 'I made the best of a bad situation. Sooner or later someone would have found out. I just speeded up the revelation.'

The words did not make sense, and Juliet wondered if she was still suffering from too much laudanum, as she had at the Duke's house. Or perhaps it was exhaustion. 'I don't understand.'

Emily gave Juliet a contemptuous once-over. 'No, you would not. Miss Prim and Proper. Always doing what is best for Papa, without a care about anything else.'

Juliet was taken aback. She knew the other woman did not like her, and she did not like her stepmother, but the venom was more pronounced than she had expected. Still, the insults fired her already edgy nerves and she spoke hastily. 'Someone has to care for Papa, for it is obvious that you do not.'

A tinkling laugh filled the room. 'I did not marry him to care for him. I married him for position and to be cared for by him.'

Juliet saw red. This woman had married Papa with no regard for anyone else. Not that she had ever doubted it, but...but there had always been a kernel of hope that she was wrong.

'If you wanted position and care, why did you not marry a man like Brabourne instead of merely dallying with one? At least then the rest of us would not be in this mess.'

Emily gave a bark of laughter, as different from her famous trill as black was from white. 'Do you think I did not try?'

Juliet looked in horror at Emily. 'So Papa is nothing to you. Only a means to an end.'

The other woman sniffed. 'All marriages of our class are arrangements. At least your papa does not need an heir. So I am free to go my own way.'

'Which you did with Brabourne,' Juliet said, her anger simmering. The small twinge of discomfort she felt at the thought of Emily in the Duke's arms was squashed.

Emily shrugged. 'For a while.'

'You are selfish. If you had been more discreet,

Papa would not have needed to challenge Brabourne to a duel, and none of this would have happened.' Juliet made her hands unclench. It was past. There was nothing she could do to change the current situation.

'So, the ever-so-dutiful and solicitous daughter has claws. Well, I never doubted it.' She turned her back to Juliet. 'If you had been less impetuous, we would not be in this situation. No one said you had to take your father's place.'

Juliet struggled to her feet, no longer willing to look up at the other woman. Dizziness made her grab the back of the chair, but she remained standing. 'Someone had to protect Papa from your folly.'

Emily sneered. 'And who will protect him from this unpleasant mess your reckless action has caused?'

'My reckless action? You are the one who let the information out, for which reason you still have not told me.' Her fingers clenched the chair until her knuckles turned white. She was so tired, but she could not let Emily leave without finding out what was going on.

Emily took in Juliet's discomfort. 'It would seem you have returned too soon. You will need to stay in bed for some time to come.'

Juliet's chest tightened in anger. 'I will do as I see fit.'

Emily arched two perfectly cared-for blonde

brows. 'Will you? We shall see what your papa has to say about your…exhaustion.'

Juliet nearly toppled over. For the first time since this argument began she realised that if Emily knew what had really happened then Papa could find out. That would hurt Papa. Something she did not want.

In a tired voice, all the fight drained from her, Juliet asked, 'Why are you doing this?'

Emily glared at her. 'Because if I cannot have Brabourne, and all that he represents in Society, I will see to it that you have him and I benefit directly from your connection to him. When the Duke decides he has to save your reputation and asks you to marry him, I expect you to accept.'

Juliet stiffened her spine, knowing she was nearly ready to collapse. 'You are crazy. He will never ask and I would never accept.'

Emily moved to the door and gave Juliet a last penetrating look. 'Do not be too sure about what either of you will do.'

Juliet stared at the door long after the other woman had left. Insanity. This was the stuff farces were made of. Brabourne would never propose. Never.

And if he did? a tiny voice asked. Juliet sank back into the chair and covered her eyes with a shaking hand. She would resist him, no matter how hard or how much it hurt. There was no other answer when a rake came calling.

* * *

Mrs Burroughs gave him the minimum curtsy required, and Sebastian could tell by the look on her face that she longed to box his ears. If anyone else looked at him the way she did, they would soon regret it. With her he merely sighed.

'Yes, Mrs Burroughs?'

'It has started, your Grace.'

He raised one eyebrow.

Exasperation lowered hers. 'The ostracism of the young lady. Just as I knew it would. Just as you knew it would—if you had let yourself consider it. You must stop it.'

This woman was one of the few people in his life he cared for, and the only woman. But, right now, irritation at her persistence in pushing him about something he did not want to do hardened his jaw. For the first time since becoming an adult he was curt with her.

'I am busy now, Mrs Burroughs, and have no time to discuss this matter. Nor will I ever.' He stood so that he towered above her rotund figure. 'Do I make myself clear?'

She inflated her chest and lifted her ample chin. 'Quite…your Grace.' Without asking permission to leave, she sailed out.

Sebastian watched her until she was gone, then turned to look out through the large window that let the meagre afternoon sunlight into the library. The roses were in full bloom and a few tulips lingered.

The girl was becoming an even bigger problem. Much as he did not want to become involved, he wanted to see her ostracised even less. She had spirit. And she cared about others.

He remembered her reason for dressing as a boy and fighting him. It had all been for her father. Never once had she mentioned or seemed even to consider the repercussions to herself. He admired that trait in anyone, since it was so unusual, but in the girl he found himself more than admiring.

Making a decision, he turned and strode to the door. He went into the hall and beckoned to a nearby footman. 'Fetch Mr Wilson for me. Now.'

'Yes, your Grace.' The young man bowed and hurried off.

Sebastian returned to the library and sprawled out in the leather wingchair that was his favourite. He did not wait long for the knock.

Jeremy Wilson entered the room, his fair blond hair glinting in the light. He was a slight man. The kind that mothers wanted to nurture and women wanted to protect. Men liked him too. Sebastian trusted and depended on him.

'Jeremy, my long-suffering secretary,' Sebastian said, waving him to a seat. 'I have yet another job for you that has nothing to do with my business affairs. And hopefully, after a short while, will have nothing to do with my social life either.'

Jeremy grinned. 'Another woman, your Grace?

Most men would be more than happy to be pursued at all hours and all days. You seek to get rid of them.'

Sebastian returned the smile from habit, not amusement. 'Ah, but then I am not most men. Besides, all women become bores sooner or later.'

A flash of pity filled Jeremy's green eyes, but only for a second. 'What can I do this time, your Grace?'

Sebastian straightened in the chair. 'I want you to find out the engagements of Lord Smythe-Clyde and his family.'

The secretary's eyes widened. The Duke had asked many unusual things of him, but never something like this.

'Yes,' Sebastian said drily, 'the same man who challenged me to a duel over his wife. And you may as well know, since I know you can be trusted and since the entire *ton* will shortly be a-buzz about it, the sick guest we housed for three days was Smythe-Clyde's daughter. She is the one who initially fought me. The later duel with her father was a sham.'

After a pause, Jeremy said, 'Interesting. I would warrant she would not be boring.'

The comment was too close for comfort. Sebastian ignored it. 'Let me know as soon as possible. If I do not receive invitations for the same events, see that I get them.'

Recognising dismissal, Jeremy rose. 'I should have some information by this afternoon. Oh, yes, you are invited to the Duchess of Richmond's ball. It is tonight. I understand that everyone has been asked.'

'Including the Smythe-Clydes?'

'I would assume so,' Jeremy said from the door.

Sebastian rubbed his right eyebrow. 'Her events are always overcrowded and uninteresting, but I suppose I must attend if I intend to put my plan into action.'

Jeremy waited to see if his employer would elaborate. When the Duke rose and turned to look out of the window, Jeremy understood he would learn nothing more.

Sebastian heard the door close. He wondered one last time why he was concerning himself. It had been a long time since he had done something for someone else who was not one of his cronies. It was a strange sensation.

Sebastian put the final crease in his cravat, his valet looking on proudly. 'A perfect Brabourne Soirée,' the servant said reverentially.

Ravensford lounged nearby on the bed, a wicked gleam in his eyes. 'All the ladies will be in awe of your sartorial elegance.'

Sebastian cut him a fulminating glance as his valet helped him into a sleekly tailored blue jacket. A thumb-sized sapphire secured in the cravat was the final touch.

'Where is Perth?' Sebastian asked.

'Carousing in some den of iniquity. He did not tell me which one, so I'm afraid we cannot plan on joining him later.'

'More's the pity,' Sebastian said, attaching a silver fob to his waistcoat. 'he will have more fun than we.'

'Without a doubt,' Ravensford said, rising from the bed and straightening his coat. 'But we are on a mission.'

'Here, my lord,' the valet said, hurrying over to Ravensford. 'Let me brush out the wrinkles and straighten your collar and cravat.'

'No need, Roberts,' Ravensford said, fending of the servant's eager help. 'I don't mind a little mussing. I am a Corinthian, not a dandy.'

Roberts backed away, but could not keep from sighing. 'You could cut such a dashing figure, my lord, if I may be so bold as to say.'

'He already does,' Sebastian said with a mocking grin. 'He is the epitome of raffishness. All the women will swoon at his feet.'

'There is only one kind of woman I want swooning,' Ravensford said, 'and we will not find that kind at this gathering.'

'No,' Sebastian said, opening the door. 'And more's the pity.'

An hour later, they finally entered the foyer of the Duchess of Richmond's town house. Their hostess beamed at them.

'Brabourne. Ravensford. I am so glad you could tear yourself away from your other amusements.'

Each man in turn took her offered hand.

'How could we resist?' Sebastian murmured, kissing her palm.

'Such devilish charm,' she said, smiling as he released her fingers. 'Enjoy yourselves. There are more than enough eligible women, even for the likes of you two.'

'Yes, but are they entertaining?' Sebastian said *sotto voce* as they walked away.

'Probably not,' Ravensford replied, before turning to greet the matchmaking mama of a girl just out of the schoolroom.

'See you later,' Sebastian said with a nod to the woman and a wink to his friend. He thought he heard Ravensford groan, but knew the Earl was too well-mannered to be so rude.

With practised ease and a cool smile, Sebastian circulated through the room. He ignored the speculative glances sent his way. People had been discussing him since he was old enough to realise what they were doing, and probably long before that.

There was no sign of his quarry.

Guests milled around the enormous room, spilling out on to the balconies and into the gardens. An orchestra played a waltz and couples swirled and dipped to the music. Dowagers sat in huddles, discussing anyone and everything. Several men wandered into another room where cards were being played. Everyone was here, including many he did not know. Except the Smythe-Clydes.

Irritation knitted Sebastian's brows together.

He stepped out on to the balcony for some cool air and privacy. This was the opening ball of the Season. Surely Smythe-Clyde and his family would be here if they had been invited. Emily would be.

A schoolgirl giggle wafted up from the walkway below him, and Sebastian took a step back towards the ballroom.

'Have you seen the Duke?' a girl asked.

'Oh, yes,' another girl answered. 'He looks so romantic. And dangerous.'

The first girl giggled again and lowered her voice. 'He is. Have you heard that he had Juliet Smythe-Clyde in his house for three days and three nights? Although they are saying she went to visit her old nanny.' Another giggle.

Her words stopped Sebastian. His fists clenched and he had to resist the urge to jump over the railing and put the chit in her place.

The second girl lowered her voice too. 'Oh, yes. Wouldn't you just love to be his captive?'

The first girl spoke soberly. 'Not if it ruined me as it has her. Mama said she and her family had been invited tonight, but when word of her disgrace got out the Duchess sent a note telling them they were no longer welcome.'

Sebastian had heard enough. If chits barely out of the schoolroom knew of the disaster, then it was all over town. Nor would he stay here and gratify the Duchess of Richmond by dancing with any of her eligible girls.

Never before had he been made so aware of the double standards of his world. Juliet Smythe-Clyde was not welcome while he was courted, even though she was innocent and he was anything but.

He entered the ballroom and scanned it for Ravensford. Catching the Earl's attention, he flicked his eyes towards the door. Ravensford nodded and began making his excuses.

Sebastian located the Duchess of Richmond and made his way to her. As furious as he was with the woman, he would not be so crass as to leave without saying goodbye. He was many things, but no one had ever accused him of neglecting the social niceties. That was for Perth to do.

He gave the Duchess a cool smile. 'Thank you for your hospitality, but Ravensford and I must be on our way.'

She tutted at him. 'Surely it is too early for the gaming hells, Brabourne. Stay awhile and dance with some of the chits who have been fluttering around you.'

He froze her with a look. 'I think not, your Grace. My morals are not up to your exacting standards.'

She blinked while his words sank in. Taking a step back, she returned his glare with one of her own. 'They certainly are not, but you are a Duke, and an eligible one at that. You can be forgiven many faults.'

'As others cannot,' he said softly, a hard edge underlying the words.

Ravensford arrived just then and took in the situation. He put a hand on Sebastian's shoulder and squeezed hard. Smiling at the Duchess, he said, 'We must be on our way. Thank you for your hospitality.'

She smiled warmly at him and gave him her hand to kiss. Ravensford performed his duty with grace and the two men made their escape.

Outside the evening air was like a cool caress after the stifling heat of the ballroom. Instead of entering the coach when it drove up, they opted to walk with the vehicle following behind.

'What was that about?' Ravensford asked, swinging his gold-tipped cane.

Sebastian took a deep breath and wondered why he had lost his temper. Usually there was only one thing that made him see red. A slight to a girl he barely knew was not in the same league. He told Ravensford what had happened.

The Earl whistled low. 'So, it has already begun. But not surprising.'

'Everyone will follow the Duchess's lead.'

'And there is nothing you can do about it. Why should you?'

Sebastian stopped. 'I don't know. But for some benighted reason I feel like helping this girl.'

'Oh-ho,' Ravensford said with a knowing look. 'So that's the way it is.'

'Hardly,' Sebastian said drily. 'I admire the chit; I don't love her. Or even care that much about her. I just don't want her punished for trying to protect her father. Few enough of our acquaintances would do what she did.'

'True. But what can you do about it?' Ravensford started walking again and Sebastian kept pace.

'I can bring her into fashion.'

This time Ravensford stopped. 'I hardly think so. That will only confirm in the old tabbies' minds that the rumour is correct.' He gave Sebastian a piercing look. 'The only way you can make her respectable is to marry her.'

'A little drastic, don't you think?'

'Depends on how badly you want to make her respectable.'

'Not that badly,' Sebastian said, signalling to the coach. 'Take us to Pall Mall.'

Ravensford followed Sebastian into the vehicle. 'I told you we would not be able to locate Perth.'

'But we shall enjoy ourselves trying.' Sebastian lounged back into the leather squabs, determined to put the chit from his mind for the night.

Chapter Five

Juliet scratched absently at her shoulder before catching herself. The wound was healing nicely; she just tired easily.

Right now, she had to plan the next week's menus. Papa's new wife had no interest in running the house and had done nothing while Juliet had been gone. Nor had anything been done during the past two weeks while Juliet had claimed illness and kept to her rooms, giving her wound more time to heal. No matter that the rumour was everywhere, she stuck to the story that she had been to visit her nurse.

Much as she hated it, she owed Emily a thank-you. The other woman had not told Papa the truth, and Papa was so wrapped up in his experiments that he did not know of the rumours.

Her brother Harry strode into the room and slammed the door behind himself, focusing her attention on him. She watched him with a fond, if puzzled look. He paced the morning room of their rented house, his red hair standing up in spikes on his head. A grin tugged at her mouth. Whenever he was agitated he ran his fingers through his hair until it resembled a hedgehog's back.

He stopped abruptly and leaned on the desk so his face was close to hers. 'Is it true?'

Her fingers tightened on the pen she held until her knuckles turned white. The urge to look away from him was strong, but she was made of sterner stuff. Carefully, she laid the pen down and forced her fingers into a relaxed clasp. Until now he had not asked her, and she could not lie to him.

'As far as it goes. Yes.'

He groaned and raked his fingers through his hair. 'Why, Ju?'

She told him about everything: the duel, her reason for going, and what had really happened during her stay. The only thing she left out was Emily's part in the mess. No one else needed to know that. Brabourne would never propose and she would never accept.

She ended with, 'I suppose I should feel shame for being in his house unchaperoned, but I don't. Nothing happened.' Or nothing of consequence, her always truthful conscience added. 'No one was supposed to find out, but somehow a servant suspected and from there it spread.'

He stood up and his mouth twisted. 'Why didn't you come to me? I would have helped.'

She saw the anguish in his eyes and knew he would be a long time forgiving her. She swallowed. 'Because I am the oldest. I am the one Mama entrusted Papa's care to. I had to do it for her.'

'I could have done it and there would have been no scandal.'

She nodded, her hands once more clenched. 'True. But I could not stand to ask you to put your life in jeopardy.'

'But you could risk yours.' Anger spotted his cheeks, making his freckles stand out like patches.

There was no way she could make him understand. She rose and went around the desk and embraced him. He remained stiff in her arms.

'I am sorry, Harry. I am so sorry. But I could not. I just could not ask you to face a man who would have had no qualms about killing you. You mean too much to me.'

He moved away from her. 'Why didn't you let Papa face Brabourne? Papa is the one who made the challenge.'

She sighed and stepped away from him. He was still too upset to want closeness. 'I told you. I had to protect Papa. To take care of him. I promised Mama on her deathbed.'

Harry shook his head, some of the colour leaving his face. 'You cannot always be taking care of him—or everyone else, for that matter. Some day you won't be here, and then what will happen?' At her stricken look, he hurried on. 'Don't look like that, Ju. Some day you will marry and leave. That's only natural. All women do it. Then Papa will have to care for himself.'

A choked laugh escaped her tight throat. 'I will never marry now. Papa's new wife may throw me out, but no man will take me in.'

His face flamed anew as he remembered the original reason he had come to see her. 'Dash it all, Ju. That ain't true. There is George at home. He loves you and will marry you no matter what.'

A sad smile tugged at her lips, and she turned away so he would not see the emotion. 'Dear George. I would never disgrace him by accepting his proposal. Not now.'

'Don't be a goose,' he said roundly. 'This is not the end of the world. All the *ton* may go to Hades. We don't need them.' His voice picked up. 'I have it. Let's go to Vauxhall tonight. We will forget all of this and enjoy ourselves. Just the two of us. There will be fireworks,' he cajoled.

She looked back at him. He had the mischievous, let's-have-fun look that had always lured her into trouble. Gone was the hangdog expression he had entered the room wearing. This was her younger brother, the boy she had also promised to look after and protect. Mama had known Papa was incapable of anything but his hunting and experimenting.

She caught his hand and squeezed it. 'What time should we leave?'

A grin split his face. 'Half past eight.'

On a much happier note, he left to prepare for their night of revelry. Juliet stayed behind and tried to finish the week's menu, but it was hard.

George's face kept coming between her and the paper. Good, kind George, who wanted to marry her. She had turned him down just before coming to London, and he had told her he would wait. She cared a great deal for him, liked him immensely, and had considered accepting him when she returned home. He would care for her and any children they might have for the rest of his life. That was a gift any woman should be glad to have.

Another visage forced its way to her attention. Hard angles and unyielding eyes made her pulse jump. Brabourne. She gave up. The menus could wait.

She rose and headed outside. The house had a small garden with a white iron bench sitting under a large elm tree. It was her favourite spot here in London. Perhaps some time spent there would ease the turmoil that threatened to tear her chest apart.

Life had been so simple before. It should be as uncomplicated now. Somehow it was not.

* * *

Juliet waited for Harry in the hall, dressed in a simple white muslin gown with green ribbons, her hair piled on her head and more green ribbon threaded through its curls. When she heard his tread on the marble floor she turned to him with a smile—and had to suppress a gasp. He was in the same coat she had worn to meet Brabourne. Visions of that horrible night threatened to close her throat.

'You look very fetching,' her brother said.

His unexpected compliment erased her tension. As her younger brother, she did not expect him even to notice her clothes.

'What is the matter, Harry? Do you have a fever?'

He grinned. 'Thought I'd start us out on the right note. Tommy says all girls like to be told they look nice.'

She chuckled. 'Coming the pretty with me? And where is the redoubtable Tommy? I am surprised he is not coming with us.'

He gave her a sheepish grin. 'He is to meet us there. He knows his way around,' he finished in a rush. 'That is why I asked him.'

'I should have known Tommy would not be far from us tonight.' She felt a twinge of disappointment that she and Harry would not be enjoying their adventure alone, but she put it aside. Young men did not like being saddled with sisters. She was fortunate to have been asked at all.

He had the grace to look embarrassed. 'Well, it

was his suggestion. Thought it would show every-one that we can't be cowed.'

'I should have known. He has been on the Town longer than you,' she murmured, leading the way to the carriage.

The ride was long and boring, but when they pulled up and Juliet stepped out, a look of awestruck wonder radiated from her face. 'It is like a fairyland. There must be hundreds and hundreds of lamps.'

'Actually,' a deep voice drawled, 'there are thousands.'

She whirled around. The Duke of Brabourne, in impeccable evening wear, lounged against one of the entry pillars.

'What are you doing here?' she said, before realising it was none of her business.

He pushed away from the pillar and moved towards her. The delight of seconds before was supplanted by an edginess that increased with each step closer he took. He made her feel so vulnerable. She angled back and bumped into Harry.

Harry glared at the Duke. 'He is here to cause trouble, no doubt. Why else would one of his reputation frequent a pleasure garden?'

Brabourne raked the youth with a frigid stare. 'We meet again, puppy, and your manners are no better.'

Harry's chest puffed up and his eyes narrowed.

Juliet recognised the danger signs and stepped between the two males.

'Enough,' she said, putting a hand on Harry to stay his forward momentum. 'Surely Vauxhall is big enough for all of us.'

'London isn't big—'

'Stop it. Now, Harry,' Juliet whispered, 'if you create a scene, then everyone will think the rumour confirmed. What then? Have you thought of that? Will you challenge Brabourne to a duel to defend my smirched honour? That would only make a bad situation worse.'

'She is right, puppy,' the Duke said.

She rounded on him. 'And what are you trying to do? Make matters worse. I am trying to reason with him and you put your oar into the waters.'

Brabourne smiled, the emotion reaching his eyes. 'A firebrand to go with the hair.'

For long seconds Juliet stood, transfixed by the change in the Duke's countenance. No longer was he the cold, sardonic man who had duelled her and then kept her in his home. This was the man who had comforted her as she lay racked by fever, the man she had thought only a figment of her imagination. The realisation was unsettling.

'I'm warning you,' Harry said through gritted teeth.

'Miss Smythe-Clyde. Harry.' Tommy's light tenor cut through the animosity. 'Thought I saw you arrive.' Tommy Montmart rushed over, his gaze darting to the Duke and back to the brother and sister. He stopped between them and Brabourne.

Tommy was a slight youth with sandy hair and hazel eyes. His chin was more prominent than necessary and his nose was not large enough to balance it. While he was not good-looking, he was friendly and helpful. You could not keep from liking him.

'We must be going, your Grace,' Juliet said breathlessly, taking each youth by the arm and propelling them down the first lane they came to.

They had not gone ten steps before Harry shook himself free. 'I can walk by myself.'

She eyed him. 'Then do so. Away from the Duke.'

'She is right, you know, old chum,' Tommy said. 'Won't do to start a fight with Brabourne. He's a prime one with his fists. Cause another scandal too. The only chance you have of weathering this one is to act as though it is all a farce.'

Harry answered with a grunt.

Juliet listened to them, but her focus was on the Duke. Why had he come up to them? Was he trying to ruin her completely?

Even now, the back of her neck tingled as though someone were watching her. Only one person had ever had that effect on her. She wrapped her paisley shawl tighter around her shoulders and forced herself to look at the sights.

Vauxhall was indeed a marvel. An orchestra played while people danced. Snatched pieces of passing conversations mentioned singing to come. Tommy and Harry talked about going to the Cascade first, a spectacle that even she, cloistered in the country, had heard of.

'Miss Smythe-Clyde.' Tommy halted and motioned Juliet to look to the right. 'It is Prinny himself.'

The Prince Regent stood in the middle of a gathering comprising both men and women. Laughter came from the group like music from a flock of gaily feathered birds. They were the élite of English society. Sudden quiet came over them as Brabourne raised his glass to the prince. Everyone toasted and the laughter began anew.

Juliet turned away.

'He comes here all the time,' Tommy said.

'Brabourne?' Juliet said before thinking.

Both Tommy and Harry frowned at her.

'No,' Tommy said. 'The Prince.'

Juliet turned quickly from their probing looks. She was behaving like a schoolgirl.

A bell chimed and Tommy said, 'We must hurry. They are about to unveil the Cascade.'

Catching their excitement, Juliet hurried after the two young men. All about them others did the same. They arrived in time to get a good position.

The curtain was drawn aside to show a landscape

scene illuminated by lights. A miller's house and waterfall were near the front. The 'water', or so it seemed to be to Juliet, flowed into a mill and turned the wheel.

'Papa would love to see this,' she said to Harry. 'I wonder how it is done?'

When he did not answer, she turned and realised he was not beside her. The crowd had separated them. A man, his complexion florid and his waist ample, grinned at her. She looked away, searching for her brother.

She felt a hand on her shoulder and jolted. It was the man.

'Here by yourself?' He leered down at her.

Shivers of apprehension coursed her spine. She yanked away. 'No. My brother is near.'

He moved closer, his gaze taking in her figure. She edged back, bumping into someone else. Instead of being thrilled by the exhibition, she was fast becoming scared. There were so many people, many of whom were becoming rowdy, and she doubted any would provide help. And Harry had disappeared.

The man reached for her again, but Juliet slipped between a group of people and headed back the way she had come. She glanced behind and saw the man trying to follow. Unlike before, when the lights had delighted her and made her think of magic, they now seemed glaring. She turned left down a small lane with no lights. With luck she would be able to hide.

She twisted around another corner and skidded to a halt. A group of young bucks strolled towards her, singing a ribald song. She looked back to see the man. The singing stopped.

'Ah, what have we here?' one of the new arrivals said, moving in front of her.

A second one edged to one side of her. 'A pretty little maid out for a walk.'

The third flanked her. 'An adventurous little maid. And we can provide her with any thrill she seeks in the Lovers' Walk. Can't we, boys?'

'Yes,' they chorused, closing the circle.

Juliet's chest pounded and the roaring in her ears almost drowned out the voices. This was worse than anything. Worse than meeting the Duke. At least that had been honourable. What these men intended to do to her was anything but.

She swallowed hard past the tightness in her throat. 'Let me pass. I am not what you think.' She was thankful her voice did not shake. It was not as strong as she would have liked, but surely it would do.

They laughed.

'I think not,' the first one said, moving close enough to run a finger down her cheek.

She knocked his hand away. 'Do not touch me.'

The other two smirked.

'I don't think she is interested in you, Peter,' the one on her left said. He reached for her.

Juliet jumped away, only to be caught from behind. Two strong arms held her immobile as the others advanced on her. Fear ate at her.

She had forgotten the man who had originally followed her. She twisted her head to look for him, only to see him gone. He must have left when these three arrived. Her jaw was caught in a vice-like grip that forced her to look back.

'Be nice to us,' the one gripping her chin said, 'and we might even pay you.'

He released her and she slapped him. The blow landed full on his cheek. He growled and swung his arm back.

Juliet was incensed beyond reason now. It no longer mattered that her knees shook so badly she was not sure she could stand up on her own. Nor would it do her any good to talk to these louts. She would fight them tooth and nail. As his arm came forward, she stared defiantly at him. His fist was a foot away from her face when she kicked him hard on the shin.

His arm dropped and he howled. The one holding her from behind snickered. Using the surprise her action had gained her, she swung the same leg back and raked her heel down her captor's instep. He gasped and his hold on her relaxed. She twisted away from him and lunged forward, flinching as her injured shoulder made itself known. The third buck caught her around the waist in a breath-snatching grip.

So close. She almost moaned aloud. The looks on the faces of the other two told her louder than words that she would not get another chance to escape. Nor would they treat her lightly now. Instead of drunkards looking for fun, they now looked for revenge.

She gulped.

'I believe you have the wrong lady,' a bored voice drawled.

Brabourne. Juliet sagged in relief. In the heat of the mêlée none of them had noticed his approach.

He came closer and, by the light of the stars and the full moon she could just make out his features. No emotion showed on his face, but there was a tension in the lithe grace of his movements that boded no good for her assailants. By his side he held a stylish black ebony cane, chased with silver that glinted like fire.

The one named Peter said, 'Go on with you. She was walking in here unchaperoned. We know the type of doxy who does that, and we intend to give her exactly what she is searching for.'

Brabourne moved closer. 'I advise you to let her go.'

'You don't scare us,' the one still holding Juliet said. 'We're three to your one. Those are the kind of odds we like.'

'I imagine you do,' Brabourne said with a sneer on his well-formed lips. 'Too bad you don't have intelligence to go with your brawn.'

Juliet had remained quiet because she was astounded at the Duke's appearance. Also, the cowardly part of her hoped he could rescue her or that they would let her go because he demanded it. Everyone else jumped to his bidding.

In one smooth, swift motion, the Duke pulled on his cane, revealing a rapier-thin blade that had been hidden in the outside case of fine black wood. Juliet felt her captor's sharp intake of breath. The three scoundrels had not expected this.

Brabourne's cold smile widened. 'I never go into dark lanes unprepared—no matter where they are. Particularly not here. It's a pity, but Vauxhall has a reputation for riff-raff such as yourselves.' He took a step closer. 'Release her.'

Still they held their ground.

A gleam of anticipation entered the Duke's intense blue eyes. 'It has been a very dreary day. Nothing would give me more pleasure than to spit you. And I would advise you not to make the mistake of thinking I won't.'

Juliet began to tremble anew. The sense of nerves drawn taut was great enough to make her reckless. 'Oh, please, Brabourne, spit them and be done with it.'

His gaze flicked to her and he saluted her with

his blade, an admiring gesture even as his eyes filled with mirth. 'You are as bloodthirsty tonight, my dear, as ever. Does the trait run in your family?'

'Brabourne,' one of the three said. 'The Duke?'

'Yes,' Juliet said. 'And he would as soon kill you as look at you. He has already killed in a duel. He could take care of you and never be penalised.'

Brabourne laughed aloud. 'She is right. The Prince will not even blink an eyelid at my dispatching filth who prey on innocent women.'

With a flick of his wrist, he marked the hand of the man holding Juliet. She was released with a push that sent her towards the Duke. He sidestepped just in time to keep her from being impaled on the point of his sword.

'That was not well done,' Sebastian growled. Before anyone knew what he was about, he moved in and flicked the cheek of the man who had held and then pushed Juliet. 'You will wear that mark for life to remind you of this night and your cowardly folly.'

The man just stood and stared while his fellows fled into the dark. 'I won't forget this.'

Brabourne looked him up and down, contempt clear in his eyes. 'I don't intend you to.'

Juliet held her breath, expecting the man to rush Brabourne. Instead he turned and seemed to melt into the darkness. Juliet, all the strength gone from her body, sank on to the pebble path. Her body shook everywhere and her shoulder throbbed from all the handling she had received.

Brabourne squatted down, still holding his sword at the ready. 'Are you able to walk? We had best get back to the lights.'

She giggled, unable to stop the release of fear. 'I…yes, just a minute.' She took a deep breath.

He stood and reached a hand down for her. She took it and he pulled her up. She stumbled and fell against his chest, fortunate that it was the side where the sword was not. He caught her round the waist and held her up.

'Steady. I cannot hold you and be prepared should they return.'

She nodded, biting her lower lip. 'I am not usually this giddy.'

'I know.' He released her and she managed to remain standing. 'Stay on my left, away from the sword, and start walking. Quickly.'

She did as he directed. Within minutes they were in the lit area again. People mingled around them, a few glancing at the sword. Brabourne quickly sheathed it.

'Come. Something to drink and eat will help restore your spirits.' He took her gently by the elbow and steered her back to the private supper boxes.

Juliet went without thinking of her reputation and how his escort must look to anyone who saw them. She was just grateful to be safe.

'Thank you. You saved me from…' she giggled again '…A fate worse than death.' She could not stop giggling.

He shook his head. 'You did not act like this when I shot you.'

She gasped for breath. 'I know. But then I anticipated the fact that I might be hurt. It never occurred to me that anyone here would accost me and…and threaten my…'

'I understand,' he murmured, his tone almost sympathetic. 'Obviously your brother and his friend failed to prepare you. Vauxhall can be entertaining, perhaps even magical, your first time here, but it is also frequented by scoundrels and thieves. You should not have been left alone,' he ended on a harder note.

She bristled at his implied criticism of Harry. 'It was an accident. We were at the Cascade and there were so many people. The next thing I knew, Harry was gone. It was my fault for not paying better attention.'

'As you wish. But next time hold on to your escort.'

'Brabourne.' A female voice intruded on their argument. 'Brabourne, I have been looking all over for you. Where have you been, you naughty boy?' She was a voluptuous woman with hair so dark it blended in with the night.

A disgusted look passed over his face, quickly

replaced by cool dispassion. 'Ah, Lady Castlerock. What a pleasant surprise. I thought you were still with Prinny.'

'Of course I am. He sent me to find you, saying it is always entertaining when you are around.' She dimpled at him.

He gave her a thin smile. 'May I introduce you to Miss Smythe-Clyde? She has done me the honour of walking the promenade with me.'

Juliet smiled at the other woman.

Shocked recognition widened the other woman's eyes and pinched her mouth. 'I will see you later, Brabourne.' Then, without a word, she turned her back to Juliet and walked away. The cut was direct.

Mortification held Juliet motionless. Fury kept her from crying.

'Mary Castlerock has been rude from the first day I met her, and that was while she was still in the schoolroom,' Brabourne observed. 'She is no better today.'

His words gave Juliet time to pull herself together. The other woman's action was not unexpected. The *ton* had declared Juliet unacceptable and Lady Castlerock was definitely *ton*. It was Juliet's fault for forgetting that she should never have been seen in public—or private—with Brabourne. Still, the woman's reaction had been extreme, and Juliet was determined that she would not succumb like a whipped puppy. But it would do her no good to stay longer in the Duke's company.

She jutted her chin and squared her shoulders, ignoring the ache that radiated from her wound. She dropped the Duke a curtsy, saying, 'Thank you so much for your help. Without you, I would have been sorely hurt. But I am able to find my brother on my own.'

One eyebrow raised, he said, 'Are you going to let her treatment of you change what you intend to do? I never thought it of you.'

Goaded beyond polite manners, she said, 'That is easy for you to say. You are no better than you should be, yet no one snubs you. No one ostracises your family for your actions. Well, your Grace, I have neither your rank nor your fortune to protect me and mine from people like Lady Castlerock.' A lone tear of suppressed hurt slid down her cheek.

The tic at his right eye started. 'Here, take this.'

He thrust his hand at her and she recognised a handkerchief. 'I don't need that.'

'Take it anyway.' He grabbed her hand, pried open her fingers and stuffed the fine linen in her palm.

In a very unladylike way, she blew her nose. The ghost of a smile curved his mouth. She saw it and blushed.

'I am not very good at being dainty.'

'You are very good just the way you are.'

Her blush deepened. 'I shall have this laundered and returned to you.'

'Discreetly, I hope.'

She searched his face to see if he joked. There was a hint of something in his eyes that made her think he might. 'Most discreetly.'

She tucked the material into her reticule which, by some miracle, still hung around her wrist. Her paisley shawl was somewhere back on the dark Lovers' Lane, and she had no intention of searching for it.

Once again he took her arm. 'Shall we try this again?'

She sighed wearily. 'I am not as good at flaunting convention as you. I think it for the best if I try to find Harry on my own.'

'So, this is where you are hiding out, Brabourne.' A booming male voice made Juliet jump.

'Lady Castlerock said she had found you, but that you were occupied.'

A florid, yet handsome man who carried too much weight headed their way. She wondered if the Duke was chased everywhere he went. It certainly seemed that way.

'Sir,' Brabourne said.

Juliet closed her eyes. This was too much. First Lady Castlerock had cut her, and now the Prince Regent would do so. She sank into a hurried and graceless curtsy, head bowed as much to hide her dismay as to pay respect.

'And who is this lovely young morsel?' the Prince asked.

'May I present Miss Smythe-Clyde, sir.'

Juliet stayed down, waiting, hoping the Prince would not snub her.

'Ahh,' he said in a knowing voice. His tone turned devilish. 'I am delighted to meet Miss Smythe-Clyde. Please rise, my dear. I won't bite— at least, not yet.'

Juliet could not believe her ears. The Prince was talking to her—flirting with her? But she had heard he had a weakness for women, preferably ones old enough to be his mother.

She rose. 'Your Highness.'

'I see why your name is linked with hers, my friend. A very rare prettiness and not at all your normal prey.'

Brabourne's face betrayed nothing, but Juliet was finding it easier to read him. The straightness in his shoulders and the grip on his cane told her he was not pleased with the Prince's words.

Fireworks started going off, momentarily catching the Prince's attention. 'I must be leaving you two. You must come to Carlton House next week, Miss Smythe-Clyde. I am having a small dinner party.'

Without waiting for a response, the Prince left to rejoin his group. Juliet gaped at his back.

'I cannot go to Carlton House alone. What would people say?'

'Nothing they aren't already saying,' he said sardonically. 'But you are right. You will need an escort.'

She nervously twisted a curl that had come loose from the knot on her head, very aware of his attention bent on her. He took her hand in his and pulled it from the hair. He gently tucked the strand behind her ear.

'That will have to do,' he murmured, his voice husky. 'I am not a lady's maid.'

She could not make herself break the rapport between them. There was something magical about the way he watched her. She felt light-headed. Giddy. Ready to twirl around.

'Ju! Where in blazes have you been?' Harry said, rushing up to her and grabbing her arm.

The moment was broken and Juliet felt as though a bubble of delight had been punctured. Everything was mundane once more.

Sighing silently, she angled away from Brabourne. 'I have been looking for you, Harry. Somehow we became separated at the Cascade.'

'I know that. You need to be more careful in a place like this. It may be frequented by all the swells, but there is riff-raff, too. Ain't safe for a girl alone.' He puffed like a gamecock protecting a solitary hen.

'I am well acquainted with the hazards here,' she said drily. Out of the corner of her eye, she watched Brabourne. He looked at her, and she knew she caught her understatement.

'You are.' Harry let her go and for the first time noticed the Duke. He glared at Brabourne. 'Has he been bothering you? For I won't have it.'

Juliet cut off an exasperated retort. 'No. He was merely keeping me company until you arrived.'

Brabourne made an abbreviated leg. 'I think, Miss Smythe-Clyde, that we have found your escort to Carlton House.'

She started, for it had never occurred to her that her brother might come. 'But what will the Prince say?'

'I will explain to him.'

Tommy rushed up just as the Duke moved away.

'Thank you again,' Juliet said softly, hoping Brabourne heard her. He looked over his shoulder and she knew he had.

'What is this all about?' Harry demanded.

'Been cosying up to Brabourne?' Tommy said. 'Not good. Not good at all, Miss Smythe-Clyde, if I may be so bold as to say.'

Juliet shook her head, finding that she was shorter on patience than usual. Normally she could let Harry and Tommy ramble on and rant and rave without any bother. Tonight she was suddenly tired. As calmly as possible, she told both young men about the meeting with Prinny and the invitation.

Tommy's eyes popped. 'Invited to dinner with the Prince Regent? That is an honour. You must go. No doubt about it. Can't refuse. Isn't done.'

'Exactly,' Juliet stated firmly. She took Harry's arm and steered him towards the entrance. 'I am tired and would like to go home. I am still not totally recovered.'

'But we have not eaten yet,' Harry complained. 'The ham is famous throughout England.'

'Thin enough to read through,' Tommy added.

Juliet managed to smile at them. 'I know— Harry, you get the coach to take me home. I shall send it back for both of you.'

The two youths gave each other long-suffering looks. Harry said, 'I shall go with you, Ju. Ain't proper for a young lady to go alone.'

She suppressed a tiny smile. They were so like schoolboys. 'No, you shan't, Harry. I am old enough to take care of myself. Why, I am a spinster. No one will think twice about my going by myself—and no one need even know.'

The two boys exchanged another look, relief replacing the former resignation. 'Capital idea,' Harry said.

They chatted on, while Juliet stood silent waiting for the carriage. The last thing she had expected tonight was to meet Brabourne. And to have him rescue her and then introduce her to the Prince—that was the stuff of any young woman's dreams. But it left her uncomfortable. One dinner at Carlton House would not restore her good name. It would only give more people more opportunities to snub her. Also, it would put her near Brabourne, something else she did not need. She was already too susceptible to him for her own good.

She would have to feign illness the night of the dinner. The tightness in her stomach eased as she thought of this excuse. She absolutely could not go.

Chapter Six

'What is the meaning of this?' Emily demanded, storming into Juliet's bedchamber.

Juliet looked up from her lending-library novel to see a cream vellum sheet clenched in her step-mother's fingers. 'Whatever are you talking about?'

'This!' Emily thrust the sheet up to Juliet's face.

Juliet drew back to be able to focus. The Prince of Wales's crest jumped out at her. Reading quickly, she realised this was the invitation to Carlton House. Only Harry and she were invited.

Juliet opened her mouth to speak, but nothing came out. There was nothing she could say.

'How do you know his Royal Highness?' Emily hovered over Juliet.

'Um…' Juliet rose and twisted around the other woman. 'Now that I can breathe again.'

'Don't be smart with me. Answer my question.'

Juliet moved to the fireplace to give herself some

time. Carefully she laid the book on the mantel and arranged it so that the spine met and ran along the marble edge.

She turned to face Emily. 'I met him at Vauxhall. A mutual acquaintance introduced us.' She waved her hand as though to dismiss the acquaintance. 'The Prince seemed to like me and asked me to dinner at Carlton House. I needed a chaperon so he added Harry.'

Emily glared, her blue eyes flashing. 'A *mutual acquaintance*? I don't believe it. Nor can Harry chaperon you. I am the person to do that. I will go in Harry's place.'

Juliet clamped her mouth shut on words better left unsaid. Harry would like going to Carlton House for all of five minutes. Then the social posturing would make him restless, while the rich foods she had heard the Prince served would not be to her brother's liking—Harry was a beefsteak eater.

'You are right, Stepmama. You will make a much better chaperon. I am sure Harry won't mind.'

The other woman flounced to the door. One hand on the knob, she said, 'It does not matter what Harry minds. I am going. If you wish to argue this, you may do so with your father.'

Juliet flinched. Emily had Papa obedient to her slightest wish. Everyone in the household knew that, and no one crossed her because of it.

Thinking of Papa made her want to see him. She

glanced at the small silver mantel clock. It was two in the afternoon. He was probably in the cellar, which he had made into a temporary laboratory for his experiments. Only his new wife's importuning had brought him to London in the first place.

She grabbed a shawl to ward off the damp cold that was always present in the underground room. She did not know how Papa could stay there all day and not catch an inflammation of the lungs, but he did.

Minutes later, she pushed open the heavy oak door and peeked around the corner. 'Papa?'

'Come in, come in,' his distracted voice said.

She slid quietly into the room. Papa was in the middle of something, and he hated to be disturbed when he was concentrating. His work table was littered with papers and scientific instruments. He fiddled with something that looked like a stack of metal plates. An arc of light that Papa said was electricity shot out. He jumped back, a huge grin on his face.

'That is more like it,' he said proudly. Dusting his hands off on a leather apron he wore tied around his ample waist, he looked over at Juliet. 'What brings you here, miss? Come to see my latest work?'

She always found his hobby fascinating, but never understood what he told her. 'Yes, please.'

'Come over here, then.'

His square spectacles perched precariously on the end of his bulbous nose. 'This is a Voltaic pile, the first electrical battery. I am trying to make a smaller and more powerful one.'

She nodded, understanding that much. But when he launched into the scientific jargon and started pulling out all sorts of machines and pieces of metal, she was lost. Still, she continued to nod and say, 'oh, yes.'

After a while, he ran down. Peering at her over his spectacles, he asked, 'What is the real reason you came down?'

'To see you,' she said, meaning every word. 'It has been days since you have come to dinner or been at breakfast.'

He puttered with his instruments in a futile attempt to clean his table. 'I am so close. I hate to take time away even to eat. But, bless her heart, Emily has food sent down to me. I don't know what I ever did without her.' A besotted look eased the line between his grey brows.

Juliet nearly groaned. She was the one who ordered the trays prepared. Emily took advantage of the opportunity and came down with the servant when the food was delivered, thus making it appear to be her idea. Still, seeing Papa's happiness, she did not tell him the truth. It would hurt him to think his new bride did not take care of his comforts.

'Shall I send one of the maids to dust and pick things up?'

His gaze sharpened. 'Absolutely not. She would

misplace everything and break my most important equipment.'

That was his standard answer. Later, when he was out for his daily ride, Juliet would come back and straighten everything. She had done so since she was a small child, and he had never realised. She was very careful to put everything back where he had it, but she managed to dust and pick up any broken pieces.

'While you are here, what's this I hear about your being invited to Carlton House? The Prince runs with a rakish lot and I am not sure I want you moving in that crowd. Brabourne is one of his special cronies.'

He took her by surprise. Normally he did not involve himself in her whereabouts. It was obvious from his question that he was unaware she was already ostracised by most of their peers.

'Everything will be fine, Papa. Stepmama has agreed to chaperon me. Surely you cannot think anything improper will happen with her there to guide me?'

'Ah, yes.' He patted her hand, his thoughts already drifting back to his experiments as his gaze shifted back to the Voltaic pile. 'That will be perfect. I shall have more time to myself for my work.'

Juliet slipped away, Papa having forgotten she was in the room. Sadness at his lack of interest in her flitted through her mind, to be pushed aside.

Papa had always been like this and always would be. She had to accept that he was the one who needed care. Still, a little voice insisted, it would be nice if once in a while he would talk to her about what she was doing.

The night of the Carlton House dinner was upon Juliet before she realised it. She wore a simple pink gown caught under the bust by silver ribbons. A matching cluster of roses and ribbon nestled in her hair. Pearls gleamed around her slender throat and dropped like tears from her earlobes. Long white gloves completed her toilette.

Her maid—Mrs Burroughs having returned to the Duke's house—handed her a silver gauze shawl. It would be no protection from the weather, but it was a charming addition. Juliet smiled her thanks and left to meet Emily in the hall.

Her stepmother was more than half an hour late, time Juliet occupied by fetching a book from the library and reading.

The other woman was ravishing, her child-like figure shown to advantage by a daringly risqué dress of royal blue silk. There was no ornamentation. She needed none because of the multi-strand diamond and sapphire necklace draping her neck. It was worth a sultan's ransom. Matching earrings dripped from her ears. Her wrists were coated in bracelets, each one enough for many families to live on comfortably their entire lives. Even with the lavish jewels, there was an innocence about her that Juliet knew to be false.

'Here you are, Juliet,' Emily said, as though Juliet were the one who had been late. 'We must hurry. I am sure this will be a sad crush.'

Juliet nearly rolled her eyes. The woman was desperate to go, yet acting as though it were a hardship.

They entered the carriage and travelled in silence. Upon arriving, they were ushered into one of the most ornate and cluttered residences in the world. Everywhere were candles and chandeliers. Nooks and crannies held priceless art. Gilt covered anything that did not move. The brilliance was mesmerising.

Juliet had heard many descriptions of Carlton House, but they had not prepared her for the reality. She stopped and blinked.

The footman paused as well, as though he was used to guests being overwhelmed. Emily continued on through the entry and into the drawing room, not bothering to see if Juliet followed.

People continued to arrive, some glancing at Juliet as they walked by. Many ignored her in their haste to reach the activities.

'You must be blasé,' a too familiar voice said softly. 'Although Prinny will be thrilled with your reaction. He likes nothing more than to know he has impressed someone.'

She turned to him, noting the elegance which did nothing to blunt his masculinity. 'Were you impressed your first time?'

She knew he had not been, but it was conversation, and her tongue was otherwise tied and her mind blank of anything but his presence. Reacting to him on an instinctual level was the worst thing she could do for her own emotional safety. She knew that. It did not matter. He made her pulse jump.

'Ah, but I watched him redesign everything. I knew beforehand what it would look like finished. Familiarity breeds...shall we say, less excitement?'

'Of course.'

'May I escort you in?' He extended his arm.

Her fingers twitched with the need to touch him. She resisted, ignoring her thumping heart. 'Thank you, but I don't think that would be wise.'

'Usually the best way to combat rumour is to flaunt it.'

She shook her head. 'I am not so brave as you.'

His arm dropped, but his gaze stayed on her as though he were searching for something he could not quite find. 'I know better than that.'

'You flatter me,' she managed to utter around the breathlessness his scrutiny created.

'Where is your brother? Since you will not have me, you should stay with him until you have been presented to the Prince and introduced to several people.'

A wry smile curled her lips. 'My stepmother is my chaperon tonight, and she was in too much of a hurry to wait while I gaped.'

His face lost all expression. 'I see. Wait here and I will send someone back for you.'

She bristled. 'I am perfectly able to fend for myself.'

'Yes, you are. But trust me in this. It will be better if someone takes you in. More proper. Less flaunting of convention.' She frowned and he added, 'Or you can reconsider and accept me.'

She accepted defeat as graciously as her competitive nature would allow. 'I will wait here.'

'A pity, but not surprising.' With a slight dip of his head, he sauntered off.

Juliet occupied herself studying each piece of art individually, the footman still hovering nearby.

'There you are, Miss Smythe-Clyde,' a booming voice said.

She turned and instantly sank into a deep curtsy. 'Your Royal Highness.'

'No, no,' he said, reaching a hand down for her. 'I don't stand on such formality. Ask anyone.'

'Such as the Duke of Brabourne?' she asked, accepting his help up.

The Prince Regent beamed at her. 'He did mention that your chaperon had gone on without you because you took too long admiring my handiwork.'

Trust Brabourne to take the truth and twist it into

something infinitely palatable. 'I have never seen anything nearly as impressive, Your Highness.'

He tucked her hand into his arm. 'You should see my pavilion in Brighton. In fact, I insist that you visit me there.'

Things were going much too fast. Juliet felt caught in an undertow of dangerous currents. 'Thank you, Your Highness. You are far too generous.'

'Nothing of the kind.' He patted her hand and led her back the way he had come.

The strains of music reached them long before they entered the room where the orchestra played. The wittiest, most glamourous and hard-living of London Society filled the vast area. Lord Holland, Lord Alvanley, and Lady Jersey to name only a few. Everyone looked their way. Juliet wanted to sink into the floor.

Brabourne sauntered up to them and, in a move unsurpassed for audacity, asked, 'Sir, please be so kind as to introduce me to your companion.'

It took everything Juliet had not to laugh out loud at his boldness. Some of her tension drained away.

'And if I do,' the Prince said, a gleam of mirth in his eyes, 'you must promise not to steal a march on me, Brabourne. For I know your reputation with the fairer sex.'

Brabourne put a hand over his heart and looked pained. 'Sir, you misjudge me.'

'Not you, but you plead so nicely that I find myself weakening.' The prince took Juliet's hand from the crook of his elbow and extended it to the Duke. 'Miss Smythe-Clyde, may I recommend the Duke of Brabourne to you?'

Juliet made a short curtsy. 'Your Grace.'

He bowed over her hand, raising it for his kiss. His eyes held hers as his lips touched her skin. Chills, followed by heat, followed by shivers raced up Juliet's arm.

'Your servant.'

He released her and she snatched her hand back to safety. Her face felt hot with embarrassment at the marked attentions the men paid her. Never had she been the centre of any group of males, and never had she thought in her wildest dreams to be the focus of two of the most sought-after men in England. Some women would have found the experience heady. Juliet found it nerve-racking and wished it over. But she could not leave the Prince's presence without first being dismissed by him, and he and Brabourne were having too much fun bantering for Prinny to remember to release her.

For the first time since she had met Brabourne, he looked as though he were enjoying himself. Despite all the Prince's faults—and Juliet thought they were many—Brabourne seemed to like the man. The *bon mots* flew between them. Some referred to people and places Juliet could not place, but the men knew exactly what each was saying.

The music stopped, and one of the women who had been dancing left her partner. 'Your Highness,' she said, interrupting the talk, 'we have a bet. Maria Sefton says there are one hundred candles in your chandelier. I say there are three. We need you to tell us who has won.'

He laughed in pleasure. 'Lady Jersey, you are always entertaining. But before I come with you I want to present you to my latest guest. Lady Jersey, may I introduce Miss Smythe-Clyde?'

Sally Jersey smiled, albeit a small one. 'How do you do? I have heard much of you.'

The Prince frowned. 'I think the young lady should come to Almack's. Don't you, Lady Jersey?'

She looked at her Prince, then at Brabourne. In a flat tone she said, 'I shall send the vouchers round tomorrow.'

Prinny broke into a smile. 'Very good of you, Sally.'

She ignored Juliet. 'Now, will you come and tell us who wins the bet, Your Highness?'

He caught her hand. 'I am yours to command. Until later, Miss Smythe-Clyde. Brabourne.'

'Your Highness,' Juliet said. At the same time Brabourne said, 'Sir.'

Juliet started to sink into another curtsy, but the Duke's hand under her elbow stopped her. 'Not now,' he said softly. 'He is very informal at these gatherings. You would look gauche. Not at all the thing, and after he has tried so hard to bring you into fashion.'

'Is that what he was doing?'

He angled a questioning look at her. 'What did you think he was doing?'

She shook her head. 'I did not know. I am not used to this kind of attention.'

'We shall have to fill that void,' he said, propelling her towards a mixed group.

Ravensford and Perth were the only two she recognised. Brabourne introduced her to them as though she had never met them. Ravensford welcomed her with a teasing smile. Perth gave her an ironic nod. Everyone else in the circle was coolly civil, their gazes going from her to the Duke. She knew they would talk about this later. Much as Brabourne had tried to maneouvre, it was not working.

One lady asked, 'Are you here alone, Miss Smythe-Clyde?'

The barely disguised disapproval made Juliet raise her head defiantly. 'No, my stepmother is here.'

'Really?' another woman said.

Juliet was beginning to feel like a mouse being toyed with—not a pleasant feeling.

'Here you are, you naughty child,' Lady Smythe-Clyde said, gliding into the group and stopping between Juliet and Brabourne. 'I saw you with the Prince, but then lost you.' She gave the assemblage a brilliant smile.

The two women who had been quizzing Juliet made their excuses. None of the men did.

Juliet watched as her stepmother proceeded to charm the males. Much to her dismay, Brabourne made his adieux shortly. She felt bereft, not a good emotion to have because the Duke had left. Without any trouble, she faded away herself, finding a secluded area and being thankful for it. She did not belong here. Even if her name was on the tongue of every rumourmonger in London, she was still not up to snuff enough for this collection of the *ton's* most rakish and wild habitués.

Several women, lavishly clothed and jewelled, strolled by. Their eyes met Juliet's and then slid past. Words drifted behind them.

'Brabourne is a devil. The nerve of him to bring his unmarried mistress here. It is just not done.'

The second woman sniffed. 'Flaunting, more like. And she nothing out of the ordinary, with that carrot-red hair and all those ugly freckles.'

They were quickly past, but Juliet imagined that their conversation continued. She bit her lip on the pain that flared to anger. The hypocrites. She might be naïve, but she had heard the envy in the women's voices. It was not done for an honourable man to take an unmarried woman as his mistress, but either of them could have filled the position as long as both parties were discreet. And she was not even the Duke's *chère amie*.

Her stomach churned at the unfairness of it. Her feelings felt raw. She would find the Prince and beg his leave to depart before dinner. Food was the last thing she needed if she was to keep from being sick with overwrought emotion.

Sebastian watched Juliet from an alcove. She looked distraught. When she started walking purposefully in the direction where Prinny held court, he began to worry.

'No sense in following her,' Perth's pragmatic voice said.

Sebastian glanced at his friend. The candlelight flickered on the other man's face, shading the side with no scar and highlighting the one with the imperfection. The slash gave Perth a hard edge that was echoed in the man himself.

'Don't be a hypocrite,' Sebastian said. 'If the roles were reversed, you would pursue.'

A slow grin eased some of the tightness from Perth's mouth. 'I would never have got into this mess to begin with. And never with a virgin.'

'Touché,' Sebastian muttered. 'I must have been out of my head ever to let her into my house.'

'You were unwilling to take the chance that she would die and make it necessary for you to flee to the Continent.'

'Oh, yes,' Sebastian muttered ironically. 'Now I remember the story of it. Remind me in future to have all my duelling opponents checked for their sex before I fight them.'

Perth chuckled.

Juliet reached the Prince, who took one of her hands and drew her into the group surrounding him. She flushed, then paled, but stood her ground bravely.

'She's a game one,' Perth said. 'But if I were you I'd leave her alone for the rest of the night. It does neither of you any good for you to seem to pursue her.'

'You are right, as usual,' Sebastian said, his attention not wavering.

'You had best marry her,' Perth said quietly. 'It will solve a lot of problems. You need an heir, and she needs respectability.'

The Duke jerked as though he had been shot. Perth was the third person, after Mrs Burroughs and Ravensford, to say that to him. As with Mrs Burroughs, he could not be cutting. Instead, he drawled, 'Are you ready for Bedlam? I am not in the marriage mart.'

'No, my friend, but there are times when one stumbles into it against one's better judgement. I believe, for you, that this is one of those times.'

Sebastian picked up his quizzing glass and surveyed the room with a bored expression. 'I think not.'

Before Perth could say more, the Duke sauntered

off in the direction of a group preparing to go into
dinner. Even though he no longer watched Juliet, he
was aware of her still standing beside Prinny. There
was something about the chit that tugged at him, but
nothing that he could not ignore.

The Prince Regent continued to hold Juliet's fingers even though he had tucked them into the bend
of his arm. She was flustered and embarrassed by
his continuing attention. Surreptitious and not-so-
surreptitious glances followed them as they walked
the perimeter of the room. The others who had been
with him when she had arrived were gone, seeing
that he had no interest except in her.

'Your Highness,' she said, her fingers clutching
spasmodically at his elaborate coat, 'if it is possible,
I should like to be excused. I…I am not feeling my
best.'

'My dear Miss Smythe-Clyde, I am so sorry. Let
me have my own physician attend you.'

She gulped, and would have bolted if his hold on
her had not been so tight, or so she told herself. 'It
is nothing much, Your Highness. Just an irritation
of the stomach.'

He tutted and they continued their walk as she
tried to persuade him to let her leave. Finally, when
they had circled the room once and were back at the
door where she had originally entered, he released
her enough to bring her fingers to his lips.

'If you are truly sick, I could not be such a beast as to keep you here. But you must promise me to come another time.'

Juliet had never stammered in her life, but she did now. 'I—I...th-thank you, Your H-highness. I should be d-delighted.'

He released her and she sank into a grateful curtsy, forgetting Brabourne's admonition not to.

'Now, none of that,' the Prince said. 'You are not at court.'

She rose, her face blushing fierily. All she wanted was to escape this awful situation. Others might pray to receive this type of attention, but she was severely uncomfortable.

The Prince signalled to a footman while she tried to think of something to say—anything that would ease the discomfort she felt. Nothing came.

The footman bowed to her and indicated she was to precede him. She made her farewells to the Prince, and left with alacrity. It was some time before her coach arrived at the door. When it did, she rushed down the steps and clambered into its safety. Even Ferguson's raised brow failed to elicit any response that might slow down their departure.

If she never went to Carlton House again in her life, it would be too soon.

Sebastian watched Juliet's hasty departure. She would not even blend well into his world. She was a country bumpkin.

A small hand crept between his arm and his side. 'Introduce *me* to the Prince.'

He looked dispassionately down at Lady Smythe-Clyde. Her jasmine scent engulfed him. He always sneezed around the jasmine plant and it was all he could do to keep from doing so now.

'Importuning, as usual?'

Her eyes narrowed and her nails scratched along his arm before he removed them. 'I saw what you did for Juliet. Do the same for me and I will do what I can to scotch the rumour about the two of you.'

'You should be doing so already. She is your stepdaughter.'

'And I am already tarred by the same brush that blackens her. No one was home today when I went calling. Previous invitations have been rescinded.'

'There you are,' he said. 'You have stated all the reasons you should be trying to protect her reputation. Whether I introduce you to Prinny should have nothing to do with your course of action.'

'Ah, but it does.' She looked up at him through thick blonde lashes, her head barely reaching his shoulder. 'If he is seen to enjoy my company, then all those old biddies who have snubbed me will have to cosy up to me. It is the way of our world.'

He looked down at her, noting the angelic curve

of her brow and the sweet fullness of her lips. Her looks belied the calculating coldness of her heart. His mother had been much like this woman.

A darkness entered his eyes, and Emily edged away from the barely controlled danger that seemed to lurk around him like a shadow. But nothing could still her tongue. 'Otherwise you would not have gone to all the trouble to introduce Juliet to the Prince.'

'Brabourne.' Prinny's voice broke between them. 'Come speak with me.' His attention moved to Emily. 'After you have introduced me to this lovely lady.'

Sebastian did the honours, a sardonic curl to his mouth as he watched Lady Smythe-Clyde simper and the Prince puff up like a peacock. They made a very unusual pair. If one were not the heir apparent, they would be said to be an amusing pair, so different in size. He easily made six of her.

It took long minutes of flirtatious badinage before the Prince remembered his original intent. 'Come, Brabourne, we must talk and have a chat.'

Sebastian bowed his head in acknowledgement. Both took their leave of Lady Smythe-Clyde.

They had barely reached a position of relative privacy when Prinny said, 'You will have to marry the chit. I have done my best to bring her into fashion, and Sally's vouchers for Almack's will help prodigiously, but neither will be enough. We are becoming a prudish lot.' His gaze swept over the gathering.

Sebastian controlled his retort. 'I don't think marriage would be good for either of us, sir.'

Prinny looked at his companion. ''Fraid it will clip your wings? Don't worry. Women don't expect fidelity from a husband, just financial support and social position. She won't care what you do as long as you keep it quiet.'

Sebastian snorted. There was no other acceptable answer other than yes, and he was not going to say that.

Accepting that Sebastian's answer would be yes, Prinny sauntered off. Sebastian turned away. He would not be forced into a situation not of his choosing.

No matter how sorry he felt for the chit.

Chapter Seven

❦

The vouchers for Almack's came the next afternoon. There was no note or anything to indicate who
had sent them. If Juliet had not known Lady Jersey
was supposed to do so, she would have never found
out. The woman had done as her Prince told her,
but in a way that made it unmistakable that she did
not want to do so. Juliet had heard that Almack's
patronesses would not bow to anyone. Perhaps Lady
Jersey was currying favour for some private reason.

Juliet shook her head. She was not normally this
suspicious. She usually took everyone and everything at face value.

Well, she did not have to go to Almack's. She
tossed the vouchers into the wastepaper basket in
the morning room. She had household accounts to
go over and no time to worry about Almack's or the
Prince or Brabourne. Particularly Brabourne.

* * *

Later that evening, as she read in her room, Harry burst in upon her.

'What brings you here this late? I thought you and Tommy were going to Drury Lane to ogle the actresses,' she teased.

'Isn't that just like a sister?' he said, hands on hips, indignation making his hair seem to stand on end. 'I've come to warn you that the fat is in the fire and you act flippantly.'

With a sigh of resignation, Juliet folded and set down her book. Perhaps she would get to read it later. Perhaps not. Harry could be as impulsive as she, and something had aroused him.

'Emily found those Almack's vouchers in the morning room, and she's fit to string you up by the neck until dead and leave your body to rot.'

Juliet snorted in an effort to cover her laugh. This was no laughing matter and Harry would not appreciate her levity. 'You are too colourful, although I am sure it is an apt description.'

'She is in Papa's laboratory right now, screaming and crying like a spoilt child.'

'Which is exactly what she is.' But Juliet knew there would be trouble. She should have burned the vouchers.

The door to Juliet's room crashed open. She was getting very tired of this. With dry resignation, she asked, 'Don't you ever knock? It is quite rude to enter without permission.'

Emily stormed into the room, dragging Papa behind her. His face was crimson and his glasses sat at a precarious angle on his nose. The leather apron he wore while experimenting still rode his ample girth. He looked flustered.

Emily was scarlet from anger, her eyes ice chips. 'What do you mean by throwing these away?' Her voice rose an octave as she waved the vouchers at Juliet. 'These are like gold, you stupid girl.'

Juliet bristled and said the first words that came to her tongue. 'Only to a social toady.'

Shocked silence filled the room.

Papa stepped forward and puffed his chest, a trait he had just before giving an ultimatum. 'Ahem... Juliet, that is no way to talk to your stepmama. She only has your best interests in mind. You will listen to her.'

'You are such a pillar of strength, dearest Oliver,' Emily said, her complexion easing back to its normal English rose. 'I knew you would support me in this.'

Juliet averted her face so Papa would not see her grimace. She saw Harry turn away in disgust. But no matter how sickened she was, she was trapped. She never defied Papa. Never. Mama had raised both her and Harry to do exactly as Papa wished. Things had gone much more smoothly that way. It was a habit Juliet was not sure she could break.

She took a deep breath and spoke as calmly as

possible. 'But I do not wish to go to Almack's. If I had known Stepmama wanted to attend then I would have been glad to give her the vouchers.'

Emily glared at her. 'They are for you and your chaperon. I shall take you next Wednesday.'

Juliet clamped her mouth shut on the defiant words bubbling up inside her. She looked imploringly at Papa, but he stood beside Emily with a complacent smile. In his mind everything was settled.

She looked at Harry. He shrugged and mouthed, What can it hurt?

He was right. She should not have made such a big issue of this. 'Perhaps Harry can go with us, Stepmama.'

His eyes popped, but he stood manfully. 'I shall escort both of you. Unless Papa wants to do the pretty.'

'No, no. I don't wish to take away your fun,' Papa said. Before anyone could pursue that topic, he left the room, muttering that he had been away from his batteries too long as it was.

With him safely gone, Juliet said, 'Are you satisfied now?'

'Immensely,' Emily said. 'This should be a good lesson for both of you on respect—to me.'

Juliet was so furious she could think of nothing scathing to say. With a satisfied smirk, Emily left.

Harry and Juliet looked at each other. Neither one wanted the signal honour of Almack's, but both were going. It did no good knowing that dozens of young ladies would give their fortunes for the opportunity to drink lemonade and dance to country tunes and, if they were lucky, be allowed to waltz.

Juliet did not want to go. It was just another opportunity for the *ton* to snub her. But she was backed into a corner.

At least she did not have to worry about seeing Brabourne there. Rakes of his ilk never went to such dry and boring gatherings.

Wednesday came much too soon, and once more Juliet found herself in the hall, waiting for her stepmother to make an appearance. Harry, never patient, paced along the black and white tiles like a caged animal.

'That will not help,' Juliet said with a smile.

He grimaced. 'It helps me.'

She was tempted to grab his arm and make him stop. 'You are getting on my nerves. At least stop for five minutes.'

He groaned, but complied. 'You look bang up to the nines in that brown stuff.'

She made him a shallow, playful curtsy. 'Thank you, kind sir.'

He flushed. 'I was just trying to practise.'

She grinned. 'Yes. For your information, this gown is made of bronze silk. My hair is threaded with gold ribbon.'

'I am sure I will need that at some time,' he said sarcastically.

'You never can tell.'

'Is the carriage ready?' Emily's demand stopped their banter. 'We don't want to be too late.'

They looked at each other and rolled their eyes. 'Ferguson has been waiting for the last twenty minutes,' Juliet said. 'And you know how he dislikes keeping the horses still. It is not good for them.'

Emily flitted by. 'It is not Ferguson's place to fret. He will do as he is told.'

Juliet's lips tightened, but she told herself not to let Emily ruin the night. Too many hours lay before them for her to let anger fester.

Hobson put a brown velvet cape trimmed in bronze satin around Juliet's shoulders. She smiled at him. He put an ice-blue satin cape around Lady Smythe-Clyde. She ignored him.

Tonight Emily wore a silver gown trimmed in pale blue ribbons. Around her neck hung a single large sapphire. Matching earrings dangled below her jaw, drawing the eye to her slender neck and elegant shoulders.

Juliet looked away, a pang twisting her stomach. The last time she had seen those jewels her mama had been wearing them on the way to a ball at the Squire's. She had thought mama looked beautiful in the magnificent sapphires. It hurt to see that the jewels looked better on Emily.

Deliberately she blanked her mind.

No one said a thing as they made their way through the London streets. Fog was drifting in from the Thames and the few street lamps were golden hazes that illuminated nothing. The clop-clop of hooves on cobbles echoed eerily.

Juliet was glad when they reached their destination.

They entered Almack's with another group, affording them some anonymity. Juliet paused to look around. Nothing was as she had expected. It was just a plain large room with no embellishments, yet this was the most famous room in London. Some of the most advantageous marriages owed their start to the weekly assemblies here. Disappointment was something Juliet had not expected.

As soon as they were in, Emily left them.

'So much for a chaperon,' Harry said. 'Good thing I am with you.'

'She did it at Carlton House, too. But I am glad of it.'

Across the room, the Earl of Perth approached the Countess Lieven. 'Madam,' he said, making her a perfect leg and giving her a wicked smile, 'would it be too much to request that you introduce me to Miss Smythe-Clyde as a waltz partner?'

She turned sharply to him. 'You are always in the

thick of trouble, Perth. Will you start first off to-night?'

'I fear I must, dear lady. The redhead has caught my interest and I would like to know her better.' His black eyes snapped with life.

She sighed. 'You always were an irresistible rogue. Come along.'

They met Juliet and Harry coming off the floor after a country dance.

'Miss Smythe-Clyde?' Countess Lieven asked.

'Yes.'

'I am Countess Lieven, and I would like to introduce the Earl of Perth and recommend him as a waltzing partner.'

Juliet blinked, then quickly dropped a curtsy. 'I would be delighted.'

'I thought so,' Countess Lieven said drily, and left.

'She does not approve of me,' Perth said.

'You are too kind, sir. I am sure my reputation is the cause of her curtness.'

'That too,' he said, surprising her by his bluntness.

Harry interrupted to say, 'I shall wait here, Juliet.'

She nodded and followed the Earl to the floor. He put one arm around her waist and took her left hand with his right. It felt strange to be this close to a man she did not know. He held her lightly and guided her with sureness.

'I am glad Harry and I spent time learning this. Otherwise I should be tripping all over your feet right now.'

Instead of flirting with her, as he had Countess Lieven, he looked down at her solemnly. The flickering candles cast his face into shadow and then in the next twirl shone directly on his scar. Juliet found him disconcerting.

'I wanted to speak with you,' he finally said. 'I believe you are the only female to ever fight a duel in England.'

Her hands went clammy, and she looked away from his intense stare. 'Why are you discussing that here?' she managed to whisper, fearful that someone might hear. That was the last thing she needed for people to find out.

'I never see you at my regular haunts, and since the incident I've been curious about what kind of female would do such a thing.' He spoke as softly as she. Anyone watching them would think they were flirting and did not want to be overheard.

'An impulsive one,' she muttered.

'A troublesome trait,' he said.

'Sometimes,' she answered with a rueful grin.

The dance ended quickly, and before Juliet quite realised it they were taking their leave of one another. She turned to speak with Harry, to tell him how exhilarating the waltz was with someone you did not know, and came face to face with Brabourne.

The breath caught in her throat and her hand went involuntarily to her throat.

'Oh, you startled me.'

'Would you care to dance?'

It was the last thing she expected from him. Shyness overwhelmed her. She would rather dance with anyone but him. No, that was not true. But it should be true. He was trouble. He was dangerous. To her. To all women. He was temptation, and she was unable to resist.

'Yes,' she murmured, dimly aware of Harry fiercely frowning at her. She gave her brother a vacuous smile and allowed Brabourne to lead her to the floor.

He did not hold her any closer than Perth had, yet it seemed as if she was pressed to the length of him. She would swear she could feel the heat of his body and the curve of his chest against hers. She tried to ease away but he held her firmly, his arm burning a swathe across the small of her back. She shuddered.

'Bronze silk is very becoming on you,' he said quietly. 'Few women wear it successfully.'

His voice glided along her nerves, making them tingle. She was so immersed in the physical reaction he evoked that she nearly missed the meaning of his words. When they sank in, they broke his spell on her and she choked back a chuckle.

'You are so accomplished. Poor Harry told me this "brown stuff" looked well on me.'

'I am a rake,' he drawled. 'Harry is but a youth fresh to life's adventures.'

'That is one way of putting it,' she muttered.

'A truthful one.'

She cocked her head to one side and studied him. He was as handsome as ever. His black hair was still longer than fashionable, his eyes bluer than blue, his mouth a sensual slash. Yet…his former cool disdain seemed muted. Almost as though he were letting her closer?

'Am I a an object of curiosity, or is there another reason you are looking so intently at me?'

She dropped her gaze and focused on the sapphire in his cravat. It was the exact colour of his eyes. He must have purposely chosen it. 'It is a bad habit of mine. Staring, that is.'

'But endearing, and not nearly so hazardous as your impetuosity.'

She could not believe this was the cynical, cold Brabourne with whom she had duelled. He was flirting with her, exuding all the charm that made him such a successful libertine. He must realised how dazed she was.

'I am not being fair. For me, our dalliance is just another incident in a string of such incidents. It is my attempt to make you smile and look less as if you have been stunned by a knock to the head.'

Cold water could not have distanced her more quickly. 'Of course. I knew that.'

'I am sure you did,' he murmured smoothly, turning her into a dipping swirl.

The dance ended then and he deposited her next to Harry with a perfunctory bow. She watched his broad back disappear into the throng, feeling as though she had lost her bearings.

Harry snapped his fingers under her nose. 'Are you in a trance?'

She blinked and focused on him. 'Brabourne has a powerful presence,' she said, wondering why her hand still throbbed and her back still felt as though he held her. She was not a schoolgirl experiencing her first dance. She definitely belonged in Bedlam.

'No doubt,' Harry said, disgust dripping from his words. 'I can see the effect he has on you, and you had best get hold of yourself. He will only break your heart if you allow him. For that matter, why is he dallying after you? You ain't in his normal style, to say nothing of how you met and the rumours flying about the two of you.'

Juliet chewed her lip. 'I think he is trying to bring me into fashion, against all the efforts of the rest of the *ton* who are trying to ostracise me. I just don't know why he should care.'

The next thing she knew, Ravensford begged her company for a country dance. Her following partner was introduced by an unsmiling Lady Jersey, who had obviously been coerced into it.

'Miss Smythe-Clyde, may I introduce Lord Alastair St Simon?'

Juliet recognised St Simon as the family name for the powerful Duke of Rundell as she curtsied. She had not risen before Lady Jersey sailed away. She murmured her acceptance and wondered why all these men, who were high in the levels of Society, were asking her to dance.

Lord St Simon smiled down at her. He was a tall man with black hair silvered at the temples and warm grey eyes.

'Would you care to dance or stroll around and talk? My wife would like to meet you.'

'Your wife? I don't understand.'

Although she had a sneaking suspicion, it was one she found hard to believe. Brabourne had said he never went out of his way for anyone. Surely he was not responsible for all these introductions? Yet she did not know anyone else who could accomplish this.

He took her hand and tucked it into his arm. 'Brabourne has said nothing to you. That is typical. He has asked the help of all his friends to bring you into respectable fashion.'

'Very kind of him, I am sure.'

'But not what you want.'

She looked up at him. The friendliness in his eyes eased some of her discomfort. 'This is very trying. I know he is doing what he considers best, but all I want is to go home to Wood Hall and leave London and all its disapproval behind.'

'It is hard to weather the ostracism of our peers, but it can be done. My brother Langston's wife was an actress before they married. She has never been totally accepted by the highest sticklers, but she has enough friends and interests that it does not bother her. You can do the same with time.'

'Thank you for the information and concern. I shall keep it in mind.'

'But not use it.'

They stopped near a woman nearly as tall as he. Her hair was the colour of a roaring flame, and her eyes were like slanted marquise-cut turquoises in the oval of her face. She was stunning.

'Liza, this is the lady Brabourne has asked us to befriend. Miss Smythe-Clyde, my wife Lizabeth, Lady Worth in her own right.'

He looked with such pride and love at the woman that for the first time in her life Juliet found herself envious of another female. The two were very much involved in one another. Most marriages among her kind were for convenience. Watching them, she wished she could marry for love. It was something she had thought about upon occasion, but never particularly longed for.   They were amusing and witty. Harry soon joined them and they treated him with a casual acceptance that won Juliet over.

A sudden hush filled the room so that one of

Liza's laughs sounded like a shout. Juliet looked around to see what was happening.

Her heart skipped a beat.

Brabourne was talking to her stepmother. Emily's hand was on his arm, and her smiling face was turned up to his impassive one. How dared Emily? Hadn't she fought Brabourne in a duel because of this behaviour?

She took a step towards them. A hand clamped over her arm and held her like a vice. Frowning, she looked to see who held her.

St Simon said softly, 'Don't. It will only make the situation worse if you intrude.'

She glared at him. 'Worse? How could it be worse?'

Lady St Simon flanked her other side. 'Things such as this are better ignored. If you make it into a large scene, it will become tomorrow's tea-time entertainment. If you do nothing, it might fade away.' She smiled gently. 'Give Brabourne a chance. He was never interested or involved with your stepmother. She is the one doing the chasing.'

Juliet digested this information. They were experienced in the ways of their world. She would do better for all involved to give way. With a sigh she accepted their advice.

Harry grumbled but, when Juliet shook her head at him he half-turned half away from the couple.

Even so, she knew that, like her, he was keeping them in sight.

Sebastian watched Lady Smythe-Clyde with a jaundiced eye. The woman was a bore, not to mention a troublemaker. He removed his arm from her grip.

'What is it you want this time?' he asked coldly.

Her smile widened, showing white, sharp little teeth. She looked like a hungry cat. 'The next waltz.'

'No,' he said bluntly, taking a step away.

Her hand gripped his sleeve again. This time her nails dug in deeply. 'You danced with Juliet; you can dance with me.'

His gut tightened. He did not like having any woman clutch at him as she was doing. He set out to put an end to her machinations. 'Not only are you vulgar, but you are stupid. After your husband challenged me to a duel, the last thing we need to do is dance together. Furthermore, you complain that no one invites you anywhere because of Juliet. Do not anger me, for I am the only reason you are here tonight. I can see that you do not attend again—or anywhere else, for that matter.'

Her eyes glinted maliciously, but she managed to keep her lips in a rictus of a smile. 'How dare you? I shall see that the little hussy suffers for your treatment of me.'

She dropped her hand and walked gracefully away, a sway to her hips that he knew was intentional. It added fuel to the fury she had fanned. He'd be damned if he would allow her to make things worse for Juliet. He had not gone to all this trouble to have that witch ruin it.

He caught himself immediately. What was he thinking? He had done everything he could and more than could be expected. Irritated with himself, he glanced coolly at the object of his thoughts.

Juliet and her brother moved towards the door, obviously planning on leaving. As they approached a group of dowagers the older women looked them up and down with haughty disdain and then turned their backs on the couple.

Cold fury filled Sebastian.

'Easy,' Ravensford said, having come up to Brabourne without the Duke being aware. 'Anything you do now will only make matters worse than they already are.'

'As usual, you speak sense.'

'But it does not make it easier when you feel responsible for the treatment the chit is receiving.'

'I am not responsible for that silly girl's predicament,' he said, more harshly than he had intended. 'I am merely sorry for her. Nothing more.'

'Of course,' Ravensford murmured.

Sebastian looked at him. 'Sarcasm does not enhance your reputation for easy charm.'

'Nor does anger over the treatment of a mere female strengthen your reputation for cool indifference towards that sex.'

'Touché.'

'Let's get out of here before anything else happens,' Ravensford said. 'White's will probably have something interesting going on. If nothing else, we can get something decent to eat and drink.'

'Agreed,' Sebastian said, leading the way. But he did not feel any less furious over the night's happenings; he just hid his emotions as he always had. His father had taught him that lesson.

Sebastian sauntered into White's, his demeanour at odds with the anger coursing through him. He looked around the heavily panelled room, taking in the regulars: Alvanley, Holland, and others. Slowly the relaxed atmosphere sank into him.

'That is much better,' Ravensford said. 'For a while I thought you were going to explode like one of Vauxhall's fireworks.'

'Those old crows and their simpering daughters are more than I can take at times.'

'Stifling,' Ravensford agreed.

The two men moved to a table where whist was being played and port consumed with a determination that was hard to match. One of the players glanced up. A worried look came over his face when he saw Sebastian.

'What's bothering you, Durkin, losing again?' Ravensford asked with a grin.

Durkin shook his head and gulped down the ruby wine in his glass, poured another and gulped that too. 'Nothing so harmless.'

Sebastian gazed down at the man whose sandy hair and blue eyes seemed to glint in the candlelight. The two of them had gone to school together and, while they were not the best of cronies, they still liked each other. Durkin's edginess meant something was not right.

'What do you know that we don't, Durk?' he asked, using their old school name for the other man.

Durkin ran long fingers through his already mussed hair and glanced warily at his partner, who nodded back at him.

'Best tell him now,' Salter said, his brown eyes looking as worried as Durkin's. 'The devil will be in the fat no matter what.'

Sebastian stiffened. There was only one topic that had ever made him lose his temper to the degree that his friends were indicating would happen here. His mother and her infidelities.

'What is it?' he demanded, his voice harsh.

'The betting book. Best look at it.'

Sebastian looked from one to the other and nodded curtly. In two strides he had the infamous book. He flipped it to the last page with writing and read the content. *When will a particular Duke tire of the lovely Miss S-C so that someone else may have a go with her?*

He slammed the book shut. His eyes narrowed to slits of blue fire as he looked slowly around the room. Most of the occupants met his gaze, a few looked away. Without a word he left, Ravensford rushing to keep up with him.

Enraged, Sebastian was glad he had sent his coach home. He needed to walk. The cool summer night air felt good.

'Bad business, that,' Ravensford said, keeping pace.

'It will be a deadly business if I learn who wrote it,' Sebastian vowed.

Ravensford glanced curiously at his friend. 'The chit is nothing to you that you need fight a duel over her honour.'

Sebastian blew out a breath and stopped. He turned to look at the other man. 'Not right now.'

Ravensford quirked one bronze brow but said nothing, waiting patiently.

'I have resisted the inevitable. Prinny ordered me to marry the girl. You even said I should do the honourable, even though it was none of my doing that brought her into my home. I resisted both of you because I don't wish to be leg-shackled. Nor do I care about flaunting Society's petty prejudices.'

He started walking again, his long legs covering distance like a thoroughbred horse racing to the finish line. Ravensford, a smile starting in his eyes, followed.

'But you can't let them vilify her, can you?'

'No.'

The curt word, with all its implications, cut through the night.

'I knew you would do the honourable thing,' Ravensford said.

Sebastian gave his friend a sardonic look. 'You did. Even I did not know I would go against my better interests because of someone else.'

Ravensford shook his head. 'You are too hard on yourself. I know plenty of people you would help at your own cost.'

'But none of them a chit from the country whom I barely know.' Self-derision dripped from each word.

'You know the old saying,' Ravensford said. 'There's a first time for everything. If there weren't we would not have the saying.'

Sebastian snorted and kept walking. What kind of hold did the chit have over him? Yes, he admired her guts and determination. He liked the way she cared for others before herself. He was even attracted to her physically, something he would not have thought. She was not the seasoned widow or courtesan he normally kept. But none of those reasons were enough to marry her.

It must be something else, but he was damned if he knew what.

Chapter Eight

'I don't want to marry Brabourne.' Juliet jumped up from her seat. The dainty yellow-striped silk chair tottered on its back legs before settling back down.

'*You* don't have a choice,' Lady Smythe-Clyde said, venom dripping from every word.

Juliet paced the room. 'Why isn't Papa here to tell me?'

The other woman's tinkling laugh filled the air. 'Don't be absurd. You know he is immersed in his experiments. Count yourself lucky he even bothered to see Brabourne. Particularly after their past.'

Juliet scowled. 'I am surprised Papa did so.'

'Ah, well, you have me to thank for that.' Emily patted her yellow curls and a complacent smile curled her lips. But only momentarily. 'Considering the state your reputation is in, you should be thrilled by this offer.'

'Well, I am not.' Juliet ground to a halt in front of the window. Outside carriages passed and people walked. A nanny and her charges trundled by like a loaded mail coach. 'If you had behaved yourself in the first place, none of this would have happened.'

Emily surged to her feet. 'Don't you dare talk to me like that.'

Juliet swung around. She was well and truly angry. Her reputation had been ruined because of this woman, and now she was to be handed off to the Duke like a piece of furniture. She was beyond calmness.

'I will talk to you any way I please. We were all fine until you came along with your London airs and little-girl looks.' She lifted her chin. 'Besides, Papa needs me.'

Emily stalked up to Juliet, her head reaching Juliet's nose. 'Don't delude yourself. Your papa is happy now, and that is all that matters. As long as he has me he has no need of you.'

Juliet frowned down at her, all the fight gone like a balloon that had been pricked. Every word the other spoke was true. Papa was besotted with her. She could do no wrong. Everything good in his life he attributed to this woman.

A pang of hurt tightened Juliet's chest. Papa had seen Brabourne because this woman insisted, but he could not be bothered to tell Juliet about the proposal of marriage. Her fists clenched and she pushed back the pain. That was just Papa. He was always like this and it had never mattered before. Except that before Mama had always been there to act as a buffer against Papa's indifference.

Mama. She had promised Mama to care for Papa. She could not do that married to the Duke. She looked at Emily. This woman would not care for her father.

A little part of her hurt seeped out. 'You don't even love Papa. You no more consider his needs than you do mine.'

Emily stepped away, having won the battle. 'In my own way I am quite fond of him. And we are married, a very permanent arrangement while both of us live.'

The supercilious tone told Juliet everything. If she left, Papa would be on his own, or very nearly so. Hobson would try, but it would not be the same.

Nor did she want to marry Brabourne. He was arrogant and cold and…and a rake. A rake of the worst sort. He would marry her, bed her and put his child in her, but he would see other women. His kind always did. 'Faithful' was not a word in his vocabulary.

He would treat her worse than Papa, only it would hurt more because he was not absentminded and focused on experiments. Brabourne's indifference would be true indifference, a cold void without emotion.

'I would rather marry a slug than the Duke.' She stalked past Emily and slammed the door behind herself. Emily's laughter tagged behind Juliet.

A good long walk in the park was what she needed. Since coming to London she did not get enough exercise. Sometimes her emotions built up to exploding point and she wanted to destroy something, anything. This had seldom happened to her in the country.

She called for her pelisse and set off towards Hyde Park. What if she was without a maid or chaperon? People already thought the worst of her; that was why Brabourne had offered. He was allowed every indiscretion imaginable. She was allowed none. Her blood boiled at the unfairness of it and what it had done to her.

When Ferguson pulled the carriage around to the front, she ignored him and continued marching down the walk. He fell in some distance behind and patiently followed.

Sebastian guided his big black gelding around a group of walkers. Ravensford rode beside him on a spirited chestnut mare. They were making the daily pilgrimage around Hyde Park, the Serpentine glinting dully in the summer sunshine.

'So you did it,' Ravensford said when they were safely past listening ears.

Sebastian grunted. 'I could not very well *not* after last night.'

Ravensford shook his head. 'Bad business, that. Sally Jersey gave her the vouchers, we all danced with her, and still some of the pinch-faced prudes cut her. And the bet.'

'When she is the Duchess of Brabourne they will all grovel at her feet. They grovelled at my mother's no matter what she did.'

Ravensford looked over at his friend's tight face. The bitterness in Sebastian's tone was unsettling. 'That was a while ago, and things have changed in the last fifteen to twenty years. If those old biddies defied Prinny, they won't think twice about doing so to you.'

'Perhaps. Perhaps not.' He turned ice-hard blue eyes to his friend. 'I protect what is mine.'

Ravensford looked away, uncertain whether to groan or laugh. 'It is time for me to return home. I have a meeting with Gentleman Jackson that I don't want to miss. Last time I was late he took someone else and made me rebook my appointment.'

Sebastian calmed down somewhat and nearly smiled. 'He is an impudent man for all that he was born a nobody.'

'He is a talented man who knows his own worth.' Ravensford slanted Brabourne a sardonic glance. 'Much like someone else I know.'

Sebastian laughed. 'Yes, but some of us deserve our sense of importance.'

Chuckling lightly, they exited the gate and headed for home. Minutes later, Sebastian saw Juliet storming down the street—alone. No maid or chaperon tailed her, as was proper. She was the most irritating and independent woman it had ever been his misfortune to meet. And he was going to marry her. He shook his head, stopped his horse, and dismounted.

'What are you doing here alone?' he demanded.

She jerked to a halt and stared defiantly at him. 'That is none of your concern. Besides, Ferguson is with me.'

He glanced at the man who had stopped the carriage and stayed put, his attention focused on the two of them. 'He is not a chaperon. Not here,' he added for good measure.

She flushed, and he knew she was remembering her time in his home, in one of his beds. 'He is sufficient. Besides, my reputation is already beyond repair—what is a little more to gossip about?'

'You are the most infuriating woman,' he said coldly. 'I am doing everything I can, and you are undoing it as fast as I try.'

She tossed her head, her magnificent red hair flaring out in an arch of curls under the brim of her chip-straw hat. 'You have gone too far this time, Brabourne. I will not marry you. That is why I am out like this, trying to burn off some of my anger at your audacity in approaching my father. After everything that has happened, I would have thought you would be too embarrassed to even talk to him, let alone ask for my hand.'

Sebastian's lip curled, but he was not amused. 'I am never embarrassed. That is something you will learn with time. As to approaching your father, I had no choice. Something has to be done. Marrying me is the only way to restore your good name. No one, and I mean no one, would dare snub the Duchess of Brabourne.'

'Really?' she said. 'You think you are that influential and powerful?'

'I know I am,' he said quietly. 'I watched my mother flaunt every convention and still be accepted by all.'

He knew from the surprise on her face that some of his bitterness must have slipped out. He did not care. Sooner or later she would hear all the sordid details. Someone would make sure of that.

'Well, that is interesting, but I don't intend to follow in your mother's footsteps.' She swept the skirt of her periwinkle gown aside. 'If you will excuse me, I find I am tired of walking.'

Sebastian watched her stalk regally to her carriage, head up, shoulders straight. He did not mount his horse until she was safely ensconced. And then he waited with Ravensford until her vehicle drove off.

'She will be a handful,' Ravensford said, a glint of appreciation in his hazel eyes.

Sebastian watched him speculatively. 'Perhaps you should marry her.'

Ravensford laughed. 'Not me. My name ain't enough to protect her. Remember? Only you can do that.'

Sebastian snorted, but took the teasing easily. What bothered him was the tiny twist in his gut when he'd suggested that Ravensford marry her. He must be getting ill or be hungry.

'Let's go back to my house. I am sure Mrs Burroughs can find us a beefsteak and ale.'

'You set such an elegant table,' Ravensford said as they set off. 'My French chef is still at Brabourne Abbey. He will be up here in time for my wedding.'

Together they set off, Sebastian putting from his mind any pang of loss connected with Juliet Smythe-Clyde. They would be married in four weeks. Time enough to ponder what to do with her.

Juliet slammed down *The Gazette*. Brabourne had posted the announcement of their marriage. How dared he? She had told him she would not marry him and she meant it. This was one instance when she would defy Papa. This was her future happiness at stake. And Papa's, although he did not realise it.

She surged to her feet and stomped to the wardrobe. She was not going to sit idly by while everything went from bad to worse. She dragged out a black cape, swung it around her shoulders and pulled the hood up to completely cover her hair.

Brabourne needed a come-uppance and she was going to give it to him.

Minutes later she was in the stable, ordering a boy to wake Ferguson. When she and the coachman were alone, she said, 'I need to go to Brabourne's house.'

He rolled his eyes. 'Lass, have ye got maggots in yer head? We are still reelin' from yer last visit.'

She tapped her foot. 'This is of vital importance. Either you can drive me in the carriage and put down a street away so no one will see the crest, or I will hire a hackney. But I am going.'

He groaned, took off his hat and wiped his brow. ''Twould be best if we both took the hackney. I will wait in the kitchen, or wherever Mrs Burroughs can hide me.'

'You are making this complicated.'

'I am trying to protect ye from yerself, lass. You're overly rash at times.'

'This is the only way. I have to stop this preposterous marriage now. I cannot wait until I happen to stumble on Brabourne at some function. It would never happen. I am not invited anywhere.'

'Aye, he will no' be makin' ye a good husband. He is too high in the instep for the likes of you.'

'Exactly. Among other things.' At last he was beginning to understand her desperation.

'A gently reared lass like yerself should no' be matched to a rake.'

'That is what I think.'

Even though her voice was firm and brisk, a small part of her—a very small part of her—sighed. There was something about Brabourne that drew her; it had started the instant she had seen him dismount from his horse at the duelling field. Whatever it was had grown stronger each time she saw him. If she were honest, it had peaked at Almack's, when she'd realised all the trouble he was going to in order to give her back her good name. His not dancing with Emily had solidified it.

She turned away from Ferguson's penetrating gaze so he would not see the distress she knew showed on her face. Over her shoulder she said, 'If you are coming, let us go now.'

Almost an hour later Ferguson was hidden in Mrs Burroughs's private sitting room and Juliet had been smuggled into the library. She hoped no one had seen them. If word got out about this visit not even marriage to Brabourne would make her respectable in the eyes of the *ton*.

Her teeth chattered in the cold room, and she wondered irritably if the Duke was even coming home. It was nearly midnight. She was rarely out this late, even though she understood that in London it was fashionable to be out much later.

Impatience ate at her. She started prowling the room, taking out a book here, another there. Brabourne had a very well-stocked library. Her irritation peaked and she decided, in a fit of uncharitable spite, that he did not spend time reading. He was not at all the type she would consider bookish.

She found a copy of Byron's *The Bride of Abydos*, and a smile of pure delight lit her face. She had always wanted to read this book, but first Mama and then later Papa, when he accidentally caught her with it in one of his rare appearances in the sitting room, had forbade her. It was not as famous as *Childe Harold*, but she did not care.

She moved a branch of candles to a small pie table set beside a large, comfortable-looking leather chair. With a sigh of satisfaction, she sank into the cushions and tucked her feet up under her. In minutes she was lost.

The mantel clock chimed four.

Juliet set the book on her lap and yawned. She was so tired. She would close her eyes for a few minutes. She hoped Ferguson was doing the same. He had to be up early.

Sebastian arrived home close to five in the morning, his mood better than when he'd left. He had won at whist, drunk three bottles of excellent port,

and enjoyed the company. He could not remember
when he had last spent a more enjoyable evening. It
had to be some time before that *chit*had come to
town.

He let himself in with the key he always kept on
his watch chain. There was nothing he disliked more
than coming home half-foxed and having servants
fuss about him. Even his valet should be in bed.

He turned around from securing the door and
nearly walked into Burroughs. 'What the…?'

'Begging your pardon, your Grace, but there is a
young lady in the library.' The always-impeccable
butler looked flustered. His gaze darted to and fro,
as though he was afraid of being overheard.

'Tell her to go home. Or, better yet, kick her out.'
Sebastian was in no mood for games and frolic.

Burroughs stepped closer and said in an undertone, 'It is Miss Smythe-Clyde, your Grace. I told
her she should not be here, and definitely could not
wait for you to return.' He sniffed and looked affronted. 'But she said she would march boldly in if
I did not help her sneak in. I could not let her do
that. Not when she will soon be your Duchess.' He
pulled himself up. '*And* her coachman is in Mrs Burroughs's sitting room.'

Sebastian's mouth thinned. 'Thank you, Burroughs.' He handed over his beaver hat and cane.
'You have gone far beyond the call of your duties.'

His greatcoat came off. 'I shall handle this now. See that Ferguson is prepared to leave.'

'Yes, your Grace,' Burroughs said, relief the predominant emotion in his voice. 'Gladly.'

With a militant click of his heels on the polished parquet floor, Sebastian went to the library. He would make short shrift of this idiotic situation. The tic by his eye started. No woman should be in a single man's house unchaperoned, and a coachman did not count. She knew that, and yet here she was.

He did not see her immediately. The room was cold and the only light came from a brace of candles near the fireplace. Closer inspection showed a figure in his favourite chair. He moved closer.

A book lay on the carpeted floor. He picked it up and a slight smile eased the harshness of his face. *The Bride of Abydos.* Interesting reading. He laid it on the table.

She lay curled into the embracing cushions of the chair, her legs tucked under her so that the toes of her half-boots peeked out from the folds of her dress. Crimson lashes swept like fire across her cheeks. She looked young and innocent. And foolish, he thought, his anger at her actions resurfacing in a rush.

He gripped her shoulders and shook her more gently than he wanted. Her eyes popped open and she stared at him. He watched confusion play in their green depths, followed by memory and then by an emotion he had seen in many women's eyes. Desire.

Her reaction took him aback. It also excited him.

Still holding her, he hauled her to her feet. 'What in blazes are you still doing here?'

Her face coloured, then paled, accentuating the freckles marching across the bridge of her nose. She pushed against his chest. 'Let me go and I will tell you.'

'Tell me and then maybe I will let you go.' It was a provoking statement, but he was in the mood to nettle her and more.

Her palms flattened against him, their shape penetrating the several layers of his coat and shirt. The urge to teach her a lesson she would not soon forget entangled with the need to feel her lips on his.

'I came to tell you I will not marry you.' The words left her in a rush. Her bosom moved up and down in feathery motions as she watched for his reaction.

A hardness entered him. 'Of course you will marry me. The statement was in yesterday's *Gazette*. Not to mention that as far as the sticklers of Society are concerned you are ruined—by me. I don't usually sacrifice myself for others, but unfortunately for me I still have enough honour left to know I must marry you.'

Her eyes widened at his cruel words. 'Don't do me any favours, your Grace,' she said, her voice dripping loathing. 'I am more than capable of living without your powerful name.'

'Are you? We shall see,' he muttered, fed up with this game of words they played. He wanted to play another game with her.

His eyes holding hers, he pulled her tight. Her fingers flexed against his coat as she tried to keep distance between their bodies. Desire coiled in him, waiting to escape in a rush of pleasure and satisfaction. Not since his first time with a woman had he felt a reaction this intense.

She licked her lips and he groaned in anticipation. But she was inexperienced, so he needed to go gently with her. Taking a deep breath, to ease some of the tension holding him tight, he lowered his head.

Softly he touched his lips to hers. She clenched her mouth and stiffened like an iron poker. Her forearms pressed against his ribs as she tried to get loose. He wanted them around his waist, pressing him close, as close as two people could be. He shuddered from the control needed to keep from lowering her to the floor and throwing caution and propriety out of the window.

'I am only going to kiss you,' he whispered against her mouth, meaning every word. 'It is acceptable for an engaged couple.'

She gasped and drew her head back. 'We are not engaged.'

His smile was feral. He traced a string of kisses from her earlobe to the top of her shoulder. She jerked against him. He pulled far enough away to see the shock on her face. Her mouth was a round O. He cradled the back of her head with one hand and, with an alacrity he refused to analyse, kissed her.

His lips moved against hers and his tongue teased her into letting it in. Tentatively she opened for him and he slipped inside her waiting warmth. Her entire body responded. He had to deepen their joining. He had to give her the unsettling pleasure she was giving him.

'Relax,' he murmured. 'I won't hurt you.'

She renewed her efforts to escape. He sighed and released her. She skittered away. He was too experienced with women to press her further. She wanted him, but was scared. He watched her through narrowed eyes. She was flushed, her lips plump and red, her chest pounding. Her hands fluttered to her neck.

'You are drunk,' she finally said after her breathing slowed. 'I could…' She edged further away from him. 'I could taste it.'

His dangerous smile returned as he narrowed the distance between them. 'No, merely enjoying myself.'

Disbelief radiated from her. She moved until the back of her knees hit the chair. 'I must go. I have accomplished what I set out to do. I will send a retraction to the paper.'

Fury hit him. He grabbed her arm and dragged her near. 'You are the most stubborn woman. What must I do to make you understand that we are marrying? Seduce you here and now?'

Fright followed immediately by innocent speculation deepened her eyes, only to end with determination. She twisted. 'I won't send anything to the paper if you release me.'

He did and stepped away. 'Bargaining already? I will meet you halfway this time. But don't try my good intentions too far.'

She nodded and warily skirted around him towards the door. 'I must get Ferguson and be gone.'

He picked up the book and held it out to her. 'Don't forget this.'

She looked longingly at it. 'I cannot take it. Papa says it is too *risqué* for me to read.'

He laughed. 'Then you shall finish it after we are wed.'

Instead of arguing with him, she fled.

Sebastian stood for long moments after she left. Her nearness and her reaction to him had left him too aroused for sleep. He might not want this marriage emotionally, but his body wanted it. Badly.

The hackney coach ride home was much too long with Ferguson sitting across from her frowning. If possible, he was even more disapproving than when he had agreed to accompany her.

'Don't say a word,' she ordered him. 'Your attitude says it all.'

He grunted and folded his arms across his chest.

She looked away, watching the London streets drift by. Soon it would be light. They had to reach home before then. So far no one had seen her—she needed to keep it that way.

Strange sensations flooded her body, making her feel heavy and lethargic. Her mouth tingled and she reached up to touch it lightly with a finger. It did not feel any different. Her neck felt branded by his kisses. She wondered if a scarlet line trailed from her earlobe to the base of her neck. She would not be surprised. She dropped her hand.

She was lucky he had stopped. She should be glad. Somehow she felt empty, not fortunate. He had opened a whole new experience to her, and for a fleeting moment, as his lips had touched her, she had wanted to explore what he offered. She had wanted it so badly that it frightened her, this power he had over her senses.

She could never marry him. He would seduce her body and then her mind. Before long she would love him—and it would break her heart, for he would never love her.

Chapter Nine

Juliet stepped into the hall, her wet cape dripping on the black and white tiles. Her arms overflowed with roses she had just cut from the garden behind the house. Their smell filled the room.

'Miss Juliet,' Hobson said, 'you have a visitor in the morning room.'

There was an edge of excitement in his normally non-committal voice. What was going on? 'It isn't Brabourne, is it? she demanded. 'For I will not see him.'

'No,' Hobson said, taking the mass of flowers, 'you have always liked this visitor.'

Curious, she started off without removing her cape. Hobson made it sound as though someone from home was there. She hurried into the room. A man with a familiar stocky figure and brown hair stood looking out of the window.

'George,' she said, breaking into a run. 'What are

you doing here? It does not matter,' she said before he could answer, 'I am so glad to see you.'

He had turned at the first sound of her voice and held his hands out to her. She took them and he squeezed.

'I came as soon as I heard, Ju.'

She saw the anxiety and hurt in his brown eyes and knew immediately what he referred to. 'It is not my choice. I have told both Papa and the Duke that I will not marry.'

Confusion knit his sandy brows. 'Then why was the announcement in the paper?'

She made a very unladylike snort and pulled her fingers from his still-tight hold. 'Because Brabourne is stubborn and arrogant and high in the instep and anything else you can think of that is derogatory.'

George's eyes widened. 'That bad, and your father is still making you marry him? That does not sound like Lord Smythe-Clyde. He is usually too engrossed in his experiments to force you to do anything, let alone something you so definitely dislike.'

'I know,' she said, wringing her hands. 'It is his new bride. She wants to be related to Brabourne to further her standing in Society. She is forcing Papa to force me.'

'What about Brabourne?' George asked, obviously confused.

'Him?' For some reason he feels he must marry me and protect me from the *ton's* disapproval.' She shrugged. 'Silly, but there it is. Once the announcement was in the paper, his pride came into play. No one refuses the great and powerful Duke of Brabourne, whether he really wants to marry one or not.'

'I am more in the dark than ever,' George said. 'Perhaps we could sit down and have a bit to eat and drink?'

'Oh, dear, I am so sorry. Of course. I was so excited to see a familiar and friendly face that I have forgotten my manners.' She moved to the pull near the fireplace and had just gripped it when the door opened and the butler entered, bearing a loaded tray. 'Hobson, you have the manners I lack. What would I do without you?'

The butler said nothing, but he straightened up at the praise. Setting the tray down, he asked, 'Will there be anything else, miss?'

'No, thank you. You have provided generous proportions of everything we may need.'

He bowed. 'I know from the past how Mr Thomas likes his food and drink.'

George beamed as he took in all the refreshment. 'That you do, Hobson.'

The butler left the room with a very satisfied air about him. Juliet sat in a gold embroidered chair across from George and began serving. She asked no questions about his preferences because she knew them all. They had practically grown up together. He was like a brother to her, which was why she had been unable to accept his marriage proposal. Unlike Brabourne, George had been sad, but had also accepted her decision.

'I owe Hobson more than I can ever say,' Juliet murmured.

'How's that?' George said around a mouthful of ham.

She told her old friend everything, omitting nothing that had happened since she arrived in London except Brabourne's mind-numbing and body-electrifying kiss. That was still too fresh and too raw and much too personal.

George chewed a mouthful of biscuit and washed it down with well-sugared tea. 'You have been busy. No wonder the Duke offered for you. It is the only honourable thing he could do.'

She nearly choked on her tea and ended up coughing until tears ran from her eyes. 'How can you say such a thing?'

He took another portion of ham and mixed it with potato. 'Because it is the truth.'

She set her cup down and crossed her arms. 'I don't wish to marry him. I won't.'

He looked up from his plate, hope sparking in his eyes. 'Then marry me. I have asked before and I still mean it.'

She leaned forward and put her hand on his arm.

'Thank you, George. You are the best friend a person could have.'

He patted her and sighed. 'I suppose that means no.'

'I love you like a brother, not a husband. It would not be fair to you.'

For the first time since his father had refused to buy him an exorbitantly expensive mare Juliet saw anger in his eyes, his most expressive feature. He was normally quite placid.

'How do you think I feel, knowing that another man will be your husband? I would rather you wed me and love me like a brother than that you go to another man. I will wait for you to learn to love me as a wife should love her husband. Will Brabourne? From what I have heard of him, I doubt it.'

His bold talk made her blush. 'Would you really rather wed me, knowing you would not be a husband in truth for some time?'

'Yes.'

His simple answer moved her more than any protestation ever could. She began to think it might be the best solution.

'What...?' She paused and took a calming breath. 'What if I never love you that way?'

Some of the hope left his eyes. 'It would still be better than having you marry someone else.'

'Oh, George, I don't want to take the chance of hurting you.'

He sat straighter. 'Then respect me enough to let me be the judge of what will hurt me. I've always known you don't love me as I love you, but I have never met another woman I am as comfortable with as I am with you. That means a great deal to me.' He gave her a lopsided grin. 'You know how I don't like to stir myself.'

'All too well,' she answered, grinning back at him.

'I won't mind how much time you spend with your father.' The look on his face told her he knew exactly what he was offering. 'And you won't have to marry Brabourne. Even he won't dare make you a widow or a bigamist.'

Uncertainty flickered through her mind and she turned away so George would not see her expression. Much as she rebelled against marrying the Duke, much as she told herself she did not want to wed him, there was still that tiny part of her that found him exciting and dangerous. That same part acknowledged that there were times when he could be kind. Chagrin at her weakness tightened her hands into fists.

Without further thought, without allowing herself to feel, she said, 'I will.'

'What?' George dropped the biscuit he was eating. It hit the carpet and spilt.

Juliet nearly smiled. 'I will marry you. The sooner the better.'

Stunned was the only way to describe George. For a second, Juliet wondered if he really wanted to marry her. Perhaps he had proposed because he felt safe doing it, knowing she would not accept. Only she had.

'Ah. Good,' he said, bending over to pick up the crumbs. When he sat back up, his round face was red.

'I will make all the arrangements,' she said.

Relief flooded his countenance. 'Very good of you. We can take my carriage.'

'I will see to food and clothing. We must start immediately, before anyone knows you are here.'

'Oh, yes, yes,' he said, gulping down the remains of his tea. 'Where are we going?'

She stopped in mid-stride and turned back to him. He looked genuinely puzzled. She shook her head. Brabourne would know exactly where they were going and he would take care of all the arrangements too. No, she scolded herself. George is not the Duke. That is why I am marrying him.

'We are going to Gretna Green, just over the Scottish border.'

'I know where it is,' he said defensively. 'I just thought that you meant to procure a special licence so we could be married here in England.'

'George,' she said patiently, wondering if she was really doing the right thing and immediately telling herself she had no other choice, 'I am a woman. I cannot get a special licence. If we were going to do that, you would have to do it. Besides, it would take too long.'

Hastily, he said, 'I will have my carriage brought round.'

She headed back to the door. 'I will be down shortly.'

'Not too long, Ju. It don't do the horses good to be kept waiting.'

'I know, George. You have told me repeatedly.'

Sebastian brought his greys to a halt in front of Lord Smythe-Clyde's townhouse. He had never been here before, but thought it best if he was seen around London with Juliet. It would make their engagement more believable.

The note he had sent her this morning asking her to go driving had elicited no answer. Never patient, he was here to bodily lift her into his phaeton if needed. The chit would not snub him.

He leapt down and strode to the door. Imperiously he banged the knocker. The door opened just as he pulled his hand away. Hobson stood in the doorway, looking down his nose.

Sebastian smothered a smile. The butler would not appreciate being found amusing.

'I am here to take Miss Smythe-Clyde driving.'

Hobson did not usher the Duke inside. 'Does Miss Juliet know you are coming?'

Sebastian frowned. 'She should. I sent round a note this morning.'

The butler looked flustered, but he maintained his ground. 'She is not available.' He moved to close the door.

Anger spurred Sebastian. He put his palm against the heavy oak and pushed. 'I will not be turned away. Show me to a place to wait and tell her I am here.'

By strength alone, Sebastian made his way inside. This was the last time the chit would treat him so cavalierly. Not waiting for Hobson to escort him, Sebastian strode across the hall and opened the first door he came to. It was the drawing room. He went in and sat down in the only comfortable-looking chair.

Minutes passed and no one came. He rose, determination hardening his jaw. No one had ever treated him this poorly. He would find where she was and drag her out. She needed to be taught a lesson.

His hand was on the doorknob when the door moved inward. He backed away. Harry stood in the archway, looking apprehensive.

'So she sent you,' Sebastian drawled, keeping his anger in check. 'I had not thought her a coward.'

Harry slid inside, keeping his face turned towards the Duke. 'Umm…she don't want to see you.'

'Do you always state the obvious?' Sebastian asked, wanting to draw blood.

Harry turned beet-red. Even his ears glowed. 'Ripping up at me won't do any good. *I* cannot make her do what she don't want. Nor can you,' he added for good measure.

'Your tongue is as sharp as hers.'

Tired of the verbal battle that was getting him nowhere, Sebastian went to the door and opened it. He walked into the entry and headed for the stairs.

'Hey,' Harry yelped, rushing after the Duke. 'What are you doing?'

Sebastian started up the steps. 'Use your brain. I am going after her.'

'You can't!' Harry pounded up the stairs and grabbed the Duke's arm.

Sebastian stopped and looked down at the youth. 'Take your hand off me,' he said, his voice deadly.

Harry blanched. His hand fell away. 'She ain't here,' he said, his voice barely audible.

Sebastian's eyes narrowed. He did not like the way this was going. 'Where is she?'

Harry looked around. Several servants were moving around in the hall. 'If you come back to the drawing room, I will tell you.'

Cold premonition stiffened Sebastian's spine. The chit had done something truly reprehensible this time. He just knew it.

Back in the privacy of the drawing room, he stared at Harry. 'Out with it.'

Harry paced the room, his fingers raking through his

hair in time to his feet. He would not meet the Duke's fierce look. 'She's left.'

'I know that,' Sebastian said, his patience at an end.

'She went with George.'

'Who is George? And make it quick and thorough. I am done putting up with your delaying tactics. Your sister has gone too far this time.'

'Don't I just know that,' Harry mumbled, his feet still moving. He took a deep breath and let it all out at once. 'She eloped.'

'She did what?' Sebastian said, his voice low.

Harry was not fooled. He knew the Duke was ready to throttle him, and heaven only knew what he would do to Ju if he got hold of her. 'Eloped. Gretna Green.'

'Bloody…' Sebastian ground his teeth together. 'And you did nothing?'

Harry swallowed, his Adam's apple bobbing convulsively. 'George will not hurt her. He left a message to be delivered to me. Seems he did not want anyone to get worried.'

Disgust flared Sebastian's nostrils. 'And that makes it all right?'

'Yes. I mean, no. That is, George is an old friend. We grew up with him. He is like a brother.'

Sebastian could not believe the naïveté. 'You do realise, don't you, that after what is being said about your sister now an elopement will be the *coup de grâce*. She will never be accepted anywhere, country or town. I imagine she will even be shunned by your neighbours.'

Harry's eyes widened. 'Surely not.'

Sebastian shrugged. 'Perhaps. However, I do not intend to let your sister succeed in this harebrained scheme. She is too impetuous for her own good.'

'You are going to chase her?'

'Someone has to,' Sebastian said, wondering why he continued to put himself through this hell. If he had an ounce of self-preservation, he would send a retraction to the papers. He might be called a cad, but he had been called worse.

'Can I go with you? I won't be any trouble and I'm her brother. I should be there to protect her.' Harry's excitement made his hair seem to stand on end. 'Not from you... That is...'

Sebastian looked the youth up and down. He would be a complication, but he did have a point. There was enough impropriety in this mess which his inclusion might help blunt.

'We are riding horses. Quicker. I shall leave in half an hour. If you are not at my house, I will go without you. Is that clear?'

'Yes, sir...your Grace.'

Sebastian wasted no time getting home and to his chamber.

'A change of shirt and linen,' he told Roberts. 'I am leaving in fifteen minutes.'

'Shall I pack a portmanteau, your Grace?' the valet said, already pulling out the luggage.

'No, thank you. I shall be on horseback.'

'What?' A horrified expression filled the servant's face. 'Surely you jest. What will people say? You have a reputation to maintain. You are one of the best-dressed men in all of England.'

'Calm yourself, Roberts. No one of importance is going to see me. I am going into the country.'

'Yes, your Grace,' the valet said in a despondent tone. 'I shall have my own bag packed in a trice.'

'You are not coming.'

'What?'

'Close your mouth, Roberts, you look like a beached fish. I am travelling alone.'

The valet clamped his teeth so hard they clicked and he winced. Not a further word escaped him as he watched the Duke leave. But his head drooped.

Juliet sat across from George, the inn's best cherrywood table between them, and watched him eat and eat and eat. At the speed he was going they would be here until it was too dark to travel and the inn's larder was empty. She had finished long ago. She muffled an irritated sigh with her napkin.

He looked up from his mutton. 'Are you all right? We can stop the night here if you would like.'

She felt as if they were barely out of London and all its environs. The last thing she wanted was to stay here. 'No, I think it best that we continue on. You could have them pack that up for you,' she ended on a hopeful note.

'Capital idea. Should have thought of that myself.' He rang the little brass bell the innkeeper had left with them.

Soon they were on the road again. Juliet took a breath of the cool evening air and wished she were somewhere else. Anywhere except eloping. But there was no help for it.

George sat on the opposite side of the carriage, snoring. He had finished everything the innkeeper had wrapped and then promptly fallen asleep. At least she did not have to worry about poor dear George trying to seduce her or in any way embarrassing her with his overtures. She was not sure he had an amorous bone in his body, for which she was heartily glad.

How different it would be if Brabourne sat across from her. First, he would not be on the other seat, he would be beside her. She had no doubt that his sensuality would overwhelm any protests she might have. He was…he was…

She sighed and looked away from her companion. The Duke was everything George was not.

That, she told herself harshly, is why you will do better with good stolid George. He will let you run things the way you wish and not bother you. Brabourne would devour you and then bed other women. Infidelity is in his nature.

This was better by far. It had to be—this was her future.

Energy coursed through Sebastian as he urged his mount onwards. 'We are not far behind,' he said, the passing wind catching his words and flinging them back to Harry.

Harry lagged behind. Even the best horse-flesh Lord Smythe-Clyde had was no match for the Duke's.

Sebastian thought he saw a glimmer of light in the distance. It flickered and disappeared, only to reappear again. He was sure it belonged to a carriage.

Wait until he got his hands on the minx. He would teach her a lesson she would never forget. He would curb her impetuosity. No woman was going to leave him after the banns had been posted and the announcement put in the paper. He had declared his intentions to the world, and his pride and heritage demanded that she wed no one else. Especially not some country bumpkin.

They closed quickly on the vehicle. In the twilight, Sebastian could see the back of the coachman's head. There were no outriders. Stupid. They would pass through stretches where robberies occurred on a daily basis, sometimes multiple ones within twenty-four hours.

'By Jove,' Harry's voice rang out, 'that looks like George's old coach.'

Sebastian drew even with the first carriage horse and shouted to the coachman to stop. The servant slowed down, but before he could bring the vehicle to a complete stop Juliet popped her head out of the window.

She gasped. 'Brabourne! Coachman, don't stop. Speed up. This is the man we are running from.'

The servant only faltered for seconds. He knew whom he took his orders from. With a flick of the whip, he urged the four horses on. The carriage, old and large, lumbered behind the panting animals like an overfed cow.

Sebastian cursed under his breath. He was not afraid of losing them. He just wanted to put an end to this charade.

The carriage took a wide turn. One of its wheels hit a large rock. The coach tottered.

Sebastian heard a loud snap and the wheel that had hit the rock cracked. The vehicle skidded on the remaining three wheels until coming to an abrupt stop toppled to one side.

'Harry,' Sebastian yelled, jumping from his horse, 'go to their heads. They are panicking.'

To Sebastian's relief, the youth did as he was told without comment. While Harry tried to calm the horses Sebastian rushed to the carriage door and yanked it open.

Pandemonium reigned.

Juliet scrambled to regain her feet, only to fall down on to the lopsided cushion. Her companion looked dazed, as though he had hit his head. Several blankets littered the floor, which was now the other side of the coach. A wicker basket, with the lid open, lay at the door. The smell of baked chicken and fresh bread filled the interior. Chicken bones were sprinkled throughout as though a giant hand had deposited them.

Sebastian's gaze locked on to Juliet. 'Give me your hand and I will help you out.'

She shook her head.

'Now,' he said, his volume low, but with an underlining of iron.

She glanced at George, who merely looked confused. Seeing there was no help there, she grabbed the strap above the door and used it to pull herself to the opening. Sebastian caught her around the waist and swung her down before she could protest.

'I could have done it myself,' she said irritably, smoothing down the brown wool of her skirt. 'I am not helpless.'

She was stubborn and belligerent. Sebastian would have smiled under different circumstances, but the anger that had driven him to pursue her still held him.

'You,' he said coldly to the coachman, 'had best help your master. He looks as if he took a hit to the head.'

'Oh, dear,' Juliet said, edging past Sebastian and leaning her upper body inside the carriage. 'Are you all right, George? You were sleeping when the wheel broke.'

'Yes, yes,' he muttered. 'Just a bit confused.'

'Where is my reticule?' she said, starting to climb back into the vehicle. 'I have smelling slats. They will help.'

She had just put her left knee on the top of the carriage when Sebastian wrapped her arm around her and hauled her out. 'He will be fine without your ministrations. You are not going back in there. No telling what will happen next. This is a relic and should never have been on the road, let alone racing.'

Together with the coachman, Sebastian helped George out. The country squire sank to the ground. One glance at the poor man told Sebastian this was no love match.

Juliet grabbed a blanket from the vehicle and wrapped it around George. 'Is that better?'

He nodded.

Harry had the horses calmed and unharnessed. They were munching on grass by the side of the road. He came up to them and said, 'I think he needs a doctor.'

Sebastian ignored him and spoke to George. 'This is going to hurt, old man, but I want to feel around your head and find out where you bumped yourself.'

George groaned, then gasped sharply. 'Damme, that hurts.'

'Shine the carriage lamp on this,' Sebastian ordered. The coachman found an extra candle and lit it, then put it close enough for Sebastian to see. 'You've got a nasty bruise forming, but it is not bleeding much. You will have a knot the size of Prinny's waist by tomorrow.'

'I…I think I'm…going…' George did not finish.

Sebastian stepped away just in time. Juliet stared and managed to suppress her own sympathetic gag. Harry turned green.

'A wet cloth will do wonders,' Sebastian said laconically.

Juliet hastened to wet one of her handkerchiefs from the jug of water. She knelt by George and gingerly wiped his forehead.

'Not there,' Sebastian said. 'On his bump.'

She glared at him, but did as he directed.

Harry sidled up to Sebastian. 'How do you know so much?'

'Had my share of over-indulgence. Head wounds too.' Sebastian motioned to the coachman. 'I want you and Mr Smythe-Clyde to stay here with your master. Miss Smythe-Clyde and I are returning to the last inn to find a doctor and send help.'

Juliet jumped up, dropping the damp cloth. 'I will not go with you. I will stay here. George needs me.'

Sebastian looked from her face to the now dirty cloth. 'I doubt that.'

'You do, don't you, George?' she asked.

'I do,' George mumbled obediently.

Sebastian took hold of her arm and steered her towards his horse. 'You are coming with me, either in front of me on my horse or on Harry's mount. Which will it be?'

She stared stubbornly at him.

'As you wish.'

He gripped her around the waist and tossed her up. She landed with a bone-jarring thud in his saddle.

'You will have to ride astride so you don't fall off,' he said. 'Unless you promise to co-operate and let me balance you against my chest without fighting; then you may ride side-saddle.'

'You know I cannot ride astride,' she hissed.

He eyed her narrow skirt. 'I can remedy that. Coachman, do you have a knife?'

She gasped. 'You would not dare.'

He met her angry gaze with his cool one. This was almost worth the chase, he thought. She might be a hazard, and too impulsive for her or anyone else's own good, but she had spirit.

'Try me,' he said calmly, taking the knife from the servant.

'Harry,' she said, 'are you going to let him bully me like this?'

For the first time in his life, her brother did nothing to help. 'Deuced stupid thing you did, eloping and all. Even if I don't think his Grace is the husband for you, I don't think a flight to Gretna Green just days before your wedding is the thing either.'

She frowned at him. 'Should I have stood Brabourne up at the chapel? For I would have.'

Harry shook his head. 'I still think you could have talked Papa around.'

She looked away from him, and Sebastian would have sworn he saw a tear slide down her cheek in the dim glow of the lantern. He almost felt sorry for her. But she had gone too far this time.

'You win,' she said softly.

He handed the knife back to the coachman and mounted behind her. Taking the reins in one hand, he wrapped his other arm around her waist.

'It should not be above an hour,' he told the three men.

Juliet shivered as Brabourne set the horse in motion. The evening was cool and her pelisse was more fashionable than practical.

Brabourne held her pinned to his chest as though he expected her to try and get away. Not much chance of that. She recognised defeat when it sat behind her.

The heat from his body penetrated the clothing

separating them. It felt good. Too good. She stiffened and tried to put distance between them.

He hauled her back.

'You are cold,' he said. 'Staying close will help.'

'I don't want your help,' she said.

'Just as you don't want my name and title,' he said harshly.

'Exactly.'

His grip tightened painfully, squeezing the air out of her lungs. Then he loosened his hold. She sensed that his reaction had been automatic. She did not think he would intentionally hurt her, not physically.

'You will have both,' he said. 'The banns have been read, the announcement is in the paper, the church is reserved, your dress is made and the invitations are out. There is no turning back. Nor are you going to botch it all by running off with some squire's stolid son.'

Anger and the urge to hurt him as she knew he would eventually hurt her drove her. 'He is twice the man you are. Ten times. A hundred times,' she said defiantly, her voice rising. 'You are nothing but a rake and a libertine who has wealth and position. I despise you for what you are.'

He reined the horse to an abrupt halt that would have sent her tumbling to the ground if not for his hold on her. He slid down and pulled her with him so that their bodies bonded.

She felt everything about him. The silver buttons

on his coat scraped against her belly and then her breast, sending sensations skittering down her spine. His arms banded her waist and back like iron, and his chest crushed hers. He held her body immobile against the length of his. It was wickedly thrilling and frighteningly comfortable, as though she were meant to be this close to him.

She was going crazy.

'Let me go.'

'Not yet,' he replied, gripping the back of her head with one hand.

She stared up at him, anxiety twisting her stomach. It had to be anxiety, she told herself as his face lowered to hers. She did not want him to kiss her. Never again.

'You are an infuriating minx,' he said, just before his lips met hers.

The kiss was hard and punishing, not gentle and coaxing like the first. This one seared.

His mouth slanted across hers, and when she would not grant his tongue entry he nipped her bottom lip so that she gasped. He took instant advantage. He plundered her, swamping her senses with his sensual onslaught.

She reeled, and would have collapsed if not for his support.

'When I am done,' he vowed, 'you won't want that man you say is worth a hundred of me.'

His kiss gentled just before he broke away to nuzzle the hollow at the base of her throat. His tongue flicked against her skin. The hand that had held her head slid down and pushed the collar of her pelisse aside to give him better access.

She gasped when his hand cupped her breast through her clothing. Even with the barrier, she felt as though he touched her bare skin. Her mind reeled.

'Stop,' she gasped.

He looked down at her, the light from the moon and stars more than enough for her to see him clearly. His eyes were a brilliant blue, seemingly lit from within. His mouth was sensual in its hardness.

She gazed at him and saw hunger in every line of his face. She exulted in her power to arouse him like that, even as she feared what he would do to her. He would make her want him.

His lips found hers again. His hand caressed her breast, making her nipple peak. His arm pressed her tightly against his hips so that she felt every hard angle of him.

She was doomed.

She felt his fingers on the button running down the back of her dress and a traitorous disappointment filled her. He would never be able to undo them. Not now. Not like this.

One. Two. Three... They opened under his fingers. The only thing keeping the garment from sliding down her shoulders was the pelisse she still wore. Soon she felt the heat of his palms moving inside the shoulders of her pelisse and edging it down her arms. All the while he held her captive with the power of his kiss.

The pelisse fell to the ground and the cool night air moved across her exposed back. Then the bodice slipped from her shoulders and Brabourne took his mouth from hers and placed it at the swell just above her bosom.

She shuddered at the moist warmth of his lips. One of his hands cupped her breast, easing it out of her chemise. His thumb flicked the aroused nipple as he raised his head and watched her reaction. She licked her lips and heard him groan.

Her head dropped back to be supported by his arm around her shoulders. He bent his head until his tongue replaced his thumb. She moaned, shock and pleasure twinning into a knot centred in her abdomen. She arched against him.

He was destroying all her resistance as though it was nothing.

Her bodice hung around her hips, followed by the top of her chemise. She was bare to his perusal, allowing him to plunder from her head to her waist. He cupped her breasts with his hands and took turns nuzzling and sucking them with his mouth until she no longer knew where she ended and he began.

The world swirled around her.

It was a cold shock when he once more raised up to look at her. 'You are more beautiful than I imagined,' he said, his voice raspy, as though too long unused.

She gazed up at him, no longer caring what else he did to her. It would all be mind-and body-exploding.

She sucked in air, more aware of him than she had ever been of anything in her life. She clung to him, her fingers tangled in the folds of his coat.

'You are more skilful than I ever imagined,' she managed to say between lips swollen from his kisses. 'I never thought seduction would feel this way. No wonder Emily wants you.'

He released her so quickly she stumbled and fell to the hard ground. He turned from her and walked away to stand head resting on the trunk of a nearby tree. Stunned, she sat still for long moments.

'What did I do?' she finally managed to say, her voice coming out small and unsure. Belatedly, she realised she sounded like a timid little mouse.

He kept his back to her. 'Do not ever again mention your stepmother to me. I did not seduce her.' He turned back and strode to her, towering above. 'Do you understand?'

His anger was like a slap in the face. She scrambled to her feet, reality returning with a vengeance. What a weak fool she had been.

She stuffed her arms back into the chemise and yanked it up over her breasts, trying to make it reach her chin. She shoved her arms into the sleeves of her bodice and contorted like an acrobat in a futile attempt to button the back. Tears of frustration and shame blurred her vision. She angled away so he would not see her weakness.

Stupid, stupid, stupid. She had been a complete fool. He had done nothing to her that he had not done to a million other women, and she had let him. No, she had revelled in his ardour.

He touched her shoulder and she jumped away. 'Don't come near me,' she ordered.

She heard him sigh, but when he spoke his voice was stripped of emotion. 'You will never be able to do up your bodice by yourself.'

'I shall do the best I can, for you shan't touch me again. I promise you that.'

His voice hardened. 'Don't make promises you cannot keep.'

'Where is my pelisse?' she muttered, looking around. The brown wool made the garment hard to see against the dirt. 'Ah.' She pounced on it and yanked it on, hoping it was long enough to cover most of the exposed skin of her back.

'You look unkempt,' his hateful voice said. 'As though you have been ravished and enjoyed every minute of it.'

She scowled, her resentment of her weakness and his skill rising to uncontrollable heights. She rounded on him. 'And you are a philanderer. A seducer of innocent women. A rakehell.'

He sneered. 'I have heard "rake" from your lips more than I like. Is your vocabulary so limited that you can think of nothing else?'

She lunged for him, her open palm connecting with his cheek. The instant her flesh met his, she knew he had let her hit him. The knowledge was in his bitter eyes.

The fury left her. 'I am sorry. I lost control, something I never do.'

His laugh was cynical. 'You do it all the time. Whenever you act impulsively you are losing control.'

Much to her dismay, he was right. It was her greatest weakness. Mama had told her so often enough. And now it had landed her in this bumble-broth from which she finally acknowledged to herself there was no escape.

'You are right,' she said in a tiny voice. 'I should never have fought you in that duel. Look where it has taken us, what it has done to us. I should have found another way to protect Papa.'

'You should have let him fight his own battle.'

'Oh, no, I could never do that. I promised Mama that I would care for him. And I shall.'

'What nonsense,' he said.

'It is a promise. I keep my promises.'

He studied her. 'And will you keep your promises on our wedding day?'

She blanched. 'You are a cunning devil, turning my words against me.'

He shrugged. 'Enough, minx. I am tired, and I venture so are you. We still have to reach that inn and send someone back for the others.

She had forgotten all else in the wonder of his lovemaking. Disgust at herself gave her energy. Briskly, she said. 'You are right.'

This time she co-operated with him when he mounted and pulled her up in front of him. She felt the tension in him when her shoulder touched his chest, but she told herself to ignore it. Just as she had to ignore her reaction to him.

She was, beyond question, a fool. Soon to be a hurt one.

Chapter Ten

For the second time since coming to London, Juliet returned home from Brabourne's protection. This time, however, Harry accompanied her and they arrived in George's carriage, which had been repaired speedily because of the Duke's intervention.

She was glad Brabourne had not come with them. After what had happened between them she never wanted to see him again. A forlorn wish. He had made it plain that he intended their wedding to take place and would brook no further evasions on her part. Nor would she get the chance for another. Her papa would have her watched, or rather Emily would. Papa never stayed focused on anything for long except his experiments.

George left them at the door and went on to his rented lodgings. No words were said between any of them.

She and Harry were met inside by Emily and Papa

and marched into the library. Anger at the other woman's obvious influence mixed with Juliet's sense of guilt over having been the cause of discomfort for Papa. Her job was to care for him, not upset him.

Harry looked at her and rolled his eyes. She nearly smiled at him, but remembered she was still angry. It was his fault Brabourne had caught her. She turned away, prepared to face the consequences without his help.

'How dare you, you ungrateful brat?' Emily started. Papa put a restraining hand on his wife's arm which she shook off. 'No, Oliver, I won't be denied my say. She has completely undone everything I have accomplished. She was about to marry Brabourne. Brabourne, the most sought-after man in all the realm. And she runs away. Not only is she ungrateful, she is stupid.'

Juliet stood stoically, but her stomach churned. The only thing that kept her standing was the knowledge that she had tried to do what was right for her. Brabourne was not the man for her, no matter how much her body responded to his and her weak emotions desired his nearness.

Emily continued her tirade.

Papa just shook his head, as though the entire situation bewildered him. It probably did. Finally he asked, 'Why, Juliet?'

'I don't want to marry him, Papa. He will make me miserable.'

'Then why didn't you say something instead of running away with poor George? It is not done. His father will be furious with him.'

She blinked rapidly, hoping no one saw the moisture in her eyes. This was so hard. Not even knowing she had been wrong eased the ache. 'I tried, Papa. You would not listen to me.'

'Of course I did, but you were wrong. Emily is right when she says this is for the best. You are ruined otherwise. No man will marry you.'

Juliet's stomach twisted again. 'George would have. Still will.'

She longed to tell Papa everything, particularly Emily's part, but for once controlled her tongue. It would do no good and only hurt Papa.

'You are too young and inexperienced,' Emily said in a condescending voice.

Juliet glared at her. 'I am three and twenty, nearly as old as you. And I may be inexperienced in the ways of the *ton,* but I am not ignorant of people.'

Emily raised on elegant blonde brow. 'Is that so? You have an odd way of showing it.'

Juliet sighed and looked away. There was nothing else to say. But it hurt just the same. If Mama were alive, none of this would be happening. But she was not.

'Go to your room,' Emily ordered. 'And be assured that you will not get a second opportunity to so disgrace us. Fortunately for you no one realises what really happened.'

Juliet cast one last imploring glance at Papa, who looked bewildered as he shook his head. She turned and left the room. Harry followed, the tread of his boots loud in the stilled house. He stayed behind her.

Reaching her door, she turned to him. 'Please go away. I know all you want to do is agree with *her*.'

He ran his fingers through his red hair. 'I'm sorry, Ju. I didn't mean for it to be this bad. Just…you just cannot run away with someone to avoid someone else. It isn't done.'

'Some of the most high-ranking people in the aristocracy have eloped,' she hissed. 'And I don't care. George and I would never even have come to London.'

He sighed. 'Those runaway marriages were mostly in our grandparents' time, Ju. People don't do it so much now. At least, not respectable ones.'

His words piled more pain on. 'But you forget,' she said sarcastically, 'I am no longer respectable.'

Her neck ached from stiffness and tension. Soon she would have a raging headache. She rubbed the stiff muscles.

'Please, Harry, just go away. I need time to myself.'

She could see his uncertainty, but he did as she asked. With feet that dragged, she entered her room and crossed to the bed. She crawled on to the large mattress and curled up, staring at nothing.

She was trapped now. No other chance to escape Brabourne would present itself. Emily would gain admittance to the select of Society. She would see some doors open and others remain closed. She might even become an intimate of Prinny. She did not care.

She rolled on to her back.

Then there was Brabourne. She did not want to marry him. Not really. Or so she told herself. He would break her heart. Perhaps he already had, if the pain in her chest was any indication.

She rolled to her other side and squeezed her eyes shut against the tears she had managed to hold in until now. They soaked her pillow.

When had it happened? How could it have happened?

There had been times when he had been kind to her. He had not shot Papa in the duel, even though he could have. That alone had endeared him to her against her better judgement. Then he had rescued her from the thugs in Vauxhall. But those events should not have captured her heart.

Yes, he made her body throb with pleasure and sensations she had never known existed. But that should not have been enough either.

Mama had once said that love was never logical

and never comfortable. Perhaps she had been right. Look what it had done to Papa.

To her.

A week later, Juliet stepped down from the travelling carriage Brabourne had sent for her family. Brabourne Abbey, the seat of the Dukes of Brabourne, was stupendous. A large, rambling abbey in the Gothic style, acquired when Henry VIII had dissolved the monasteries, it had been in the family ever since. The grey rock blended in with the cliff on which it perched, the English Channel visible from all the south-and east-facing rooms.

To Juliet's mind it suited Brabourne perfectly. Dark and arrogant.

She had not taken three steps from the carriage before footmen in the Duke's green and black livery were there to assist. Brabourne was right behind them.

'Welcome to my home, Juliet,' he said, taking the hand she had not offered. Watching her the entire time, he kissed her fingers.

Even though she wore gloves, the feel of his lips was distinct and unsettling. Memories flooded back of their minutes in the dark night. Her pulse raced and her heart pounded. She could not look away from his knowing eyes.

'I believe Prinny was right. You will set a new fashion for freckles, my dear,' he said *sotto voce*.

The spell broke and she snatched her hand back. 'I seriously doubt that. No one likes freckles. They are too much like blemishes.'

Before he could further discompose her, she turned away. Emily and Papa exited the coach with Harry close behind. The carriage that carried their luggage drew up and more servants converged on it. It was organised mayhem.

Brabourne welcomed her papa. 'Come this way, Smythe-Clyde. My butler and housekeeper will show you to your accommodations.'

'Yes, yes,' Papa said, his gaze darting all around. 'Nice place you have here, Brabourne. If it were mine, I should never go to the city.'

Emily rolled her eyes. 'Oliver, don't be ridiculous.'

The small group headed to the marble steps that led to the front door. Juliet lagged behind, marvelling that Papa was acting as though he had never challenged the Duke to a duel. Men were so strange. Or Papa was.

She was not surprised to see Burroughs waiting for them. Not even with the blink of an eye did he reveal that he knew her. He assigned a footman to show Harry to his room and took Papa and Emily to theirs himself. Juliet was left standing in the entry with Brabourne.

Old muskets adorned the walls in circles like radiating suns. Many-antlered deer gazed down at them with sightless eyes. The Brabourne crest and motto, a jousting knight and the words *Never Fear*, were emblazoned above the entryway. Soon they would be hers too.

'Not nearly so ornate as Carlton House,' the Duke said drily.

'Not enough gilt,' she managed to remark with a slight smile.

'I will take you to your chamber,' he said abruptly. 'Come with me.' He held out his arm.

The ease that had started to slow her pulse ended. She glanced apprehensively up at him. He stood implacably, waiting. Juliet knew when she was up against a wall. With ill grace, she accepted his escort.

The muscles of his lower arm were sinewy and strong beneath her fingers. She knew their power from his rescue and his lovemaking, thoughts she did not want to have at this moment.

They progressed up a flight of stairs wide enough for three ladies to walk three abreast while wearing the wide skirts of a generation ago. Gleaming marble overlaid with a fine red carpet stretched ahead. Periodically they passed a footman, who bowed until they were past. It was overdone and overwhelming.

'You are like a potentate here,' Juliet said, hard pressed to keep the distaste from her voice.

'Do I detect displeasure? You will have to get

used to this. Anything less would not be fitting for my station.'

Was there bitterness in his last words? She looked at him as they walked. His face, as usual, was unrevealing.

They stopped in front of two double doors with the Brabourne crest and motto carved across them. She got a strange feeling in her stomach.

With his free hand, Brabourne opened the doors. Juliet gazed into a room big enough to be a ballroom in many houses.

He ushered her in, leaving the doors open. 'This is your sitting room. Beyond is the sleeping chamber and a room for your maid.'

Done in shades of pale green and black, the Brabourne colours, it was enough to take her breath away. A settee and several chairs grouped around a table where tea had been laid out. A large secretary and several bookcases took up part of one wall. The wood floor was covered in carpet. Many-paned windows, with green brocade curtains with black trim pulled back, presented the view of a stormy English Channel. She imagined that during a storm she would hear the waves pound the shore.

'Magnificent,' she breathed.

'It is the suite of rooms traditionally occupied by the Duchess. My rooms are connected through a door in your sleeping chamber.'

She was not surprised. Even a house as grand as

this could not have many rooms this fantastic. Still, he was bucking respectability by putting her here before their marriage.

He must have known her thoughts. 'By tomorrow it will no longer matter. I am tired of being dictated to by narrow minds.'

There was nothing she could say. She was not yet mistress here. Besides, a large part of her agreed with him. She was heartily tired of having her life tossed about because of what others expected.

'I will leave you now,' he said, releasing her. 'We keep country hours here, in spite of Prinny's presence, but we do dress. The dinner bell will ring at five.'

'Prinny is here?' She had known he was close to Brabourne, and that he intended to attend the wedding, but she had thought he would arrive tomorrow.

'He came several days ago. He likes the hunting.'

The Duke's voice was non-committal and Juliet wondered what else the Prince liked. But it was none of her business.

'We will be twenty for dinner,' he added as he left.

Juliet stood looking at the closed doors long after he had gone. Twenty might be small for him, but to her it was too many. The day had been long and the preceding weeks even longer. Tomorrow was her wedding day, the ceremony to be held in the estate chapel. She really did not want to spend the evening trying to appear excited and eager.

A knock on the door signalled the arrival of her trunks. More would follow over the next week or so. Striding into her sleeping chamber and seeing the massive wardrobe and tallboy, and a separate room specially designed for her gowns, Juliet began to wonder if she had enough clothing for the life she was entering into. She would worry about that later. Right now she needed to direct the unpacking and find a gown suitable for tonight's activities. Pleading sick on the eve of her wedding was not the thing to do.

Several hours later, she studied herself in the large bevelled mirror. She wore the same bronze silk gown she had worn to Almack's, with the same single strand of pearls. Gold ribbon threaded through the curls her maid had let fall like autumn leaves on to her shoulders from a gold clasp on top of her head. Something was missing.

She looked like a schoolgirl. The last thing she wanted. It had not bothered her before, but now she felt gauche in these magnificent surroundings. Out of her depth.

And, a small part of her acknowledged, she wanted to stand out so that Brabourne would notice her and admire her. As much as she told herself she did not want to marry him, she still wanted him to be proud of her. For what reason, she could not, would not admit to herself. The need was just there, nestled in her chest and demanding satisfaction.

She sighed and stood. This was silly.

The smooth sound of wood sliding on wood alerted her. The door to Brabourne's room opened. He stood in the entryway, watching her, a velvet box in one hand.

He was magnificent, everything she had ever dreamed a man should be. There was a powerful grace about him when he moved, showing his lean body to advantage. His longish hair brushed his shoulders, its darkness nearly lost in the midnight colour of his coat. Black breeches moulded to him.

She gulped and looked away.

'I have something for you,' he said, stopping too close for her comfort.

He flicked open the box and held it out to her. On a bed of black velvet lay a necklace that caught the candlelight and split it into many shades of yellow, orange and red. It was a choker made up of three strands with a large, canary-yellow oval stone in the centre. Around it was a circle of red stones with an orange tinge. More yellow stones made up the three strands. It was stunning. Matching earrings and bracelets lay beside it.

'I have never seen anything so…so striking,' she said.

'They are the Brabourne diamonds. The centre

stone is one of the largest yellow diamonds in existence. They will look good on you.'

She looked from the jewels to him. 'I cannot wear them. What if I lost them?'

'You are impossible. I had them cleaned and the catch strengthened. The settings are also good.' He took the necklace out and set the box on a table. 'You will not lose them unless you get into a skirmish with someone, which I don't expect tonight.' A slight smile curved his lips. 'To my knowledge, there are no thugs present.'

She returned his smile with a grimace. 'One never knows.'

'True. You are prone to finding trouble. Now, turn around so I can hook this.'

She looked at him, noting the implacable gaze he bent on her. No argument would sway him. That much she had learned about him. With a reluctant sigh, she did as he ordered.

His fingers brushed the nape of her neck just seconds before her pearls slid down so that one end came to rest where the fabric of her bodice ended. The smooth feel of pearl slid along her skin as he pulled them free. The breath she had not realised she held slipped through her parted lips.

She had barely regained her composure when his fingers once more touched her. A *frisson* shot down her spine. The cool kiss of diamonds and gold rested against the heated flush of her reaction to him.

For a fleeting instant she thought she felt his lips against her neck and across her exposed shoulder. Shivers joined the *frisson* that continued to move through her. Then he stepped away.

'Turn around so that I may see you,' he said, his voice a harsh sound in the utter silence.

She did as she was told, unable to do otherwise. His voice held the same sound it had the night he had nearly ravished her. When she saw him, the hunger in his gaze took her aback.

He reached out and with one finger traced the line of the necklace. Where his flesh met hers fire erupted. He bent forward and kissed the base of her throat, just below the centre diamond. She moaned in shocked surprise and delight, her fingers reaching out to grasp something so she would not fall. Her nails dug into the fabric covering of the chair behind her.

He raised his head and stared down at her. Her chest rose and fell in small panting gasps.

'They become you,' he murmured. 'I knew they would.'

She stared at him, her eyes wide with reaction while his were slumberous. If he crooked his finger, she would fall willingly into his arms. It was a shameful admission, but she knew it for the truth.

She was his—body and soul.

Instead, he stepped further away. 'We must go down. Our guests are waiting.'

Disappointment made its insidious way through her emotions. She caught herself up short with a shake of the head. Would she never learn?

'You are right,' she said, her voice remarkably level for the turmoil her thoughts were in.

Holding her head high, she preceded him through the door. After his bestowal of the jewels, anything else would be anti-climactic.

She was right.

The next morning, Juliet stood across the altar from her groom in the small chapel situated on the Brabourne estate. This was not her choice of place, but Brabourne had thought it best after her attempted elopement. Behind them stood her family, Prinny and Perth. Ravenswood stood as groomsman to Brabourne. She had no bridesmaid.

George had not been invited.

In half an hour all the rich and powerful who were not already here would be arriving for the wedding breakfast.

Right now, she had to turn to the Duke and allow him to kiss her. Her hands shook, so she hid them in the folds of her white silk and silver lace gown. Please let it be chaste. She did not want to succumb to him in front of these people. She never wanted to melt against him again.

He touched his lips to her cheek before holding his arm out for her hand. Relief flooded her. She laid her fingers lightly on him and hoped he did not feel her shivers.

He graciously accepted congratulations, even smiling at his friends and the Prince. She managed to keep her lips parted in what she hoped looked like a smile. It was the best she could do.

'Beautiful bride, you lucky devil,' Prinny said with a wink.

Before Juliet realised what the prince intended, he planted his mouth full on hers. She gasped, but managed to keep from jumping back. She could not stop the blush.

'Thank you, Your Highness,' she said, grateful her voice did not tremble.

'Oh, Your Highness,' Emily cooed, having come up beside him, 'you are such a charming rogue.'

He took her hand and beamed down at her. Together they left the chapel. Juliet glanced at her papa, who stood to one side watching.

'Why don't you ask him to go in with us?' Brabourne said quietly.

Juliet gave her new husband a speaking look, torn equally between gratitude for his kindness and irritation that he was so thoughtful, which weakened her resolve to dislike him. She could not control her heart, but she was determined to control her mind.

She rushed to Papa, only to have Harry get there first. 'Come with us,' she said to both of them.

Harry grinned and shook his head. 'We will follow. This is your moment—and your husband's.'

She frowned at him, but knew from the stubborn light in his eyes that he would not change his mind. With ill grace, she returned to the Duke, who once more held out his arm.

'You can do better than that,' he chided, his face once more masked by his cool reserve. 'After all the trouble we have gone to, there is no sense in defeating our purpose by having the tongues wagging that our marriage is a sham.'

'Why should they think anything else?' she hissed. 'Everyone knows you only married me to save my reputation.'

He shrugged. 'That does not mean you have to confirm their suspicions. They can just as easily believe it is a love match. After all, I compromised you. Let them guess.'

She gave an unladylike snort.

They entered the large ballroom that Brabourne had had made into a bower of flowers. Through the many french windows she saw white silk tents set up on the acres of lawn. Beneath them were more tables laden with food. Her husband had spared no expense.

People were everywhere, dressed in the height of fashionable morning dress. She had to endure the next couple hours and into the evening. Many of the important guests had arrived last night and stayed over.

Brabourne led her to the largest table, where a many-layered bride's cake reposed. His French chef had been working on it for days. Crystal, china and silver sparkled like constellations around it. With luck, she could spend the rest of the morning and early afternoon cutting the cake.

Then there was the night.

Chapter Eleven

Juliet could stand the waiting no longer. With a huff of ire, she jumped out of the massive four-poster bed and marched to the mantel. She grabbed a brass poker from the stand and attacked the coals. Heat jumped out at her from the reinvigorated fire. It was small satisfaction.

This was her wedding night and she had come to bed hours ago, or so it seemed to her heightened nerves. Many of the guests had left that afternoon. The only ones remaining were her family, Prinny, Perth and Ravensford. She had left Brabourne drinking with his cronies, thinking he would soon follow.

She was a fool.

She returned the poker to its stand and went to the large window. Pulling the curtains back, she peered out at the night. Clouds scuttled across the sky, obscuring the stars. The moon was only a sliver. If she listened hard enough, she could hear the waves hitting the rocky shores. This was a primitive, vital land, like its owner.

She let the curtain close. Some hot chocolate would be nice, and might help her to sleep, but she did not want to let anyone know of her shame. Her husband was not interested enough in her to come and do his duty. She must have been mistaken when she'd thought she saw hunger on his face after he had fastened the diamonds around her throat.

Her temples began to throb.

Everyone had gasped the night before when they had entered the salon. Emily had turned green. The large gilt mirror over the mantel had shown her the necklace sparkling like a miniature sun around her neck. She had been beautiful, if only because of the jewels. She had even felt beautiful for the first time in her life.

Now, the diamonds were back in their case on her dressing stand. She was back to her normal self.

She returned to the bed, crawled in and burrowed under the covers. It might be summer, but being so close to water kept the abbey too cool for comfort. She turned into the embrace of the fluffy pillows and told herself she was better off without Brabourne in her bed. He was too expert at what he did to leave her unscathed.

Sebastian paused at the door separating his room from Juliet's. He had drunk everyone under the table and now felt a cool detachment about his new wife. The desire that had driven him lurked beneath the haze caused by good French wine. Yet he knew that if he crossed the wooden barrier separating them, all his good intentions would be for naught. He would have her to wife and be damned to anything else.

The cynical part of him said do it. He would ensure her first child was his.

The side of himself he showed only to those few people close to him said wait. For her first time with a man she deserved to have someone who was sober enough to give her pleasure and to care about how she felt. Right now he was not that person.

He should not have drunk so much, trying to exorcise the spectre of his mother and her infidelity to the man the world had known as his father. His marriage had opened wide the already-weeping wound of his bastardy. Telling himself Juliet was not his mother did no good. Juliet was a woman, and he did not trust women.

Hands clenched, shoulders tight, he turned and went to his bed. He snuffed the single candle he carried and set it on the side table, then undid the sash of his navy robe and let the silk slither to the floor. Naked, he got under the cold covers.

It was going to be a long night.

The next morning Juliet rose before the maid came to her room and made her bed. Raised in the country, she knew the first servant in to tidy the room would realise she and Brabourne had not consummated their marriage. She had never thought herself prideful, but having people know her husband could not bring himself to make love to her on their wedding night was more than she could bear.

She pulled the bell; when a footman came, she told him she wanted Mrs Burroughs. It was not so strange a request for a new bride. Brabourne had introduced her to the staff yesterday after their marriage. It was plausible that she intended to speak to the housekeeper about the running of the abbey...what if it was a little too early? She was eccentric.

Mrs Burroughs arrived promptly, making a curtsy to Juliet. 'Your Grace?'

'Please, Mrs Burroughs, don't treat me that way. I am not used to it.'

The housekeeper smiled warmly. 'Used to it or not, you are a Duchess now and must learn to accept what comes with it.'

Juliet wrung her hands and paced the floor of her chamber. How did one go about asking for help to hide this sort of thing? If only Ferguson or Hobson were here.

Reaching the sticking point, she stopped short and blurted, 'Mrs Burroughs, I need your help. The Duke did not visit me last night.' Embarrassment was like a flame that burned her face.

The old woman's round cheeks turned ruddy even as sympathy softened the lines around her eyes. 'Oh, dear. I knew he would have problems, but I was so sure he was attracted to you enough that he would… Well, anyway. We must get you dressed, and you need to go to the Long Gallery to see the pictures. That will tell you. Meanwhile, I will tidy your room. No one must know what did not happen last night. Least of all your stepmother.'

Relief eased the constriction in Juliet's chest. She had found an ally. She dressed in a pale lavender morning dress, with a white paisley shawl around her shoulders to ward off the morning chill. Mrs Burroughs gave her directions to the Long Gallery and she set off, wondering what she was supposed to learn that Mrs Burroughs did not want to tell her.

She got lost twice, and finally asked a footman to show her the way. The young man made her a very impressive bow, which made her more uncomfortable. She was going to have trouble getting used to her new rank. At her destination he bowed again.

'Please,' she said, then stopped herself. She could not tell him to stop bowing. 'Thank you.'

He raised one eyebrow, but otherwise managed to keep an impassive face as he took his leave. Her impetuosity had nearly got her into trouble again. Being a Duchess was going to be hard work.

Drawing the shawl close, she started slowly walking the length of the room and studying the portraits as she went. The style of clothing changed with each painting, as did the women. Each Duchess differed from the one before or after her. Blonde, brown or black hair, and blue, brown or grey eyes, graced the women randomly. Some were plump and others thin. Some were tall and others short.

The men never seemed to change. Their clothes reflected the time period, but their features and bearing never altered. All the Dukes had blond hair and heavily lidded pale blue eyes. Their noses were arrogant hooks that turned down at the tip. Their lips were thin. Even the last Duke, Brabourne's father, looked like all those who had gone before him.

She stopped at the end of the gallery and studied the portraits of the last Duke and Duchess. The Duchess looked like Brabourne, the same raven-black hair and piercing blue eyes. Her lips were full and sensual like her son's. Her nose was straight and well defined and, like her son's, had no hook. She was willowy and he was lean. Brabourne had a squarer jaw, but that was the only major difference.

Juliet felt a presence and turned to see her husband. He stopped beside her and looked up at the picture of his mother.

'We are much alike.'

There was a harshness to his voice and an intensity to his body that told Juliet he was disturbed. He glanced down at her and his eyes were hard.

'I don't look anything like the last Duke.'

'Your father,' she said, before realisation hit her. She had been so stupid.

He stiffened. 'The man the world calls my father.'

Instinctively she reached for him. He moved as though to look somewhere else and managed to avoid her touch. She drew back, hurt.

'I have his name and title, but I am really a bastard,' he said softly.

She did not know what to say, but had to do something. The gulf between them was widening. 'You cannot know that for sure.'

'He told me.'

'Oh.'

'I was ten. It was my birthday. He never forgave my mother for doing it to him, and he never forgave me for living. I never forgave her either.' His voice was void of emotion, as though he spoke of someone else.

Juliet was appalled by the pain the last Duchess had wrought. She longed to comfort Brabourne, but did not think he would let her.

'I am so sorry,' she whispered, knowing the words were inadequate.

He turned back to her. 'Don't be. It is in the past.'

'But not forgotten or overcome.' Even as she said the words she knew she spoke the truth. When he said he had never forgiven his mother, he also meant he did not trust women. 'I will not do that to you, to our children.'

He looked at her for long minutes, then walked away without saying a word. Her heart ached for him as she watched his proud back disappear around a corner. Her heart ached for herself. She had known her marriage was far from perfect, but she had never imagined there was so much past pain that had to be put to rest before they could start to make the best of their life together.

One step at a time, she told herself. He would never love her, but she would make him trust her. She could live with that. She would have to.

For dinner that night she wore the palest of lavender. Brabourne sent her a magnificent set of amethyst and diamond jewellery. Her maid fastened the necklace. Juliet missed the electrifying sensuality of her husband's touch even as she wondered what maggot had taken up residence in her brain. She should be glad he was keeping his distance. It was what she had wanted from the beginning.

The Prince was still with them. During the meat course, he announced, 'I will be returning to London tomorrow, Brabourne. I hope to see you there after your wedding trip.'

'Within the week,' Brabourne answered without looking at Juliet.

No one said a word about there not being a trip.

'Really?' Emily said, 'Oliver and I were just talking about when we were returning to town. We have decided to go tomorrow as well.'

Juliet watched her papa, noting the look of confusion on his face.

Harry said, 'That is news to me. The hunting here is excellent, and Papa likes hunting above everything except his experiments.'

'Don't be ridiculous,' Emily said quickly. 'Oliver wants to get back to his experiments, don't you?'

'Yes, yes. Quite, m'dear.' He returned his attention to his meal.

Juliet watched her stepmother and wondered just what the other woman was up to. She had used Juliet's connections to Brabourne to better her position in Society. Was she now going to use her budding acquaintance with the Prince to further boost her position? Was Prinny aware?

Prinny smiled warmly at Emily. 'Delightful to have you coming back so soon, Lady Smythe-Clyde. The two of you must come to Carlton House.'

Juliet glanced at her husband. Brabourne was watching the exchange with a jaundiced air. He obviously knew something was going on between the Prince and Emily and did not approve. Papa seemed oblivious, his food holding all his attention.

What a mess, Juliet decided, grateful dinner was essentially over. She signalled for herself and Emily to leave the men with their port.

Her relief at escaping the quickly deteriorating dinner was short-lived.

With an insinuating tone, Emily asked, 'Was last night everything you thought it would be? Brabourne is reputed to be the best lover in England.'

Juliet's hated blush came in full force. Pulling herself together, she gave Emily a supercilious stare. 'How unladylike a question.'

Emily's eyes narrowed. 'High in the instep, now that you are a Duchess.' She moved nearer and said in a venomous whisper, 'But don't expect him every night. He has a reputation. No woman has ever held him exclusively.' Her tinkling laugh filled the room as she went to the sideboard and poured herself a glass of sherry.

Juliet left while the other woman's back was turned. She would not stay and hear Emily's bold words and hurtful insinuations. The truth in them was something she did not want to face tonight.

In her own rooms, she quickly dressed for bed. Her last request to her maid was for a cup of hot chocolate. She intended to sleep.

An hour later she sighed and threw the covers off. She got out of bed and lit the candle left near. By its golden glow she found her lavender wool robe and donned it, tying the sash tightly. She should have known oblivion would evade her.

A chill hung in the room. She crossed to the fireplace and stirred the banked coals. Sparks jumped up and rode the air currents like fairies. She smiled, remembering the tales of little people her nanny used to regale her and Harry with before bed.

A click and the smooth slide of a door across carpet froze her, poker in right hand. Very careful not to appear startled, she put the tool back, then pivoted around.

She swallowed hard.

Brabourne was a dark figure in the entry, the glow of the fire barely reaching him. He stood there, watching her for long moments before stepping into the room. The door slid shut behind him.

Juliet's heart pounded.

In one hand he held a bottle of wine, in the other a velvet box. He set them down on the table nearest the bed, then continued towards her, not stopping until he was close enough so that she could see every nuance of his face and feel the warmth from his body. Much too close.

Her stomach knotted and butterflies seemed to fly up her throat. This was the moment she had been dreading as much as she had been longing for it. He was finally going to consummate their marriage.

'Juliet,' he said softly, taking her hands in his, 'it is time.'

She nodded, allowing him to lead her back to the bed. He released her and poured them each a glass of golden wine. She took hers and sipped. It was champagne. The bubbles floated up her throat. A surprised smile eased some of her discomfort.

He watched her with an intensity that brought back her sense of impending disaster. Intuitively she knew that when he was finished with her nothing would ever be the same. She swallowed down the wine in one long gulp.

He shook his head. 'Fine wine is for sipping, not quenching your thirst.' Still, he poured her more.

This time she sipped, allowing the effervescence to cascade down her throat as she wondered what he was going to do next. Anticipation was a delicious tingle in her toes. None the less, it was a shock when he undid the belt on his robe and allowed the silk to fall to the floor.

He stood naked before her, his magnificent body glowing in the light from the fire. She gaped, taking in his splendour before squeezing her eyes shut. Her cheeks flamed. The empty glass would have fallen from her nerveless fingers if he had not rescued it.

'Get into bed,' he murmured.

Without opening her eyes, she backed away until her knees hit the mattress. His hands gripped her waist and lifted. He held her against him so she could feel his arousal pressing into her. She gasped and put her hands on his shoulders and pressed, trying to put some distance between them.

'Don't,' he ordered. 'This is only the beginning.'

The beginning of the end, she told herself. He

would take her and make her his. She licked her dry lips. He laid her on the bed.

'Here,' he said, handing her another glass of champagne. 'It will help relax you.'

She opened one eye and took the wine. She needed a lot of relaxing. He grinned indulgently at her as she gulped down the contents.

'Remind me not to waste good wine on you again,' he said, taking the empty glass and setting it on the table.

She began to feel a little giddy and drowsy. It would be so nice to sink into the comfort of the feather bed and sleep.

'You cannot go to sleep yet,' he said, untying the sash of her robe. 'I have things to show you.'

It was an effort to open her eyes, but she managed. He loomed over her, his face golden on one side where the firelight hit it. Overwhelming curiosity drew her gaze downward. Dark hairs scattered across his chest, swirling around his nipples. The temptation to touch was great.

'Go ahead,' he murmured, his voice husky. 'Feel me.'

'How did you know?' she asked, her words only slightly slurred.

'Your face. Every thought you have shows on it.'

When she did nothing, he caught one of her hands and placed it on his chest. The invitation was irresistible. With wonder, she explored the textures of his upper body.

His skin was firm, not as soft as hers, but not coarse either. The dark hairs that had beckoned her twined around her fingers, their wiry toughness so much like him. Firm muscles twitched. When she finally found his nipple, it hardened with an alacrity that enthralled her. She swirled her thumb over the nub until he groaned.

'For a beginner you do very well.'

She smiled, hearing the need in his voice. 'I am a fast learner.'

But she knew it was bravado. She had no idea where they were going or how to get there. He was the one who would control their joining.

With infinite skill, he eased the robe off her shoulders. She shivered as the cool air caressed her exposed skin.

'How can you stand being naked?' she asked.

'Anticipation.'

'Ah,' she murmured, memories of his caresses returning. 'I can understand that.'

'Can you? Then help me get your nightrail off.'

That stopped her. 'Can you not do it with me dressed?'

'I could,' he said, leaning down and catching her nipple in his mouth through the fine linen. He sucked and nibbled until she shivered with delight.

He raised his head to watch the wonder moving over her face. 'But it is not nearly so nice.'

'If it were any more so, I would not be able to stand it,' she murmured.

'Oh, you will,' he promised, easing the material over her head.

He dropped the clothing on the floor with his robe, the two garments entwining as he imagined their bodies soon would. His heart hammered with desire. It was all he could do not to enter her now.

She flinched, but did nothing to stop his hand from cupping her breast. His warmth felt good, adding another layer to the sensations he gave her. This time when he took her into his mouth his tongue slid smoothly over her flesh.

'Oh,' she whispered. 'I see what you meant. This is much better.'

He chuckled. For an innocent she was certainly hedonistic. All the better. Her arousal would intensify his reaction.

He reached across her for his half-full glass of champagne. With a tilt of his wrist, he poured some on to her flat abdomen. She flinched, pushing her breasts up against his chest.

'What are you doing?' she asked, raising her head so she could see.

'Patience,' he said, lowering his head to her belly.

With flicks of his tongue he licked up the wine. Her muscles spasmed at each touch.

Juliet had never known such pleasure. She caught his hair in her fingers and held him to her. He chuckled and his warm breath on her skin was like torture. Divine torture that she knew was only the beginning.

Some of the champagne slipped down to the secret place between her legs. He followed it.

Juliet stiffened and tried to pull his head up. 'Please, no.'

He looked up at her, his face implacable. 'Yes.'

She shook her head.

He smiled and slipped his hand where his mouth wanted to go.

She gasped, her eyes wide. 'What are you doing?'

'Making love to you,' he murmured, watching carefully as his fingers slid along the moist warmth of her skin. When he slid one into her, she tightened, and a groan of anticipation escaped him.

Juliet licked dry lips and stared up at the ceiling. She could not watch what he was doing. It was too intimate, too depraved. But it felt so good. She moaned.

'Relax,' he crooned. 'This night is for pleasure.'

Still unable to look at him, she murmured, 'This is so…so unladylike. I never imagined it would be so—'

'Delightful?'

'That too.' She gasped as he found a particularly sensitive spot.

He chuckled, and in her moment of weakness

moved her legs apart and touched her with his tongue. Juliet cringed, only to have shivers rack her body with each caress he gave her. Her stomach clenched.

'What is happening?' she gasped.

He raised up on his elbows to better see her face. 'You are becoming aroused.'

She gulped as his fingers replaced his mouth. 'Oh.'

It was a small sound and all she could make. Her world was spiralling down to the way he made her feel. Nothing else mattered any more. Not the indignity of her position or the crudity of what he was doing. Only the way he made her feel.

Sebastian watched her, his own need mounting. She responded with such sweet intensity he did not know how much longer he could put off entering her completely. He felt her muscles contract and knew she was close.

Never taking his fingers from her, he slid up until he lay in the valley between her legs. Her whimpers drew him on.

In one smooth motion, he pulled out his fingers and inserted himself. He slid in with only a slight hitch.

'Ohh! That hurt.' Her eyes opened and she stared up at him where he lay above her.

He clenched his teeth. 'I...I took your maidenhood.'

She said nothing.

Driven nearly beyond his celebrated control, Sebastian kissed her. He kissed her as if there was no stopping them. Only when she started to kiss him back did he start slowly moving.

She gasped.

He grinned, not knowing it was nearly a grimace. 'Move with me,' he murmured. 'Match my rhythm.'

'I cannot,' she whispered, eyes wide in shock at the knowledge he was inside her. Yet it felt good. Terribly good.

'Yes, you can,' he said, catching her face between his hand and taking her mouth again.

His tongue slipped into her mouth and teased hers. His body slid over hers, his belly meeting hers in shivering pleasure. He moved faster.

Juliet gave in to the demands of his desire. Her hips met his and withdrew in response to his. Her back arched and her breasts pressed tightly against his chest. Sensations drenched her nerves. Her nails raked down his back until her hands clutched his buttocks and urged him on.

Her gasps matched his.

'Now, now,' he moaned.

She thrust up and exploded. Spasms of pleasure tore her apart. She could hardly breathe.

His mouth still covered hers when he lost control. His shout filled her lungs as he bucked into her.

It was a long time before either could move. She

lay beneath him her legs still wrapped around his hips, her eyes slumberous jewels that watched him with satisfaction.

'You are very, very good,' she murmured, running her fingers along his spine. 'I never imagined it could be like that.'

He grinned, enjoying her feather touch on his back. 'Not a fate worse than death after all?'

She smiled and tightened her legs, making him wonder if he would soon be able to repeat what had brought the glow to her body. He certainly wanted to.

Soon he was moving in her again as she moaned and thrashed beneath him. He began to wonder if he would survive the night. If not, he could not think of a better way to end.

Chapter Twelve

〜〜〜〜〜〜

Juliet woke up the next day with a sense of well-being. She sighed and tried to roll over. A heavy arm held her pinned to the bed. Soft snores gently blew the curls from her face. Brabourne had stayed the night with her.

She smiled, remembering all they had done to and with each other. Never in her wildest imagination would she have created the things he had done to her. Not even *The Bride of Abydos* had prepared her for the bliss of making love. She flushed as desire quickened her blood.

His eyes opened and she wondered if she had spoken aloud. He gave her a slow, sensual smile, and before she knew it she had straddled him. She lowered herself until he filled her.

'Do your duty, wife,' he said, his voice a hoarse growl.

Feeling her power over him in this position, she

took her time, drawing it out until he begged. When she felt him jerk and his eyes close, she knew he had taken his pleasure.

After his breathing returned to normal, he opened his eyes and said, 'Now it is your turn.'

She squealed as he flipped her over and began doing things to her that she remembered only too well. They had not slept much the night before.

He teased her with mouth, tongue and hands until she was hot and ready. Then he slipped into her.

She watched him with eyes glazed by passion, waiting for him to start the rhythm that ended in such delight. He began slowly so that her tension mounted.

'Brabourne,' she pleaded, her hands on his hips urging him to greater speed.

'Sebastian,' he said.

'Yes, yes,' she muttered. 'Faster, please, I am so—'

'Sebastian.'

She gazed up at him, not knowing what he wanted. She wiggled her hips, hoping to entice him into doing what she needed so desperately.

'Call me Sebastian,' he said, holding back so his face was a grimace caused by the effort it took not to ram into her and take them both to the top.

'Brabourne. Sebastian,' she said, wriggling beneath him. 'They are both your names.'

'Sebastian,' he gritted. 'That is my Christian

name.' He panted as he held back. 'Call me Sebastian and I will end this torture.'

'What's in a name?' she muttered. 'Sebastian.'

He released a pent-up sigh and thrust deep. She arched up to meet him, their bodies straining.

Some time later she woke to find him gone. The bed seemed too large and very cold without him. She rose and wrapped her robe tight before going to the window. Pulling the curtains back, she saw it was dusk. She had spent the entire day in bed. She never did that. But, then, she had never made love to a man all night and day either.

When she finally went downstairs, Burroughs met her in the foyer. 'His Grace is waiting in the library, your Grace.'

She glanced at him to see if he had kept a straight face while sprinkling all those 'Graces' in one sentence. He was the perfect butler, his countenance betraying nothing, not even the ridiculousness of the situation.

'Thank you,' she said, and headed off in the direction he indicated.

She knocked and waited for permission to enter. Once it was given, she opened the door and walked through.

Bra—Sebastian stood by the window looking out, his back to her. He was casually dressed, like a country squire, only on him the simplicity was actually striking. Juliet sighed. He was a magnificent man.

He turned and smiled, the emotion actually reaching his eyes. 'Come here. I want to show you something before it is completely dark.'

She moved to him until they stood side by side. He slipped an arm around her shoulders.

'Look out there,' he directed.

An expanse of grass stretched to the horizon. Every imaginable tree dotted the earth. Manicured gardens of roses, nasturtiums, honeysuckle and much more tempted the beholder to walk through them. A lake in the distance reflected the red rays of the dying sun. Further still were cultivated fields and the smoke from tenants' cottages.

'It is impressive,' she said, not knowing what his point was.

'Yes. And it is mine.' His voice firmed. 'And it will pass to the first male child you bear.'

She stiffened.

He turned her to face him, but she refused to look at him. He caught her chin and made her eyes meet his.

'I know you were a virgin last night, so I know you are not carrying another man's child. Don't betray me as my mother did my father.'

She gazed at the flat blue of his eyes. She now understood that his feelings on this subject were so strong he hid them behind a blank surface. Still, his assumption that she might be unfaithful hurt.

She took a deep breath before speaking. 'I am not your mother. I have already told you I will honour my vows. Obviously you did not believe me.'

He stared down at her, his countenance still inscrutable. 'Ours was not a love match—I don't expect fidelity. Just wait until after I have an heir.'

She slapped him, her reaction instinctual. 'How dare you accuse me of your sins? When I said I honour my vows, I meant I honour them for my lifetime.'

She wrenched from his loosened embrace and stormed to the door and through it.

Sebastian watched her go before turning back to the view. He was sorry to have hurt her, but she had to understand. He would not brook raising another man's bastard as his heir. He would divorce her and disown the child first.

Still, he wished it could have been different. A part of him wished he could have trusted her. But trust was something he had never learned to have for women.

That night he came to her and she let him make love to her, knowing he would visit her every night until she conceived his heir. It was bitter-sweet knowledge as she dissolved under his caresses.

* * *

The next morning Juliet woke to an empty bed, the warmth and intimacy of their first night together gone. The loss brought tears she could not stem. For a while she had allowed herself to enjoy her husband's attentions without feeling the future press down on her.

The door between hers and Sebastian's rooms opened. He entered, dressed for riding.

'I am touring the estate today. Would you like to come along?'

'Why?' she asked without thinking, concerned only with concealing the fact that she had been crying. She swiped at her cheeks.

He flinched before his cool hauteur returned. 'I deserved that. I would like to show you around and introduce you to some of the people. This is your home now, and will be so for the children you bear.'

Her stomach churned. The children she bore, not *their* children. 'Any children I have will belong here.'

He nodded. 'Are you coming?'

He was implacable. She was tempted to throw his invitation back in his face, but she was also curious. As he had pointed out, she would spend a large part of her life here.

'Give me a few minutes to dress.'

'I will be in the library.'

She made a fast toilet and descended the stairs in her leaf-green riding habit. A jaunty black hat with a lone peacock feather tilted rakishly on her auburn curls. She looked her best and knew it. Somehow she did not think it would make any difference. Sebastian had his pick of beautiful women and trusted none of them. Beauty would not win him, but it gave her courage to know he would not be embarrassed to introduce her as his Duchess.

They wasted no time.

Juliet rode a placid gelding while Sebastian rode a spirited mare. He led the way down a dirt road.

Rich fields spread out around them. She could see people working the earth. Up ahead was a cottage with a woman and child standing outside.

Sebastian reined in. 'How are you, Mrs Smith?'

The woman bobbed a curtsy. 'Well, your Grace. The harvest will be large this year.'

'We can use it,' Sebastian said. 'I have brought my bride. You will be seeing a lot of her.'

The woman made another curtsy. 'Your Grace.'

Juliet smiled. 'How old is your child and what is his name?'

'He be eight. We call him Tom after his pa.'

Juliet smiled at the boy who stood bravely beside his mother, taking in the novelty of the lord and lady speaking with them. He raised his hand to a lock of hair and tugged it.

'We must be going,' Sebastian said. 'Let my steward know if there is anything you need.'

At the next house a young girl met them. She bobbed respectfully. 'Your Grace.'

Sebastian nodded and introduced Juliet. After the acknowledgments, he asked, 'Where are your parents?'

'In the village getting provisions.'

'Tell them someone will be out within the week with materials to repair your roof.' And they were off again.

By the end of the afternoon Juliet felt as though she had met more people in the past few hours than in the last year. All of them were well fed and seemed contented. Sebastian was a good landlord. She was not surprised.

That night she fell into bed, tired and aching. It had been a while since she had spent so much time in the saddle. Not even a hot bath had helped. Her eyes were drowsily shutting when the door opened. She suppressed a groan of pure exhaustion.

Without asking permission, Sebastian got under the covers of her bed and snuffed the candle he carried and set it on the table. He reached for her.

Juliet scooted back. 'Please, not tonight. I ache in all the wrong places.'

'Ah. Too long on horseback.'

She rolled over on her back. 'Yes. I have not ridden like that since before Mama died. Coupled with the soreness from our activities, I feel I am splitting apart.'

He chuckled. 'Poor Juliet. Come here and let me rub your back and legs.'

She snorted. 'I know where that will lead.'

'I promise.'

She knew he would keep a promise. And it did sound divine.

'Just for a little bit.'

'Of course,' he murmured.

She rolled onto her stomach and let him do as he would. His fingers dug into the sore muscles of her lower back and thighs. At first it hurt, but soon she loosened as his massage continued. Shortly she purred contentment.

'Glad now?' he asked, his voice husky as his fingers moved down from the small of her back.

Little jolts of pleasure shot through her as he rubbed. 'You are very good,' she murmured.

Instead of answering, he turned her on her side and cuddled her close. 'I will leave you alone tonight,' he said, wrapping his arm around her waist so that his hand cupped her breast.

'You have a very unusual way of doing that,' she muttered, wiggling into him.

'And you have a very tempting way of getting comfortable.'

She stopped all movement. As much as she enjoyed his lovemaking, she was truly sore and tired. With a sigh she closed her eyes and tried not to let hope flare in her heart. He was staying only because he was determined she would have *his* child. Sadness filled her instead as she drifted to sleep.

The next morning Juliet drifted awake, feeling warm and cosy. She snuggled into the source of her delight.

'Time to wake up,' Sebastian murmured, his lips skimming along her face.

She opened her eyes and looked straight into his. Their blue depths were filled with desire and she knew there would be no denying him this time. Nor did she want to.

Two days later, she sat in the Duke of Brabourne's travelling carriage, the Brabourne crest emblazoned on the glossy black paint outside. The thick gold velvet seats were the most comfortable she had ever ridden in. Sebastian rode his favourite horse.

Brabourne Abbey disappeared from sight and Juliet leaned back into the cushions. They were going to London. She had not wanted to leave, thinking that with time and no other distractions she might win her husband's trust, if not his love. He had not given her that time.

She sighed and forced herself to read the book she had brought along. The journey would be too short.

* * *

Juliet could have done without dinner at Carlton House, but Brabourne—no, Sebastian—was still one of Prinny's intimates regardless of being married now. She supposed she should consider herself lucky she had also been invited.

Resigned, she took another bite of salmon and smiled at her dinner partner, Lord Appleby. He was tall and slim, an elegant man with blond hair and a dimple when he smiled. He was also a witty talker and a wicked flirt. Innuendoes fell from his lips like water from an icicle.

Sebastian was further up the table near Prinny. So was her stepmother, but that did not bother her much. What ate at her was the woman beside her husband. She was beautiful and endowed in ways Juliet never would be. She also constantly touched Sebastian, and he enjoyed it if his sultry smile was anything to go by. Watching them was like twisting a knife in her heart. If she could, she would leave. She could not.

She took another bite and looked away. There was nothing she could do, no matter how much it hurt. She would worry about something else, such as the way Papa was watching Emily flirt with the Prince. He had the same gleam in his eye that had been there the night she had overheard him tell Hobson about challenging Sebastian. He absolutely could not challenge the Prince. That was treason.

'Lady Brabourne,' Lord Appleby said, breaking

into her thoughts, 'you have not heard a word I have been saying and now dinner is over. You owe me the pleasure of your company for a walk.'

She turned and blinked at him. She owed him? She pulled herself together and glanced at her husband, only to see him still flirting with the same woman. Perhaps she did owe Appleby after all. He rose and she allowed him to take her hand.

Sebastian watched his bride walk off with one of the most notorious womanisers in London. Michael Appleby had been chasing skirts since their days at Eton. Appleby left his own wife in the country while he pursued his pleasures in town.

A spurt of anger caught Sebastian unawares. He did not want Juliet consorting with the likes of Appleby, not after all he had done to improve her reputation. With a murmured excuse, he extricated himself from his companion's clutches.

The couple sauntered ahead. Sebastian knew exactly where their roundabout walk was taking them. He had entertained his share of women there, too.

Juliet allowed Appleby to guide her down ornately decorated halls where footmen stood around doing nothing. All the while he kept up a witty monologue. He stopped at a door that was indistinguishable from the others, but he seemed to know where they were.

Smiling down at her, he said, 'There is an Italian picture in here that I would like your opinion on.'

She studied him in the light provided by wall sconces. His hazel eyes dared her, and his dimple teased her. She wondered how many women he had charmed with those two assets.

'An Italian picture?' She grinned at him. She was married to Brabourne and knew what a rake looked like when he was bent on conquest. 'That sounds perilously close to a walk in a darkened garden.'

His smile widened. 'You are too astute for me. Brabourne must have taught you well.'

She shrugged. The last thing she intended to discuss was her husband.

With a mock sigh, he extended his arm once more. 'Let me escort you back to the salon.'

'That will not be necessary,' Sebastian said, coming round the corner where he had stopped to see what Juliet would do.

Appleby frowned before stepping away graciously. 'Over-protective, ain't you?'

Sebastian gave him a feral parting of lips. 'I know you too well, my friend.'

Appleby's gaze went from Sebastian to Juliet and back. 'I once thought the same of you. But things seem to have changed.'

'Precisely.'

Juliet watched the two men and wondered what they were really saying to each other. With a mock bow, Appleby sauntered off. Sebastian turned his attention to her.

'What was that all about?' she asked. When he did not answer, she narrowed her eyes. 'Don't look at me like that. I did not do anything wrong.'

'I know,' he said solemnly. 'But you need to know I am not my father, my dear. I will not share.'

She clenched her teeth and glared at him. 'Neither will I. So you had better remember that!'

The corner of his mouth twitched. 'What is good for the goose is good for the gander?'

'Absolutely,' she huffed.

Head high, she skirted past him, resisting the urge to stay close. It was a battle she fought every time he was near. But this time she was not going to weaken. How dared he tell her to be faithful when he was not? And then to be amused when she told him he had to be equally true to her. More amazing than anything was that she had told him anything. He was not a man one gave ultimatums to, and she had told herself she would never do so. She would do her best to accept his infidelities.

She shook her head at her bravado. A giggle of nervous reaction bubbled to her lips which she smothered with a hand.

She rounded a corner well ahead of Sebastian and came to a dead halt. Down the long hall, in plain sight for anyone to see, the Prince stood kissing and embracing her stepmother. All thought of her bold words to Sebastian evaporated in the anger that gripped her. Her hands fisted. More than anything she wanted to hurt Emily. How dared she do this to Papa?

'I would be careful about what I do. Attacking the Prince could be construed as treason,' Sebastian said in a sardonic whisper.

Juliet shot him a fulminating glance. Keeping her voice as low as his, she hissed, 'It is Emily I wish to kill.'

Sebastian took her arm and steered her back around the corner and out of sight, shaking his head the entire time. 'I shall be careful not to anger you for I am looking forward to a long life.'

He was teasing her, and at a time like this. She rounded on him, hands on hips. 'This is awful. What will Papa say if he finds out? It will break his heart.'

Sebastian moved his hands to her shoulders and scowled. 'You cannot protect him from everything. You certainly cannot fight a duel with Prinny. It isn't done.'

'Then what am I supposed to do? Stand by and let that…that *woman* hurt Papa? I do not think so.'

He shook her. 'Don't be ridiculous. Your father is a grown man. He can and should take care of his own problems.'

Her face scrunched up and it was all she could do not to shout in her frustration. 'I promised Mama. I have to take care of him.'

'No, you don't, Juliet. What she made you promise was unfair. You were hurting and under duress. You must let it go.'

She twisted in his hold, but he tightened his grip. Part of her knew he was right, but a larger part could not release her from her promise. Not yet.

'Remove your hands, please,' she said hoarsely. 'I need to find Papa and make sure he does not come this way.'

Sebastian did as she asked, but stayed close, blocking her from an easy exit. 'You are the most stubborn woman it has ever been my misfortune to meet. Your father is a grown man. Let him solve his own problems, especially since he seems to make all of them. No other man in his right mind would have married Emily Winters. Forget the past.'

She lashed out at him. 'Then what about you? Instead of carrying your hatred of your mother around like a mountain on your shoulder, why don't you forget? Do as you order me to do.'

He stepped away and all emotion fled from his face. 'You hit below the belt, madam.'

'So do you,' she muttered.

Not meeting his burning gaze, she started edging around him. Fortunately, the walls were as wide as they were opulently decorated. The Prince Regent skimped on nothing. She looked up just in time to see Papa rounding the nearest corner. She groaned.

Sebastian heard her and pivoted to find out what

was the matter. He put a hand on Juliet's arm. 'Don't interfere.'

Ignoring him, she stepped in front of her parent. 'Papa, are you lost? Let me show you the way back to the drawing room.'

He did not even glance at her, only swerved to miss her and continued down the hallway. She shook off Sebastian's hand and ran after him. Papa turned the corner and halted so quickly the tails of his coat were still visible to her. She reached him and wrapped both hands around his right arm.

'I am sure there is a reason for this,' she spouted, without thinking how inane her words sounded.

He stared at his Prince and his wife. As though sensing they were no longer alone, the couple slowly separated and looked towards where Juliet and her father stood. The Prince had the grace to flush, the colour heightened by his ruddy complexion. Emily gasped and moved further away from her royal conquest.

Juliet dug her nails deeper into Papa's arm. He seemed impervious to anything she did or said, his focus completely on the couple.

'You cannot challenge *him* to a duel,' a dry voice said. 'It's considered treason.'

Juliet breathed a sigh of relief. Even though she knew Sebastian would not interfere, having him close gave her a sense of strength. If nothing else, he might keep Papa from doing something rash.

'Just showing Lady Smythe-Clyde around,' the Prince said, moving away from Emily as he walked towards the trio.

Emily loosed her tinkling laugh. For the first time since Juliet had met the woman, the noise sounded strained.

'Oliver, darling, Prinny has been so kind as to point out his works of art to me and tell me where they are from.' She stopped by her husband and linked her arm in his.

Juliet watched everything, eyes wide, ready to jump between everyone if that seemed necessary. Sebastian's light touch at her waist would not stop her.

Lord Smythe-Clyde stared down at his wife for a long time. His jaw worked and the hand of his free arm clenched and unclenched. Juliet held her breath.

With no warning, her father gave the Prince a curt bow. 'Your Highness, we must leave.' Nor did he wait for permission. He moved off so quickly that Emily stumbled and would have fallen if Smythe-Clyde had not had a death grip on her arm.

Juliet released her pent-up breath, nearly sagging in the process. Sebastian's arm slid completely around her waist and held her. His solid strength and warmth felt good.

Sebastian shook his head. 'That was not well done, my liege. You know Smythe-Clyde's propensity for violent retribution.'

Prinny shuddered. 'Yes, but he could not challenge me.' He watched until the other couple were gone from sight. 'I almost feel sorry for her.'

'I don't,' Juliet retorted. 'She needs a come-uppance.' She gave the Prince a jaundiced look that said she thought he did as well. Once more he flushed.

'Well, I must be getting back to my other guests,' he blustered.

After sufficient time had passed, Sebastian turned Juliet in the circle of his arms so that she faced him. 'That was not so hard, was it?'

After a second's resistance, she allowed herself to sink into the comfort of his strength. Now that the crisis was past, she began to shake. He held her closer. When the short reaction had run its course, she pushed away from him. He let her move several inches so they could see each other's face.

'It was certainly not easy. I thought for a moment Papa would either challenge him or hit him.'

She closed her eyes on the picture of mayhem that would have ensued. Sebastian's lips on her forehead brought her back.

'He handled it on his own. I doubt Emily will be quite so free with her favours in the future.'

'Papa has never done that before,' she said in wonder.

He raised one brow. 'I doubt you or your mother ever let him before.'

He had a point, and rather than argue she said, 'We must return or people will begin to wonder.'

The slow, sensual smile that made her stomach flutter parted his lips. She gulped, but could not look away from the deep blue of his eyes.

'Let them. We are married. Remember?'

His voice was deep and caught on the last word. She knew what that meant.

'We cannot,' she said, panic rising. 'We are not at home.'

His smile turned sardonic. 'There are plenty of places here, believe me.'

Pain flared, squeezing her chest, at this reminder of how experienced he was. She twisted in his arms. 'Thank you, but I don't wish to have that experience.'

His grip tightened. One hand caught her jaw and forced her to meet his gaze. 'Juliet, I have been a rake. You knew that when we wed. Nothing can ever change that.'

'Yes,' she whispered. 'That is why I did not want to marry you.'

His eyes darkened as though she had hurt him. 'But because of that I am skilled and you enjoy my lovemaking.' Memory lit fires in his body. 'You like it a lot.'

She closed her eyes, not wanting to see the hunger in his, not wanting to be drawn into the passion he did nothing to control. 'Yes, but not here. Please.'

It was an eternity before he released her. She had begun to despair that he would listen to her plea. With cold formality, he offered his arm. With the best face she could summon, she laid her fingers on his coat, barely touching him.

That night he came to her bed and made fierce love to her as though demons drove him. She lost herself in his passion and was glad for it. Nothing else mattered.

Chapter Thirteen

Juliet laughed from sheer pleasure. The veil of her riding hat billowed out behind her as her mare flew along the bridle path in Green Park. She heard the pounding hooves of Sebastian's gelding gaining on her. She urged her mount on.

Out of the corner of her eye, she saw Sebastian's horse edge closer until it was even with her. Sebastian reached out and grabbed her mare's bridle. Juliet grinned at him.

Rather than risk either of them or their horses being hurt when it was not necessary, she pulled in on the reins. Her mare slowed until she walked. Sebastian did the same. They continued to walk their horses while the animals cooled down.

After a time, they meandered to the early-morning shade provided by a huge oak tree. Sebastian dismounted, then went to Juliet and grabbed her waist.

She put her hands on his shoulders and slid down the length of him. Excitement curled in her stomach.

He held her a long time.

'Why are you staring?' she asked, her brows furrowed. 'You have seen me look a mess before.'

He tucked several tendrils of hair behind her ear, a gesture she had come to expect from him when she was dishevelled. Then he righted her riding hat so that it sat at an angle on her head and the ostrich feathers tickled her cheek.

'You are so vibrant,' he said. 'I have never met a woman before with your enthusiasm for life, and not just in bed.'

This was so unlike him that she became embarrassed. 'I am sure you exaggerate.'

'No.' He abruptly released her and turned away.

She reached for him, wanting the security of feeling his body. Something was very wrong this morning. He did not draw away from her touch, but neither did he cup his hand over hers as he usually did.

'What is the matter?'

'Nothing,' he said curtly. Before she could remonstrate with him, he asked, 'Do you recognise this tree?'

Nonplussed, she stepped back and looked at the tree. It was obvious Sebastian was not going to tell her what troubled him. Absent-mindedly she studied the oak. Then it came to her.

'This is where we duelled. It seems like an eternity ago.'

He nodded, his mouth curling sardonically. 'It certainly seems that. So many things in our lives were changed by that one act.'

Dismay swamped her. She knew he would not have married her without being forced, but she had fooled herself into thinking he was at least contented with their union. He definitely seemed that way in bed. But then he was a man and a rake. Lovemaking was his forte. All the pleasure of the morning and the ride evaporated. She wanted to go home.

'We should be leaving. There are so many things to do today. I have to return Maria Sefton's visit, and I must write to Papa.' Sebastian raised an eyebrow in disbelief. 'I know he very likely does not read my letters, but it gives me comfort to tell him how things are going in London. Since he forced Emily to return to the country, I find I miss them. Silly, but Papa has always been a large part of my life.'

She stopped. She was rambling on in an attempt to cover the hurt his mood had brought on. Better to be quiet.

'Thank goodness they are gone, and good riddance. Heaven only knows what you would have done next in your misguided efforts to protect him from the world. I don't like to think of it.'

She hoped he was trying to be amusing, but there

was no glint of humour in his eyes. He was deadly serious. The knowledge added to her discomfort. Just a week ago she would have argued with him, but not now. Not here.

'Please help me to mount. If we don't get home soon, I shall not have time to change for my visit.'

He did so and they cantered home, neither saying anything.

At the townhouse a groom helped Juliet dismount. She thanked him and went inside. She smiled at Burroughs and a nearby footman. Burroughs gave her a disapproving look while the footman smiled shyly.

'Your Grace,' the butler said, taking her riding crop. 'I hope you enjoyed yourself.'

'Oh, yes. Since we returned to London I have missed riding more than anything.'

'You ride,' Sebastian said, entering behind her and handing Burroughs his hat and crop.

'In Rotten Row,' she said derisively. 'That is meandering.'

He flicked her cheek. 'I must finish some work. I will see you later.'

She watched him go, wondering how long she would be able to stand the sham of their marriage. She knew everyone married for convenience, as had they, but her feelings had gone beyond that. She loved him.

Sebastian went up the stairs and she watched him

avidly. She wanted so much for him to love her as well as desire her. It was an ache in her heart.

'Ahem.' Burroughs interrupted her thoughts. 'Mrs Burroughs has the week's menus ready when you have time, your Grace.'

'Thank you. I will meet with her later.'

Burroughs bowed and left to perform his other duties.

Juliet turned to see if any notes, invitations or messages were on the silver tray by the door.

Only one envelope lay on the salver. There was no visible writing so she picked it up and turned it over. An overly ornate feminine hand had written 'Sebastian'. That was all, except for the heavy scent of tuberose.

Juliet licked suddenly dry lips. Her hand began to shake so that it was a supreme effort to return the note to the tray without dropping it. She stared at nothing, wondering why having the truth staring her in the face was so much worse than just thinking about it. Sebastian had never promised to be faithful.

'Your Grace?' Burroughs asked, louder than normal.

'Yes,' she said, her voice a croak.

'Are you all right? Should I send a footman for the doctor?'

He must have returned while she stood numbly. She turned to him, still dazed from the heartache eating away at her chest. 'A doctor?' Could a doctor mend a broken heart? She was ready to cry. 'No, thank you.'

Before he could ask something else, she walked past him towards the back of the house and went out into the garden. She needed to be alone. She had Sebastian's name and as much of his lovemaking as any woman could want. They were not enough. She wanted his love.

She wandered down the path leading to a white gazebo where roses climbed towards the sun. The peace and scent of fresh roses always made her feel better. Perhaps they would help. She sank on to her favourite bench and cupped a blossom in her palm, inhaled the wonderful fragrance. It was lovely, but, as she had known, it was not enough. Nothing would ever be enough to dull the pain of her husband's infidelities. Nothing.

Hands clasped in her lap, she closed her eyes and let the tears fall.

Sebastian found her half an hour later, his fore-head creased in worry. Burroughs had come to his rooms and told him her Grace was not feeling well. From the butler's tone, Sebastian knew he wondered if Juliet was pregnant. Sebastian wondered himself. Part of him hoped so.

She looked pale and tired. He should not have talked to her this morning the way he had, but he had not known exactly what was happening to him.

He still did not know. The oak tree had brought back the memory of their duel and for an instant he had been glad she had fought it. Which was preposterous. She had entered his life and nothing was the same. He did not even visit his former lady-friends.

He sat beside her and took her hand. 'Are you sick? Is your shoulder still paining you?'

She opened her eyes and looked at him. Their green depths sparkled with unshed tears. 'No, I am fine.'

He traced the path of one tear with his finger. 'Then why have you been crying?'

She turned away and her voice came out barely audible. 'I am tired, that is all.'

'Are you in the family way?' He caught her chin and gently drew her face back so he could watch for her reaction.

She shook her head. 'No. I don't think so.'

'Ah.' Disappointment he had not thought he would experience shafted through him. There is plenty of time for that, he told himself. 'Then it must be too many late nights and too much of your husband's attentions,' he added with a lecherous smile.

She gazed dully at him. 'Perhaps. I think I should lie down.' She stood and looked down at him. 'Alone.'

He rose and took one of her hands in his. 'Are you sure?'

'Yes.'

He released her and stepped away. He had seen people look as she did, usually when they had lost everything. It made no sense for her to feel that way. He had given her their world.

Maybe questioning Burroughs more thoroughly would bring something to light.

That night at dinner she looked no better for her rest. Sebastian watched her pick at her food, moving it around on her plate and cutting it into small pieces she did not eat. Nor did she drink any wine.

She looked up from her activity and caught him watching her. The circles under her eyes accentuated her high cheekbones. 'Will you be staying in tonight?'

She had never asked him that before. He pondered her question before answering. Did she know about his summons and who it was from? He did not think so.

'No. I am to meet Ravensford and Perth at White's,' he lied with smooth proficiency.

'I see,' she mumbled. 'If you will excuse me?' She pushed back her chair before the footman could help and left the room without glancing back.

Sebastian rose, his only thought to follow and comfort her. He got three steps and stopped. This was not the time. Something was upsetting her and he could not spare the time to find out what.

His mother waited.

* * *

Juliet pulled the hood of her black cape more securely around her face. Her fingers clenched the heavy wool so tightly her nails went through, and she had to blink rapidly to rid her eyes of the moisture blurring her vision. Ahead of her, Sebastian moved quickly through the early evening shadows. He was going to another woman.

Thankful it was dusk and the shadows were settling, she edged into the doorway of a closed shop. A few people still milled around, some with purpose, others aimlessly. They helped keep her hidden as well. Not that Sebastian would look. He thought she was safely at home reading a book while he cavorted.

She knew she was making a mistake. A wife did not follow her husband to his mistress's abode. It was very improper. It also hurt as nothing else she had ever experienced—except, perhaps, finding out about the infidelity.

He was heading towards Piccadilly. She hastened to keep up, his height the only thing that allowed her to keep him in sight. Without once looking back or around, so she knew that he did not know she was following him, he entered the Pulteney. It was where the Tsar and his sister had stayed when they'd visited London in 1814.

She was surprised. She had thought his mistress would be set up in a house somewhere. Still, if she was a member of Society, she might meet him here.

However blasé her husband might be, he would not want his wife meeting another man in their own home. Even Juliet understood that much about dalliances.

She could not follow him into the hotel without drawing attention she did not want. No one must know what she was doing. With a sigh, she settled into a shadowed alcove across the street to wait, thankful she had remembered to bring the little one-shot pistol Harry had given her a number of years before. No matter how decent an area might be, a woman alone was at risk. She had learned that lesson well in Vauxhall.

Sebastian strode through the lobby of the Pulteney towards the stairs and the room the note had indicated. This was the last place he wanted to be. His jaw twitched and the tic at his right eye was a constant irritant. But he had no choice.

Reaching the door, he stood and did nothing. Many years had passed since he had last seen his mother. He did not want to see her now, but neither did he want her setting up house in England. He had given her plenty of money to move to Italy. He still gave her a very generous quarterly allowance.

Girding himself for the encounter, he knocked sharply. Her imperious 'Come in' filtered through the door, making her voice soft like a young girl's. Sebastian grimaced and entered.

She sat straight-backed in a chair pulled close to the fire. Her once-black hair was streaked with silver. It was the most obvious change in her.

'Have a seat,' she said, motioning with her hand to another chair. 'I have much to say to you and would prefer not to look up. It puts a crick in my neck that later gives me a headache.'

That was just like her, Sebastian thought, doing as she said. Even knowing it was crazy, he acknowledged that his mother had a hold over him. First it had been the love of a child for the parent. Later it had been disgust at her stream of lovers, and later than that it had been hatred when he had learned he was not the son of the Duke of Brabourne. Her hold on him now was curiosity. He needed to learn why she had returned and speed her removal back to Italy, preferably without her meeting Juliet.

'Would you care for some wine?' she asked.

'No, thank you.'

He crossed one booted leg over the opposite thigh and studied her. In spite of the greying hair, she had aged well. There were lines around her blue eyes and crinkles near her mouth but her skin was still a creamy white with no age spots. Her bearing was regal and her figure slim. She wore a very stylish gown, its simplicity drawing attention to her magnificent bosom and small waist. A multiple strand choker of pearls circled her neck; he assumed it was to hide the wrinkles that were inevitable on that part of the body. Her vanity would make that a necessity.

'Why have you come back?' he asked, determined to finish this quickly.

'You always were brash and disrespectful.'

'Not always,' he murmured.

She cocked her head to one side. 'No, I suppose not. When you were young you were loving and eager to do anything asked of you. You changed.'

He was surprised to hear regret in her words. He had not thought her capable of anything but self-interest. 'I changed because of what you did.'

She sighed and her gaze dropped to her folded hands. Her black lashes hid any emotion that might show in her eyes. 'I did what was necessary. I am sorry if it hurt you.'

A sharp bark of laughter escaped the tightness in his throat. 'Sorry? You should have thought of that while you were busy sleeping with every man in England.'

Her laugh was bitter. 'I was not talking about that. I meant marrying Brabourne, even though he was not your father.'

'You married him while you were carrying me? Did he know it?'

'No,' she murmured. 'I told him you were early. At first he believed me, but the nurses talked and he heard them. They said you were too big for a premature baby.'

'Why did you do it?' He could barely believe what she was saying. Not only was the man he had considered his father for years not, but he had been tricked into marrying a woman he did not know was pregnant.

She twisted a large pearl and diamond ring she wore on her wedding finger. As soon as the late Duke had passed on, she had returned the heirloom engagement ring Juliet now wore. Sebastian had not had to ask for it back.

'It was the only way. I would have been ostracised. You would have been a bastard. I could not let any of that happen.' For the first time since they had started talking she sounded anxious.

He stared at her. 'You tricked him. The least you could have done was tell him and let him make the choice.'

She shook her head. 'No. He would not have married me. He was a proud man. Much as you are. I could not have had you out of wedlock. I could not do that to you or myself.'

She was right. He would never marry a woman who carried another man's child, no matter what the circumstances. Except…perhaps Juliet. No, he quickly told himself. Not even Juliet.

'What about my real father? Why didn't he marry you?'

She looked back up at him and he thought he saw moisture in her eyes. He had to be mistaken. Never in his entire time with her had he seen her display this much emotion. He did not expect it now.

'He was already married. He said he would leave her and we would go to the Continent. I loved him. I believed him.' She sighed sadly. 'I was a fool.'

Appalled, Sebastian sat like a statue. 'But the other men?'

'You have never been in a loveless relationship. I did not love Brabourne and he never loved me. Ours was a marriage of convenience. Once he realised you were not his, he did not even maintain a semblance of civility to me. He insulted me in front of everyone—our friends and family and the servants. He made my life a living hell.' Anger sparked from her eyes, making her resemble her old self for the first time since her confession had started. 'I hated him, and openly sleeping with other men was the only way I could hurt him. His pride and arrogance could not withstand the public humiliation.'

Sebastian felt the first glimmer of sympathy for her, this woman he had hated all of his adult life. As a child he had not been in his parents' company much, which was normal for the nobility. He had known there was something uncomfortable between them, but he had never understood exactly what it was. Then he had learned of his own background and of his mother's infidelities. After that, nothing had been able to penetrate the wall he put around himself for protection from emotional pain.

'Is this why you came back, to tell me these things?'

She nodded. 'When I heard you were married I felt you needed to know the truth behind my actions. I have always known you hated me. I did not want you to take that hate out on your wife, who is innocent of anything I did.'

Nobility of character in a woman he had always considered to have none—it tugged at the part of him that worried about honour.

It was hard, but he finally managed to say, 'Thank you. I know this could not have been easy.'

She gave him a weak smile. 'No, but I had to do it. I owed you that much. If you hold your wife at arm's length because of what I did, you will forge yourself a miserable life. Even if you did not marry for love, marriage can give you children to love and raise together and bring companionship for your older years.'

For the first time he realised how lonely she must be, exiled to Italy and away from her family. He had not thought of it before, and if he had, he would not have cared. Now it mattered.

He stood and paced the floor, unsure of what he was going to say and how to say it. But he felt impelled to do something. Juliet would certainly expect it of him if she knew about this. He found he expected it of himself.

He stopped and made a conscious effort to ease

the knotting of his shoulder muscles. 'I think my wife would like to meet you. If you have the time.'

She looked up at him and the tears he had imagined before became real. 'I would like that very much.'

Sebastian had never felt so awkward in his life. It was not a pleasant experience. 'Then I will send my carriage round for you tomorrow,' he said gruffly. 'Now I must take my leave and let Juliet know to expect you.'

'Of course,' she said, some of her earlier strength returning. 'Until tomorrow.'

She held out her hand, which he took. He raised it to his lips and brushed her knuckles with his mouth. With her, kissing her fingers was an old-fashioned, courtly action, a gesture from her youth.

He took his leave, wondering where all this would end. The things she had told him eased some of the old hatred, but anger still lingered in the back of his mind. There was too much hurt and not enough time to resolve it. Not yet.

As to how it related to his marriage, he just did not know. Trusting was not easy for him. Trusting a woman was the hardest of all.

Juliet saw him exit the Pulteney. He had been there barely thirty minutes. She knew from their own lovemaking that half an hour was not nearly enough for Sebastian. At least not with her.

Hope rose. Perhaps she had been mistaken. But who could have sent the note and when would he meet with her?

He headed back the way he had come.

It was starting to rain. She huddled into her cape and glanced around, looking for a way to watch him and still keep out of the wet. With a sigh of regret she realised there was no way to avoid the moisture. She would be as soaked as he by the time they got home.

One more look around and she started out.

Something moved in her peripheral vision. A man dressed in black moved along the side of the buildings. If she did not know better, she would think he followed Sebastian. Still, she watched the dark figure for a while. There was something elusively familiar about the way he walked and the tilt of his head. She did not know what exactly, but it was there, teasing at her memory.

A hint of something wrong made her follow behind him as he kept some distance from Sebastian. She edged closer to the man.

'Brabourne,' the man said, his voice carrying in the damp night.

Sebastian turned to see a pistol aimed at his heart. His pulse speeded up and his senses sharpened. This was not the time for him to die. He had too much to do and all of it centred around Juliet.

'Ah, it is you,' he drawled, hoping to keep the

man off guard. 'I see your cheek has healed nicely. The scar becomes you.'

The thug from Vauxhall stepped closer, his face a furious mask. 'You will not be so smug when I have finished with you.'

Under the guise of a bored yawn, Sebastian looked around for some means of distraction. All he needed was to divert the man's attention for a moment. The figure sneaking up on them would do. He was sorry to draw the other person in, but he did not think the thug had the skills to kill both of them. With luck, no one would even be hurt except the would-be killer.

'Don't look now,' Sebastian said drily, 'but there is someone behind you.'

'I don't believe you,' the other growled.

Sebastian shrugged. 'It is your party.'

Doubt flitted across the other man's face, which was a pale oval in the light from a street flambeau. Though not many people were around, this part of Piccadilly was well lit. Soon, however, the light would be gutted by the water coming down.

The rain had soaked Sebastian's hair and made his greatcoat heavy. The man holding him up looked worse, as though he had been waiting in the wet for some time. Sebastian hoped the thug would slip on the cobbles.

The man edged around, keeping the pistol aimed at Sebastian but looking over his shoulder to see if

Sebastian spoke the truth. The figure that had been following them stopped. For the first time Sebastian saw that the innocent he had dragged into this wore a cape. A woman.

'Blast,' he cursed, lunging forward. He could not put a female in danger. No matter what.

He heard a bang and saw a flash of light from the barrel pointed his way. He jerked his torso around so that the ball entered his shoulder instead of the centre of his chest. Pain raked through him.

Another shot rang out.

The figure in front of Sebastian bucked just as Sebastian tackled him. Ignoring the fire radiating out from his shoulder, Sebastian straddled the thug and punched his jaw. The man's head jerked.

'Sebastian. Sebastian, is that you? Are you all right?'

Sebastian could not believe his ears. His head came up just as he landed the thug another facer. 'Juliet? What in blazes are you doing here?'

She fell to her knees beside him. 'I…oh, I cannot tell you. But I am so glad I did. This villain has been following you.'

'Ah, yes.' Sebastian looked down at the man he still straddled. Blood flowed freely from a wound on the thug's right side, soaking through his coat. 'I think he is completely incapacitated.'

'Will he die?' Juliet asked. 'He deserves to, for that is what he intended to happen to you.'

'You are the most bloodthirsty woman I have ever met,' he said, catching the back of her head with one hand and pulling her to him for a long, hungry kiss. 'But I am glad to see you. I think he might have killed me otherwise, instead of just injuring me.'

She blinked water from her eyes. 'Injured! Where? We must get you home. You will catch an inflammation out here.'

He smiled at her, feeling his energy of minutes before seeping out. 'First we must take care of this fellow.'

'Leave him for the night watch, Sebastian. You are more important.'

He staggered to his feet and offered her a hand. She took it and he pulled her up. 'Remind me not to anger you.'

She glared at him. 'Your levity is out of place.'

Ignoring her, he pulled out his handkerchief from inside his coat and wadded it into a ball. With a grimace, he pushed it inside his clothing and pressed it hard to his wound. It was not much, but it was the best he could do under the circumstances.

His teeth started chattering and he noticed her lips were blue. Both of them needed a warm fire and a hot drink, but first he had to take care of this villain. For good this time.

'Juliet, go to the Pulteney and tell them to send

out several servants to help us. I do not intend for this scum to get away.'

She clamped her mouth shut on what he was sure was another reprimand. With a sweep of her soaked cape, she stalked off. His wife had more spirit and courage than ten men. But why had she been following him, for that was the only explanation for her presence? He would find out soon enough.

Chapter Fourteen

Sebastian relaxed into the chair, grateful for the warmth of the nearby fire. A tumbler of whisky and a full decanter sat on the table beside him. The doctor had just left. He had a flesh wound, more painful than serious.

They had taken care of the scoundrel who had shot him and come straight home. Juliet fussed around him, plumping the pillows on the bed and getting his robe.

'You must be cold with just your breeches on,' she said, bringing the fine woollen garment to him.

He leaned forward and allowed her to wrap it around his shoulders. She was careful not to touch his bandage.

'Thank you.' He took a big swallow of whisky, enjoying the warm sensation all the way down his throat. 'Why did you follow me?'

'Why did you go there when you were supposed

to be with Perth and Ravensford?' she countered, meeting his gaze without any hint of remorse.

He swirled the burnt brown liquid and sniffed the woodsy aroma. 'I had to meet someone.'

'Your mistress?' She moved away from him.

He could tell by the tightness around her mouth and eyes what the question had cost her. She had not taken the time to change out of her wet clothing and she looked exhausted, worse than this afternoon.

'No. Before we discuss this, and we need to, will you please get out of that wet dress and into something dry? I don't want you getting an inflammation of the lungs when I need you to nurse me.'

Her face turned mutinous. 'I am tired of you telling me what to do all the time. I will change when I am good and ready. As for getting sick, it would serve you right if I did and Burroughs had to take care of you—or Roberts.'

He sighed. 'You are the most stubborn woman. At least come over here, where I can see you better and the warmth from the fire can reach you.'

She edged closer.

He finished the whisky and poured another glass. Dutch courage. What he had to say to her was not going to be easy. He had never said this sort of thing to a woman. He hoped it was not too late.

'I went to see my mother.' He waited for her reaction, dreading that she might feel disgust for the woman who had birthed him.

'Your mother? I thought you hated her.'

'I thought I did. I don't know any more.' He stood and went to her. Putting his hands on her shoulders, he asked, 'Are you happy with me?'

'What kind of question is that?'

She looked wary, as though she expected him to say something that would hurt her. He knew he had made her feel that way by his actions. He had kept her at a distance.

'This is not easy.' He released one of her shoulders and held his hand out. 'See, I am shaking.'

'That is very likely from your wound and all the whisky you have consumed,' she said drily.

His mouth twisted. 'You are not being very helpful.'

'I did not know I was supposed to be.'

'It would help.'

She eyed him speculatively. 'I don't think I want to help you. Remember, you did not help me when Papa caught Emily and Prinny.'

'That was between your father and stepmother. This is between us. And you are not happy with me anyway,' he finished for her. 'You thought I was unfaithful.'

Juliet nodded. A sense of dread weighted her down and her stomach was a tight knot. Was he going to tell he had a mistress, as she suspected? How cruel.

'Don't say anything else,' she said hastily. 'I don't want to hear any more.'

He caught her chin and made her look at him. 'I have never been unfaithful to you,' he said solemnly. 'I have not been with another woman since you burst into my life on the duelling field.'

Juliet stared at him, not sure she had heard correctly. She swallowed the lump that had lodged in her throat. 'I…I—'

'Don't believe me,' he said bitterly. 'I never thought I would regret my past, but you are fast making me do so.'

He abruptly released her and went to the window, his back to her. She staggered before catching her balance.

'I don't understand,' she said, her voice barely above a whisper.

'Neither do I,' he said, sounding as though the words were dragged out of him. 'I thought I had everything under control. You are a woman, and women cannot be trusted. I was going to stay faithful until I got you with child, then I was going to go my own way and let you do the same.' He turned to face her, a haunted look in his eyes. 'But I can't. The thought of you with another man tears me to pieces.'

Her mouth dropped.

He gave her a wry smile. 'Amazing, isn't it?'

'What are you saying?' She held her breath, hoping against hope.

'My mother told me everything tonight. About her being pregnant with me when she married the Duke. How he hated her for it and treated her badly. Everything. It gave me a lot to think about. Especially about us.'

She took a step towards him, but stopped. She did not know what he was really saying.

His smile disappeared. 'Come here.'

'Why?'

She knew that if she went to him and made everything easy he would never finish what he had started. Or so she told herself when she held back. She wanted him more than anything. But she would not be hurt by him again. She could not go through that.

'You don't trust me,' he said.

'You are the one without trust,' she said sadly. 'You made that clear from the beginning. You told me that you have no mistress. I find that hard to believe, but I am willing to do so because you tell me it is so.' In her heart she added that she was willing to believe because she wanted so badly for him to belong only to her.

'I know. And I am still not sure. Not completely.'

She bit her lip to keep from saying something she would regret later. 'Then perhaps it would be better if I left for a while.'

Leaving him would be the hardest thing she had ever done but if it would give him a chance to decide what he wanted she would do it. More than anything she wanted their marriage to work. Having him love and trust her would be heaven, but if he could not do that she would settle for his companionship. She loved him that much.

He came to her and wrapped her in his arms. 'No. I want you to stay with me. I am just not sure that I can give you everything you deserve.'

She kept her head lowered, not wanting him to see the need in her. His words, that said so much but not enough, left a bone-deep ache in her chest.

He stroked her hair, tucking a loose strand behind her ear. 'I have not trusted a woman in a long time…since I was ten and learned what my mother had done. Yet she came back to explain everything to me, things I had not been willing to listen to before. She told me not to take my bitterness and distrust out on you. She made me think.'

Juliet began to shake.

'Don't,' he said, stroking her back. 'I don't want to cause you pain.'

She nodded, her head rubbing up and down on his chest. She still refused to look at him.

'I wanted you from the beginning. At first it was physical and…curiosity. I had never met a woman like you. Then it was more. I could not stand the thought of you being hurt.' He took a deep breath.

'After we were married, it was more. I wanted to make love to you all the time, and when we were apart I wanted you by me, just to be near.'

Tears started to seep from Juliet's closed eyes. She was so anxious about what he was saying, what he was going to decide.

'I want you to stay with me, Juliet. I don't know for sure if I love you, but I want you. I am not sure that the two are not the same.'

She slowly slipped her arms around his waist. It felt as if she had longed to hear those words from him all her life. 'I love you so much, Sebastian, it is a constant ache.'

'Then look at me,' he said. 'Tell me to my face.'

Taking her courage and determination in both hands, she angled her head back. 'I love you. I think I always have.'

'Ah, Juliet,' he murmured, bending down and kissing her.

It was a sweet melding of flesh. Desire was there, but it was like a banked fire waiting to flare to life later. They could wait. Right now they were committing themselves to one another.

When the kiss was over, she gave him a tremulous smile. Tears still seeped occasionally from her eyes. Only one thing remained. As much as she did not want to ask, she had to know about trust. Without it their love would not last. That much she knew.

'What about trust, Sebastian? Do you trust me? Can you?'

He groaned. 'You cannot leave well enough alone, can you?'

She shook her head. 'No. If you don't trust me, then what will happen to us? You will forever torture yourself, and consequently me, with your doubts about me and about our children.'

His arms tightened around her. 'I know. That is what I have wrestled with all night, and I cannot answer you for sure. Trust is too new. I want to trust you, but I fear there will be times when I slip. When I hurt you with my lack of faith.'

'Oh, Sebastian,' she whispered.

'But I want to try. If you will give me the chance.'

She heard the doubt and longing in his voice. 'I don't think I can live without you. I am willing to try with you to make this work. I know it will not be easy, but I want to be with you.'

'Juliet, my love,' he vowed.

Epilogue

❧❧❧

Twelve months later...

'Sebastian,' Juliet called, 'what are you and Timmy doing? Your mother will be here any minute, and you know how she dislikes not seeing Timmy.'

The Duke and a baby with a head of peach down came out from the dining room, where they had been for the last hour. Sebastian handed the boy over. 'I think he needs changing.'

'Oh, no,' Juliet said, crossing her arms. 'You can take him to Nurse as easily as I can. And you had better hurry.'

'I will call Mrs Burroughs,' Sebastian said with a wicked gleam in his eyes.

'No, you will not,' Juliet said, humour tipping up her mouth.

Sebastian gathered a gurgling Timothy close with one arm and pulled his wife in with the other. 'You are a stubborn woman, my love.'

She grinned up at him. 'And you are a scoundrel, always trying to foist the unpleasant aspects of parenthood off on me.'

He returned her grin. 'The boy is the spitting image of you, therefore you should be the one to do the nasty things.'

The smile left her face and she paled. 'He is your son, too.'

Sebastian's eyes darkened and Timmy squirmed. 'I am sorry. I told you it would not be easy, but that was a year ago. I know these past months have not always been the bliss we could have wished, but I don't doubt Timothy's parentage. He is mine and yours. No one else had a part in his creation, and I believe no one else will have a part in the begetting of our next children.'

'I would not trade them for the world. But are you sure?' she asked, doubt still a tiny kernel lodged in her heart.

'Yes,' he said. 'Now and for ever.'

Joy replaced the disquiet. She clung to her family with an intensity that she knew would increase with time.

'I love you, Sebastian.'

'And I you, my love.'

Timothy, caught in the middle of his hugging parents, laughed in sheer delight.

* * * * *